PRAISE

Drums of War continues the story from *West Point* with a mix of humor, romance, and drama of the onset of terrorism and the military missions to keep the United States safe. Another great read. — A.S. Romberger, NMMI69

Once again, J. M. (Mike) Patton has knocked it out of the park! After just a few sentences into the novel, the reader moves from his own reality into the main character Jake's, Reading is experiencing *Drums oWar!* — Tommy "T" Tatom

This story is the very fast-paced and exciting sequel to his first book *West Point*. I highly recommend it as not only an entertaining read but a look into the development of the bond between our military men and woman created by their unselfish service. — Greg Graves, NMMI69

I recommend Patton's books to any reader of any genre. The characters are vibrant. The emotions enkindled are universal. He has captured not only the details of the WPMA experience, but also the character traits that embody a graduate's service as an officer in the U.S. Army: Duty, Honor, Country. *Drums of War* reads like a thriller. — Wayne Springer

As a fan of military novels, I really liked reading Patton's second work, *Drums of War*. It ties in perfectly with his first book, *West Point*, of the trilogy. Its storyline and characters are both captivating and true to life. Patton's trilogy is an appealing story of military service during a very trying time in our national history, and I eagerly await the final book of this series. — Mike Herbert, CAPTAIN, USN (Ret)

I have read the first two books of the A *Full Measure* trilogy, *West Point* and *Drums of War,* and found them connected and exceptional. As a cadet at USMA, 1963-67, I had similar experiences as those described for Jake Jacobs. — Dr. Daniel P Schrage, Professor Emeritus, Georgia Tech; COL USAR (Ret); Former SES Level 3, U.S. Army

Drums of War kept my interest throughout, making it hard to put it down. It was a journey of emotional extremes: highs and lows, laughter and tears. Great read! — T.C. Berry

In *Drums of War,* author J. M. Patton continues to entertain his readers with the second installment of his trilogy – *A Full Measure.* In this book, John Paul "Jake" Jacobs begins his career as a West Point graduate and Special Ops Ranger. He is immediately thrust into action, with the reader living Jake's perils and achievements throughout. *Drums of War* is every bit as intriguing and exciting as *West Point,* the first in the trilogy. My wife and I highly recommend this exceptional book as a must read. — L. D. & Dana Swift

From the first page to the last, *Drums of War* had me intrigued by characters and plot. I have now read the first two books of the trilogy and can hardly wait for the third. I thoroughly enjoyed every minute of reading these books. I highly recommend the novels *West Point* and *Drums of War.* — J. Oliver

ALSO BY J.M. PATTON

West Point

West Point, book #1 in the *A Full Measure* trilogy, is a tale of honorable military commitment, love, and conflict. It gives the reader the experience of attending West Point—featuring the humor and heartbreak of daily life that slowly develops the panache of a West Point leader during the Vietnam Era.

DRUMS OF WAR

A NOVEL

J.M. PATTON

Publish Authority

This book is a work of fiction. Names, characters, places, and incidents are products of the author's imagination or are used fictitiously. Any resemblance to actual events or locales or persons, living or dead, are entirely coincidental.

Copyright © 2021 J.M. Patton
Drums of War (*A Full Measure* series, Book 2)

All rights reserved. No part of this book may be reproduced or used in any manner without the prior written permission of the author, except for the use of brief quotations in a book review.

ISBN 978-1-954000-22-3 (Paperback)
ISBN 978-1-954000-23-0 (eBook)

Cover Design Lead: Raeghan Rebstock
Editor: Nancy Laning

Published 2021 by Publish Authority,
300 Colonial Center Parkway, Suite 100
Roswell, GA USA
PublishAuthority.com

Printed in the United States of America

Chief Petty Officer Donald R. Patton, USN- Hospital Corpsman,
3rd Marine Division, Vietnam (2) – RIP.
For his service many Marines lived to go home

And

Midshipman First Class Steven O. Coats,
United States Naval Academy,
Class of 1973 – RIP.
In our hearts and minds, he will remain forever young

And

Jim Roth, Sr. - RIP
An Exemplary Individual

This is as true in everyday life as it is in battle: we are given one life and the decision is ours whether to wait for circumstances to make up our mind, or whether to act, and in acting, to live.

GENERAL OMAR N. BRADLEY

AUTHOR'S NOTE

I would like to give a special thank you and acknowledgement of appreciation to James Roth for agreeing to co-write portions of this novel with me. James is a skillful writer, and he is an accomplished marksman, active in pistol and three-gun competition. His knowledge of firearms is extensive, and his ability to weave that knowledge into the story is impressive. His writing skills and adeptness at bringing a scene to life are simply awe-inspiring.

Readers can look forward to forthcoming novels written by James Roth. They will be well written and thrilling.

Thanks again, James, for graciously contributing to the writing of *Drums of War*. Your participation is of incalculable value.

J. M. Patton

FOREWORD

J.M. (Mike) Patton's *Drums of War*, the second in his trilogy *A Full Measure*, is a valuable work of art, thought, military history, and political science.

In the first book, *West Point*, Patton laid out the key actors and their character formation at the United States Military Academy (USMA) at West Point. The *Drums of War* novel focuses on special forces operations and the training required to be successful. It also delves into what makes men tick in combat, what moves them forward when every nerve in their body tells them to run. He successfully captures the stress that builds when preparing for a short notice deployment, the ferocity of the action, and the quiet and solemn return. For Special Forces, much of this goes unnoticed and unpublicized due to the classified and sensitive nature of their operations.

As the author depicts the growth of US Army Special Forces post-Vietnam and the JSOC, or Joint Special Operations Command, he also touches on the war in Vietnam, the nadir of American military services. The failure of our political and senior military leaders, along with a press bent on

FOREWORD

stopping the war at any cost, shading every story in the worst possible light, was and is a national embarrassment and disgrace.

Drums of War is a novel but reads like a biography, and a manual on lessons in leadership at both the platoon and flag officer (Generals and Admirals) level, and an after-action report on small unit actions, and the value of true friendship solidified by difficult situations and stress. A soliloquy by Admiral Hollifield to Jake on his combat experiences and losses in Korea is worth, by itself, reading the book.

This book is also a foretelling of the war on terrorism that has consumed us as a nation since September 11, 2001, but that we should have and could have ameliorated to a large degree had we read the tea leaves correctly after Beirut in 1982; and after the airline and cruise ship hijackings in the 1980s and 1990s; and after the embassy bombings in Kenya and Afghanistan and Khobar Towers and on and on during the Clinton Administration.

Mike very deftly shows us the impact that faith has in the military as a force multiplier, a counselor, and comforter. It is essential for maintaining balance in what can be a hectic world. And finally, he reveals to the reader the sustaining power of a women's love for her soldier, sailor, airman, or Marine, as he tracks Jake's unrequited love for Sara.

You have to read this book.

Scott B. Cottrell
Colonel, US Army (Ret)

PROLOGUE

DRUMS OF WAR is the second novel, following *West Point*, in the trilogy *A Full Measure*. The entire trilogy is a work of fiction. The setting for this novel is the final days of the Vietnam War. Cadets John Paul (Jake) Jacobs and Patrick McSwain near graduation from West Point and prepare to don the army blue for a career in the Army combat arms.

Jake, Patrick, and Jake's lifelong friend, Steve Ross, a midshipman at the Naval Academy, have developed an unbreakable bond, typical of those who share hardship and commitment in military life. Unfortunately, Jake has lost the love of his life, while Steve has joyfully found his. Coming to terms with his loss, Jake buries his emotions and stays the course by navigating through the demanding requirements of West Point. The first book of the trilogy, *West Point*, gives the reader a clear view of who and what the characters of *Drums of War* have become. *West Point* demonstrates the development of the character traits of a follower, which is a prerequisite to the development of leadership characteristics dramatically shown in *Drums of War*.

Sukarno Bangjar, an Indonesian already wealthy and privileged, hates America and the influence it has had on the understanding of faithful Muslims. He particularly despises the West's lack of appreciation of the Islamic impact on society centuries ago while the West loitered in the Dark Ages. His anger and ambition have precipitated the murder of his family and fueled a quest to use appalling tactics against Americans on American soil. As a result, destiny dictates that Sukarno and Lieutenant Jake Jacobs will collide violently. Jake is committed to protecting America, and Sukarno is likewise committed to destroying it.

With a backdrop of the final days of the Vietnam War, *Drums of War* is a compelling read where each of the characters is on a collision course with intense difficulty. As in life, the intersection of these lives is perhaps providential but unknown, where seemingly insignificant decisions and choices weave the tapestry of reality.

J.M. Patton

CHAPTER 1

2130 Hours
19 December 1971
United States Military Academy
West Point, New York

ANY CHANGE in routine at West Point is reason enough to be in a festive mood. It does not happen often. But the reveille cannon at 0600 hours tomorrow would signal departure for Christmas leave, and now that meant no six to eight hours of study for another day of the academic grind. John Paul (Jake) Jacobs from Texas, Patrick McSwain from Tennessee, and Wayne Barnes from California had survived two and a half years together as roommates. They shared an unbreakable bond forged by the rigor of West Point.

"Why don't you just come to Tennessee with me?" Patrick said to Jake as he swung his feet to the top of his desk and clasped his hands behind his head. "You'd have a great time. Tennessee has the most beautiful women in the world."

Jake smiled. "Tennessee probably does have the most

3

beautiful women. But, as Wayne and I can attest, they also have the ugliest men."

Wayne laughed, and Patrick stuck his lower lip out to indicate his feelings were hurt. "Alright," Patrick said. "Be that way. You go on down to Texas. I'll just have to take care of all those Tennessee gals myself. Don't you come back here moaning about how dull Comanche, Texas is. You had your chance."

Jake sat down in his chair, assuming the same position as Patrick by throwing his feet on top of his desk and clasping his hands behind his neck. "Thanks for the offer, but I need to spend a couple of weeks in Comanche. I haven't seen mom and dad for a year. They need me to show up."

"Understand," Patrick said. "This is your first trip back there since Sara got married. How weird is that going to be?"

Jake brought his feet to the floor and leaned forward. "Well, the hardest part about going home is that everyone I know will start gossiping all over again. At least Steve will be there from the Naval Academy. I thought I would start getting myself in shape for the fight against Cruikshank in March, and I'll twist Steve's arm to run with me."

With a look of surprise on his face, Patrick said, "Huh? I didn't know a navy man could run more than a block or two."

1800 hours
19 December 1971
Dallas, Texas

A COLD DRIZZLING rain fell on Dallas's dark streets as commuters fought their way through foul weather toward home. The freeways were packed, slowed by the rain, and Brent Mosher cursed under his breath as he downshifted from 2nd to 1st in his Porsche. Though the drive from downtown Dallas to Methodist Hospital was less than twelve miles, the weather made it an hour's drive, bumper-to-bumper. The Porsche struggled against overheating, and so did Brent Mosher.

Sara had called two hours earlier. She said she was in labor and was having the next-door neighbor take her to the hospital.

"She's had false labor before," Brent grumbled. "It's another damn false alarm. She loves doing this to me. Brent slammed the brake pedal to the floor to keep from rear-ending the car in front of him and simultaneously slapped the steering wheel in anger. He glanced at his watch again. "Damn!" he said aloud, knowing that Sara was going to be mad because he had not left the office to meet her at the hospital after she called. Brent dreaded the confrontation. He had meant to leave. But the meeting he had with the advertising agency was too interesting to skip. The minutes suddenly accumulated into two hours.

"I'll simply have to tell Sara I was tied up at the office and just couldn't get away. She might not like the explanation, under the circumstances, but she'll have to accept it," Brent said, practicing his excuse, as he slammed the palm of his hand on the horn in frustration.

———

1730 Hours
20 December 1971
Comanche, Texas

JAKE AND STEVE startled Laura Jacobs by bursting through the back door into the kitchen. "Good grief! You two scared the wits out of me. I'm not used to having anyone move that fast around this house anymore."

"You mean dad has slowed down, Mom?" Jake jokingly asked as he opened the refrigerator.

"Well," she said teasingly, "he slowed down some, but he's still too fast for me."

"Yeah," Steve said. "We saw him sound asleep in the recliner. That's why we came in the back. Guess he's just resting so he can move fast, huh, Mrs. Jacobs?"

Laura Jacobs giggled and playfully slapped Steve's arm. "You just wait, young man. Someday a recliner will feel pretty good to your tired old bones, too."

"Won't be long either, the way Jake has me running twice a day." Steve had not counted on Jake deciding that now was the time to start working hard for his brigade fight with Cruikshank in March. Frankly, he had been looking forward to ten days of sleeping late, lying around the house totally inactive, and being grossly overweight when he returned to Annapolis. Jake had asked Steve if he would like to work out with him during leave. Though Jake did not expect Steve to rise faithfully at six in the morning for a brisk five-mile run and a repeat performance again late in the afternoon, Steve felt some overwhelming obligation to be a part of Jake's quest for whipping the tar out of Cruikshank. This support was all he could offer. He would be absent from the actual fight.

The phone rang, and Laura Jacobs lifted the receiver from

the wall phone as she wiped her hands dry with a linen towel. "Hello," she said, trying to hear the voice on the other end while Jake and Steve continued their banter. Again, they argued and made vastly exaggerated claims for or against the two branches of military service. It was no wonder they could run so far twice every day, with neither willing to admit he was tired and quit in the presence of the other. Oliver Jacobs had commented that they were likely to run each other to death by the end of the week.

"Valerie, I'm so happy for you, and I'm glad Sara and the baby are doing fine. A boy, you say? That's wonderful. I'm sure the Moshers are thrilled with having a grandson as well."

Laura was happy for her friend and Sara, but at the same time, she was acutely aware and terrified of the deafening silence that prevailed behind her. This was not how she would have chosen for Jake to hear the news. His hearing this one-sided conversation felt as unfair to her as her images of Jake standing behind Bob Lowell's unopened screen door precisely one year ago. Although Valerie Lowell continued to chatter in her excitement, all Laura could think of was how Jake must be feeling at the moment. Last year his world crumbled with Sara's marriage. This Christmas, it was Sara's baby.

"Yes, Valerie, Jake is doing just fine. We are so glad to have him home with us for a few days. It's been a year since we've seen him, you know?"

Laura Jacobs turned to sit on the stool next to the phone and looked at Jake with expecting eyes. He stared back at her. His eyes were void of expression.

"A visit to Omaha would be nice, but I doubt we'll have a chance to come for a while. Thank you for asking, though. You could always fly to Dallas. I could meet you there, and we could spend all of Bob's and Oliver's money."

Laura kept looking at Jake's face, expecting some sort of reaction of visible hurt, or anger, or disappointment. But what she saw was nothing. It was like he wore a mask with complete concealment of his feelings, as though the news of Sara's baby was a non-event that had no impact on him whatsoever.

"Well, thank you for calling. And give our best to Sara. Tell her we love her. Bye, now. Don't wait so long to call next time."

Laura replaced the receiver with slow deliberation, still watching Jake for a reaction as Steve leaned against the refrigerator, feeling he was in the wrong place, the wrong house, and possibly in the wrong town for the news he had just heard. He knew Jake well—all his life. But he did not have the slightest idea how Jake was going to handle the fact that Sara now had a baby. A full minute passed in complete silence while Jake and his mother stared at each other. Steve stood motionless, feeling out of place. Finally, Jake broke the silence. Without expression, he said, "What's for dinner, Mom? This sailor and I are starved."

1600 Hours
20 December 1971
Dallas, Texas

SARA WAS TIRED. The delivery of Stephen Patrick Mosher had been typical. But even so, all deliveries, even at best, are painful and exhausting. The doctor had warned Sara that depression was something she should expect over the next few weeks, but she had no comprehension of just how depressed one could feel.

On the one hand, her baby's birth was the happiest moment of her life, while on the other, she felt utterly betrayed and deserted by her husband. Brent destroyed her expectations of sharing this moment. There was no happy moment celebrating together that they had a healthy new son and that they were together in this life. But reality and fantasy were far apart.

The baby was born without the father present. Sara was an hour out of delivery when Brent casually strolled down the corridor toward the nursing station to inquire about his wife. Since Sara was asleep in her room, he peeked in, then slipped into his coat before going home. He was at the office as usual until mid-afternoon the following day before he returned to the hospital

"We'll name the boy Jonathan Stanley Mosher, after my grandfather," Brent said firmly, knowing that Sara had resisted that idea since she had discovered she was pregnant.

Sara did not show a reaction. She was too tired for that. She simply stated, "No," in a calm, firm voice.

Brent was indignant. "What do you mean, no? We decided on that name long ago. It was my grandfather's name. My family expects us to name the kid Jonathan Stanley."

Sara stared at Brent with fire in her eyes. The look of hatred was piercing to the man who stood looking down at her.

"Since you were not concerned enough to even show up for the birth of our baby, you can take your grandfather's name and shove it. I had this baby alone, and I named him alone. I already signed the papers. His name is Stephen Patrick, and right now, I'm disgusted that his last name is Mosher."

"Stephen Patrick! What kind of name is that? Where did that come from?" Brent was angry and concerned about the criticism and ridicule he would receive from the Mosher family. However, at the moment, he was even more intimidated by the fierceness in Sara's eyes and voice. He had never seen her this way. He paced toward the door, then back toward Sara's bed. With her arms crossed, she looked even more resolute than she had only seconds before. He started to argue the point, then reconsidered. Following a frustrated glare, Brent Mosher stomped out of the room and down the hall.

Sara was still angry long after Brent was gone. Something had turned inside her. She no longer felt intimidated, at least not now, by Brent or his family. The desire to name her son John Paul was almost overwhelming, but she knew all too well that to do so would cause upheaval on both sides of the family. The Moshers would certainly pitch a fit, but her family would, too. They would all point their fingers at her and claim that she had named the baby after Jake. No. Not the same, but as close as she could come was to call her precious newborn son Stephen Patrick, after Jake's two best friends. To her, the name claimed all that was good in how a child should grow straight and tall and honorable. Every time she spoke his name, she would be reminded of the models she would like her son to emulate, and at the same time, whip herself repeatedly the rest of her days for the soul-crushing mistake she had made in her life. Sara often tried to understand the blindness she had to the reality she had experienced. The delusional imaginations of being married to the charming Brent Mosher and the trappings of his family's wealth led her to make catastrophic decisions. When the consequences of those decisions— based on delusion—came to greet her, they only came in terms of reality. The blindness was an enigma.

0800 Hours
26 December
Comanche, Texas

THE PACE WAS FASTER on this run. Jake led by only a yard, and his legs and arms and lungs were working harder than on the runs they had before. He ran with his mind someplace other than on the pain that came with each stride. Steve's mind was in the present. The pain was horrid, and they had already covered seven miles. He was very much aware of the agony he felt in his legs and lungs. And he was aware that Jake ran silently.

Another quarter mile trailed behind them when Steve said, "I'm not doing this, jerk!" and immediately slowed to a walk. Jake was stunned at the comment and came to a halt a dozen feet further down the road. Steve's comment had snapped him back to reality. Both stood looking at each other, breathless and dripping sweat.

"This sailor can run with you step for step, Jake, but I'm not stupid. You want pain; you run by yourself. I'm not the least bit interested in wasting my leave. You want to be mad—you do it by yourself." Both were stooped with hands on their knees, gasping for air from the long run.

"Sorry," Jake said, straightening his body and walking in a circle around Steve while trying to bring his breathing back to normal. "Guess I lost track of how far we've run."

"Look. I know you're mad about Sara. But you don't need to take it out on everyone else. I want to run with you, but I've got no reason to let you punish me for you being mad at her."

Jake stopped his pacing, threw his head back in a roaring laugh, grabbed Steve in a bear hug, swung him around a full turn, and turned him loose. Steve stood completely confused.

"I'm guilty as charged. At least guilty as far as having my head somewhere else and pushing us too hard. But I wasn't thinking about Sara." Jake started slowly walking toward town, and Steve fell in beside him, silent, patiently waiting for Jake to explain.

"Don't get me wrong," Jake finally said as they walked. "I didn't get much sleep last night for thinking about Sara. I reckon it shouldn't have bothered me that she had a baby, and more specifically, she had a baby, and it wasn't mine, but it did bother me. I mean, she is married to this Mosher guy. Kinda stupid for it not to dawn on me that someday they'd have a baby. Pretty natural, don't you think?"

"Mosher? Is that her husband's name?" Steve asked.

"Yeah," Jake replied. "Mother said his name is Brent Mosher. Some wealthy family in Dallas. That's all I know about him. Anyway, I guess sometime during the early hours, I let it go. Hearing the news of Sara's baby is just the same old hurt. It's not new—you know what I mean? Sara has the life she chose, and the baby is just part of that life, no more, no less. I'm not upset about her having a baby. I just still miss her. Sometimes I lose sight of the fact that she's gone and that I'll never see her again. Sometimes it seems unreal to me that we are on such different paths in our lives and that they will never cross. I hate it. But I don't hate Sara." They walked in silence another tenth of a mile, their breath visible as it hit the cold hours of early morning.

"I miss her, too," Steve said seriously. "I guess you and Sara not being together changed my life, too. If things were the same, we wouldn't be out here running ourselves into the ground. Comanche isn't the same anymore."

"Nope. It's different. Not bad, mind you, but different. Change. Guess we have to learn how to roll with it."

They continued to walk, the old bridge and the houses on the outskirts of Comanche in sight. "So, if Sara wasn't bothering you, what was? You weren't running that hard just for grins."

"I was thinking about that colonel. You remember Colonel Strong, whom we met in Philadelphia at the Army-Navy game? And I was thinking about Charlie," Jake replied without hesitation.

"What about them?"

"The colonel asked me to consider going Special Forces when we graduate next year. I'm going to do it."

Steve was not surprised at Jake's announcement, but he certainly had his doubts about the wisdom of the decision. He did not know much about the Green Berets, but he was familiar with the Navy SEALs, and it was the same thing, different mission. They were an elitist group, hush-hush type operations that smacked of CIA shenanigans and generally disregarded by the real Navy as a bunch of wild cards that were sure to give the service and the country a black eye somewhere along the line. Special Forces served a useful purpose in Vietnam, but the war was winding down quickly, the lack of public support would see to that. It was generally felt that there would be no need for the Special Forces types in another year or two. It was a dead-end for someone who had invested four years at one of the academies and planned a career.

"I always thought I'd be with the 101st. Just like Charlie," Jake said sadly. "I miss him."

Steve paused. "You're a lot like him, you know? What do you think Charlie would say about this Special Forces idea?"

Jake thought for a moment before replying. "I reckon that's what I was thinking about while we were running. I think Charlie would tell me to go with my gut feeling and go where I think I have the talent. I remember talking to Charlie late one night, right before he went to Vietnam. He was in exactly the right place for him, which was an airborne infantry company. He was technically very good at the job, but then a lot of guys are. They know tactics like the back of their hand. The thing that made Charlie really good was his natural leadership ability in a combat infantry environment. He truly cared for his men. He had empathy for them, and he felt that each man deserves the very best he could give to keep them alive and bring them home. The infantry needs men like Charlie. It's so rare to find an officer who has the capacity to care the way he did."

"Yeah, but I see you the same way. You're like that. If you want infantry, then I think you'd be great at it," Steve said.

Jake smiled as he kicked another rock to the side of the road. "Do you believe in Providence?"

"You mean a God-driven fate for everyone, a predestination kind of thing?" Steve replied.

Jake chuckled. "Not really predestination. More of a God-chosen path to which we're led. And, of course, we make our own choices when we follow that path. People often fail to choose or recognize Providence when it's right in front of them. You studied the Civil War at Annapolis just as I did at West Point. Robert E. Lee and Stonewall Jackson are perfect examples of men who possessed military mindsets that functioned with a total belief in Providence. Personally, I think failure to take Providence seriously is responsible for half of the self-induced misery in the world. People make the wrong decisions that set the course of their lives. Well, I feel like I'm facing one of those providential decisions right now."

"You mean whether you should go Special Forces or not?"

"That's right," Jake replied firmly. "Look at the facts, or at least what I think are the facts. On the one hand, there is every reason in the world not to choose Special Forces. It smacks of a lousy career decision from top to bottom. There may not even be a Special Forces in a few years, and everyone caught inside will be an outcast to all the regular combat units. What's worse is that it's perhaps more dangerous than being a combat officer in another branch. Nothing too safe about jumping behind enemy lines with a half-dozen men and being ridiculously outnumbered. The way I understand it, I could get dropped somewhere hostile at a moment's notice, and no one would know if I were alive or dead, ever."

"Yeah. Sounds dumb to me. I agree with your assessment. In fact, you don't need to give me any positives. I'd feel much better if you'd get yourself a nice slot in the Quartermaster Corps moving boxes around some warehouse." Steve was attempting to switch this serious conversation to a more light-hearted tone.

Jake laughed. The houses of Comanche grew larger with each step. "Dumb? Sure, sounds like it, doesn't it?" Jake did not expect an answer. "The list of positives is short but powerful."

"Okay, let's hear them," Steve said with resignation. "You've already said you've decided to go Special Forces. You've already made up your mind. Why?"

"It's simple. It's the right thing to do. It's the right decision for me, for my life."

They continued their slow pace down the country road. Steam rose from the fields as the morning sun warmed the cold earth, and the birds began their daily activity of searching for food on a wintry landscape. Steve continued to walk in silence, trying to understand the commitment he had heard behind Jake's words.

"You're going to get yourself killed, Jake," Steve said sadly.

Jake stopped immediately. Steve took three more steps, then stopped to face Jake. The possible consequences of Jake's decision were exposed between them like a nerve exposed to air on an open wound.

"That's not something we have to worry about," Jake said. "We all have an appointment to die. The victory comes in living our lives to the fullest with the confidence that God will handle the when and how. That kind of confidence is what allows us to perform our duty with courage. Rest assured, Steve, no matter what circumstances I might find myself in, I'm not going to die without God's authorization."

Steve nodded his head in acceptance of Jake's decision and his beliefs—then they continued their walk toward town. The conversation changed to trivial subjects, indicating that the discussion of Jake's choice to join Special Forces was forever complete and accepted. Sitting on the Jacobs' back porch a half-hour later, untying their soaked and muddy running shoes, Steve inhaled deeply and said, "For now, let's do what we do best. Eat."

CHAPTER 2

1000 Hours
12 March 1972
United States Military Academy
West Point, New York

JAKE SLIPPED the C4 t-shirt over his head and tucked it into his academy gym shorts. Wayne had tried to talk him into wearing a bright yellow shirt he had brought back from Christmas leave emblazoned on the front with a large hand, the middle finger extended. But Jake preferred the simplicity of giving Cruikshank the finger by smacking him in the mouth with his fist. In less than an hour, he would have the opportunity.

The intramural boxing season had gone as everyone had hoped. Both Jake and Cruikshank were undefeated and had fought their way to the finals. The Corps of Cadets wanted to see them in the ring for a rematch. If not for the honor of a plebe named Benson in Company A3, Cruikshank almost failed to make it to the finals. The plebe had fought him well in the semi-finals, and with one round remaining, knew that he was ahead of Cruikshank in points. The crowd had roared, "Jacobs! Jacobs! Jacobs!" Benson knew what the cadets wanted. They wanted Cadet John Paul Jacobs to have his chance to get a piece of Cruikshank. Benson backed away, walked to his corner casually with his arms victoriously in the air, grabbed a towel on the lower rope, and threw it into the center of the ring. He capitulated in the fight to move Cruikshank to the finals against Jake. The crowd went crazy as Cruikshank stood red-faced with anger, embarrassment, and fear.

Cruikshank had alienated the Corps with his fight against Jake last year, and he had done nothing to redeem himself. He acted like it was his God-given right to cheat his way to victory in every fight throughout the boxing season and to deliver debilitating pain to each opponent. Cruikshank was the personification of arrogance. Last year, he had at least used some discretion as he approached the Brigade Boxing Championship. His victory over Jake seemed to have unleashed a form of savagery in him. Jake was the first real victim of Cruikshank's foul play, at least in terms of physical damage. But since then, there was a string of victims sent to the infirmary because of Cruikshank's outright disregard for the rules or sense of fair play. The academy staff seriously considered disciplining Cruikshank, but no one did. The fact was that the staff, together with the Corps of Cadets, felt that the only justified punishment would be a severe whipping at the hands of Cadet John Paul Jacobs. It was not a sure bet by a longshot. But the hope for it was worth the gamble.

"You've got a visitor, Jake," Wayne said

Jake wiped the sweat from his forehead and turned. Cadet Benson stood in dress grays at rigid attention. Jake looked at the plebe from top to bottom, and he was pleased with the young man's bearing and adherence to plebe custom in such an informal environment. It showed that the plebe had respect for the upperclassmen and the system.

"At ease, Mr. Benson." Jake smiled.

Benson relaxed slightly with the recognition that Jake was maintaining the requisite formality while at the same time being as friendly as an upperclassman could be to a plebe. If anyone found out that Jake, or any upperclassman, recognized Benson before June week, Benson's life would be made miserable for the remainder of the year. Jake was showing his respect and concern for him in West Point fashion.

"Sir. I just wanted to drop by before the fight to wish you good luck. I hope you defeat Mr. Cruikshank, sir."

Jake walked within a step of Benson and extended an unexpected hand. Benson took it, and their eyes met in mutual understanding. "Thank you, Mr. Benson. Thank you for allowing me to have this fight. Throwing in the towel when you could be fighting for the championship yourself says a great deal about you and your love for the Corps. Not many men would be so unselfish. "

"You deserve this fight, sir. And the Corps, too."

"Well, I'll try not to disappoint either of you. Perhaps next year it will be you and me."

"I'd like that, sir," Benson said.

"So, would I, Mr. Benson. And I don't think I'd even mind losing to you. You deserve the title. I wish you had it this year, but as you already know, there's more involved than just a title. If I could fight Cruikshank without the title at stake, I'd do it."

"Yes, sir. I have three more years to earn the title."

Benson turned to leave, and Patrick motioned that it was time to walk to the ring. Jake pitched the towel on the bench and purposefully opened the door. Immediately, sounds of excitement from the crowd filled the hallway, and his anticipation grew with each step. Two years ago, when he fought Captain Scott, he had a definite plan of attack. Patrick and Wayne both had tried to get him to do the same for this fight, but he had refused. He had said he felt it best merely to rely on the skills he already knew. Right or wrong, it was now time to find out. If he were wrong, Cruikshank would again likely get away with a dishonorable victory. Worse yet, the Corps would be disappointed.

As Jake came through the double doors to the main gymnasium, the crowd went wild. "Jacobs! Jacobs! Jacobs!" The Brigade Boxing Championship finals always drew a full crowd, but somehow, they seemed packed even tighter than in prior years. There was an assortment of banners from various companies rooting for their favorite cadet in the fights, but Jake noticed right away that most of them had something to say about this fight. A total stranger to West Point would have no trouble determining that this was a grudge match and that some cadet named Jacobs was the Corps' unanimous choice to win. There were numerous banners colored with bright markers depicting Cruikshank in one debilitating condition or another. As Jake walked toward the ring, he noticed that Cruikshank played his championship title to the hilt by waiting for him to enter the ring before making his grand entrance.

Jake crawled through the ropes, and Patrick followed. The roar of the crowd increased, highlighting the collective excitement. Immediately, Jake went to his corner and continued to stretch against the ropes while waiting for Cruikshank to appear. And appear he did. Cruikshank entered the gym as though he was the world champion, and the event would be televised. Two plebes from Cruikshank's company served as his entourage, jogging through the crowd in front of him. The captain of his company boxing team and coach for this fight trudged along with obvious reluctance behind him. For this third fight, Jake again felt underdressed. His standard-issue shorts, C-4 t-shirt, and black tennis shoes just did not stack up to the costume worn by Cruikshank of black silk shorts, a silk shirt with "1971 Brigade Middleweight Champion" sewed professionally on the front, expensive goatskin boxing shoes, and a black silk robe with his name on it, just like Joe Frazier or George Foreman. Cruikshank must have thought he looked magnificent, and he did, but the Corps reacted with laughter. No one had ever entered the ring at West Point with a robe and a coerced entourage of plebes as far as anyone still alive could recall. A bit much, but then, they thought Cruikshank a bit much, too. That is why they wanted so badly for Jake to pound him into the ground. The crowd roared their disapproval of him, but it did not faze the current champion. He strutted around the ring with his arms extended over his head to make sure everyone got a chance to see his fine duds, like a peacock in the barnyard.

Patrick leaned over the rope and shouted above the roar of the crowd into Jake's ear. "If you don't beat the crap out of that creep, I personally will have to drag you back to our little room and bayonet you. I'd rather give up women than to see you lose this fight to him."

Jake laughed. "He's a sight to see. It will be great to watch him perform in that getup. Why don't you fight him, so I can just watch?"

"I'm the manager. Remember? You know, the one with the brains. You're the one that likes to get hit in the face, not me."

The crowd grew silent as the referee stepped to the center

of the ring and motioned toward each corner for the fighters to come forward. "Ladies and gentlemen. The next fight is the title fight for the 1972 middleweight brigade championship. On my left in black shorts and a black shirt is the defending champion, Cadet Craig Benjamin Cruikshank." The crowd sounded its disapproval as Cruikshank danced around the ring. "On my right is the challenger, Cadet John Paul Jacobs of company C4 in gray shorts and white shirt." The crowd raised the roof, yelling and screaming their approval while stomping their feet and waving their banners.

The referee gave his instructions to the fighters as usual, and Cruikshank did as he had done last year. He ignored Jake's extended hand and snarled as he turned to go to his corner. Jake shrugged his shoulders. With only a few seconds before the bell, Patrick started to offer advice and encouragement. Jake held his glove over Patrick's mouth then winked at Wayne.

The bell rang, and Jake turned swiftly to move to center ring. Cruikshank was playing the game. He walked slowly with his arms down, an arrogant grin on his face, and started circling to Jake's right, knowing that Jake was right-handed. He circled to avoid Jake's power. Another three steps to the right, inches out of reach, he continued to circle. Jake followed each step, well aware of the distance between them. Deliberately, Jake took a step backward, and in doing so, dipped one shoulder as though he had slightly stumbled off balance. Cruikshank did what Jake thought he would do. He took a long step forward, thinking he could easily slam his fist into Jake's face at a weak moment. But before Cruikshank's extended foot touched the mat, Jake quickly shifted his weight and stepped solidly towards his opponent. Jake's left fist slammed into Cruikshank's rib cage with a loud pop, and a high arcing right followed to his left temple. Cruikshank's feet left the mat, and he landed face down at Jake's feet. The crowd roared while Jake strolled to his corner.

"Holy mackerel," Patrick said excitedly. The referee started the count, and Cruikshank struggled to clear his head and get to his feet.

At the count of seven, Cruikshank was up and cleared by the referee to continue the fight. A slight cut above the left eye trickled blood down the side of his face. He saw that Jake's facial expression was all business as he again approached. The game was over. He was scared, and it showed in his eyes. The arrogance was now gone. He was in for the fight of his life, and he knew it.

Jake became the hunter now, and Cruikshank the prey. Jake began a circle to his right, positioning his moves in support of his powerful right arm. A half-circle completed; Jake took the offensive. A lightning combination to the head staggered Cruikshank, and he retreated to catch the rope. Jake backed off, forcing Cruikshank again to move to the center. He did. But when in range, Cruikshank threw a wildly ineffective combination then spun a full turn with his elbow held high, intending to crush Jake's face, just as he had done a year ago. Jake reacted instinctively. He held his ground. He moved his head a fraction backward, enough for the elbow to miss. In his attempt to fight dirty, Cruikshank was again off-balance. Jake slammed his fist powerfully into Cruikshank's exposed armpit, lifting him off the mat and nearly dislocating his shoulder. Cruikshank shrank to the mat on his knees, holding his arm. Jake turned and again strolled to his corner as the bell rang for the close of the first round.

The crowd watching was delirious with excitement. A poll of the conversations in the stands would have delivered a consensus that Jake Jacobs was in the process of punishing the cheater with slow, deliberate precision. Cruikshank deserved it. They were glad to see dignity returned to the Corps.

Jake sat on his stool, wiping the sweat from his face without expression. "How are we doing?"

"How are we doing?" Wayne repeated credulously. "Good grief! Cruikshank is sitting over there thinking he got hit by a train, and he hasn't even touched you yet."

Patrick chuckled as he took the towel from Jake and wiped his own face. "You don't need this towel. You haven't even broken a sweat yet. I'm the one that needs it."

"It's not over yet," Jake said seriously. "Not by a long shot. Let's just take it one round at a time. That jerk has more dirty tricks than I've got hairs on my head."

"That ain't saying much. Not around here anyways," Wayne said as he ran his hand over Jake's closely cropped hair.

The bell rang, and Jake walked cautiously to the center of the ring. Cruikshank did likewise, shaking his right arm, trying to overcome the excruciating pain in his shoulder. The crowd continued its roar, but neither Jake nor Cruikshank heard it. Each was buried deep in concentration as their respective subconscious whispered warnings of danger that heightened the senses.

Cruikshank took the offensive immediately. He caught Jake with a left jab then a right to the cheek. Jake felt only the first punch. The second lacked power, and the shoulder was too weak to exploit the opportunity. Jake stepped back, circled a half-turn, then attacked with deliberation. For a full minute, Jake pursued Cruikshank around the ring with two and three punch combinations. Cruikshank tried to counter, but Jake evaded the hits and continued to deliver deliberate scoring punches to the head. Swelling began to take form around

Cruikshank's eyes and cheeks, and Jake continued to methodically press the job he had crawled into the ring to do. Moments before the bell, Cruikshank grabbed Jake and shoved both of them into a corner. The referee tapped him on the shoulder to break and return to the center of the ring. As he released Jake, Cruikshank slammed his knee into Jake's groin, stepped back one step, and delivered a vicious two-punch combination.

Jake was stunned with pain. Though standing, the muscles in his stomach contracted, bending him toward the mat. The crowd screamed their disapproval from every direction, and the referee shook his finger at Cruikshank in reprimand. Cruikshank smiled arrogantly at the referee. Jake straightened himself the best he could, taking one step at a time towards center ring. Cruikshank stepped forward with a newly found confidence to attack. Jake stood stationary, ducked a hard-thrown right, then crossed over the top of Cruikshank's swing to slam his right to the bridge of his nose. Again, Cruikshank hit the mat with his body weight's full force, his nose broken and gushing blood. The bell rang. Jake did not look back as he walked to his corner.

Patrick slid the stool under Jake as he dropped to sit, confident the stool would be there. Wayne handed him the water bottle and asked if he was all right. "Can't believe he kneed you in the groin."

"Are you okay?" Patrick pressed.

"I don't know. What do you think?" Jake asked in a voice four octaves higher. Patrick roared with laughter, then popped Jake lightly with the towel. "You've got one round left, buddy. No doubt you've already given this guy a boxing lesson, but apparently, he still hasn't learned how to be nice. What are you gonna do about it?"

"Well, I think I'm warmed up now. It's time for the real fight to start, don't you think?"

"Attaboy!" Wayne said enthusiastically.

The bell rang for the third round, and Jake told Patrick to let him know when the first two minutes of the round had lapsed. Jake approached the center of the ring, oblivious to the sounds around him. The noise from the crowd was at a pitch that made it almost impossible to hear anything. The crowd was hopeful that the final round would finally put Cruikshank where he belonged, as if the first two rounds had not already done just that.

Jake was lively in his step as he approached, but Cruikshank was visibly tired and battered. His cheeks were swollen, the cut over his eye had swollen it almost shut, and his nose was stuffed with gauze to stop the bleeding. Jake would ordinarily find compassion for an opponent in this condition, but Cruikshank walked to the center and spat at Jake's feet. His arrogance, as yet, was unbeaten. It was arrogance. Pride alone might make a man want to continue the fight. That was natural, but illusions of self-importance and superiority strictly generated Cruikshank's attitude about himself and toward others. Even amid this humiliation, Cruikshank had convinced himself that he was the knight in shining armor while the entire world was blindly against him.

Jake disagreed. Before Cruikshank could react, Jake slammed his left fist into the ribs, lifting Cruikshank's feet from the mat, then recovered quickly for a hard left jab to the swollen cheek. As Cruikshank moved his arms to protect the right side of his face, Jake's powerful right connected with Cruikshank's nose. Blood spattered both of them as the packing from the prior break tore free. Cruikshank staggered back, and Jake pursued with deliberation. For the next full minute, Jake concentrated on scoring punches thrown with less than full power. He was not ready to end this fight. Cruikshank was angry, frustrated, and embarrassed. Every punch he tried, Jake blocked and covered him with painful combinations. Cruikshank tried to grab Jake to keep him from hitting him, but when he did, Jake rocked him with pain by slamming his fist into Cruikshank's ribs. He tried to kick Jake twice. The first time, the referee scolded him with an accusing finger. The second time, Jake attacked viciously with a wild flurry of punches to Cruikshank's head that dropped him to the mat. Nothing was working against John Paul Jacobs. Nothing.

"One minute remaining!" Jake heard Patrick yell over the noise of the crowd.

Jake walked to a neutral corner to give Cruikshank a moment to gather himself off the mat. Cruikshank's eyes were desperate. Jake had beaten him badly in this match, and there was no place to escape. There was no way to save face amongst his fellow cadets.

A quarter of the minute passed, then Jake slowly moved towards his opponent. Cruikshank circled toward his corner, grasping for any degree of security, knowing that even his corner was taking pleasure in his defeat. Jake moved in and cornered Cruikshank against the ropes.

Cruikshank had to fight. He could not run. Jake stepped forward, and Cruikshank wildly flailed his arms with no chance of striking a severe blow. Without retreating or delaying the inevitable, Jake calmly thrust his right to the point of Cruikshank's chin with all his body weight. Cruikshank's eyes rolled back as his knees buckled simultaneously. Jake caught his unconscious opponent in his arms, then gently laid him on the mat. The crowd was no longer yelling and screaming their approval. They clapped as though they had attended an opera. There was something profound about the fear and hopelessness that Cruikshank displayed in the final round and the graciousness Jake had displayed as the victor when he laid Cruikshank on the mat so caringly.

The Corps had gotten much more from the fight than they had expected. Cruikshank had brought undignified and ungentlemanly conduct to the ring. Jake had returned to the Corps a sense of integrity and compassion in victory.

The referee held Jake's hand in the air to finalize his victory, then Jake crawled through the ropes and walked without expression for the locker room. Patrick and Wayne were close behind as the crowd continued to clap.

"Great fight, Jake," Wayne said admiringly.

Jake untied his gloves with his teeth and pulled them off in silence.

"You feeling a little low about this, buddy?" Patrick asked. "You shouldn't, you know. Cruikshank acted like a total jerk, and you took him to the cleaners just like you were supposed to do. I think you're feeling bad because he looked so pathetic out there. But Jake, you don't need to feel bad about it. You simply outboxed him, even with him trying to cheat the way he did."

Jake held the palm of his hand toward Patrick, indicating enough said. He wiped the sweat off the back of his neck with a clean towel then took a long drink of the Coca-Cola Wayne handed him.

"I don't really feel bad," Jake said as he slowly gathered his thoughts on exactly how he did feel. "I fought a good fight. And I fought a clean fight. For that, I am pleased." He took another swallow and leaned back to face his roommates.

"What doesn't feel right is that it was a grudge fight. Don't get me wrong. If there was ever a guy that needed a whipping, it was Cruikshank. And I did that. But you know, now that it's over, I realize I was out there in that ring today for all the wrong reasons. I was out there to punish Cruikshank for what he did last year and for being a jerk."

"So, what's wrong with that?" Wayne asked incredulously.

"Wrong reason," Patrick answered. "I see your point, Jake. Yes, we are all guilty of that—you, me, Wayne, the whole Corps of Cadets. None of us were interested in the sport today, the good old-fashioned competition. We all just wanted to see Cruikshank bleed all over the floor."

Jake paused. "Makes me feel like maybe I'm no better than Cruikshank. Maybe my attitude was just as arrogant as his, just in a different way."

All three fell silent as Jake stripped and walked toward the showers. The realization that the fight had been a travesty, at least on one level, took the elation of victory away and left them glad that it was over.

Five minutes later, Jake emerged from the shower and stood dripping wet against a locker. "Well, guys. We took a victory today. And we took a defeat. It didn't turn out to feel exactly the way we wanted, but let's feel good about the fact that we worked hard to win, and we did. We accomplished what we set out to do, even if we didn't do it with the right attitude. We will learn from this. I think what I've learned is that revenge motivation is a slippery slope. I wanted my revenge on Cruikshank, and now I wonder who the winner truly is."

"Oh. You're the winner, Jake." Patrick said as he leaned against a locker with his arms crossed over his chest. "In every way. Do you think Cruikshank is in the locker room trying to think about how he's going to be a better person, or officer, from his experience today? I don't think so. You're a leader, Jake. Cruikshank, not so much. I'd follow you anywhere."

Wayne sat on his bench, watching his two roommates, and smiled. He would follow either one of them or both. They were both exceptional leaders, in his opinion. Academics were his forte, not leadership, and living with Jake and Patrick for three years had helped him prepare for a military career in countless ways. If it were not for them, he might have dropped out the first year. Patrick instilled in him a sense of humor to live the Mickey Mouse life, and Jake had given him the courage to search his limits and achieve. "Well, how about me, guys? I'm a leader of men. Wouldn't you follow me anywhere?" He asked while laughing.

"Wayne," Patrick said with false seriousness. "The next time we go to Disneyland, you lead. Anyplace else, you better stick to being the brains of this outfit. You will make general's stars, Wayne, but it'll be because you're smarter than everyone else. MacArthur or Patton, you ain't."

"It's a good day," Jake said after they had finished laughing. "Let's go fatten me up with some greasy, fried food. Training camp is now officially closed."

CHAPTER 3

0900 Hours
20 March 1972
New York, New York

SUKARNO PUT the receiver of the phone back on its cradle and sipped his morning tea. Central Park's view was beautiful this time of year from his Manhattan apartment, and the day was young enough to be comfortable outside on the balcony. But Sukarno was not concerned with the weather or the view. He had other things demanding his concentration. By mid-morning, he would be at the Chase Manhattan bank.

As predicted, he had had visitors. Two well-dressed officials from the Indonesian Embassy had come to his apartment two months ago, and Sukarno greeted them with cordiality. Why not? Unless he implicated himself, the President of Indonesia and his specialized army would not harm him. He did not have the slightest idea where his father had vanished. And yes, he was dismayed and ashamed to learn that his father

31

was a traitor and embezzler. Of course, he would do the right thing and contact Indonesian officials if he heard from his father. After all, he was an Indonesian who had greater loyalty to his country than love for his father and family. The officials left. They did not believe a word Sukarno had said, but they had no other choice but to leave the young man alone for now. If they could prove that Sukarno had been in touch with his father and complicit in the embezzlement, then he, too, would die. Time will tell. Time was on their side. They knew that eventually, Kuwat Bangjar would surface. A man with half-billion dollars did not remain hidden forever.

Sukarno agreed. The question he had asked himself repeatedly during the past months was how he could use all the complex realities of the situation to his benefit. He had access to all the money. His father had seen to that in his naïve trust in him to carry out their joint goals. Fool. He, too, had dreams of a united Muslim world, but history indicates that such unity is not likely ever to happen. More realistic was Sukarno's potential to achieve inordinate wealth and power in his own right. There had to be a way to keep the money or a large portion of it and still stay alive.

Sukarno had already solved the problem of whether anyone would catch his father. He knew that he would be dead, too, if he had not found a way to disassociate himself from his father without question, and at the same time, utilize the fortune his father had stolen. The problem now was how he could keep the money? Killing his family had clouded the proof of his collusion with his father. Indonesia wanted Kuwat alive to recover the money. They wanted to get their hands on the money first, then kill him. Would his father have told them that his embezzlement also involved his son? That his son had access to the bank accounts? That they, together, had a plan? Of course he would. Kuwat Bangjar was not a physically strong man. Interrogation, properly applied, would tell the authorities everything his father ever knew or even thought. That problem solved—Sukarno now sought a way to maximize his gain and simultaneously satisfy the Indonesian government.

The limousine driver opened the door for Sukarno promptly at 10 o'clock and drove him to the Chase Manhattan bank. The limousine was not out of the ordinary, nor was the young man in the immaculate black suit. The driver thought Sukarno looked the part, a foreign mega-millionaire going to the bank to count his stacks of gold.

"Mr. Stavanos will see you in a moment, Mr. Bangjar," the young secretary said politely.

Sukarno took a chair in the private waiting room adjacent to the executive vice president's office and inhaled deeply. This part of his plan was easy. It was completely legal, and Stavanos would have no trouble carrying out his wishes.

The secretary walked from Stavanos's office with its ornate double door and coyly stated that Mr. Stavanos would now see him. Her flirtation went unnoticed. Sukarno had more important things on his mind than some American bimbo who brought coffee to an overstuffed bureaucratic banker.

"Mr. Bangjar. How good to see you. I'm sorry we haven't had the opportunity to meet before. Please have a seat."

Stavanos was not as Sukarno had pictured. He was not an overstuffed Greek puffing on a cheap cigar. Instead, Stavanos was in his mid-30s, quite handsome, and obviously in good physical condition. "Miss Stiles, please bring a tray of coffee and danish for us."

Miss Stiles nodded and again smiled at Sukarno as she closed the door. Stavanos immediately extended cordiality and demonstrated his adeptness in the art of conversation. He made Sukarno feel comfortable in a matter of seconds. He was impressed with this young executive's skills and was surprised that time had passed so quickly when the flirtatious secretary returned with the tray. But when she left the room, Stavanos made a transition. Stavanos was all business.

"Are you here about your father?" Stavanos asked directly.

Sukarno had not expected anyone at the bank to know much about his father's situation, let alone for the banker to confront him in such a blunt manner. He paused to sip his coffee and to regain his composure. "Yes and no, Mr. Stavanos. Do you know my father well?"

"Of course, I know a great deal about your father. I will not beat around the bush with you, Mr. Bangjar. The Indonesian government has already been around to question me about your father and about you, too, I might add. I lied. I told them I haven't heard from or seen your father in over a year. But you and I know different, don't we?"

"Yes, we know different, Mr. Stavanos," Sukarno replied. "You must be aware that my father opened some new accounts, personal accounts, in this bank in the past year. Did you handle those accounts personally?"

"That's right." Stavanos was extraordinarily relaxed, as though they were discussing baseball rather than embezzlement. "And, no one knows who owns those accounts except you, me, and Kuwat. The funds are in the name of three U.S. corporations. Right at $500 million, if memory serves me correctly. The funds are spread to correspondent banks, of course, so as not to create too much interest in them."

"I am a signatory on those accounts, am I not, Mr. Stavanos?" Sukarno asked arrogantly, knowing the answer.

Stavanos burst into a hearty laugh and bit into a Danish. "You should try one of these. They're wonderful. Did you have breakfast?"

"I'm not interested in breakfast, Mr. Stavanos," Sukarno said, visibly frustrated that Stavanos clearly thought he had the upper hand and was toying with him. "I'm interested in talking about the money in those accounts."

Stavanos wiped his mouth with a linen napkin and took a long sip of his coffee. "I know why you're here, Sukarno. You don't mind if I call you by your first name, do you? After all, Kuwat talked about you often. In fact, he gave me some idea about the grand scheme he cooked up some time ago. I must tell you. I was surprised that he actually had the nerve to steal money from the Indonesian government. They would string him up if they could find him, wouldn't they, Sukarno?"

Sukarno squirmed in his chair while struggling to maintain his composure. He thought frantically. Was this a trap? Stavanos' sly facial expression indicated that he knew that Kuwat was dead. Was Stavanos about to turn him over, or had he already done so? This meeting was not going as planned.

"They will, and you know they will." Stavanos continued with a hard stare into Sukarno's eyes. He sipped his coffee again and leaned back in his chair. "Let me tell you why I think you are here, Sukarno. Correct me if I'm wrong."

Sukarno sat forward instinctively, anxious to know how much trouble he would have from his banker, who seemed to know everything he was not supposed to know.

"You know as well as I do that your father has made an egregious error. I don't believe for a minute that you thought your father was going to get away with this. And, that's why he's dead. And we know who made sure that he was."

Sukarno was shocked again. Stavanos knew about São Paulo, which meant that he could destroy everything. Stavanos could turn Sukarno over to the Indonesian authorities. He could blow the whistle, and all the money would wash right down the drain.

Stavanos leaned forward. "Don't look so shocked, Sukarno. I have banking resources in Brazil. Your father's murder is not widely known, but it will be soon. You're here to get the money, aren't you?"

Sukarno did not answer.

"Listen, Sukarno. I don't much care about you, your father, the Indonesian government, or your grand plans. But I do care about what happens to the 500 million dollars. I haven't told anyone about this situation yet. What do you want to do? As far as I'm concerned, it's your money."

Sukarno was cautious. Stavanos appeared to be wanting to make some kind of deal. "I want to withdraw a portion of the funds you are holding."

"How much?"

"100 million dollars," Sukarno said nervously. "I want to transfer the money to another corporate entity."

"And the rest?" Stavanos was confident.

"I want to leave the funds where they are, for the time being."

"I see." Stavanos leaned back in his chair and sipped his coffee. "So, what you want to do is to strip a mere $100 million from the pot for yourself, then be positioned to turn the remainder over to the Indonesians. Is that about it, Sukarno?"

Being outsmarted was foreign to Sukarno, and he did not

like it. Stavanos had him cornered. "I didn't say that, Mr. Stavanos."

"You didn't have to. What about Kuwat? What about your father's wishes? That is, what about his connection with Darul Islam? Are those fanatics looking for a share of the money?"

The question of Kuwat being angry was no longer pertinent because he was dead, and Darul Islam was not aware of his father's wishes. Nevertheless, Sukarno credited Stavanos for recognizing that the Indonesian government was a threat concerning the money. Sukarno saw the direction of the conversation clearer. Stavanos was trying to see if he could profit from the situation himself, but he needed assurances that he would be safe. Like himself, Stavanos knew the money was useless if it killed him. Stavanos wanted to make a deal. If he could not make a safe deal, he would simply cooperate with the Indonesian government and continue to earn his six-figure salary every year.

"Mr. Stavanos, my father's plans will not be a problem. I think you have a grasp of the situation. First, somebody must return the bulk of the money my father stole. The world is too small for one to hide that kind of money. A portion of the money might still be missing without much question, but certainly not an overly greedy portion. A fifth of the money is pushing the limit. Second, my father could not ever have been taken alive. That would not have been healthy for you or me. My father is no longer a consideration. The Indonesian government is."

Stavanos chuckled. "Well, Sukarno, you are just about as bright as your father said you are. So, Kuwat is no longer among the living. That takes care of one problem. That's fine, so long as I allow you to walk out of here with 100 million dollars. I could just blow the whistle on the whole deal, and your problem with the Indonesian government would not mean diddly-squat to me."

Sukarno returned the smile. "Yes. Well, I suppose we must see that we come to a mutually agreeable solution to this dilemma. Let's not beat around the bush any further, Mr. Stavanos. What do you suggest?"

"More coffee?"

"No, thank you, Mr. Stavanos." Sukarno tried to hide his anxiety.

Stavanos slowly poured himself another cup, then relaxed in the chair before speaking. "I don't altogether trust you, Sukarno. Nor do I have delusions that you trust me. That's why our agreement has to be very straightforward." Stavanos sipped his coffee again then set the cup on the table beside him.

"I want to transfer 10 million dollars to a little company I own down in North Carolina," Stavanos said without emotion. "A consulting fee of sorts, you might say. We will do that today if that's all right with you. That will be the end of any conversations you and I will have where I'm concerned. You see, we Americans consider well-off to be much less than a half-billion dollars. I'm not greedy." Stavanos chuckled at how relative wealth was. Ten million dollars would be astoundingly adequate. I don't want some ghouls sent by you or the Indonesian government to come knocking on my door in Connecticut, scaring the hell out of my family or me."

Sukarno sipped his lukewarm coffee, buying a few moments to think. "Why wouldn't I just go to one of the other banking institutions that are holding funds and deal with them? I doubt they would charge me a consulting fee for withdrawing my money, and I doubt there would be any delay."

"You could do that," Stavanos said calmly. "It would be

stupid, but you could do it. You see, Sukarno, none of the other banks involved have the slightest idea whose money they are holding or from where it came. I know because I arranged the accounts. The minute you walk in and ask for a withdrawal, they will likely start asking serious questions. No. That would be a bad idea. You are already lucky that you came to see me first."

"Why shouldn't I simply turn you in?"

Stavanos laughed. "Because you have big plans, my boy. You're not going to run around the rest of your life broke, or worse yet, find yourself dead. Quit stalling and quit asking stupid questions. We will do business today and do it my way, or you won't even get down to the first floor before I am on the telephone blowing the whistle. You know, I'd probably get a big fat raise from the almighty Chase for doing it."

Sukarno chuckled. He was disgusted at having been beaten at this step in the game. Never had he planned on the likes of Mr. Stavanos. Never would he fail to plan thoroughly again. "Very well. You win."

"Good," Stavanos said calmly. There's one other matter. I have recorded this entire conversation, Sukarno."

Sukarno's mouth dropped open.

"If you get any bright ideas about ever bothering my family or me, someone will still blow the whistle. If anything happens to me, ever, these tapes and all the documentation will spring to life. Do you understand?"

Any ideas of eliminating Mr. Stavanos in the future were suddenly clouded. Stavanos had covered every angle and every fear. "What happens if you die in an accident or merely have a heart attack? That's not acceptable. I can't control those things."

"You better hope I don't have an accident or die of a heart

attack. You better hope I stay healthy, Sukarno, for a long time." Stavanos smiled. "We'll work together on this. You'll have nothing to worry about from me so long as you go about your business and stay out of mine."

Sukarno did not like having this threatening loose end, but he did not see any way to avoid it. It was not perfect. As Stavanos waited for his answer and finished his danish, Sukarno realized that as time passed and his long-term plans matured, the threat from Stavanos would diminish. If he did die, his heirs would likely prefer to keep the money than to surface with any documentation and lose the money to Indonesia. There would come a time when this event would be insignificant, and then, he would have the option of either taking care of Stavanos or continuing to let him live. For now, the proposal met his needs. He could always deal with the loose ends later. Perhaps there was even a permanent need for a man like Stavanos. After all, a good banker is hard to come by.

"Where do I sign, Mr. Stavanos? We have some money to transfer to North Carolina."

1300 Hours
15 May 1972
Dallas, Texas

STEPHEN PATRICK MOSHER slept in the playpen in the center of the den after his customary early-morning feedings. Sara was continuously amazed at how much fulfillment he brought to her life. He seemed to give it purpose. His hair was fine, like corn silk, and of the same color. Blonde hair and light blue eyes had everyone saying he looked like her, and that pleased her. She had expected all the horror stories of midnight feedings and hours of crying to be true, but Stephen Patrick has surprised her. He slept through most nights and mostly only cried when he was hungry. The remainder of his waking hours were nothing but pleasure.

Sara was gladly lost in caring for Stephen Patrick. His every need consumed her day in a pleasurable way, and the added benefit was that she did not have to focus on the dynamics of her marriage or what was left of it. Brent did not seem to mind. He was glad that Sara had something to tend to that kept her from disrupting his hobbies. He was perfectly happy spending as much time as he possibly could away from home. He preferred to stay at the office, the club, or wherever else he could dream up a reasonable excuse to be. She now had her life, which was the boy, and he had his. The less actual contact they had, the better.

Brent's attitude and desire for distance in their marriage was not lost on Sara. It was more than acceptable to her. She painfully chuckled to herself when she thought back on how hard she had tried to have what she believed to be a normal relationship with Brent. Gone were the delusions that he loved her or even that she loved him anymore. It seemed now that maybe she never did love him. The past eight months were not good, as far as marriage goes, only tolerable. She had accepted that "tolerable" was all there was to have and that she would spend the rest of her life just as it was today.

Divorce? It had crossed her mind often, but she immediately forced the thought away as impossible. There was no need to even think about it. There were a thousand reasons why she could never divorce Brent, no matter what. She believed divorce was morally wrong for her and wrong for

Stephen Patrick. No. She had made her bed, and now she must sleep in it for the rest of her life, no matter how miserable she was. She would just have to make her life happy in other ways. Ways that did not depend on Brent. Dreams of love and marriage, companionship, friendship, and respect would never be. Loving and caring for Stephen Patrick was all she needed. He was already the center of her life.

CHAPTER 4

1600 Hours
10 August 1972
United States Military Academy
West Point, New York

SECOND DETAIL OF BEAST BARRACKS, the month of August, is easier on the upperclass cadre than the first detail but less exciting. The new plebes had already learned the basics after four weeks of terror and functioned admirably as cadets. They could now march, knew most of the required fourth-class knowledge, and knew how to survive three meals each day in the mess hall. They had learned a great deal in four weeks. Many of those who could not learn fast enough or could not handle the rigor of the plebe system were already gone. West Point was quick to weed out those that could not survive or did not have the aptitude to learn to become an officer in the U.S. Army. It was an objective environment where those that had it—stayed. Those that did not were gone.

Jake was a part of the process. He was assigned a job as the company commander of the 7th New Cadet Company and had been in command for the last ten days. Four black bars on his collar, designating him as cadet captain, seemed strange to him. Had it actually been three years ago that Captain Jonathan Scott had worn those same bars and stood in front of the same company? Every day since he had returned to West Point from leave, thoughts of Captain Scott crossed his mind, and Cantrell, as well. Beast had been hard, just as it was hard for these new cadets, but Scott and Cantrell had done a tremendous job for them. A widely known statement heard from West Point graduates is, "I owe everything I am, or ever will be, to my First Detail squad leader in Beast Barracks." Jake had not realized it at the time, but he knew now that every minute had been wholly dedicated to their best interest. They had done their duty to prepare his class to be West Point cadets and future officers, precisely as he was charged to do for the terrified new cadets in front of him today. The sense of Duty, Honor, Country had never been stronger in him.

Jake had trained for the position during June and had spent all of July in Comanche on summer leave. He spent most days helping his uncle, John Fritz, build a new barn and corral. He enjoyed the physical work and being outdoors. It was such a change of pace from his usual routine that he felt rested and relaxed. There were no formations, no academic grind, no uniform, and no fixed schedule that demanded maximum performance every minute of the day. He regretted he had not known his uncle John well over the years. John was his mother's distant cousin, and she was a Fritz herself. Jake was fascinated with the stories Uncle John told about his great-great-great-grandfather Fritz, a soldier in the Confederate Army, an Indian fighter in the Oklahoma territory, a Texas Ranger, and finally, a settler and farmer in Comanche. Each day, he went home in the evening, quizzing Laura Jacobs about his ancestors and the history of the town he had assumed had no remarkable history at all. The more he learned, the more he wished he had known Grandpa Fritz. It amazed him how one man could have been so blessed with being an active participant in so much critical history.

For a short week during July, Steve had been home and then packed his meager bag for a month at sea aboard a frigate. He complained incessantly about being away from Julia.

"Better get used to it. Being a sailor means being away from your sweet-britches months at a time, forever," Jake kidded. "Maybe you could transfer to the Army next June. We may have to go to the field for a few months, but we certainly don't have to set sail three times a year for the rest of our careers."

Steve shoved Jake off-balance in a blast of aggravation. "You've got to be kidding. I wouldn't be an Army scum for anything. I may be on a boat, but at least I'll have three squares a day and a dry bed. As for you, it's the mud. It amazes me how anyone who is seemingly as intelligent as you can go to Ranger school and still not catch on that humping a pack and eating snakes is a bad deal."

"Snake ain't so bad," Jake said defensively.

"You're hopeless. I'll stick with the Navy where all the intelligent human beings serve their country."

Jake let the insults slide, but only temporarily. They had filled the week taking turns delivering the most derogatory remarks they could imagine about the other's choice of service. The only thing clear to anyone who heard one of their discussions was that they surely hated each other.

Jake had mixed emotions when his leave was close to an end. In some ways, his leave passed much too quickly, and in other ways, he was anxious to get back to West Point. It was his last year. Another ten months and the fastest four years of his life would be finished. West Point was nearly done, and he was starting to look forward to a life beyond the granite walls on the Hudson. It would be nice to have a place of his own, maybe an apartment or a nice room in the Bachelor Officer Quarters (BOQ) on whatever post was assigned to him. And the car. At the age of twenty, the simple privilege of owning and driving an automobile was a desire well past due. Graduation and the rest of his life were anticipations starting to grow and would ripen to burst by the first week of June. Thousands of the Long Gray Line had preceded him, and they had all felt the same.

———

"GET your scrawny ass to the position of attention, mister!" Jake barked. "Mister Higinbotham, you walked past me and didn't salute. How long you been here, mister?"

"Sir. I have been at West Point for..."

"You've been where, mister?" Jake barked again.

"Sir," the plebe barked. "May I begin again, sir?"

"Yes, Mister Higinbotham, I suggest you start over."

"Sir. I have been at the United States Military Academy for four weeks, six and a butt days."

Jake smiled. "Seems like a lifetime, doesn't it, Higinbotham?"

"Yes, sir!" The plebe popped off.

Jake slowly took a deep breath and stepped an inch closer to Higinbotham's face. "I can guarantee you, smack, if you fail to salute an upperclass cadet again, you'll have spent your last day in my beloved Corps. You can go back home and tell your mama that you didn't make it at West Point because you spent all your time with your head up your butt. You got that, mister?"

"Yes, sir!"

"Get out of my sight," Jake said with disgust.

The plebe did an about-face and ran toward the sally port like a robot. Wayne came sliding up next to Jake, and both laughed. "Bet that plebe will salute anything that moves from now on," Wayne said. "Dogs, post squirrels, bellboys."

"Yelling at them seems to be the only way they get the stuff through their thick skulls. Of course, we weren't that thick when we were plebes, were we Wayne?"

"Of course not, Captain," Wayne chuckled. "We were the smartest class of plebes ever to go through John Wayne University. Maybe they should quit all this harassment of plebes. Don't have Beast Barracks. Put an end to the plebe system altogether."

"Can't," Jake said matter-of-factly.

"Why not?" Wayne asked, expecting some rational answer.

Jake smiled. "Because then we would be the Naval Academy, and we already have one of those."

"Or maybe the Air Force Academy, God forbid," Wayne said as they resumed their walk toward the field house. New cadets bustled all around them, running like Higinbotham in every direction.

Jake asked, "How's your platoon doing?"

"Good. I have great squad leaders. They're doing a fine job with the new guys, and my platoon sergeant, Bill Urich, is so good I hardly have to lift a finger.

"That's great," Jake said reflectively. "That means that our team is well motivated and that our chain of command is working as it should. We've only been here a few days, but it seems to me that the new cadets need a little more chow. First detail did a good job. They rode these guys hard. It shows. I hate to admit it, but I think they are doing better than we did after our first four weeks. Pass it down to your squad leaders. I want to keep the pressure on these guys but let them get a little more to eat. They know how to do it without appearing to be letting up. These new cadets are doing fine, but I want them really prepared to go into the regular companies in another month. They might hate our guts when this is over."

"Might? They already do. But that's okay. Getting them ready is our job."

"That's your job," Jake said jokingly. "My job is to stand up in front of the company and look cool and sound official."

Wayne smiled. "Sure, Jake. That's why you haven't been in the rack before 0200 since we got here. Somehow, I don't think it takes that much effort just to look cool. Well, then again, in your case, maybe it does."

"Trust me," Jake said, "I've never been so busy. I didn't know there was so much to do to keep the training on track. It seems like I've been at a dead run for the last three days. If you ask me, the plebes have it easier than we do. At least they get to close their eyes and sleep a few hours."

"I hate to change the subject during one of your greater philosophical moments," Wayne said, "but what's this I hear about you being on the list of hot shots for brigade commander in September?"

Jake laughed. "Can you imagine how difficult my life would be if Patrick were here to give me a hard time about this? He'd make me miserable with his dramatics."

Wayne came to a dead stop and bowed at the waist in front of a few hundred other cadets on the slab. "So, it is true, O

Great One." He threw his arms in the air and slowly bowed like a Muslim in prayer. "Have pity on me, O Great One, allow me to touch the bottom of your nasty feet."

Jake threw his head back with a laugh but was also embarrassed. Somehow, Wayne and Patrick had seemingly learned in three years to make a career out of getting their classmates, mainly him, in embarrassing situations with their exaggerations and dramatics. Patrick was born to it, while Wayne was an excellent student of the art. "Rise, you despicable peon," Jake said, playing his appointed role. "Never, never can the likes of you touch my nasty feet. But, take heart, you lowlife scumbag, it would please me much if you would make my bed every morning."

Fat chance of that!" Wayne said. "Seriously. What's the scoop? You gonna make brigade commander?"

With Wayne's antics finished, they continued their walk. "I don't think so," Jake said with ease. "I think Jeff Robertson will get the position. But there's a chance I might get the slot for the regimental commander of the 4th."

I'd like that better," Wayne said with sincerity. "If you got the brigade, we hardly ever see you. Besides, regimental CO is still pretty hot stuff. It's one of the five permanent ranks in the Corps."

Jake grinned. "I hope it's for the regimental job, too. I really don't want to leave the fourth regiment. It's our last year. I'd like to spend it with my friends."

"I'm touched, O Mighty One of the 4th Holy Regiment."

———

2300 Hour
3 October 1972
United States Military Academy
West Point, New York

JAKE'S LEGS were crossed on his desk, bunny ears occasionally twitching as he prepped for an advanced chemical engineering writ or test. Wayne was also concentrating on his textbook, but Patrick was at his desk, thumping the eraser end of a pencil on the arm of his chair and gazing at everything in the room except a book.

"I thought that commie was dead," Patrick said of Jake's bunny slippers.

"No," Jake said. "As it turns out, he wasn't a commie. He was just a reporter for the New York Times working to ingratiate himself to the anti-war crowd. You know, a wanna-be commie but not willing to give up his Diners Club card."

Patrick grinned. "Maybe we should have done him in and helped the Times with some objectivity."

"Don't hold your breath for objectivity," Jake said as he slid his feet off the desk to sit upright. "There wasn't a peep of objectivity in the Times last spring when the Harvard track team refused to compete in a meet if the Army and Navy teams were going to be there."

"That was interesting," Wayne piped into the conversation. "Half of those Ivy League geniuses end up in Washington, D.C., formulating the very decisions that get us into a war, then they criticize and blame someone else for the outcome. I took psychology. That's narcissism."

Jake threw himself on his bunk and pulled his old baseball cap down over his eyes. "What kind of car you gonna get? I think I'll keep the ole Woo Poo tradition and get a Corvette."

"Damn," Patrick said in mock aggravation. "What'd ya bring that up for? I need to study. Now I'll spend the rest of tonight dreaming about my gorgeous black Vette and the almost as gorgeous blonde riding with me."

Jake remained silent and chuckled under his cap. He knew Patrick's daydream would take some wild and entertaining tangent from reality.

"Yep," Patrick continued, looking at nothing in particular as his mind drifted. "She's in love with me, all right. She wants my body. She likes the Vette okay, but she just can't keep her hands off me. I've told her a thousand times to keep her hands to herself while I'm drivin' Mach-one down the freeway, but she can't help it. Poor kid. You know what I mean?"

"Five-and-a-butt months," Jake sighed. "Mobilization Day. I can hardly wait. I still wish I had my old '57 Chevy, but I reckon a royal blue Corvette with a 327 and a four-speed will just have to do. Steve is going to get a red one. Wayne a yellow. I can just see us flying down the highway. Blue Vette, red Vette, yellow Vette, black Vette."

"You mean black, red, yellow, and then blue, don't you?"

Jake sat upright on the bunk and shoved the cap to the back of his head. "I'm good with that. I'm just ready to get out of this place."

Patrick turned back to his textbook and sighed. "It won't be long, buddy. The real world is coming around the corner at us."

———

3 October 1972
London, England

THE WEST GERMAN wiped the sweat from his brow then replaced the handkerchief in his oversized suit's side pocket while Sukarno hid the contempt he held for the fat merchant. Franz Siegel was well-known in the arms market, albeit somewhat unreliable in his promised deliveries. Even if impeccably reliable, that would not make it any easier to enjoy his company. The cool December weather did not influence Siegel's obesity, which caused him to perspire constantly, soaking his shirt and causing his suit to rumple within minutes of a fresh pressing. He was self-conscious about his appearance, but he had ceased to try to do anything about it years ago. His obesity was a battle he simply could not win.

Siegel leaned over the table, thumbed the stack of negotiable bearer bonds, then placed them in a large black briefcase.

"Are you so trusting of your new clients that you do not wish to inspect the bonds more closely?" Sukarno raised an eyebrow to emphasize the question.

Siegel smiled, then laughed loudly, his fat belly bumping against the table. "I have no trouble trusting you, my friend. You came to me. You obviously know my reputation in the arms business. If you cheat me, I know who you are. Men who do such things do not live long. It is a very small world for men who try to cheat Franz Siegel."

Sukarno smiled. "I do not need to cheat anyone. And I think you understand that the world is, indeed, very small. A man in your business must assume that one who wishes to buy arms is also willing to use them against his enemies."

Again, Siegel laughed but nervously. "The ship will dock

in Libya on or about the first of February. You will be pleased with the merchandise. I can assure you of that."

"And delivery to Berlin?" Sukarno asked. Siegel slapped his shirt pocket. "I have the address here. No later than a month after unloading in Libya."

"Very well, Herr Siegel. It has been a pleasure doing business with you."

Siegel nodded, struggled out of his chair, then walked out of the hotel room with his briefcase and four hundred thousand dollars worth of bearer bonds.

Rokus Sogiarto, the commander of Komando Jihad, the extremist splinter organization from the now near-defunct Darul Islam, settled on the sofa and poured himself a glass of wine from a bottle that had not been touched during the meeting with Franz Siegel. "Do you think he will deliver?"

Sukarno glanced at the athletically built Indonesian and paused before answering. "Of course he will. Siegel deals with dangerous people. He's not about to jeopardize his life by getting too greedy. He's smart." His statement sounded confident, contrary to his actual thoughts. Sogiarto's age of mid-forties, his presence, and his military bearing intimidated him. Sukarno found it disconcerting that he felt inferior to Sogiarto, though Sogiarto was subordinate in their newly formed alliance.

Sogiarto had never dreamed that his organization, Komando Jihad, would ever have the capability it now had. The parent organization, Darul Islam, though centered on Dar-al-Islam, the House of Islam, where Muslim government unyieldingly rules and Muslim law prevails, was too conservative for his taste. This core tenet of Islam has two houses of Islam, not one as Darul Islam claimed as their focus. The second house is that of Dar al-Harab, or House of War. The world not ruled by the House of Islam is ruled by infidels, and Komando Jihad's article of faith was that the House of Islam could only be obtained by the sword. Violence carried to the populace engendered conversion to Islam, rather than violence aimed directly toward a government as an institution. Though Sogiarto would prefer to confine operations to Indonesia, Sukarno's funding made a broader field of operations acceptable, and to some extent, desirable. With Sukarno's money, Komando Jihad was to be more than a philosophical sect incapable of action.

Sukarno sat in the overstuffed chair adjacent to the sofa, poured himself a glass of wine, and held it in the air. "A toast, Rokus, to our first victory against the Americans in Heidelberg."

Sogiarto hesitated, then completed the toast with Sukarno. "Are you absolutely sure you want to attack the Americans? There are targets in Indonesia. On our soil."

Sukarno stared coldly into Sogiarto's eyes. "Are you afraid, my friend? Does an American army headquarters frighten you?" He paused long enough to see Sogiarto's eyes drop to the contents of his glass to avoid those eyes staring at him so intently. "We must take the battle to the enemy. We must make him understand that we will destroy him anywhere in the world. Komando Jihad will no longer be insignificant. Komando Jihad soldiers are soon to become the most feared warriors in the world, and glory is to Allah. And you, my leader, the most feared man in the world.

CHAPTER 5

1000 Hours
1 December 1972
Seventh Army Command
Heidelberg, Germany

AS THE ARMY ambulance with its characteristic green paint and a large red cross on a circle of white passed through the main gate, Sukarno busied himself miles away in his Berlin hotel suite, preparing for a flight to Rome at noon. He glanced at his watch. Another half-hour and his plan would add another layer of fear and chaos to the Western world.

Ahmad, a twenty-year-old Indonesian from a small coastal town in southeastern Java, drove calmly but was inwardly excited that Rokus had selected him over the others to glorify Allah. The others wanted this assignment, but Rokus had favored him because he spoke respectable English. He learned it from the American oilfield workers and merchant seamen that moved cargo on the docks. He hated them all, not because they had done anything in particular to harm him, but because their mere presence was disrespectful to the Muslim way of life. His father was a deeply religious man, and he had been taught the values of generations before him. With their drunkenness and money, the Americans had destroyed life as he had known it and valued it. They lacked respect. They had no respect for the traditions and beliefs of the people whose land they exploited for themselves. Rokus had shown him a way to preserve those values though he knew from the start that it would someday cost him his life. He did not mind.

A jeep marked *Military Police* passed Ahmad going the other way as he accelerated away from the gate. He waved, and they did the same. Passing through the gate had been as easy as Sukarno had said it would be. It was an open post. The guards at the gate were not there to strictly survey everyone entering. They were primarily there to provide information or to give directions. Ahmad had slowed as he approached the gate, giving a cursory wave and nod to the guard, who waved him through. No one was the wiser, just as he had been told.

Ahmad stopped at a stop sign a mile down the winding road and cautiously made a slow left turn. He had studied the maps for hours and had been tested many times by Rokus and Sukarno. There were too many chances for error or just plain bad luck, should he have to pull over to check his map. There was too much risk that an MP might stop to offer assistance, only to become overly curious about Ahmad's broken and often incorrect usage of the English language. Suspicions might lead to an inspection of the cargo in the back of the ambulance, which would mean a disgraceful defeat.

A right turn, then a left. Within twelve minutes of passing through the gate, Ahmad pulled the ambulance to the curb. He pulled his cap off his head, wiped the sweat from his brow, then wiped his sweating palms on the olive drab uniform pants while staring straight ahead. He replaced the cap and surveyed the road to the front, then the rear by glancing in the side mirror. There was nothing unusual. Even the pedestrians on the street thought nothing of an ambulance parked across the street from the post-elementary school.

Ahmad lit a cigarette, then relaxed in the seat, his left arm resting on the window frame as he surveyed the school's front door. Through the door and the waist-high windows that extended in both directions from the doors, he could see the young students and teachers as they went about their daily routine. The cigarette slowly burned, and Ahmad studied it carefully after each long pull of the smoke into his lungs. Every exhale had suddenly become a ceremony, a countdown to the most significant event of his life.

When the cigarette had burned too far to hold it, Ahmad dropped the butt to the street outside the window, turned the key, and started the ambulance. It roared to life without hesitation. As it idled, Ahmad rummaged through his shirt pocket and withdrew a small red capsule, glanced at it briefly, then put it into his mouth and clenched it between his teeth. Next, he pulled a radio transmitter from under the seat and flipped the chrome switch on the top of the box. When he did, a small red light immediately began to flash.

A quick glance in every direction confirmed that the time was perfect. Ahmad slipped the transmission into gear with his foot pressed heavily against the brake pedal and simultaneously revved the engine. The ambulance shuddered for a moment under the strain of the opposing forces of the engine and brakes, and then he released the brake. The ambulance sprang to life. With both hands on the steering wheel, he made a smooth arcing curve toward the school's double doors. The ambulance jumped the curb, which slammed his head against the roof of the cab, causing him to almost prematurely bite through the cyanide capsule he held between his teeth, then bounced violently up the steps before crashing through the double doors. Ahmad pressed the detonator button as the doors gave way, and the plastique exploded. The ambulance's momentum continued to carry it another twenty feet into the school hallway, and the explosion sent shards of metal in every direction. The plastique was intended to do minor damage to the building, which was accurate enough in its planning, and the three fifty-five-gallon barrels in the cargo area ruptured exactly as planned. Within seconds, a cloud of gray gas swelled from the wreckage and found its way down each hallway toward the classrooms, where three hundred eighty-six students and teachers sat stunned from the noise and reverberations of the explosion.

1300 Hours
6 December 1972
J.F.K. Memorial Stadium
Philadelphia, Pennsylvania

IT WAS THAT TIME AGAIN—THAT special time. The Army-Navy game was about to be underway. For Jake, Patrick, Wayne, Steve, and sixteen hundred other cadets and midshipmen, it was their last such event in their respective academy's uniform. For the first classmen, this game was filled with mixed emotions in that they were excited that the four years of academy life were near an end, but equally sad that never again would they experience the annual Army-Navy game in quite the same way. They might attend the game many times in the years to come, but never again would they experience it from the perspective of a cadet or midshipman. None of those in attendance, or the millions watching on television, wanted their team to win more than the first classmen of Army and Navy. This game was special to them.

Jake heard the command of the brigade commander in the distance and immediately snapped an about-face. In the drawn-out cadence of a perfectly timed and executed military command, one that can take six seconds to sound two words, he bellowed out the command, "Ba-tal—yons! Atten—shun!" The three battalion commanders of the 4th Regiment repeated the command, and the three company commanders of each battalion did likewise. In short order, the one-thousand-man command of Cadet Captain John Paul Jacobs snapped to attention as one-fourth of the United States Corps of Cadets, the world's finest marching unit of its size, prepared to march. "For—ward! March!" Jake commanded.

The United States Corps of Cadets began its entry into the stadium, and Jake, as the regimental commander of the 4thRegiment, felt a surge of pride rush through his body. He had never dreamed that one day he would hold one of the five highest cadet ranks at West Point. The march-on for the Army-Navy game at the head of his regiment was the major highlight of his cadet career. Though he could not hear it himself, his parents watching the game at home heard the television announcer say, "… and commanding the 4th Regiment for the Corps of Cadets is Cadet Captain John Paul Jacobs from Comanche, Texas." While insignificant to the world at large, it was a monumental moment for a twenty-year-old and his parents who had lost a son in the mountains of South Vietnam. Nothing would bring Charlie back to them. Nothing would vindicate the sorrow. But the moment brought joy in the knowledge that if he were alive, Charlie would be bursting with pride at the magnificent sight of his little brother leading the 4th Regiment onto the field.

1300 Hours
6 December 1972
Dallas, Texas

THE MILITARY MARCH played through the speaker as Sara kneeled three feet from the television, staring excitedly at the sight of four thousand cadets in gray uniforms perfectly formed on the football field. She watched intently as the camera panned for closeups of different cadets as they marched. She hoped against all hope that out of the four thousand, she would be lucky enough to see him. And she did. The camera slowly zoomed in from a distance for a closeup as they announced his name. Sara was both elated and stunned.

Though brief, the sight of Jake brought a lump to her throat, and her chest tightened from a rush of adrenaline. The announcement and the camera moved on to events unfolding, but Sara continued to stare at the screen, seeing nothing but the scene of Jake marching toward her. Tears rolled down her cheeks as she vaguely realized that her momentary glance at Jake was gone, and a beer commercial had replaced him.

1500 Hours
6 December 1972
J.F.K. Memorial Stadium
Philadelphia, Pennsylvania

THE CANNON of Navy and the Howitzer of Army fired simultaneously as the last second rolled off the clock at halftime. Army led the Navy 17-10, but the midshipmen still had thirty minutes of fight remaining before the day was done.

Pre-game antics had started during the march-on. The Brigade of Midshipmen had marched into the stadium first. They had received strict orders before leaving Annapolis to show respect for their sister academy by demonstrating their maturity as future officers of the United States Navy. But, as with any organization that is composed predominately of eighteen- to twenty-one-year-old men under the stress of enthusiasm, orders have a way of breaking down. The cadets of West Point entered the stadium and formed perfectly by regiments, battalions, and companies to execute their precision opening ceremonies. It started with merely a ripple of voices, but it was not long before the entire Brigade roared "Big Deal" after every movement made by the Corps of Cadets. The Corps handled the immaturity of the midshipmen with dignity, maturity, and professionalism. Their duty was to not be distracted by the childish behavior of the Navy. The superintendent of West Point stood proud. Then, the Corps of Cadets executed their final about-face and shouted in unison, "Up yours, Navy!"

There was no time wasted in the traditional declaration of war. Two Army cadets, camouflaged in Navy long overcoats and white hats, casually strolled within proximity of Billy, Navy's handsome goat, and furiously spray-painted him with water-soluble paint in black, gray, and gold. Across the field streaked the two cadets running as hard as they could, shedding the enemy's uniform with thirty midshipmen close behind. The laughter from the West bounced from wall to wall of the stadium, and old Army gridiron songs flowed from the band. Navy was indignant at the attack. Pearl Harbor had been low, but this was lower.

The stadium roared again as A-Man ran to the center of the field. A-Man looked like Spiderman dressed in black with a gold cape and a large gold "A" on his chest. A knight in black armor sat astride Hannibal the Army mule, following A-Man, brandishing his broadsword at the East. Ten cadets, dressed as midshipmen, encircled A-Man and the black Knight to unfold a drama at center field. A-Man and the Black Knight quickly dispatched the undercover midshipmen, as any two heroes would, and stood victorious over their enemies. Those in the East shouted their disgust and disapproval. Those in the West cheered their heroes and sang their songs of victory.

The first half of the game had not been a disappointment. The game was hard-fought by the players on both sides, and the cadets and midshipmen made the stadium vibrant with their cheers and traditional yells. As always, Army and Navy were well-represented by their team, and no one on the field of honor was literally vanquished.

Meeting under a goalpost at halftime had by now become a tradition. Jake and Patrick spotted Steve and Julia Dane and hurried to meet them. "You look great, Steve," Jake said as he shook hands with his friend in the white hat. Steve returned the compliment with a broad smile on his face. "And you, Julia. I've never seen you look more beautiful. This sailor must agree with you."

Julia nearly leaped into Jake's arms and kissed him affectionately on the cheek. "He does agree with me. Or at least he better," she said as she glanced at Steve. "I sure have missed my favorite Army man, though."

"How about me," Patrick said. "Where's my passionate hug and kiss. I don't know why you bother with either one of those two, Julia. You're looking at the best right here."

Julia grabbed Patrick and gave him a hug and kiss on the cheek. "I've missed you, too, you smooth talker you. I see you've been taking good care of Jake for us."

"Yep. That's me—guardian angel. With Jake, it ain't easy, though. These Texas boys ain't got enough sense to get outta the rain. But I reckon you know what I mean."

"Six stripes," Steve said, admiring the chevrons covering Jake's arm. "I wouldn't want you to get the wrong idea and think I give a hoot about you, but I sure was proud to watch you lead your regiment into the stadium today. I always knew you'd be a big shot."

Jake laughed. "What are you talkin' about? You're a squadron commander. Besides, the word I get is that you stand number three in academics. I'm the one that's proud."

"Don't you just hate a mutual admiration society when you're not in it?" Patrick said to Julia.

"I'm proud of all of you," Julia said.

Steve removed his hat and gently raised Julia's left hand for all to see. Obvious to all was the miniature class ring, traditionally worn as an engagement ring. "Between this ring and Rear Admiral Dane, Julia has no escape now from being all Navy."

"I figured you would be calling him Admiral Daddy by now," Patrick said. "And I'm downright disappointed, Julia. I was hopin' you'd be over this Steve business by now. I was gonna ask you to marry me. Just as soon as the game is over."

CHAPTER 6

1930 Hours
10 January 1973
United States Military Academy
West Point, New York

FINALS WERE COMPLETE, and a long weekend of three days was welcome. It always seemed so depressing to return to the Gloom Period and immediately be faced with the semester exams. Wayne had explained his theory that the academy did not want you to study for finals. In harmony with the rest of West Point's good deals, those in charge figured that a cadet either knew the material or he did not. Cramming for an exam was not acceptable. And, they knew that not one cadet would bother to crack a book during Christmas leave. Occasionally a plebe took a few books home, but they soon learned that all they had gained was a little exercise from lugging the books through airports.

Christmas had been fun and relaxing for Jake. Julia Dane

had flown with Steve to Dallas, and the three of them spent a good part of the week together. As expected, Steve's parents fell in love with Julia, which made everyone delighted with the upcoming graduation and wedding. If Julia felt ill at ease in the Ross home, no one was the wiser. She seemed more relaxed and at home than Steve or Jake had ever seen her. Jake mentioned it to Steve, and he remarked about having just the opposite feelings in her parent's home. They were nice enough, and they tried to make him feel at home, but it was hard to forget that the man of the house was an admiral. In fact, it was not often that the admiral forgot that he was an admiral.

In terms of amusement, the week's highlight for Steve was on Saturday night when the women coerced Jake into arranging for a double date. At his mother's and Julia's strong suggestion, Jake called his high school classmate, Jamie Slaughter, and she readily accepted. Jamie seemed to be a non-threatening choice. He had not been with a girl since Sara, nor was he ready to be. Jamie was the most non-threatening choice if he had to do this.

"I already know Julia," Jake pleaded. "Why don't you escort Jamie, since this is no big deal, and I'll escort Julia?"

"No can do, Jake. She's an engaged woman. Besides, I promised Admiral Daddy that I'd protect her with my life against the evils of all Army men. A promise is a promise."

"You'd make a fine catch," Julia stated in her firm demand that there was to be no backing out.

"Catch? Who said anything about getting caught? Things are just fine the way they are," Jake defended. "I may take some girl to a movie with you two, but that's it. Finished. Over-and-out. Adios! I've got better things to do than to get my head all out of joint over some female."

Steve looked at Julia and laughed. "It's worse than I thought. This boy is scared to death."

"He should be scared. We females are dangerous. Boxing champion Jake might get whipped if you know what I mean," Julia said, giggling as she snuggled close to Jake. She had never in her life failed to melt a frown, and she was not about to give up on Jake either. She ran her fingers through his hair and allowed her perfume to attack his defenses. "You like me. I'm a woman. Do you like my perfume?"

"Yes. I know the dangerous part very well," Steve said with a grin. "But are you sure you have the right girl to get Jake's head turned around? Not only was Jamie Slaughter the smartest girl that has ever gone to Comanche High, but she could have won an Einstein look-alike contest, too."

"Trust me," Julia said sternly with her hands on her hips.

"Fine," Jake said with a tone of resignation. "The date is on. But I'm drivin'. When I say the date is over, it is over. I'd be an idiot to let Steve drive me down some dark road and leave me sitting in the back seat with some girl I didn't want to go out with in the first place while you two moan and slurp all over the front seat."

"You could use a little moanin' and slurpin'," Steve said jokingly.

For the next two days, Jake vacillated between the temptation to cancel the date and the acceptance that he would enjoy visiting with an old high school classmate. Jamie was nice, and he had always liked her, but he had never considered having a date with her. Jamie had probably never considered having a date with him either, or anyone else for that matter. The two days passed, but not without a sense of uncertainty and dread hanging over him.

At 2000 hours, or eight o'clock, sharp, Jake slammed the

car door to muffle the giggling from the back seat and walked solemnly to Jamie's front door. He knocked. The door opened.

"Hi, Jake," the woman said. "Let me get my coat, and I will be ready."

Jake stood speechless. It was Jamie Slaughter. It had to be, but it sure did not look like her. This woman was the same height as Jamie, but that was about the only similarity she had with the Jamie he remembered. It was a metamorphosis. Jamie's large-framed, black glasses were gone, her figure was exquisite, her hair was immaculate, and she had matured into one of the most beautiful women he had ever seen.

Jake had a wonderful time. Jamie was still the nice person he had known in high school, and she liked being with all of them. California Institute of Technology, better known as Caltech, had failed to convert her small-town, Texas values to those of hating the military and soldiers. She and Julia became immediate friends. While still at dinner, Julia and Steve told her about Jake's collywobbles over his date with her. Jamie laughed with them and hugged Jake.

"Jake," she said with a smile on her face. "You dear sweet man. I was thrilled that you asked me out tonight. You and Steve, and a few others, were the only ones that treated me nice in high school. Most of our classmates gave me a hard time about being good at academics and being plain-looking. You treated me like a person. Thank you."

"I'm the one that's thankful," Jake said. "I'm having a great time."

"And you should have a great time, Jake," Jamie said in a motherly tone. "I was sad to hear about you and Sara. But it's time for you to get out there and enjoy life. You don't have to get serious with everyone you take out. Just go out to have fun. Look at us. Good friends, talk of old times, talk of the future."

She was right, and Jake knew that she was. He was having fun again, and he did not feel pressured or out of place. He was simply enjoying himself.

"Make me a promise," Jamie continued. "You graduate in June and have sixty days of leave. Come to California for at least a couple of weeks. We'll have a great time. I'll introduce you to all my friends, and we'll go and do everything there is to do. My roommates and I have a house on the beach. You can sleep until noon, watch bikinis during the day, and play all night. What do you say?"

Jake was dumbstruck. "Say yes," Steve said emphatically. "The only thing that could be better than that for sixty days is to be in my shoes, which you won't be, by the way. I'm gonna be on a sixty-day honeymoon with the most beautiful woman in the world."

"Okay," Jake said without hesitation. "If you're sure, I wouldn't be a bother. I'd love to come."

Dinner was perfect. The two couples stayed at the restaurant laughing and talking until midnight and skipped the movie. The evening still felt young to Jake as he and Jamie walked slowly toward her door. Time had passed so quickly, and it was so exhilarating to him that he wanted to ask her out again for the next night, but she was leaving for California. When they reached the porch, Jake wanted to kiss Jamie, but he was afraid. It had been so long, and it had always been Sara. He felt like he did not know how to act or what to do. Jamie sensed his fear and stepped close to him with a thin smile. She wrapped her arms around his neck and kissed him with a passion reserved for lovers only.

Jake now lay on his bunk, covered from head-to-toe with his comforter to ward off the constant chill in the room and thought of California. He had forced Wayne to call his parents and tell them to send every brochure they could find. He was anxious for graduation, his blue Corvette, California, and time with Jamie. It felt good to have a friend of the female persuasion again, and it did not hurt that she was smart and drop-dead gorgeous.

1930 Hours
10 January 1973
United States Military Academy
West Point, New York

WAYNE THREW OPEN the door and walked into the cold room. "Shake a leg. Brigade CO has called a little get-together at HQ for all you big shots. Just ran into the deputy brigade commander."

"Go away," Jake mumbled. "Leave me alone. Can't you see I'm fantasizing?"

"Well. Sorry to bother you, O Great One, but duty calls. See? That's what you get for being a big shot. If you were a screw-up like me, nobody would give a hoot where you are."

Jake moaned his displeasure at having been disturbed as he tied his shoes. "Where's Patrick? I haven't seen him for hours."

"He is over at the boodlers in Grant Hall sipping a coke and trying to sweet-talk Brad Noonan's girlfriend. He wants you to come over as soon as you finish with the CO."

"That boy is going to get killed one of these days," Jake said as they walked down the hall together. "Brad Noonan is likely to stomp Patrick's head into dust. Where is Noonan?"

"On the area. Walking tours."

Jake snickered. "I'll go make the CO happy. You go back to

Grant Hall and keep Mr. Personality out of trouble. As soon as I finish, I'll meet you there."

"So, you want me to get my head stomped into dust, too, huh?"

"I'm not worried. Patrick isn't really trying to beat Noonan's time. He's just practicing. Of course, Noonan wouldn't know that."

Jake turned up his collar against the freezing wind blowing from the Hudson and walked briskly to brigade headquarters. He noticed the solemn look on the staff's faces when he entered the room. Normally it was a lighthearted group, even under the worst of stresses. Not today. The room was quiet. The other three regimental commanders were milling around the coffee pot, each lost in his thoughts, while Jeff Robertson, the first captain or brigade commander, talked in a barely audible tone to his second in command.

"We have a situation here, gentlemen," Robertson said. "Have a seat. This may take a while. I'm sorry I had to bother you."

"What's the problem?" the commander of the 1st Regiment asked.

"A yearling from Company B-2 was found on an honor violation last week. Cheating on a statics and dynamics exam. The honor board was convened, and a true bill was found. The name is Kelly. I reviewed the proceedings, and there is no question the honor board acted responsibly. There was a professor and two other cadets who saw Kelly cheat. The file is on my desk if you'd like to review it."

"How did he cheat?" Jake asked.

"He had a crib sheet of formulas, and he wrote in some multiple-choice answers as the professor gave the approved solution." Everyone present could easily visualize the violation. A writ, or test, was given every day. When the professor had given the order to cease work on the writ, the procedure was for all cadets to set down their pencils while the professor gave the correct answers. The purpose of this ritual was to let the cadets see how they had done and have an opportunity to ask questions or clear up misunderstandings. Operating under the Cadet Honor Code, the procedure is an effective form of instruction. "Mister Kelly palmed a short pencil to write in answers."

Cheating at West Point was rare, but it did happen occasionally. The code was clear. Whatever work that was not one hundred percent the individual's work was defined as cheating. On written papers due, a cadet signed the outside cover, which represented a statement that everything in the paper was his work. The signature constituted assurance that the cadet did the research himself, wrote the paper himself, and typed it himself, no one helped him spell a word, and no one proofread it. At West Point, the work was one hundred percent the work of the cadet.

"So, what's the problem? It's a true bill. He is to be separated from the Corps," the 3rd Regiment commander said.

Jeff Robertson leaned against his desk and rubbed his chin. "Kelly requested an Officer's Board, which he is permitted to do, and the Uniform Code of Military Justice rules that board. Mister Kelly found a loophole. The professor technically prejudiced the case in a discussion he had with the other two witnesses immediately following that class."

The commander of the 3rd Regiment bolted upright in his chair. "Don't tell me they let him off the hook! They didn't throw it out on a technicality, did they?"

"That's exactly what they did, Bill," Robertson said in a

tone that sympathized with the question. "The entire transcript of the board is in the file if you care to read it."

"I think I know what you are going to say next, Jeff, but you need to lay out exactly how you want us to handle our people on this," Jake said calmly.

Robertson nodded his head in agreement. "The Corps will silence Kelly. If he doesn't resign, which I don't think he will, we will silence him. It's been years since the Corps silenced a West Point cadet, but I don't see any way around it."

The four regimental commanders sat without a word. The silencing of a cadet was the most dreaded situation that could occur at the academy. The Honor Code belonged to the cadets because they were the ones that lived it, individually and collectively. The Honor Code did not belong to the officers, the administration command, not the United States Congress, and not even the President. The Honor Code was a way of life, and each cadet lived it every day and made it work for the Corps as a whole. The Corps of Cadets only had the power to request that a cadet found guilty of an honor violation resign of his free will. They did not have the power to dismiss him formally. Only the officer board could do that, and they did not do so with Kelly due to the technicality. The only recourse the Corps had was to silence the cadet. The Corps would cease to recognize that he was a member of the Corps or even existed. Silencing meant that the cadet would have his room far from the barracks, live by himself, eat at a table by himself, attend classes by himself, and no one would talk to him, ever.

"I don't think any of us agree one hundred percent on every detail of how the honor system works, but I do believe it's good for West Point as it is," Robertson continued as he sat on the edge of his desk and crossed his arms. "I think that silencing is our only course of action. Kelly shouldn't be here.

And, it makes me mad that Kelly doesn't at least have enough honor to take responsibility for his actions. The entire Corps will suffer from this."

The New York Times will love this one," Jake said, shaking his head from side to side.

"Are you saying you disagree, Jacobs?" the 1st Regiment commander asked defensively.

Jeff Robertson lifted himself from the top of his desk. "What about the Times, Jake?"

"I mean, it's too bad there isn't a different way to handle this. The New York Times takes a whack at us almost every day. We have the intellectuals from Harvard who think that refusing to participate in athletics with baby killers, like us, is a rational protest against Vietnam. We also have some unbathed super-geniuses from a few of the all-women bastions of higher learning that stick flowers in our faces and call us names as we walk to class. These people seem to take a moral imperative when burning our flag or throwing bags of human feces on a soldier. They are likely to say we are morally bankrupt for silencing a cadet who violated the Honor Code. That line of thinking makes no sense to me either, but then, we weren't smart enough to get into an Ivy League school."

They all chuckled at the prospect of any of them choosing to attend an Ivy League university over West Point. Had they done so, they would certainly be a different person than they were today.

"So, what's your point?" Robertson asked. "Are you saying we shouldn't silence Kelly?"

Jake thought for a moment, then leaned his chair back on two legs. "Nope. I don't see that Kelly has given anyone much choice. All I'm saying is that Kelly has hurt West Point more than appears on the surface. I think this situation is explosive and that a little pow-wow with the general is in order. The Corps will silence Kelly all right, as they should, but when things heat up in the outside world from it, the men are going to get angrier and angrier with Kelly. We have an obligation to the Corps, and to West Point, to keep order. This silencing is about honor. We have to make sure that it doesn't turn into dishonor."

"I agree, Jeff," the 2nd Regiment commander said. "This has to be done right. Otherwise, we have done more harm than good."

"What do you suggest, Jake?" Jeff Robertson asked.

"Well. Perhaps we need to gather the entire Corps of Cadets together for a little chit-chat about this. They need to understand that Kelly's civil rights must be protected and that if they aren't, then the consequences to West Point will be severe. It's been years since the Corps silenced a cadet. I think the Corps will handle it fine if we give them a little instruction on how to do it."

Jeff Robertson rubbed his chin again as he thought, then moved to the other side of the desk to sit. "Dang, Jake. When are you going to learn to keep your mouth shut?" He laughed. "You're in charge of putting together a plan to instruct the Corps on this matter. I want specifics on what considerations each cadet should give to the silencing and how we should get the word out to the Corps. I want it on my desk at 0800 hours in the morning. I'll set an appointment with the general. We'll meet here for a formal briefing by Captain Jacobs, and by sundown tomorrow, we'll have it ready to implement. Any questions?"

"No, sir," the four regimental commanders replied. Robertson had given the order. All the commanders respected Robertson, and he had made the command of their regiments meaningful. He delegated command and allowed each commander to do as he saw fit. Quick summation of a problem and a viable solution was one of his strengths. The officials at West Point had chosen the first captain well. Jake and the others had no doubts that Jeff Robertson would one day wear four silver stars.

Jake hurriedly walked to Grant Hall and found Patrick, Wayne, Brad Noonan, and his girlfriend at a table in the corner. He immediately noted that they were all laughing. If Noonan had thoughts of murdering Patrick, he had his emotions well hidden. Jake pulled a chair from the table nearby and straddled it backward.

"Well, if it's not our mighty leader," Patrick said. "Hope you got the brigade CO all straightened out. What I'd like to hear is that you guys did something useful, like cancel classes until June."

Jake avoided the comment. It was not the time or place to debate the honor system or the silencing of a cadet. The Honor Code was politics, character issues, and religion all mixed, West Point style. "Brad. Has my roommate been charming your girl while you were walking the area?"

Sue Pratt giggled. "He tried. But Patrick's not nearly as smooth as he thinks he is."

"I resent that," Patrick said in mock indignation. "I'll have you know, Sue, I was holding my best lines in check out of respect for my classmate here. Just wouldn't be fittin' for a cadet to make time with another cadet's girl."

"Since when?" Wayne asked. "Wasn't it just last month that you snatched Brenda what's-her-name out of the clutches of that guy from the 1st Regiment?"

Patrick leaned back in his chair and smiled. "That was different. He was from 1st Regiment. Those guys are too warped to know how to treat a lady. If she married a 1st Regiment guy, she would find herself having to make breakfast in fatigues, and a Jeep would be the family automobile. I was just saving her life, that's all."

"Patrick. You're so full of it. You should be a Marine," Wayne said.

Jake laughed and stood. "I have to run. Sue, it was good to see you again. Brad is a lucky man. I hear there's a wedding scheduled in the chapel after graduation. Is that right?"

Sue coyly held her left hand in the air to show everyone her engagement ring, a West Point miniature. "Four more months, and I'll be Mrs. Brad Noonan."

"And four after that, you'll be crying for mercy," Wayne said. "Noonan here is a good man, but you sure can pick the ugly ones, Sue."

Sue slapped Wayne's arm and giggled. Brad cracked a genuine smile, knowing that the disparagement was a compliment, and squeezed Sue's hand under the table.

Jake excused himself again and started the long walk back to the barracks. He was halfway when Patrick and Wayne caught up with him. "Slow down, hillbilly. Don't you know it's bad for a firstie's image to be seen running?"

Jake chuckled at the image he had of first classmen when he was a plebe. During the last semester, most of them looked like overweight executives, and their attitude toward military trivia was nowhere to be found. All they could think about was Mobilization Day and graduation. Patrick was right. It was difficult to find a firstie out of his rack during free time, much less running across the area.

"What's the scoop?" Patrick asked. "I hear we have one cadet who has done screwed the pooch."

"Screwed," Jake said. "He did that, all right. It looks like we're going to have to silence a cadet named Kelly. He refuses to resign, and the Officer's Board had to dismiss the case."

"Maybe he will mysteriously disappear in the middle of the night," Patrick joked.

Jake stopped dead in his tracks with a stern look on his face. "Well, that's exactly the kind of attitude we have to get turned around. This Kelly is a sure-fired, number-one numbskull for not having enough courage and honor to resign at the Corp's request, but he still deserves his civil rights, just like any other American citizen. We have to make sure he is not harassed or physically harmed one little bit. We will silence him according to the protocol of silencing, and that is it."

Patrick was thoughtful and started walking. Jake and Wayne automatically fell into step with him. All three remained silent, each lost in his thoughts until they had climbed the five flights of stairs of the 50th Division and closed the door to their room.

"I see the problem," Patrick earnestly said. "My first instinct, I'm ashamed to say, was to lynch the bugger. It's not the right way to handle the situation, but most cadets in the Corps will have about the same reaction."

"So, what kind of plan do we need to put together, Jake? Patrick and I will be your slaves. What do you want us to do?" Wayne asked.

"It's an all-nighter. I'm sorry your evening is going to get ruined. I appreciate the help," Jake said, somehow feeling content that he could always count on Patrick and Wayne whenever he needed them.

The hours to dawn passed quickly with drafts and redrafts of outlines, speeches, and organizational charts. But, at the first crack of light, a full-scale plan had taken form. They had prepared outlines for each regimental commander to use when addressing his regiment in North Auditorium. They prepared a special order for the brigade commander's signature, which outlined the particular set of regulations that would be enforced along with the consequences to be imposed on any violators. They then prepared a short speech for delivery in the mess hall by the brigade commander and prepared a press release for the New York Times. They established time schedules for every detail. At 0700 hours, Jake stripped and took a hot shower with only an hour remaining until he presented the plan to Robertson and the other commanders. The brigade CO had not said whether Jake would accompany him to the superintendent's office but a shower, shave, and a fresh uniform seemed a reasonable precaution.

1830 Hours
11 January 1973
United States Military Academy
West Point, New York

JAKE SLOWLY STROLLED the length of the walls of a room on the first floor of the library. The Corps was in the mess hall, and for a few minutes, he was alone. It felt strange to be in the room without a dozen cadets hunched over books or passing to another section of the library. It was a special room for Jake. He stopped in front of the large window and fixed his eyes on General George S. Patton's larger-than-life statue standing outside, illuminated by lights. The darkness around the figure, and the large falling snowflakes, delivered flashes of history from pages once read about the general and the snow, of him leading components of the 3rd Army to rescue the 101st

Airborne at Bastogne. Jake turned and faced the center of the great room. On one end hung a huge oil painting of General Robert E. Lee with his gray hair and kind eyes, graduate and twice superintendent of West Point, and brilliant commander of the valiant Army of Northern Virginia that fought through some of the nation's most dramatic battles. Chancellorsville, The Wilderness, Gettysburg, Petersburg, and finally Appomattox revealed the American Civil War's rich history. On the opposite wall, Jake stared at Lee's counterpart in the war, fellow West Pointer, and President of the United States. Ulysses S. Grant's visage loomed from the canvas with a sadness in his eyes, perhaps from the destruction seen and ordered in combat with Lee. Jake walked to the far end of the room and delicately touched the wood and glass case where dozens of West Point class rings rested for all to contemplate. The case seemed to make one aware that Eisenhower, MacArthur, Stillwell, Jackson, Beauregard, and others whose contribution to the nation's military history would never die. Jake was no different from the hundreds who entered the Civil War Room each year, where a sense of history and the purpose of West Point came to life before their very eyes. It could be seen. It could be felt—down to the marrow of the bones.

"Sir. Cadet Kelly reporting to the commander of the 4th Regiment, as ordered, sir."

Jake turned from the case, startled by the disturbance from his thoughts, and motioned Cadet Kelly to have a seat. Jake pulled up a chair and sat across the walnut table from him. "Do you know why I asked you to see me here?" Jake's manner and tone were relaxed.

"I have a pretty good idea, sir. I imagine you want to talk me into resigning."

"That's an honest answer. I've been ordered here, too.

And, you're right. The brigade commander and the superintendent thought you might resign if we had a talk."

"I'm not going to resign, sir. You're wasting your time," Kelly said defensively.

"Ok. As far as I'm concerned, you have a right to make that choice and decision. The regulations say that you have that right under the circumstances, so let's just forget you resigning and accept that you are going to stay." Jake shifted casually in his chair. "My job for the past couple of days has been to make your silencing conform to regulations that will prevent you from being harassed or physically abused."

"This silencing is a bunch of bull, sir. I'm innocent. I don't deserve to be silenced."

Jake paused and looked at his fingernails. Kelly became more uneasy, knowing that Jake didn't believe his lie. "Mister Kelly, there is no one here but you and me. The rest of the Corps is in the mess hall. Captain Robertson and the superintendent are talking to them, as we speak, on how to silence you —which is a potential action every new cadet is made aware of during his earliest days at West Point—and at the same time preserve your rights. This conversation will never leave this room. You've made a decision to stay in the Corps of Cadets, though the Corps has asked you to separate yourself from them. Don't sit there and compound this problem by lying to me. I won't tolerate it. The Officer's Board has seen to it that you have the choice to go or stay, but don't you dare lie to me again. This conversation is confidential. It is just you and me. I want the truth. This is probably the only opportunity you're going to have to get all this off your chest."

Kelly stared at Jake for a few seconds, and then his chest started heaving as the sobs rose in his throat. He tried to make himself stop, but he could not. "Oh, God, what have I done? I'm sorry. I'm so sorry."

Jake sat forward in his chair and reached across the table to touch Kelly's arm. Kelly gripped the hand as though the touch of a caring being was the most important thing in the world to him.

"Tell me what happened. Tell me all of it."

Kelly got himself under control and sat back in his chair. "I thought I was going to flunk statics and dynamics. I just couldn't keep up. Every day it was something new that I didn't understand. I just couldn't take it anymore."

"So, you had a cheat sheet and wrote some of the answers in during the approved solution?" Jake asked.

"Yes, sir. I'm sorry I shouldn't have done it. I just didn't know what else to do," Kelly said as he wiped the tears away from his eyes with his sleeve.

Jake could see the relief on Kelly's face. He had fought for days to maintain his innocence under impossible evidence. "Did you try additional instruction, or did you go to the academic sergeant in your company?"

"Yes, sir, but I still couldn't keep up."

Jake sighed and leaned back in his chair. "Where you from, Kelly?"

"Provo, Utah. My folks have a hardware store there."

"Why did you come to West Point? Did you want the Army as a career?" Jake asked, trying to learn from Kelly why silencing seemed like a better solution to him than admitting he had made a mistake and going home.

"The Army is all right. At least I thought it was. I thought I wanted to be in forestry once, but I don't think I ever will be"

Jake reflected a moment on what Kelly had told him. "Tell

me, did you come to West Point because you wanted to, or did you come because someone else wanted it for you?"

Tears welled up again in Kelly's eyes. "Oh God, everyone back home will be so ashamed of me. My father. This will kill him. I can't go home. I just can't go home like this."

"Did your father want you to come here? Was West Point more his idea than yours?" Jake asked with concern in his voice.

Kelly thought for what seemed a full minute, then wiped his eyes again roughly as though he were angry. "My father has wanted me to go to a service academy since I was in the seventh grade. My coming to West Point has been the most important thing in his life. I mean, I'm glad I came, but he wanted it a lot more than I ever did."

"You know, Mister Kelly, I'm glad you've been straight with me. I think I understand where you are coming from and how you feel. I understand better the pressure you are under, and I can sense how you feel about West Point."

Kelly looked at Jake with sad eyes. "Yes, sir. I love West Point and all it has done for me. That's why I can't bear to be thrown out this way."

Jake paused and felt sad himself. He empathized with how Kelly felt about West Point and the strain he was under to avoid disgrace. "Look, Kelly. I'm not going to tell you what to do. It's up to you to make that decision. You have to make a decision here for yourself and West Point. You know you have broken the Honor Code, and you know how black and white this part of our life is. I don't totally agree, but the code has no mercy. You've learned a lot of good things here. One of them is courage, for you to apply to whatever decision you make. There have been good men who had to walk out those gates for one reason or the other. You've seen guys who couldn't make the academics, guys with medical problems, and guys who have broken the Honor Code. None of them wanted to leave. You are a West Pointer, Kelly, and that is all I am going to say."

Kelly stared at the stripe on his sleeve. He found it hard to look Jake in the eyes because his words rang true. He had a classmate who had shattered a knee in gymnastics, and a medical board dismissed him from the academy. His classmate had been heartbroken, but he walked away, loving West Point and the part he had played in its long history.

"Well, Mister Kelly," Jake said in a friendly manner, "I can hear the Corps coming out of the mess hall. I'm glad we had a chance to visit about this. Take a little time to think about what is really important to you, then act on it. It's not an easy choice, I know. Whatever you decide, I wish you well. It may not seem like it now, but you have a long life to live, and I'm sure it will be one of many blessings. Whether you choose to stay or resign, this incident has changed the course of your life. Personally, I believe you will conquer this obstacle. West Point has given you the power to do so." Jake smiled compassionately at Kelly as he rose from the table and patted him on the shoulder before walking away.

At 0830 hours, 12 January 1973, Cadet Gregory P. Kelly officially resigned from the United States Military Academy.

CHAPTER 7

0900 Hours
12 January
The Pentagon
Washington, D.C.

"COLONEL, send in Mr. Hanraty. Is he still in the waiting room?"

"Right away, sir." Colonel Carpenter closed the door behind him, leaving Admiral Hollifield focused studiously on the ten-page report lying flat on his desk. The admiral had only been a month transferred to the Pentagon for a tour as the Navy's highest-ranking officer and a member of the Joint Chiefs of Staff. Being Chief of Naval Operations (CNO) was the pinnacle of a military career. The admiral was excited about the opportunities he might have to favorably restructure a military organization completely demoralized by the Vietnam War. Much needed to be done, even if no one could seem to agree on precisely what was required. If the politicians and the country's youth had their way, the military would be disbanded altogether. Absurd. These were hard times. He hoped he could somehow help rebuild what should never have been destroyed, the American serviceman's morale and fighting capability.

The door opened, and Admiral Hollifield aimed his eyes over the top of his glasses to survey the young civilian in front of him. Hanraty was thin, had poor posture, was thirtyish, and by the look of his rumpled blue blazer and gray trousers, exhausted.

"Have a seat, Richard. I'd like for you to be in on this." Colonel Carpenter nodded and took a seat next to Hanraty in a leather chair in front of the admiral's desk. The admiral leaned back in his chair and removed his glasses. "Interesting report, Hanraty."

John Hanraty repositioned himself in the chair, obviously trying to present an air of comfort where none existed. In the eight years since finishing graduate school at Notre Dame, he had worked for Naval Intelligence as an analyst. This was the first time anyone above his immediate supervisor wanted to talk to him personally about a report. Before, his reports had been assigned, turned in, and had disappeared to the trash as far as he knew. Anxiety was clearly written on his face.

"Heidelberg Military Police says their investigation shows that some inexperienced terrorist group is responsible for the bombing. Fact is, they don't have much of an opinion on what the terrorist was trying to accomplish. I mean, only the terrorist was killed. There were not enough explosives involved to do much damage, and that ammonium nitrate has everyone baffled. Fertilizer? It was contaminated to the point that it was useless. I suppose if everyone in that school had sat still and consciously tried to breathe that stuff, it might have killed someone, but everyone got out with only a few minor chemical burns."

"That's true, sir, this time," Colonel Carpenter interjected. "But if the terrorist had a decent cargo of ammonium nitrate, we would have had a disaster on our hands."

"What do you mean, Colonel?"

"Well, sir, ammonium nitrate can be made to be more powerful than military TNT. If they had useable ammonium nitrate and saturated it with fuel oil, that school would be nothing but a hole in the ground."

Admiral Hollifield was agitated by Carpenter's assessment that they had been lucky. "Do you agree, Mr. Hanraty?"

Hanraty again squirmed in his chair. "Yessir."

"You didn't mention that in this report of yours. Why don't you explain why you think we have a serious problem developing here?"

Hanraty stared at the admiral's expectant gaze for a moment, then glanced at Colonel Carpenter. When he realized that he had to reply, he twisted his fingers together as though in pain. "Well, sir, all this looks like some inexperienced guys put this together. In that, I agree with Heidelberg and Colonel Carpenter. But here are the facts, Admiral." Now that Hanraty had started talking about a subject in which he had confidence, he forgot his anxiety and became quite animated in his presentation. "The bomber was blown up and burned beyond recognition. We have no idea who or what he was. The small amount of explosives? Not enough there to do much more than destroying the ambulance he was driving since they didn't rig good ammonium nitrate, and there was no sign of fuel oil or anything else that would make ANFO (Ammonium Nitrate Fuel Oil)."

"Okay." Admiral Hollifield sat forward in his chair and lit a cigar. "No argument there. But why would some idiot kill himself to fill the school with ammonium nitrate fumes? I mean, I reckon we eat that stuff on just about everything. What was their purpose? The only point he made was to prove he was ignorant."

"That's right, Admiral, but I don't think he knew his weapon was chemical fertilizer. I think that he, and whoever sent him, thought they were detonating a deadly chemical agent. A chemical weapon, or perhaps some biological agent. That guy thought he was going to kill everyone in the school."

Admiral Hollifield puffed on his cigar. His silence encouraged Hanraty to continue.

"Sir, if you were a terrorist and wanted to be as powerful as the big boys, you'd have to have weapons of destruction like the big boys. But no terrorist group is going to have the resources to develop a nuclear bomb. They could instead have chemical weapons to scare the bejesus out of the entire world. If that attack had killed nearly four hundred kids, on a U.S. military facility, with a car bomb, I bet there'd be some excited congressmen this evening."

"No doubt about that," Hollifield said. "Sure wasn't the Vietnamese. They've all but got us out of Vietnam. They wouldn't do something like this. Not now."

"I don't think it is Southeast Asia, Admiral, or Europe. I think it's likely the Middle East."

"So your report says." The admiral flipped through the pages again slowly as Hanraty and the colonel sat silent. "So, to sum this up, you think we have some Arab out there, who is a new player in the game, who wants to make a name for himself. And, according to your report, he's after American targets." The admiral paused and looked sternly over his glasses at Hanraty. "Chemical?"

Hanraty nodded.

"Colonel Carpenter?"

"Yes, sir."

"I'd like to borrow Mr. Hanraty from his section for a few weeks, longer if necessary. Make the arrangements and find him a desk."

"Yes, sir."

"Hanraty. Go home and get some rest."

With wide eyes, Hanraty acknowledged the order with a nod and started to rise.

The admiral frowned, and Hanraty sank back down into the chair. "There's not enough here to prove you're right. But we're going to find out. Get in here in the morning and go to work. If your theory is right, I want to know everything. I want to know who, what, when, and where. You got that?"

"Yes, sir." John Hanraty was both nervous and excited about the assignment. He wanted to do a good job for the admiral. It was his first chance in eight years to work on something important and to use his instincts.

"You're dismissed. See you in the morning, John."

1900 Hours
1 March 1973
Dallas, Texas

Sara sat upright in the leather recliner and strained to see out of the library window when she heard the Porsche's distinctive roar in the circle drive. It was not unusual for Brent to come home much later than this on a weekday, but he was late for a Saturday. He had left the house early that morning with his golf clubs, which was also typical, but Rex

Snyder called before noon, asking where the missing member of their foursome had disappeared. They had not seen him.

Brent did not like being at home. Sara knew that. He did not like her. He did not like being around Stephen Patrick, and he avoided anything that resembled family togetherness with the most obvious of lies. The routine, week after week, had become life. Brent would stay out until midnight during the week doing what Sara had grown to accept him doing, and then he would quietly get into bed with her while she was either asleep or pretending to be. Neither minded that part of the routine. The most uncomfortable of situations for both of them was when some degree of conversation was required. Sara did not want to ask where he had been, nor with whom he was keeping company, and Brent had run out of flimsy excuses months ago. The weekends were a different routine, but of the same result.

The front door opened, and Brent walked to the library. "Hi, babe. Didn't expect you in the library. What have you been doing today?" He tried to act casual, but finding Sara in his library when he expected her to be elsewhere had unsettled him. He knew Sara might question him about his whereabouts.

Sara smiled and continued to sit in the recliner with her leg over one arm. "Stephen Patrick and I went shopping this morning, then came home. How was your day? Did you have a good round of golf?"

"Not bad," Brent said casually, staring at a letter that had come in the mail. "I've played better, but I've played worse."

"Did Rex play well today, or is he still having trouble with the shoulder he dislocated?"

"He is playing better," Brent said, putting down the letter

and picking up another. "He beat me today. I guess the shoulder's not bothering him much anymore."

"Brent." Sara paused. She could tell by the way Brent stiffened his neck that he knew she was well aware that he did not go to the club. She put both feet on the floor and leaned forward. "Stephen Patrick and I are leaving you. I want a divorce."

"Divorce? What are you talking about?" Brent's face turned red as he stalled for time to think. His father would go through the roof if he were to get a divorce, and his mother would complain for a year because of the scandal it would cause. He hated being trapped in this marriage, but he had done a fair job of making it livable in that he did pretty much what pleased him, and Sara and the boy had everything they could want.

Sara retained the same calm tone of voice. "I am going to divorce you."

"But why? Why would you want to throw all of this away?" Brent was confused. He waved his arm in the air, alluding to the grandeur of their home and all that it meant. "You and Stephen Patrick have everything you could ever want. If you don't have it, just tell me, and we'll get it. I love you, Sara. Don't do this."

A thin, false smile crossed Sara's lips as she slowly shook her head from side to side. It was all she could do to control the anger that raged inside of her. "I want a divorce, Brent, because I despise you for sleeping with half the women in Dallas."

Brent masked his face in the act of shock at the accusation. "Sara, I swear. I've never been with another woman."

"You're a liar, too, Brent Mosher. I've had you followed by a private investigator for the past month. I know all about Lisa

Perkins, and Trina Carone, and your father's secretary. I've known all about your life away from home for weeks. I've known almost since we were married. Rex Snyder called today looking for you. You may have played a good game today, but it sure wasn't golf. It was Trina you were playing. The private investigator called an hour ago to tell me he has pictures of you leaving her apartment."

Brent sat listening to Sara and clutched the arms of his chair. His mind raced frantically for a defense, but there was none. A private investigator following him for a month probably had enough hard evidence to hang him in any divorce court in Texas.

"As far as Stephen Patrick and I having everything we wanted, you are wrong. All I wanted from you was for you to be a decent and faithful husband and father. You're none of that, Brent, and I'm through with you." She had been afraid that once she started, she would cry or become hysterical with anger. But with each passing minute, she was gaining strength in her conviction and determination. In days gone by, divorcing Brent was only a delusion full of uncertainty and guilt, but it was now the reality that felt wonderfully right.

Brent stood from his chair and knocked the lamp to the floor with the swing of his left arm. "You bitch. You won't get one dime from the Mosher family or me. You think you can pull this and get away with it? I'll see to it that you get nothing. Go ahead. Leave. I don't care. And take that kid with you. I don't want him around to remind me of you. You've betrayed me, Sara, and I don't ever want to see you in my house again."

Sara smiled. She was feeling like her old self again. She felt good about standing up for herself and Stephen Patrick, and she was confident in her decision. She had not felt like this for a long time. "Sit down, Brent," she said sternly.

Brent swung his hand again at the desk, knocked a stack of mail to the floor, and then sat as Sara had told him. He was angry, but he felt intense danger in a threat of great proportions to his money and his social standing in the community. Sara had the upper hand, and he knew it.

"Stephen Patrick and I will be leaving tomorrow for Colorado. I have an aunt and uncle in Durango. I want you to stay somewhere else tonight, and I don't care where. I want a divorce, and I don't want a big fuss about it. You and your family can keep your millions. All I expect from you is to take care of Stephen Patrick. You owe him that."

Brent sat stunned. He looked like a little boy that had just had a reprieve from his mother for eating cookies before dinner. Though his mother would rant and rave, divorce was beginning to sound like an event of less consequence than expected.

"I'll be signing the divorce papers tomorrow that the lawyers have already prepared. I'm suing for divorce on the grounds of adultery."

Brent winced but said nothing. Whatever evidence she had from the private investigator put him in the weakest of bargaining positions.

Sara stared hard into Brent's eyes. "Brent, if you fight me on this divorce, on custody of Stephen Patrick, or if you harass us one little bit, I swear I'll rip you to shreds in court and take every dime you have. Do you understand the terms, Brent?"

Brent stared back at Sara with his jaw hanging open. He understood. He had never seen Sara so calm yet vicious. There was no doubt that she meant every word she said. "Yes, I understand. How much money do you want?"

Sara laughed and shook her head again. Leave it to Brent to think of money as the most important thing. "I'll leave it up to you and your lawyer to contact me with an acceptable proposal. I'll leave you with a number and address in Durango. Don't dilly-dally around, Brent. I want this over as quickly as possible, and I want to hear from you within a week."

"Well, can you give me some idea of what you expect?" Brent asked.

Sara sighed. "Okay. I want reasonable child support until Stephen Patrick is twenty-one. I want you to pay for all his educational needs, and most of all, I want you to have minimal visitation rights. I never want to see you again. As for your son, I think the less he has to do with you, the better."

Sara could see Brent calculating and thinking about numbers that would satisfy her meager demands. "Unless you have something to say, I would like for you to leave. I have packing to do. We'll be gone by noon tomorrow."

Brent stood and started to say something but changed his mind. He walked slowly to the door without so much as a word, then left the house. Sara sat in the quiet and heard only the Porsche's roar as it turned into the street.

2000 Hours
1 March 1973
United States Military Academy
West Point, New York

JAKE PRESSED the new Corvette's accelerator to the floor and felt the surge of power at his command. A smile stretched across his face, and his heart pumped fast with the excitement of driving his very own car after so many years of waiting. A glance in the rearview mirror told him that the headlights close behind were those of Patrick's black Corvette, and the lights behind his were those of Wayne's canary yellow. All three had chosen Corvettes at the car show in January. The only difference between them was the color and the maniac behind the wheel. Jake slowed, and Wayne pulled into the passing lane. Within seconds, a yellow streak and a melodious roar ripped through the cold, spring air around Patrick and Jake. On their way to nowhere in particular, they took turns at the lead getting there.

Mobilization Day had finally arrived, and the first classmen had not slept in a week. The anticipation of this day made everything in the way of duties null and void. The cars had arrived three weeks earlier and were parked neatly on the lot adjacent to Michie Stadium. The firsties could not drive their new dream machines, but they could sit in them and admire them for hours at a time. The first weekend after the cars had arrived, just under eight hundred vehicles sat on the lot with engines revving and stereos blaring. At least a full tank of gas had passed through each without driving a single mile.

Wayne pulled the yellow 'Vette down the exit ramp and into the drive of an all-night restaurant. Jake and Patrick followed close behind. They parked the cars side-by-side near the windows so they could sit inside and admire them. It had taken them almost four years to get the cars, and they were not about to let them out of their sight.

The pert little waitress took their orders and seemed to enjoy the flirtatious advances the three cadets made. She had been around. Today was not the first Mobilization Day she had seen in her twenty-five years, nor the last. It happened every year, and the residents and business people in the neighboring towns had grown accustomed to seeing intoxicatedly happy cadets with their new cars. She thanked the three for their order with a smile and walked to the kitchen with a little extra swing of the hips, knowing that she was watched—every step.

"Unbelievable how good it feels to get behind the wheel and drive finally," Wayne said excitedly. "I've been dreaming about Ole Yeller for four years."

Jake grinned. "Just think, week after next, we get to take off for spring leave. Five days. What's the plan?"

"Let's all go to Chattanooga. We'll run a convoy. It'll only take us about twelve hours or so, and my folks would love for all of us to show up for a week."

"You sure we wouldn't be too much trouble?" Jake asked.

"Of course not. Besides, I'd like to show you around and introduce you to the best people in the world. You'll love Tennessee. It's a lot like Texas."

"If you ask me, both places are a little backward," Wayne piped in.

Patrick smirked. "Well, we don't often let California surfers into Tennessee, but we'll make an exception in your case. That is if you'll promise not to stay too long."

Jake was staring out the window at the three Corvettes and thinking how fast this last year at West Point had passed. In another two-and-a-butt months, they would leave John Wayne University and have sixty days leave before taking their first duty assignment.

"Having second thoughts about not fighting in the Brigade Boxing Championship next week?" Wayne asked.

Jake smiled and turned to answer the question. "Not at all. Fact is, I'm really excited about not fighting this year. Having the excuse that I've been too busy with the regiment to train for it is just that, an excuse. I think the decision not to fight is best. I fought for three years. That's enough. It's Benson's turn."

"Benson, huh?" Wayne was skeptical. "What's he got to do with it?"

"He was gracious enough last year to step aside for me to have a crack at Cruikshank. He didn't have to do that. If he hadn't, I think he might have taken the championship title last year. That kid is good."

"Not better'n you, partner."

"You're prejudiced. Besides, what's a hillbilly know about anything?"

Patrick bristled like his feelings were hurt. "I'll have you know us hill folks are smarter than we look."

"Couldn't be by much, though," Wayne said.

Patrick was about to respond when four men in their mid-twenties stepped in front of the table. They were appropriately dressed for a sit-in at the White House and evidently had not seen a barber in recent years. The three cadets stared up at them, each with dread in their eyes. The routine was well known.

The largest of the four was naturally the spokesman. "They let you warmongers out of your cages tonight? We were sitting over there having a nice quiet dinner until you baby-killers came in."

Patrick and Wayne glanced at Jake. Patrick had fire in his eyes, but he thought it best not to jump up and stomp a hole in the hippie's head without permission from the regimental commander. Jake slid his chair back, leaned against the table, and casually wiped his mouth with his napkin. "What seems to be the problem, sir? My friends and I just came in here for a bite to eat and a little conversation. We don't want any trouble."

"You filthy military scum. We don't want you eating in here with us. We want you to leave. Right now." Heads were beginning to turn all over the restaurant at the commotion. It was apparent that trouble was about to infect them all.

Jake smiled, then astonished his two friends. "All right. We'll leave. We don't want any trouble, and we don't want any of these other people involved in any kind of incident. If you'll excuse us, we'll be on our way."

Jake started to rise from his chair, but the man pushed him back down. "Not so fast. Do you soldier-boys think you can just waltz in here and sit with decent folks? You think you can just do whatever you want to this country, don't you?"

Jake instantly saw the man's hand come from behind his back and the blade that was in it. With movements based on pure instinct, Jake threw his cup of coffee at the stranger's face and charged toward him. The man flinched at the hot coffee, which was enough time for Jake to seize his wrist with his left hand, forcibly turn it, and slam the back of the man's elbow with the palm of his right hand. The crack of the elbow breaking could be heard throughout the restaurant but was quickly drowned out by the scream that came from deep in the man's throat. Jake spun the man around and threw him on top of the table, sending plates and glasses in every direction, then grabbed the man's testicles in his fist, squeezing and twisting as the man writhed in agony.

Patrick and Wayne stood back and watched with wide eyes, then glanced toward the door to see the other three retreating toward the parking lot.

Jake squeezed tighter. "That wasn't nice to pull a knife, mister. Where do you get off calling us warmongers? Seems to me that you're the one wanting to spill someone's blood."

A man in his late forties, dressed in gray slacks and a blue sweater, quickly approached the table and tapped Jake on the shoulder while everyone else sat stunned. "Excuse me. I'm

Sergeant Collins, New York State Police." Collins dangled his badge in front of Jake's eyes; since Jake had not taken his off the man spread across the top of the table. "You can let this man loose whenever you're ready."

Jake paused, then slowly loosened his grip on the man's groin. When he did, the man sighed some relief, but he was in so much pain from his broken arm that he continued to moan and whimper.

"I saw the knife," Sergeant Collins said. "Just give me your names, and I'll notify the academy about the incident. This dummy didn't give you much choice."

Over the next half hour, two squad cars and an ambulance arrived on the scene, as did a Military Police car from West Point. Sergeant Collins explained to the Military Police what had happened and faulted Jake not in the least for his conduct. The major on the scene asked all three of the cadets separately about the incident, then he and Collins took Jake a few yards from the crowd.

"Mister Jacobs," the major said. "I don't see that you or your classmates have anything to worry about here. Sergeant Collins said that you tried to leave without any conflict. It's too bad that guy pushed his luck. Not only does he have an arm that's broken, but he'll also be charged with assault with a deadly weapon. Still, I think it's important for you to know that you were absolutely right to try to leave without any trouble. I'll report to the commandant tomorrow morning on this incident. I'm sure he will see to it that this is properly stated in your permanent file. So why don't you and your buddies drive on back to The Point and call it a night."

"Yes, sir."

"Jake." Patrick put his hand on Jake's shoulder. "I guess you got a brigade fight after all, huh?"

CHAPTER 8

2200 Hours
22 May 1973
United States Military Academy
West Point, New York

JAKE PLACED the week's duty roster neatly on the clipboard and hung it on his bulletin board. Sunday nights were always the longest because there was so much regimental paperwork to do for the start of a new week, so preparation for the next day's classes was delayed. He was lucky if he got to crawl between the sheets before two in the morning. He did not mind much now. Much of life at West Point was routine, and time often passed more slowly than a soul could stand, albeit there was an element of bitter-sweet that graduation was upon them. It was only ten more days until June Week's festivities started, and graduation followed five days later. Patrick was studying for a Russian history exam, and Wayne was lying prone on his bunk, flipping through the pages of a catalog from

Duke University. Much to everyone's excitement, Wayne had been selected for medical school.

Spring leave had come and gone. Steve met the trio of Corvettes in Washington, D.C., with his shining red one, making a convoy of four to the Tennessee hills. The 'Vettes made good time on the back roads by traveling at speeds in considerable excess of the posted speed limits, and they often stopped for gas, food, and idle bragging about which Corvette was the prettiest. Patrick's mother and father were delighted when the four cars rolled into the driveway, and the uniformed young men stepped out. Mrs. McSwain did everything she could to keep more food on the table than an army could eat, and Mr. McSwain spent much of his time out in the yard bragging to the neighbors about his son and his beautiful new Corvette. The neighbors were impressed. It was one thing to have a new Corvette on the block, but four looked like an auto convention. Men and boys alike walked around each with admiring eyes and envious hearts.

Shortly following spring leave, all the first classmen had nervously entered North Auditorium for their branch selections. The event was usually one of pleasant anticipation for those who stood high in the class academically and terrifying for those in the bottom quarter. There were only a fixed number of slots for each combat branch, except for the infantry, and the names were called for selection by General Order of Merit. When a branch was full, it was closed for selection, often leaving many with dashed hopes of serving in the branch of their choice. Many of those at the top of the class would choose the combat engineers as it was considered the most prestigious, yet it was not uncommon for members of the top tier to choose the infantry or any other branch. The higher the General Order of Merit, the more likely one was to do what he wanted to do in Uncle Sam's Army. Of the three, Wayne's name was called first. He was number sixteen out of a class of seven hundred eighty-three. Wayne stood and announced the branch of Armor, though he would probably never see a day in a tank because of medical school. Patrick and Jake had to wait a while. When number two hundred and one was announced, Patrick stood and chose Armor. It was from this branch that he hoped to get into Army Aviation and fly helicopters. When number three hundred twenty-two was called, Jake stood and announced the branch of Infantry. All that knew Jake well chuckled and smiled. He could have stayed in his room. Everyone had known since day one that Jacobs was infantry.

The May nights were still cool, and a breeze blew through the open windows. Jake thought about changing out of his dress gray uniform before starting to study but then decided to remove only his coat. It was late already. Any delay meant just that much longer before he could get horizontal for a few hours of sleep. He settled himself at his desk and opened his text to the proper chapter.

The door burst open. "Sir! The general is on his way up here!" The CQ, a yearling Cadet in Charge of Quarters, was clearly flustered. Very seldom did a general, any general, make an appearance in the barracks. A visitation during study hall was even more unusual. "Colonel Brinkman called and said the general would be here in fifteen minutes."

"Brinkman? That's the superintendent's aide. What is Lieutenant General Parker doing strolling around the barracks at this hour?" Jake was standing, angered that the general would pull a surprise inspection of the regiment. "Where in the regimental area is he going to be?"

"Colonel Brinkman specifically said the general wanted to

see the three of you. He's coming here. To your room," said the CQ breathlessly.

Patrick and Wayne both reached for their dress grays without a word. Entertaining the three-star general in your quarters called for a uniform, not sweats, and a t-shirt.

"Thank you, Larry. When the general arrives, escort him to our room." Jake was about to dismiss the CQ then thought it best to be prepared for anything. "Call the battalion commanders immediately. Put them on notice that the Supe is in the barracks. If they think it best, they can pass the word down their chain of command. It's optional. They can do what they think best." Having notified his men, Jake nodded, and the CQ closed the door behind him.

"What's up, O Great One?" Wayne zipped his dress gray coat and bent over to tie his shoes. "Somebody must have screwed up big time to merit the Supe paying us a visit."

Patrick stood straight as though he were ready for inspection. "I hate this kind of stuff. God, I just know he's coming over here to rip me apart for something I've done, but for the life of me, I don't know what I've done that would hack off the Supe. Can you guys think of anything?"

Wayne slapped his belly and laughed. "He doesn't have a daughter, does he?"

Patrick threw Wayne a frown. Normally, a comment such as that would have a certain degree of complementary flavor, but not at the moment. One did not jack around with three-star generals unless, of course, the subject daughter was extraordinarily worth the risk. "No. There ain't no 'daughter of the general' problem."

Jake smiled as he put on his dress gray coat and zipped it to the neck. "Well, the general doesn't have a daughter, but if he did, at least we'd know why there is all the commotion. Wayne and I could just shove you out the door and be done with it." He checked a clipboard on the wall to ensure there was nothing on the schedule he had overlooked. There was no oversight.

Patrick checked himself in the mirror and mumbled something inaudible as he realigned his closely cropped hair. Jake and Wayne leaned against their desks, awaiting a knock on the door. The general was due any minute.

"I sure don't get it, guys," Jake said. "If the general wanted to chew me out for something someone did in the regiment, this might make more sense. But the CQ said he wanted to see all three of us. If he's mad at me, why has he involved you two?"

Patrick turned from the mirror. "Blessing by association, I reckon. They're gonna skin and quarter you, and they don't want no witnesses. Me and poor Wayne are just innocent victims, pure and simple. I figger one of the thousand guys in this regiment probably flipped off the general and his old lady, and they've come to lynch you and your poor roommates. You're in charge, you know?"

Jake laughed. "The flippin' off is believable, but the poor innocent roommate part is a total distortion of reality."

A knock at the door sent all three of the cadets to the position of attention. Jake tugged at the bottom of his dress gray coat to straighten it and opened the door. Square in front of the door stood Lieutenant General Lloyd S. Parker. The general was no less than six-foot-three, a trim two hundred and twenty pounds. He had played football at West Point in the class of 1949, and he looked as though he could still play a full game. It was Parker's first year as superintendent, but he had already established himself as a friend of the Corps. He had changes he wanted to make, most of which had to do with officer interaction. But still, he was a three-star general, which meant that the Corps, down to the last man, felt ill at ease in his presence.

"Good evening, Mister Jacobs. May I come in?"

"Certainly, General. I think you know my classmates, Cadet McSwain and Cadet Barnes."

The general shook hands with both, which was a good, if not puzzling, sign. For the general to do so meant that the call was more along social rather than business lines. "Aren't you from California, Mister Barnes? And didn't I see your name on the list of cadets going on to medical school?"

Wayne smiled. As far as he was concerned, there was no particular reason for the general to know who he was or care. The general knowing those things about him was pleasing. "Yes, sir. I'm from Venice, California, and I will be attending Duke Medical School in the fall."

"Congratulations. Do you plan to make the Army a career as a doctor? We could use you."

Wayne looked at the general as though he were making a lifetime commitment backed by the Honor Code. "Yes, sir. I still want to be a part of the Army."

The general nodded his head in approval. That was precisely the purpose of the medical school program. The Army did not have to let him go. He owed them five years minimum. If they did not think a good many of them would stay for twenty years or more, they would stick a rifle in their hands instead of a stethoscope.

"Mr. McSwain. I see you selected Armor, and I understand you have aspirations to fly."

"Yes, sir."

Until now, the general had performed the customary

pleasantries, but it was apparent from the change in his facial expression that he had more on his mind than idle chit-chat with the troops. "You'll do well, Mister McSwain. The Air Cav can always use a good man." He paused. "Gentlemen, I'm afraid I have some bad news for you. Some very bad news."

All three stiffened. Jake leaned against his desk and looked at the general's stern but sad expression.

"I received a call from Admiral Hollifield about an hour ago. I know how much you gentlemen think of the admiral, and I can assure you that he has strong feelings for all of you."

Jake stiffened even more. His first thought was that something had happened to the admiral or Mrs. H. Admiral Hollifield would not have called the superintendent unless it was some kind of emergency.

"The admiral called and asked me to come to see you personally. A close friend of yours, Midshipman Stephen Ross, was killed in an automobile accident earlier this evening."

Jake was stunned. He could not move. He could not breathe.

"Mister Ross was on his way back to the Naval Academy this afternoon when a truck ran a stoplight."

Patrick and Wayne were dumbstruck. It had only been a few weeks since Steve and his red Corvette were winding through the hills of Tennessee with them. He was one of them. He was family. He was a brother.

Jake's eyes filled with tears, and he choked on the words he wanted to come out of his mouth. "Was he alone?" He finally managed to ask, afraid of the answer.

"Yes. Admiral Hollifield specifically wanted me to tell you that Julia Dane was not with him. She is home with her parents."

"Thank God for that." Patrick turned his back. He did not want the general to see him cry.

General Parker sat in a desk chair and unbuttoned his tunic, then leaned forward, his elbows resting on his knees. The news silenced the room, and it was obvious that the general was upset from having to deliver it. "This is my first tour of duty back in the states. I was in Vietnam before this assignment, commanding the Americal Division." He looked at Jake and saw the tears, which in turn made his eyes cloud from the pain he saw in the three cadets. "I've had to tell so many that their loved one is dead. I thought I was finished having to do that."

Jake nodded his understanding. After four years at West Point, he had seen many officers return to teach who were heartsick from the war. The general was one of them. Obviously, the general hurt badly from telling another living soul that a brave young man in uniform had died.

General Parker wiped his face with the palm of his hand as though that act brought back the courage to keep moving. He sat upright in the chair. "The funeral will be at the Naval Academy day after tomorrow. Admiral Hollifield has requested your presence as soon as possible, and permission is, of course, granted. My aircraft will take all three of you to the Naval Academy tomorrow morning. You'll need your full dress uniform and dress grays. My staff car will arrive for you at 0800."

The general stood and walked slowly to the door, and then he turned to the sad-faced cadets. "Mister Jacobs, I know how much this hurts and how impossible it is to understand how a young man like Stephen Ross could be taken from us, but try to remember that God takes every man only when He is ready. Death is God's prerogative. Not ours. God has a purpose for everything, even if we don't see that purpose or understand it."

Jake nodded. He understood what the general was saying, and he believed him, but for now, any useful purpose for this waste seemed impossible. "Thank you, General. I mean, we appreciate you coming over personally to tell us."

"I wouldn't have had it any other way, Mister Jacobs. Come see me in my office when you get back." General Parker closed the door as he left the room in silence.

―――

IN HIS SKIVVIES, Patrick crossed the dark room to the figure sitting in the chair, hunched over, staring out the window. It was just past 0400 hours, and Patrick had watched Jake sit motionless for over an hour. Wayne was either asleep or only silent, consumed by his thoughts. Patrick softly put his hand on Jake's shoulder and knelt by the chair. "You ought to get some rest, Jake. Today and tomorrow are going to be long, tough days.

Jake looked at his friend and smiled. "I was sitting here remembering all the great times Steve and I had together. God, we were inseparable. We did everything together, just like you and me."

"Yeah. I guess I know how you feel. Probably about like I would if I ever lost you."

"Better me than you. After this, with Steve, I don't think I could do this again. I really couldn't. First Charlie. Now Steve. What a waste. Two of the finest men I've ever known, and they're gone. I think the general was wrong. There's no purpose. You knew Steve. He never hurt anyone. Steve was good through and through. There's never been a nicer, kinder, more gentle man than Steve Ross. Why would God let something like this happen to someone like Steve?"

Patrick felt himself swelling up again with tears. It hurt him to see Jake ravaged with pain and doubt. Jake was always steady as a rock when it came to his faith. He studied it, and he worked at it. Patrick did not always agree with Jake's frame of reference, but he did admire him for living what he believed because it made him who and what he was. It appeared that Steve's death was testing those beliefs in the strongest sense of the word. "Let's get some sleep, Jake. Julia and Steve's folks are gonna need you in a few hours."

Jake nodded and followed Patrick across the room. He swung himself to the top bunk, sighed in anguish, and drifted into a half-sleep.

1100 Hours
23 May 1973
Madrid, Spain

"THANK you for meeting with me, Mr. Bangjar. I trust you have traveled well?" asked Colonel Oleg Lebedev. Lebedev was a functionary of the Union of Soviet Socialist Republic's diplomatic mission in London. He was also a tenured Colonel of the *Komitet Gosudarstvennoy Bezopasnosti*, the KGB, the secret police force of the Soviet Union. His specialties included the recruitment of mercenary agents for purposes of strategic disruption. Sponsorship of such agents was a high-risk/reward gambit but often worked remarkably well.

Lebedev cared not one whit for this dreadful little man, but he could be useful. Sukarno Bangjar already possessed the resources for financing operations through laundered money and had clear connections with a known terrorist organization, making this a particularly attractive enterprise. However, Lebedev was interested in what motivated him. Bangjar's dossier suggested he was a secular Muslim, not like the typical Komando Jihad cadre of Islamic fundamentalists. Lebedev's superiors had made it clear that he would be Bangjar's handler, responsible for directing his actions.

Sukarno took in the scene. The Russian was dressed immaculately in a dark grey bespoke Saville Row suit. The Madrid safe house was nondescript, just another Moorish-style home in a sea of Muslim-inspired architecture. Sukarno was keenly aware that this location was overtly symbolic. Muslim culture transformed the Iberian Peninsula into a center of art, science, architecture, medicine, and worship. As far as the eye could see, the Islamic influence was evident. The Islamic empires were glories of the so-called Dark and Middle Ages when Europeans were still wallowing in filth and ignorance. *They are ignorant still,* he thought without expression, simultaneously masking his disdain for this *apparatchik* of the Soviet Union. Alas, time for pleasantries. Lebedev motioned for him to be seated at a parlor table set with a modest tea service.

"Yes, thank you, Mr. Lebedev. I am well. Please call me Sukarno. What can I do for you?" he intoned abruptly.

Lebedev threw back his head and laughed uproariously, startling Sukarno only slightly. "You certainly do not waste time with small talk, eh? Very well, let us set the formalities aside and talk man to man. Tea?"

Sukarno braced himself and pressed on. "No, thank you. I know that you are a Soviet diplomat. What interest do you have in meeting with me?"

"Very well, I hope you don't mind if I indulge myself,"

said Lebedev as he simultaneously ignored the question and poured himself a cup of tea, one sugar. He passively stirred his tea, staring deeply into the cup. Without looking up, he asked, "Sukarno, what do you know of the attack on the school located on the military base in Heidelberg, Germany?"

Sukarno recoiled internally, his face revealing nothing. "Why, Mr. Lebedev, I've no idea what you're talking about." How could he possibly know anything? Perhaps someone had compromised that German fool Siegel. *I must deal with that swiftly,* he thought.

"My dear Sukarno, let us dispense with the façade. Surely you realize that I have access to resources you could only hope to imagine. I am here to help you. In return, you will be helping me," said Lebedev. He continued, "I would like you to realize that we have common goals, a common enemy. The ideologies differ, but the endgame is the same. I am here to assist you with those objectives, to bring fear and death to Americans." Lebedev paused for effect, allowing the offer to penetrate Sukarno's psyche.

Lebedev continued, impressed with Sukarno's self-control, "we know who supplied you with the explosives, a bungling dolt of an arms dealer named Franz Siegel." He sat back and smiled benignly. "Surely you don't deny that you met with him and purchased his services with negotiable bearer bonds?"

Sukarno slumped, then quickly recovered his composure, which subsequently gave way to anger. Sukarno fumed audibly, "that fat fool," dispensing with all pretense.

"Now that we understand each other, let's talk about the future," continued Lebedev.

"I would like to know more about you. You do not adhere to your Komando Jihad brethren profile since you don't appear to practice Islam actively. Given that, why do you so despise Americans?"

Lebedev had shaken Sukarno once again. "You have me at a disadvantage, I'm afraid. How do you know these things?"

Lebedev explained in a kindly, almost fatherly way, "My dear Sukarno, I am more than a diplomat, as you must know by now. I am a Colonel in the Committee for State Security. You must believe me when I say we have common interests, and I wish to partner with you."

Sukarno visibly stiffened as he realized who was sitting across the table from him. Frantic now, he attempted to think soberly to himself, *This man is a KGB agent, and he knows who I am.* It suddenly occurred to Sukarno, who had provided information about his father to that criminal banker, Stefanos, in New York City. It also occurred to him how he might now be able to tie up that loose end. These thoughts sobered Sukarno instantly. He saw his opportunity to benefit from this situation, after all.

"Very well," began Sukarno deliberately. "My disdain for the West is not limited to Americans, but Americans collectively personify all that is worst in the West. The American, the West, dismisses Muslims as members of yet another archaic and primitive religion, practiced by austere authoritarian misogynists who hide their women under outlandish garments."

Lebedev chuckled at the image.

Ignoring Lebedev and gathering momentum, Sukarno went on. "Islam shaped the world we live in today, but thankless, ignorant infidels have assimilated all that was contributed by Islam. Their appropriation of our culture is my motivation, Mr. Lebedev. Islam demands that we struggle against the political domination of tyranny. We are commanded to conduct

Jihad. We must reclaim our culture and our destiny. There must be demonstrations of resolve over such people, and they must be public and personal. Yes, and very violent demonstrations. It is the only way the Americans know. Islam must experience its own Renaissance and be restored to its glory, regardless of the price."

Lebedev patiently nodded as Sukarno vented his apparent anger. This was going to be easier than he thought. "Sukarno, my friend, I can help you achieve your goals. Naturally, we will achieve my objectives, as well," he began. "Weakening the United States of America will be attained by a multi-faceted approach, and you will help lead that effort," emoted Lebedev, playing to Sukarno's ego.

He continued, "Americans are driven by capitalist greed, always hungry for possessions and pleasures, even at the cost of their countrymen. Where there is profit, there is corruption and the eventual disintegration of that culture."

Lebedev paused for effect. "We will work to take away the things that Americans take for granted and replace them with things that will weaken them from the inside out. While they are awed by the spectacles that your activities will create, they will be unprepared for what is going to take their children and families."

Sukarno Bangjar solemnly nodded his assent. "Colonel Lebedev, I am ready."

"Excellent, Sukarno. This is the last time that you and I will meet in person," explained Lebedev. "From this point forward, we will communicate via intermediaries. Someone will inform you of who they are at the appropriate time. Is that understood?"

"Of course. I realize the importance of security, thank you," replied Sukarno. His mind reeled as he pondered the vast number of possibilities now before him, with many more questions than answers.

Lebedev calmly set down his teacup and rose, indicating that the meeting was over. "Good day, Sukarno. I look forward to working with you."

Still lost in his thoughts, Sukarno replied, "Good day, Colonel Lebedev."

CHAPTER 9

1300 Hours
23 May 1973
United States Naval Academy
Annapolis, Maryland

THE ADMIRAL'S car pulled to the curb in front of the Bachelor Officer's Quarters, and a lieutenant commander opened the door to the rear seat. "Gentlemen, I am Lieutenant Commander Eagleston. Admiral Hollifield asked me to help you get settled in the BOQ and brief you."

Jake stepped out of the car and saluted. "Thank you, sir."

The cadets followed the officer up the steps to the double doors and were given keys to their rooms. "The car is at your disposal. The driver will take you wherever you need to go. I've prepared an itinerary for you, a map of the academy, and a list of telephone numbers."

Jake looked at the organized piece of paper and tried to orient to the events scheduled. The lieutenant commander continued, "Mr. and Mrs. Ross are guests of Admiral Hollifield. They will arrive later this evening. The admiral asked that you do whatever you like for a couple of hours, and he will pick you up here at 1600 hours. The ride to the Tingey House at the Washington Navy Yard is only thirty minutes."

Jake folded the paper, unzipped his coat halfway, and placed the paper in the inside pocket with his wallet. "Yes, sir. We will be here at the curb at 1600 hours. Is there anything helpful that we can do in the meantime?"

Lt. Commander Eagleston smiled. "No. Just make yourself at home." He started walking toward the lead car, then turned around. "I didn't personally know Midshipman Ross, but we are all saddened. The Brigade is glad you are here to share this loss with us. My numbers, office and home, are on the list. If there is anything we can do for you, let me know." Eagleston nodded to indicate his sincerity, then drove away.

Two hours passed quickly, and the cadets waited patiently on the front steps of the BOQ. Admiral Hollifield's car pulled to the curb, and the admiral exited without waiting for the driver to open the door. The smile on his face told them that he was, as always, genuinely glad to see them. "It's been a while since Philadelphia. You men look like you're ready to graduate. A few extra pounds, eh, Mister McSwain?"

"It's a first-class privilege, sir." Patrick saluted along with his roommates and respectfully waited for it to be returned. The admiral returned the salute, then shook each cadet's hand heartily and exchanged pleasantries.

"Let's go to my quarters. Suzanne is anxious to see you. We would have loved for you to stay with us, but I felt you might be more comfortable here at the BOQ."

"The BOQ is fine, sir. After living in the Lost 50s, one of the oldest barracks at West Point, for four years, the BOQ is like living in a grand hotel.

The admiral sat in the back seat with Jake and Wayne while Patrick sat in the front seat with the driver. The car made the thirty-mile trip up U.S. 50 East to the Washington Navy Yard, then pulled in front of a large white house known as Quarters A, or the Tingley House. It was the traditional residence for all serving Chiefs of Naval Operations. The yard sign indicated that it was four-star Admiral Hollifield's residence, one of a long line of distinguished seamen to reside there.

When the car came to a full stop, Jake could see Mrs. H. walking down the sidewalk to the car with a grin on her face. She, too, was glad to see them, albeit the circumstances were sad beyond belief for all of them. Mrs. H. hugged the cadets, then took Jake by the arm and led them back into the house.

"What time do Mr. and Mrs. Ross arrive?"

Suzanne Hollifield gave Jake's arm a light squeeze. "In about two hours. We're glad you are here, Jake. I think it will help that Steve's parents have someone here that they know."

"How's Julia?"

They sat in the den, and an aide set a tray of refreshments on the large table in the corner of the room. Suzanne poured Jake a cup of tea and handed it to him. "Julia is not holding up very well. She'll be here, briefly, sometime this evening. She wants to see Steve's folks, but she's torn all to pieces. In two weeks, she would have been a bride. I went to see her this morning. She was lying on her bed with her bridal dress draped over a chair. She just stared at it. The poor dear. It breaks my heart to see her this way."

"Jake, would you step into the study with me?" Admiral Hollifield's tone indicated a command, and Jake set his tea on the table to follow him.

Jake walked to the center of the study and remained

standing while the admiral walked to the desk, opened the humidor, and removed two cigars. He snipped the end off of both and handed one to Jake. It had been years since he and Steve tried to smoke cigars under the bridge on Chandler's Creek, and the thought of those days made him feel even more saddened. The admiral struck a match and extended it toward Jake. He coughed while the admiral lit his.

"Patrick tells me you are taking Steve's death hard."

Jake looked at the admiral in disbelief. "Of course I'm taking it hard, sir. The boy I grew up with and loved like a brother is dead. His life was snuffed out as simply as you blew out that burning match."

Admiral Hollifield sat in an overstuffed chair by the window overlooking the front lawn and motioned to Jake to sit in the matching chair next to him. Jake sat, and the admiral took a long draw on the cigar.

"Did I ever tell you about Korea, Jake?"

"No, sir." Jake's anger stirred. It would be easy to be disrespectful at the moment. Somehow, now did not seem the right time for war stories, even from the man he had more admiration for than anyone in the world.

Admiral Hollifield took another long draw on his cigar. "I was a lieutenant, junior grade, assigned to the 2nd Marine Division as a forward observer. My job was to direct naval gunfire and close air-ground support for the grunts. I was with them for four months. We landed at Inchon, fought our way north, then fought our way back, inch by inch from the Chosin Reservoir."

Jake already knew about the admiral and Korea. It was where he had been awarded the Navy Cross.

"You're going infantry, aren't you, Jake?"

"Yes, sir. Green Berets," Jake replied.

"Well, someday you'll know what I'm talking about. I hope you don't. But you probably will."

"I don't understand, Admiral." It seemed that the admiral suddenly was lost in his unpleasant memories of those many years ago.

"Four months. I ate, slept, pissed, shit, and suffered alongside those jarhead sons-of-bitches." The admiral sat forward in his chair and rolled his cigar nervously between his finger and thumb. "Never in my life have I come to love a bunch of guys more than I did that platoon of ignorant bastards. My roommate here at Annapolis went Marine. That idiot. He was the platoon leader, and he was the best friend I ever had." The admiral paused and stared into Jake's eyes. "He died in my arms at the Chosin Reservoir. There is something about the smell of death all around you and up close that eliminates all the bullshit in your life. Things that seemed important last year, or yesterday, suddenly don't mean diddlysquat when your best buddy just got his face blown off, and you're trying to keep some Chi-com from shoving his bayonet up your frozen ass. You know what I mean, Jake?"

Jake squirmed uncomfortably in his chair. "Sort of, sir. I guess one has to experience that before he could truly understand."

Admiral Hollifield blew smoke out of his nose and narrowed his eyebrows. "Bullshit. You know exactly what I'm talking about."

Jake squirmed again.

"You just lost one of your best buddies, Jake. You lost your brother, too." Admiral Hollifield sat on the edge of his chair, leaned forward, and pointed the cigar butt at Jake for emphasis. "As a man, you have chosen the toughest profession known to the human race. It's tough because people you love can and do die, and you have to keep standing up straight and keep moving forward. None of us understand why death takes some and not others, but I do know that so long as God Almighty leaves you standing, leaves you alive, then He has a plan and a purpose for you. You have a brilliant career ahead of you, Jake, but to be the kind of soldier I know you are capable of becoming, you have to conquer death."

Jake drew on his cigar, coughed, and leaned forward. "I'm not afraid of dying, Admiral."

Admiral Hollifield smiled. "Hell, Jake, I know that. You have too much faith in your Maker for that. But conquering the fear of your death is only half of it. The harder part is conquering the death of others, of those you love. It's easy and normal to feel like you're falling apart when someone dies. In combat, you have to keep standing strong for the men still alive. They'll need you. They may fall apart, but you can't."

Jake lowered his head as a tear rolled down his cheek. Admiral Hollifield reached across the narrow span between them and put his hand on Jake's knee.

"They need you. Julia will be here. She needs you." The admiral patted his knee, then rose from his chair. "I'm sorry about Steve. You probably knew him better than anyone. What do you think Steve would tell you if he were here, in this study, alone with you for five minutes?" Admiral Hollifield slowly walked out of the study and left Jake sitting with his thoughts.

1500 Hours
24 May 1973
Durango, Colorado

THE SPRING RAIN fell gently around the log house with the promise that wildflowers would grow knee-deep in the meadow. Sara had leased the house from a couple who lived in Phoenix and found they could spend less and less time every year in the higher altitudes due to their health. The couple was hopeful that Sara would buy the house and often called to try to excite her more about it than she already was.

The house was perfect, at least at this point in her life. It was located almost midway between Durango and Lake Vallecito in some of the most beautiful country created. Tall pines surrounded the house, and a sloping meadow provided a breathtaking view of the valley in all its splendor of wildflowers and grazing horses. The house itself was modern in its convenience, but it was constructed entirely of logs. It made Sara feel that she had stepped back in time, back to a time when simple pleasures and solitude were norms. She took long walks through the meadow every day, pushing Stephen Patrick's baby stroller down a path that meandered through the tall grass, and sat for hours on the broad front porch smelling the clean pine air.

Brent had delayed as long as possible through his lawyers, but Sara's quiet determination was soon accepted. He often called, at first, pleading for Sara to reconsider the divorce. His mother, Delia Mosher, was making his life miserable. She did not like being on the other end of the gossip chain. Two drafts of the divorce settlement arrived for her review, but she sent both back to Dallas with notations made in red ink, scribbled in the margins. Sara gave him some credit. Brent was voluntarily sending a generous check every two weeks, and she was glad that she could afford not to put Stephen Patrick in a daycare center. Not working, for the time being, was a luxury. The time alone in the mountains with Stephen Patrick was a healing therapy for the disappointments and failures she felt so deeply.

As the rain continued rhythmically, Sara sat on the front porch in jeans, a light cotton sweatshirt, barefoot, wrapped in an old down comforter. She enjoyed the porch, especially during a rain. Stephen Patrick was down for his afternoon nap, leaving her with only the sounds of the rain and her thoughts.

The phone rang. Sara knew that, in all likelihood, it was her mother or Brent. She had remained so isolated the past three months she rarely received a call from a local. Sara reached inside the screen door, then returned to the chair on the porch before answering it. "Hello."

"Sara." Valerie Lowell usually called every two or three days to assure herself that everything was all right. She did not like Sara and Stephen Patrick being so far away, living in the mountains.

Sara smiled. "Mother. It's so good to hear from you. I haven't talked to you since last night." Sara wished her mother would not worry about them so much. Sometimes her calls irritated her in that they repeatedly interrupted the very peace and solitude she sought.

"Well, dear, I'm sorry to call you again so soon. I don't mean to be a bother, but I'm afraid I have some news, and I knew you would want to know about it right away."

Sara signed, wondering who had run off with whom or who is pregnant that should not be? "Okay, Mother. What's the news?"

"Steve Ross is being buried today at Annapolis."

Sara was stunned. She could not believe what she had heard. "What did you say?"

"Helen Murray, from the flower shop in Comanche, just called me. She said that Steve was killed in a car accident. Everyone in town is sending flowers, and she thought we might also want to send some. That dear boy. I can't imagine him being dead. He was such a nice boy."

Sara was on her feet. Adrenaline pumped through her body as if she were prepared to fight for her life, the life that had so many pleasant memories and brought bits and pieces of calm to her otherwise troubled soul. Tears rolled down her cheeks, and the lump in her throat made it almost impossible for her to talk.

"Mother. I'm too upset about this. I'll call you later tonight. I promise."

Sara stared down the rain-soaked valley as memories of Steve flashed through her mind. When the sobbing started, she cried loudly while the mountain shadows darkened. Stephen Patrick stirred from his nap, which brought her to her feet. She wiped her eyes on her sweatshirt sleeves before she went to him.

Stephen Patrick was oblivious to her pain as she rocked him in the living room. He tugged on her hair and pulled her finger.

Tears ran down her cheeks again as she thought of Jake and the friendship he and Steve had. She remembered grade school days, with Jake and Steve teasing her and showing off, lazy summer days with the two of them bored on the front porch, high school where they were seldom seen apart, and the proud smiles they wore as they drove away from Comanche to attend the academies.

Sara bounced Steven Patrick on her knee and rubbed

noses with him. "I'm so glad I named you Stephen. I named you after one of the most wonderful persons I've ever known. He would have been happy to know I named you after him. He would have been proud, and he would have loved you so much."

1400 Hours
22 May 1973
The Pentagon
Washington, D.C.

JOHN HANRATY BURST through the door to Admiral Hollifield's outer office and grabbed Colonel Carpenter's sleeve in his excitement to get the colonel's attention. "Colonel. We've had a breakthrough on the Heidelberg bombing. I need to see the admiral right away!"

Carpenter grinned. He had grown to like Hanraty. The little analyst was like a dog chewing the meat off of a bone. He was persistent, untiring, and mentally consumed until the task was done. Over the past six months, Hanraty had followed every lead, no matter how insignificant, and had never lost interest or drive to see the mission to its completion. What he had uncovered, above and beyond what the investigators on the scene had done, was quite remarkable. Tracing hundreds of manifests, he had discovered the movement of what was labeled as a relatively small amount of ammonium nitrate that had been purchased by one Franz Siegel at the Cherbourg, France port of entry. It was held on a wharf for less than thirty days and subsequently loaded on a Libyan freighter for destinations throughout the Mediterranean.

Military Intelligence had a sheet a yard long on Siegel. He was well known as a nickel and dime arms dealer who primarily sold illegal small arms to malcontents. He wasn't a player in the worldwide business of selling weapons in quantity to legitimate governments, but he was a pest for those whose job it was to know who was buying arms around the world and for what purpose. Assuming that Siegel would peddle inoperative ammonium nitrate to a naive buyer as a lethal weapon was not at all farfetched. Hanraty had been engrossed in that assumption for weeks and was convinced, albeit without proof, that Siegel's shipment of chemical fertilizer was responsible for the Heidelberg bombing.

"Slow down, John." Carpenter wasn't about to barge in on the admiral without good reason. The admiral was busy, and it was his job to decipher and filter information critical to Hollifield. He would be a poor aide if he bothered the old man every time John Hanraty got excited about a new lead. "Tell me what you've got. You know the procedure. If I think the admiral should know in person, then I'll get you in to see him."

Hanraty grimaced. "Okay. But this is good. He'll want to know right away."

"No doubt." Carpenter crossed his arms across his chest and leaned against a desk, prepared to listen.

"You know my theory about Franz Siegel, the two-bit arms dealer out of Germany. Well, he's dead. Found him stuffed into a fifty-five-gallon barrel in the Thames River outside London."

Carpenter shrugged. "So what? He was a fat crook in a dangerous business. It's not so surprising that somebody bumped him off."

"Yeah, but it's how he was bumped off that's interesting." Hanraty put his hands on his hips and smiled.

"So, tell me. Or am I supposed to guess?"

"Well, first, he didn't drown. His throat was cut. And to make it even more interesting, his genitals were cut off and stuffed down his throat."

"Good grief!" Carpenter made a face, showing his disgust at the mental vision he had of Siegel's death.

"I was right. The bomber in Heidelberg was Middle Eastern, or at least Muslim. The genitals and cut throat are Muslim one hundred percent. They've been doing that for centuries."

Carpenter quickly thought through the possibilities. "Okay. A traditional Muslim killed Siegel. But that doesn't tie him to Heidelberg. That just means he may have screwed some Middle Eastern guy on another deal."

"Aha! But guess what else was in the barrel besides Franz Siegel?"

Carpenter's eyes grew wide. "Ammonium nitrate?"

"You got it. That stuff ate him up. If we can find out who was in town, we might build a legitimate list of suspects. We know now what part of the world we are dealing with, and we just might get lucky if any of the security agencies kept tabs on who was in the country at the time."

"Sounds reasonable." Colonel Carpenter checked his watch. "Five minutes with the admiral at six o'clock. Good work, John."

J.M. PATTON

0930 Hours
6 June 1973
United States Military Academy
West Point, New York

JAKE FASTENED his full-dress coat's high collar then pulled the waist down over his starched white trousers. Next came the sword and crimson red sash. As he stood in front of the mirror, he could feel both the excitement and the sadness in the knowledge that this was the last time he would wear West Point gray. In a few hours, he would be commissioned and wear Army blues for what he hoped would be a long career.

Patrick and Wayne felt much of the same. But for the sounds of three men dressing, the room was silent. Each was lost in his thoughts and memories of the past four years—the good times and the bad. The days they had long counted were behind them, and they suddenly seemed too short.

The shock of Steve's death was still with them, but Jake had surprised his roommates by having a miraculous change in attitude while at the Naval Academy. Patrick recognized it first, and a surge of pride ran down his spine when he saw Jake emerge from Admiral Hollifield's study to greet Steve's parents. The hours would have been much harder on everyone if Jake had not stepped in to take charge. He was strong. Jake's strength carried them through the most painful hours of their lives and renewed their pride in Steve's commitment to the United States Navy. Jake had spent time with Mr. and Mrs. Ross, Julia, and Mrs. H. His pride in Steve and his obvious love for him was infectious, making the sight of the three midshipmen and three cadets carrying the oak coffin bearable. In their mind's eye, it was a moment of which Steve himself would have been proud. It was a salute to him. It was a salute to his commitment to the service of his country.

Jake centered his white hat and pulled it snugly into the correct position. "You two ready to get that sheepskin?"

"I'm ready." Patrick put on his hat and began to put on his white gloves.

"Me, too," Wayne said. "But before we go, I've got something to say." He paused while Jake and Patrick turned from the door to listen to him. "I just want to say that I couldn't have had two better roommates. West Point would have been a lot more difficult if it hadn't been for you. I mean, I want to say thanks before we go out there and put these four years out of its misery."

Jake and Patrick smiled. Within seconds, all three were laughing in celebration, not only for graduation but for the bond they had for each other. It was the end of an era in their individual lives, but even more so, it was a beginning—the Long Gray Line. The essence of West Point was who and what they had become, and they were the personification of West Point, forever.

CHAPTER 10

1800 Hours
15 August 1973
Ft. Benning, Georgia

JAKE SAT on the bar stool in the officer's club, twirling the ice in his drink as he waited for Patrick. It had been nearly three months since he had seen him, and he was anxious to see what jump school had done to the Volunteer. As much as Patrick disliked anything that smacked of infantry, his bitching and moaning was bound to be highly exaggerated and another lesson in dramatics.

Being a workday and after hours, the officer's club was crowded. Most were dressed in fatigues and boots, as Jake was, and every possible rank was present. Many of Jake's classmates in the Infantry Officer Basic Course (IOBC) were in the club to kill a couple of hours before going to their quarters to study. Jake smiled to himself as he thought of the course. It was six months of physical and academic grind. It was indeed a myth that the academics were over for your life when you leave West Point.

On the contrary, Infantry Officer Basic Course was hard work at the books, and the competition was fierce. Jake's classmates came from all over the United States and had mostly come out of ROTC programs at various universities. They were sharp, bright, and excluding what he had learned at Ranger School, one step ahead of him in the skills required of a junior officer. Most had spent at least two summers with active units. It was an advantage. They had experienced the real army and knew how the system worked from a practitioner's perspective.

Wally Bidet had become Jake's closest friend at Benning and was constantly giving him the benefit of his wisdom on the evils of West Point and how ROTC and OCS types were better soldiers. Jake did not argue. It did not seem to make much difference how one got his commission. West Point certainly was not a guarantee that one would be a good officer. Likewise, neither was the Citadel, or VMI, or Texas A&M, or any other university for that matter. Bidet was a graduate of LSU, Louisiana State University in Baton Rouge, and thought that any place outside Louisiana was a foreign country. Jake could see his point of view but thought Wally was the foreigner. Texans might have a twang in their dialect, but Louisiana patois was a mixture of English, Spanish, and French. Wally could not make a complete sentence without throwing in some Cajun word, and he was impossible to understand on a field radio. An artillery shell was likely to land most anywhere, with Bidet calling in the fire mission.

"How come you ain't a general, yet?" Patrick grabbed Jake. Patrick had not looked more fit since their plebe year. Airborne had run the firstie blubber off his bones, and his blonde hair was cut extremely short, the sides shaved to the skull.

"Airborne! You look like a soldier. I knew there was one inside that mess you call a body somewhere," Jake said with a broad grin on his face.

Patrick pointed to the jump wings on his chest with pride. "Can you believe it? Me? One of those idiots jumping out of perfectly good airplanes."

"Never." Jake laughed. "When did you get out of school?"

Patrick sat on the empty stool next to Jake and nodded his head toward the bartender for a draft. "We graduated yesterday. Man, am I ever glad to see you. Why didn't you tell me this airborne business was this much fun? I might have gone gung-ho infantry like you."

Jake smiled, knowing that Patrick's high would crash as soon as he got a taste of Ranger School. He suspected that Patrick would curse every minute for the next nine weeks. "When does Ranger School start?"

"Tomorrow." Patrick took two long gulps of his beer and grinned. "If you can do it, I can do it."

"You'll do fine. Just put your mind in neutral for nine weeks and your butt in gear. You'll come out lean and mean."

"So, how was California?" Patrick asked as he smiled and moved his eyebrows up and down like Groucho Marx.

Jake blushed. "California was fine. But unlike some people I know, I never kiss and tell."

Patrick teasingly looked disappointed. "Shoot. I've been waiting for months for all the grubby details. After hearing Wayne describe California bikinis for four years, I figgered you'd have war stories aplenty to warm a man's heart."

"No war stories," Jake said. "Let's just say that two weeks

in California with Jamie destroys the myth that Camp Buckner is the best summer of your life and leave it at that."

"Is tis t famous Tenn-see bo you been braggin' bout so long?" Wally Bidet slapped Jake on the back and gave Patrick a friendly smile. "I been lookin' fo-wrd ta meet ya."

"Patrick, this is Wally Bidet," Jake said. "He's from Louisiana and talks like he didn't graduate from the third grade. Don't let him fool you. He has a degree in chemical engineering from LSU, and if he can ever learn to talk right, he'll graduate number one in IOBC."

"That be t facts," Wally said with a smile. "Yo frien, tell me yo r gon-ta-fly helicopters."

Patrick grinned. "Hope so. Say. Bidet. Isn't that some kind of fancy toilet with no seat that squirts water up your butt?"

Jake and Wally burst out laughing. Wally had spent his entire life with the misfortune of having a last name that was easily ridiculed. Though a fairly common French name in Louisiana, those living elsewhere likely had the same thought cross their mind, but most didn't say anything, not wanting to insult Wally. But there were a few, like Patrick, who couldn't resist.

"Yes. It is t same," Wally said.

Patrick laughed. "I like it. I love Louisiana, by the way. I love Cajun food, Cajun music, and Cajun women."

Wally put his hand on Patrick's shoulder. "Roadtrip."

———

J.M. PATTON

1300 Hours
3 October 1973
Fort Benning, Georgia

JAKE REMAINED IN HIS CHAIR, softly drumming the eraser of his pencil against his notebook as his classmates hurriedly gathered their books and crammed the aisles, trying to leave as quickly as possible. It was Friday. The young officers either had wives, girlfriends, or some yet unknown adventure awaiting the attention of their free time. The schedule at Benning during the week was hard work, and weekends were hard play. Either way, every minute counted.

Jake was in no hurry. He enjoyed his weekends as much as anyone else in the class, but more often than not, whatever he found to entertain himself was spontaneous in nature. In fact, the adventures of spontaneity had become addictive. It was exciting to move about without plan or expectation. One excursion outside the gates of Fort Benning for the weekend had led him to the porch of an old country store in the Georgia backwoods, where he had met a black man named Jess. Jess didn't know exactly how old he was, but his best guess was that he was over one hundred years old. He had never been more than twenty miles from the very porch they sat on. Jake sat for hours listening to Jess talk about periods of American history that were recognizable to him only from the books he had read. Reconstruction as a small boy, the revolutionary automobile, the civil rights years, the changes in technology from the eyes of a man whose entire world was forty miles in diameter. Another spontaneous adventure brought him to a mountain bed and breakfast inn as nightfall closed around a Saturday's drive down curving back roads. Jake swam in the bracing waters of a clear natural lake and tall grasses wavering on a gentle breeze under a full moon. There wasn't a special someone to meet for the weekend. There was simply himself, comfortable with meeting whatever Providence might place in his path.

"Lieutenant Jacobs."

Jake, startled to hear his name, snapped his head toward the voice. It was Colonel Strong.

"Colonel. It's good to see you," Jake said as he rose, smiling.

The colonel returned the smile and extended his hand. "Why aren't you scrambling out the door like the other young bucks? It's Friday, you know?"

"No hurry, sir. I don't really have any plans. I'd be honored if I could treat you to dinner tonight at the officer's club. That is if you don't already have plans."

"Thanks for the invite, but I have to catch a plane in an hour back to Fort Bragg." Colonel Strong frowned, demonstrating that he had something serious to discuss, and motioned for Jake to sit.

"I'll get right to the point, Jake." Strong pulled a long cigar from his breast pocket and lit it with full attention. "You remember that little discussion we had at the Army-Navy game awhile back?"

"Yessir."

"Well, I don't know what your plans are after you finish here at Benning, but...."

"I still want to go Special Forces, sir. That is if it's still available to me."

Strong paused and stared into Jake's eyes. "Maybe you better hear all the facts, Jake. You may want to retract that statement."

"What do you mean, sir?"

"Things are changing. Fast. Two years ago, when I talked

to you, Special Forces had a tough but bright future. Today, Special Forces is all but dead. Kaput."

"I don't understand."

"The desk warriors upstairs have decided to eliminate us. They will recall the 5th and the 25th from Vietnam and Thailand to the states, and they will shut down the whole shooting match. That's the word, and it's official."

Jake was stunned. Not only had he spent most of five years preparing for Special Forces, but more importantly, the Pentagon was putting *legendary* units out of business. They were eliminating a critical concept in modern warfare. How could the Pentagon be so shortsighted?

Colonel Strong slumped his shoulders in reaction to Jake's disappointment. He had spent the best part of his career trying to recruit top personnel like Jake into the units, and now he saw his life's work destroyed at the stroke of a pen.

"You'd be better off going with an infantry unit or a Ranger battalion if they are reformed, Jake. That's why I dropped by to see you. You deserve a fighting chance at a career. Special Forces would kill your career now unless our mission changes, just like it may kill mine and a few other hardheads."

"Wait a minute, Colonel. You sound like Special Forces are down but maybe not out. What is the status of Special Forces?"

"Well, for the most part, it's over. Of course, we still have some support in the Pentagon, but your conventional warfare types are tickled to death to see us disbanded. We still have our training facility at Fort Bragg and a directive to hold a small unit together. We don't have a mission concept yet, but we're working on it. I'm still convinced that small, specialized unit tactics are just beginning, Jake. A few of us will hold it together, by hook or crook, until those jerks in Washington wake up. And they will. It's only a matter of time until they realize that terrorism is the name of the game for the eighties and nineties. We'll come back, but it's going to be a hard, tough road."

Jake rubbed his chin in deep thought, then stared at the colonel through squinted eyes. "You still looking for a few dumb butter bars to carry this matter forward?"

Strong smiled. "You're a glutton for punishment, aren't you? You sure you still want in?"

"If you have a slot for me, sir, and you can train me, then you can still count on me. I haven't changed my mind. I agree wholeheartedly with the program. I'm willing to take the chance. I think it's important."

Strong stood with a smile on his face. "Welcome aboard, sucker. Be at Bragg 1 March ready to go to work."

0900 Hours
2 February 1974
Fort Benning, Georgia

JAKE PACKED THE CORVETTE TIGHTLY, with only necessities for the month of February. He shipped the remainder of his gear to Fort Bragg. Jake tightened the clamp around the pair of snow skis he had bought at the post exchange and grinned at the thought of finding plenty of snow in the Rockies. He had less than thirty days of leave to relax and have fun before reporting to Colonel Strong. He could have reported in early, but after a second of thought, he realized that with the Special Forces in the condition it was, he would be lucky to see any leave at all for the next year or two. A month in Comanche did not sound too appealing. He had been home for two days during Christmas, and though he had enjoyed seeing his family, he was glad for the excuse to return to Georgia and the Infantry School. He had reconciled himself to spending a week in Comanche during this leave but had decided to do it after chasing the snow through New Mexico, Colorado, and Utah for a couple of weeks. It was another adventure. He had never been to any of those states and was looking forward to wandering from ski resort to ski resort. After visiting Comanche, he would find Patrick at Fort Rucker, Alabama, see if he had managed to drive any helicopters into the ground, then drive to North Carolina.

Jake climbed into the Corvette, turned the key, and pulled out of the Bachelor Officer's Quarters' parking lot. As he passed through the main gate, he felt a bit strange leaving the home he had known for the past six months. *I wonder if I'll be at Benning again?* Good memories here. Good friends. Young in his career, Jake knew he would likely see Benning many times over the years. Most infantry officers do. In Special Forces, Fort Bragg would be his real home from now on, but he would return to Benning and spend time at other posts as well. Driving away, Jake knew the hardest part, and yet in some ways, the best part was leaving the friends he had made, only to reunite with them another day on perhaps another post. It was part of the Army life to build a network of friendships stationed all over the world. Jake smiled. Thinking of friends brought back memories of Patrick, Wayne, and Steve. His West Point memories were already recognized as the foundation for fond recollections of an old man yet to be.

1700 Hours
2 February 1974
Durango, Colorado

SARA STOMPED her feet on the top step of the cabin to shake loose the snow that stuck to her boots and switched the heavy load of groceries to the other arm to unlock the front door. She was pleased with her decision to buy the cabin and make the vicinity of Durango her home. It was a good place to be. She had her solitude to the extent she wanted it, and Durango was close enough for easy shopping and civilization when needed. Before signing the papers, she had visited each school in Durango, and though years ahead of time, she was satisfied that Stephen Patrick would receive the education he needed when the time came. Her initial and temporary retreat was now home.

The divorce was final in November, and Brent had been thrilled with Sara's demands for child support and property settlement. Sara did not mind that Brent thought she could have gotten much more and that he had escaped the marriage with his financial well-being intact. She was satisfied. The settlement was comfortable, and that was all she cared about. It allowed her to buy the cabin and only work part-time so she could spend half her day with Stephen Patrick. She got a part-time job with a local dentist doing general office management work and picked Stephen Patrick up at the daycare center at lunch.

Sara set the groceries on the kitchen counter, then walked again through the living room to get Stephen Patrick. He had managed to climb the stairs himself and tracked huge clumps of snow stuck to his tiny feet into the room. "Aren't you a big boy now? You made it from the car all by yourself, didn't you?"

Sara lifted him in her arms and hugged him before unbuttoning his coat. Brent had not called in the two months since the divorce. On the one hand, she was glad for herself, but on the other hand, she hurt for her son. It was obvious that Brent would never attempt to be a father.

Stephen Patrick waddled off toward his room and his toys when his heavy coat was no longer confining him, and Sara poked at the fire, stirring hot cinders to stoke a flame and warmth. It was a mindless task that hypnotized while the mind wandered to either the past or hopes for the future. As usual, thoughts of Brent and his lack of fatherly instincts kept memories of Jake constantly at hand. How different it would all be if Jake were Stephen Patrick's father.

Sara jabbed at the log, which was now ablaze, irritated at herself. Thoughts of Jake and how happy they would be in this cabin and what a good father he would be for Stephen Patrick were pointless, hopeless, and depressing. She knew from daily experience how consuming such fantasies could be. Those fantasies pleasantly passed the daylight hours but left tears on her pillow when darkness and futility surrounded her. She knew nothing about him anymore. She didn't know where he was or what he was doing. She had lost touch with him completely since her parents had moved to California, and that intensified her sorrow and lack of tranquility. She wanted him to be happy, but in contradiction to her desires for him, she was inwardly horrified that he might have found someone else to love and was now married. One day she would pray for his happiness with another woman so she could get on with her life, and the next day, she'd pray that the hope of being with him again would become a reality in her life.

CHAPTER 11

2000 Hours
14 February 1974
Durango, Colorado

SAM GALE, a local rancher, had pleaded with Sara a dozen times to have dinner with him, but she had always refused gently but quickly. But today, she just could not. It was Valentine's Day, and Sam had come to the dental office shortly after they opened, with a dozen roses and a box of candy. Again, he pleaded for a dinner date, and reluctantly, she accepted on the condition that she could meet him in town at the restaurant. She wanted to be in control. Only dinner and with her own transportation. Sam was ecstatic with his victory and told her to meet him at the Ore House, one of Durango's better steak houses.

Sara arrived sharply at eight o'clock, and Sam was already seated at a table overlooking the busy street full of tourists roaming from shop to shop. He had his back to the window so he could see Sara when she entered. When she did, he stood with a nervous smile on his face.

Sara forced a smile herself. She did not want to be here. "Sam. Thank you for inviting me to dinner. It was sweet of you."

Sam stammered in puzzlement as he held Sara's chair for her to sit. "It's not the first time. I'd about given up on you ever taking me up on dinner. You look great tonight."

"Thank you, Sam." The compliment made her nervous. She did not want Sam to get the wrong idea about her accepting the dinner invitation. She felt awkward because she knew that Sam saw her acceptance as a real date, and she did not feel that way about it. After agitating over it all afternoon, she had decided to be up-front with Sam and tell him that she was not romantically inclined toward him or anyone else.

―――――

JAKE HAD MADE the most of the past twelve days. He had skied Taos, Aspen, Vail, and the last two days at Purgatory, twenty miles from Durango. When the slopes closed for the day, he decided to check out of the resort and start his trip south to Comanche. Driving to Durango for the night would put him within driving distance of Amarillo, Texas, in one day and Comanche the next.

He checked into a small motel, showered, and asked the clerk at the front desk where a hungry skier could get the biggest steak in town. The Ore House was the recommendation. Jake drove to the downtown area and wandered through the busy streets for an hour with the other skiers and tourists. It was a fascinating little town with plenty of resort area atmosphere, and he had no trouble finding directions to the Ore House when hunger overcame him.

Jake entered the restaurant, and a pretty young waitress greeted him before leading him to a table for two against the wall. It was a good table in that he could see the street from where he sat, and like airports, it offered the opportunity to people-watch.

"Can I get you a drink before you order?"

Jake thought a moment. "Sure. How about a hot apple cider with whatever it is they put in those things to make you feel like melted butter?"

"You must have been skiing up at Purgatory. They serve that drink there. A lot of people come in asking for it."

Jake smiled. "It hits all the sore spots."

She handed him a menu. "Will there be anyone else joining you?"

"No. I'm alone."

"That's a shame. Don't you know it's Valentine's Day? You should have your wife or your girlfriend with you."

"Valentine's Day. I didn't realize." He fidgeted with the menu and half-smiled.

"You SEE, Sam. I like you and all, but I'm just not ready for a relationship right now. You're such a nice man. You need to find someone you can be with and get to know. I'd like for us to be friends, but that's all we can be. Just friends."

Sam visibly tried to show his understanding. He twirled the swizzle stick from his drink tightly around his finger repeatedly. "I reckon that ex-husband of yours really hurt you."

Sara relaxed, realizing that Sam accepted what she was

saying and was trying very hard to be the friend she had asked him to be. "Yes. But I'm so thankful it's over. It was a nightmare. I'm just glad to be away from him."

"And that other fella? The one from back in Texas. Where you were from?"

Sara smiled. "Jake? Oh, I don't imagine I'll ever see him again. I blew it."

"What do you mean, you blew it?"

Sara suddenly felt much better about being in the restaurant with Sam. She had not realized it before, but it felt good to have someone to talk to, and Sam seemed genuinely interested in what had happened to her and how she felt. It felt right to be open with him.

"We were childhood sweethearts. We were going to get married. Have a family, you know? He graduated from West Point last June."

"An Army man, huh? I had a West Point officer when I was in Vietnam."

"Jake will make a great officer. I just know he will. We had plans to get married in the chapel at West Point on graduation day." Sara bit her lip lightly.

"So, what happened?"

"Well, I went off to the University of Texas, met my ex-husband, and married him. I thought I loved him. He was charming. Kind of swept me off my feet. His family is very wealthy, and I think I got caught up in the fantasy of marrying him and living that kind of life. And, I was in a sorority. My friends all thought it was awful that I was planning to marry Jake, a military man. I look back on it all now, and I don't know why I married Brent. It was foolish, and I shouldn't have let my sorority sisters influence me the way they did."

Sam motioned to the waitress for another round of after-dinner drinks, then leaned back and put his hands in his pockets. "Sounds like you still love this Jake guy. I was in the Army. I am all too familiar with how people feel about the military. A lot of people try to shame me for being a soldier. But the fact is, I'm proud of my service."

Sara's moist eyes stared out the window to the snow-covered sidewalk where people exaggerated their steps to keep from falling. "I'm proud of you for your service, Sam, and I do still love Jake."

―――

JAKE SHOVED the empty plate away from him and leaned back as the waitress approached the table with another hot cider. She cleared the table as he sipped the steaming cup.

"Can I get you anything else?"

"No. Thanks. A steak like that, a hard day on the slopes, and spiked hot cider has me wondering if I shouldn't just sleep right here in this chair tonight."

"I'm sure the boss wouldn't mind. You're not the first to ask. Skiing can make a person dead tired. Thank you, and I hope you have a nice Valentine's." The girl smiled at him and walked away with a load of dishes stacked along her extended arm.

Jake sipped his drink and turned his attention beyond the other diners to the window with its activity outside. The tiredness, the meal, and the hot apple cider made him dwell on the depressing fact that it really was Valentine's Day again, and for the fourth year, it had absolutely nothing to do with him.

Jake reached behind him and pulled his wallet from his pocket, fumbled through pieces of paper, and stared forlornly at the old ragged picture. Sara's picture resided in his wallet for nearly five years and had been soaked a dozen times by sweat, rain, and swamps. It was still here, though. It still brought a rush of memories that would never fade as the picture had done.

As he put the picture back, Jake glanced around the restaurant and noticed that most of the customers were couples celebrating Valentine's Day. Best he could tell, he was the only one alone. "Good grief. From the back, that girl over there even looks like Sara. I wish it were her," Jake said to himself.

Jake sighed, gulped the remainder of the cider, then walked slowly out of the restaurant onto the snow-covered sidewalk. The light breeze was cold around his neck, and he pulled his coat collar around his cheeks and walked past the Ore House window.

0500 Hours
15 April 1974
The Pentagon
Washington, D.C.

"SORRY TO HAVE GOTTEN you out of bed at this hour, sir." Colonel Carpenter was in a crisp uniform, but his face showed exhaustion. He had been in the office with Hanraty all night and had finally decided that the situation warranted awakening the admiral.

"Don't worry about that. You did the right thing. Get some coffee, and let's huddle in my office. I want you to brief me on the entire situation."

When Admiral Hollifield hung his coat on the rack in the corner, Hanraty returned with three large cups of steaming black coffee and a pocket full of sugar and powdered creamer. He had not said a word since the admiral marched in. His time was coming. If the admiral was fully awake, he knew he would ask a hundred questions not anticipated. Admiral Hollifield had an uncanny knack for getting information faster than anyone he had ever known, and he thought exponentially, looking for all possibilities and potentialities.

Without sitting down, the admiral started. "Let me have it, John. Facts only. We'll speculate later."

"Well, sir. Hijackers took two airliners less than eight hours ago at Heathrow in London. Both were American Pan Am 707s. Both loaded to roughly seventy percent capacity. One hundred fifty passengers on one and one hundred forty-three on the other. There were three terrorists on each plane, and they identified themselves as Komando Jihad."

"Jeez. Where do these characters come up with the names?" The admiral plopped down in his chair, irritated, and sipped his coffee.

Hanraty interpreted the admiral drinking his coffee as a cue to continue. "Their demands were typical of this sort of thing. That is, release a half-dozen of their brothers from prisons. They..."

"So, are these guys Middle Eastern? Palestinian?"

"No, sir. They are Muslim. They're Indonesian, based in Java. The organization has been around a while, but until now, no one has paid much attention to them."

Colonel Carpenter took the chair next to Hanraty. "Go ahead, John. The planes."

"Yeah. Sure. Ah, it was a typical hijack situation, sir, until about two hours ago. The British were on top of the situation. The negotiations were going as well as could be expected, but then those idiots made a farewell speech about American imperialism and BOOM! They blew up one of the planes."

Carpenter interrupted. "A high-velocity explosion, sir. No survivors. Roughly one hundred fifty passengers and crew are dead. Most of them were American."

Admiral Hollifield slowly sat forward in his chair, deliberately placing his arms on the desk. He was angry.

"Admiral, the blast was extraordinarily violent. Intelligence on the scene said that the plane was literally obliterated. It's almost a certainty that the primary explosive was made from ammonium nitrate and fuel oil, generally known as ANFO. You could level a mountain with that stuff. At least the fumes and gases delivered by the explosion indicate it was. If so, then maybe, just maybe, these are the same terrorists responsible for the bombing in Heidelberg that John has been chasing."

"How did they get enough ammonium nitrate on board for that kind of explosion?" Hollifield asked.

Carpenter flipped the page of his notes but answered without looking at them. "It wouldn't take a lot, sir. Even a small amount would ignite the twenty-three thousand gallons of fuel onboard."

"What's the status on the other plane?"

"Still sitting on the runway, sir. No new developments. That's why I called. The Brits are frozen in their tracks. Can't blame them. They're afraid to make a move out of fear of killing another one hundred plus. It's a touchy situation for them, sir. They'd like for us to handle this problem since it's primarily our people at stake, assuming there is time to react."

"Tell me more about Komando Jihad, John. What's with them? What do they want?"

"Like I said, Admiral. We don't know very much. I dug

through the files over at Naval Intelligence, and all I came up with is a short brief. All we really know is that they want the Indonesian government to be run by strict Islamic law. They are a splinter group from Darul Islam. But the Indonesians pretty much eliminated them some years ago. Komando Jihad has not been on our radar."

Hollifield slammed the palm of his hand down on the desk, spilling coffee over the edge of the Styrofoam cup. "Not good enough. By 1200 hours, I want to know every detail there is to know about this psychopathic outfit called Komando Jihad. I don't care where you get the information, but get it." The admiral was shaking his finger at Hanraty in a fatherly manner, which indicated he was deadly serious, but at the same time, warm-hearted toward the object of his scolding. "Drag out that list you brought back from London of possible bad guys when that German got himself killed. Find me a match, John. I want to know who these people are so I can personally see to it their agenda is terminated."

Hanraty sat silently with a meek expression on his face. He had never seen the admiral so mad.

"Now, get out of here and get to work. Colonel Carpenter and I have to figure out what we can do to save those people on the other plane."

Hanraty closed the door behind him, and Carpenter pulled his chair an inch closer to the desk. There was no time for formality, just quick action.

Hollifield lit a cigar and coughed. "These things taste bad this early in the morning."

Carpenter smiled but said nothing.

"Okay, Colonel. You have any ideas?"

"Yes, sir. Call Strong down at Fort Bragg."

"Special Forces?"

"Yessir. This terrorism game is exactly what they've been working on down there. Of course, timing is critical. Fort Bragg is one hell of a long way from London. They might not get there in time."

"How about the Navy SEALs?"

"The same kind of program, lately. Both are shifting their emphasis to counterterrorist activities. I'm sure they could do as good a job. I'm just personally not as informed on the state of readiness or the precise capability of the SEALs for this kind of situation."

"Me either. I could find out, but we don't have time to waste. I've known Colonel Strong a long time, and I know he is one dedicated soldier. If something can be done to save those people, Strong is as good of a shot as we are going to get."

"You want me to call, sir?"

"Yes. Use a dedicated line and get him up here this morning. Give him a general mission order so his teams can get ready while we do a little fly-by-the-seat-of-the-pants planning. I'll brief the Joint Chiefs, and then the President, providing this scheme gets off the ground."

"Yessir." Carpenter rose and headed for the door, then turned again to the admiral. "Sir, Colonel Strong is right. This country has to get serious about handling this kind of crisis. We're going to see a lot more of this, and we can't stop and try to re-invent the wheel every time."

"I know, Colonel. We're moving as fast as we can, but in all likelihood, it's probably too slow. We may have a total of three hundred dead Americans before this day is done."

0600 Hours
15 April 1974
Fort Bragg, North Carolina

"Lieutenant Jacobs. The major wants to see you at the command post." Sergeant Mallory placed the handset back in the radio pack and continued to stir his rations over a small burning piece of C-4 explosive. Issued heat for rations was too cumbersome, and the C-4 burned hotter.

Jake set his rations to the side and walked briskly toward the command post. They had been in the field for three days after having spent the week before in the classroom. The Special Forces School had been more than he had hoped. The training was specialized, the instructors were professional, and he was made to feel a part of the team the moment he stepped on post. It was hard work, but he had learned skills he had never dreamed of and had fine-tuned skills he had already acquired. Six weeks into the course, he had begun learning the arts of survival, fieldcraft, emergency medical care, use of weapons from around the world, including improvised weapons, deadly use of hand-to-hand combat, communications, and hostage rescue tactics. He had earned his wings for HALO, high-altitude/low-opening, jumps at thirty thousand feet, scaled and rappelled every conceivable rock formation, and was becoming familiar with demolitions and the handling of a dozen small arms. Colonel Strong had promised him the best training in the world, and he was not disappointed in the promise made good.

"Sir. Lieutenant Jacobs reporting as ordered."

Major Hearn motioned for Jake to have a seat in his office, a large rock under a lean-to. "Tell me, Jacobs, if you were given the opportunity to go on a real mission today, a hostage rescue mission, could you handle it?"

Jake was stunned by the question. *Is this a course question that everyone is asked two weeks before the first training phase is over?* he thought.

"Just give me an honest answer. I need to know, and we don't have time for you to think about it."

"Well, sir. An honest answer is that I feel prepared for a mission as a team member, but I don't think I'm prepared to lead a team on a real mission. I still have to think about what I'm doing on the exercises. It's not second nature yet."

Hearn laughed. "I like that answer. And I agree with your assessment. If I had a choice, I wouldn't offer you a mission yet, but we have a situation that's developed, and I think you can be of help."

Jake's eyes grew wide at the realization that the major's question was for real. There really was a mission.

Hearn sat on the rock in front of Jake and sipped a canteen cup of hot coffee. "We have one hundred forty-three hostages on an airplane in London, and we're going to try to get them all out alive. I think you could be of value to the team going in because you're the best shot I've ever seen with a handgun. If the team gets into the plane, picking out a target and quickly killing it will be critical. They already blew up one plane, killing a hundred fifty people, and we have to bring them down before they can detonate another bomb. I figure pistols are our best resource. Automatic weapons are out of the question because of the passengers, and rifles might be too cumbersome. Are you sure you want to go?"

Jake shook his head affirmatively but could feel the muscles tighten in the back of his neck. He had prepared for combat for years, and now that the time for it had arrived, he felt fear. He felt fear of making a mistake and fear of getting killed.

Major Hearn slapped his knee. "You'll do fine, Jake. Just let your training take over." He rose from his rock, and Jake stood with him. "Go get your gear. We are being extracted in ten minutes. We'll be on our way to London in less than an hour."

CHAPTER 12

2000 Hours
15 April 1974
London

SUKARNO AND ROKUS Sogiarto anxiously paced the hotel suite's floor, agitated by the lack of knowledge about specific events at Heathrow. They had no communication with their soldiers, and the public radio and television coverages were sporadic. Ann Borden, a BBC, British Broadcasting Corporation, news correspondent, was the most accurate in her speculations. Her accuracy was not because she had any more precise information than the press at large, but rather because she had experience with such events. It was her specialty. She traveled the world covering hijackings and other acts of terrorism. Sukarno amused himself with her constant assumptive chatter about the hijackers' motives and how the captive passengers were behaving.

"I am no longer sure our men can delay another twelve hours. This woman reporter may be right. Our men may already be near exhaustion. What was it she said? The auxiliary power unit on the plane is no longer functioning?" Rokus needed a shower. He was tense and sweating profusely, though in a cool room miles away from Heathrow Airport.

Sukarno silently despised Rokus's mental weakness. "Do not worry so much, my leader. Our men do not need lights and air conditioning. They do not mind suffering before they die. It is all part of their sacrifice to Allah."

"That is true," Rokus said, still concerned. "They will do their duty."

Sukarno sat at the table near the radio and reduced the volume. "And even if our soldiers do become exhausted prior to our target time for destroying the plane, we have still won a major victory. The longer they hold out, the better. The world is getting a good dose of how powerful and dangerous Komando Jihad is. It is just the beginning, my leader."

"You are sure there is no way for the authorities to capture our men and prevent the explosion, aren't you?" Rokus had asked the same question repeatedly until Sukarno was out of patience.

"There is a chance for anything in these matters, Rokus, but it is not likely that our men will fail to carry out their mission completely. And, even if they were captured, so what? They would ultimately be forced to tell all they know. But isn't that the purpose of this mission in the first place? We don't care that the world knows about Komando Jihad or you as its leader. We've already told the world who hijacked those planes. Our men know nothing that we do not want the world to know."

"Yes. As always, you are right."

Sukarno smiled. Rokus misinterpreted his counsel as

loyalty. "We must leave. It is time for us to drive away from this city."

2200 Hours
15 April 1974
C-130 Flight to London

AT THIRTY THOUSAND feet above the Atlantic, the C-130 flew at its ceiling and its maximum speed of three hundred miles per hour. Heathrow was less than two hours distant, and the team rested without regard to the aircraft's loud drone.

Major Hearn and executive officer Captain Rigdon served as the commanding officers of the B-Team for the Operations Detachment A-Team. The A-Team consisted of a commanding officer, Captain Bradley Badger, an executive officer, temporarily assigned to Jake but normally filled by a warrant officer, and ten noncommissioned officers. Though Colonel Strong and his staff were developing a specific new doctrine for hostage rescue missions and a new operational structure to meet its needs, the A-Team still consisted of its previous components of specialties manned by NCO's concerning operations, weapons, intelligence, medical, communications, and engineering. It wasn't a perfect organization for this type of combat, but each man had cross-trained in at least one other team area as a specialty, and for the moment, it was the best they had.

During the first five hours of the flight, the team had devised a plan, as best they could from the sketchy intelligence they had from Heathrow, then practiced their maneuvers in the space available. Afterward, Jake reviewed his weapons inventory one more time. The armory Staff Sergeant had issued him a specially outfitted version of his trusty M1911A1 Colt .45, one that had been accurized and equipped with a couple of "non-standard upgrades," as the sly Sergeant had put it. In addition to custom sights, he had pinned the weapon's grip safety, leaving only the thumb safety active. This would prevent any stress-related issues that two safeties might introduce. He had also provided a dozen 7-round magazines, all filled with something called "frangible" ammunition. Frangible ammo was very new, delivering incredible takedown power combined with the reassurance that it would not over-penetrate. The Sergeant told him it would not penetrate sheetrock or a plane fuselage, but it would "ruin anyone's day who got in its way." Jake inserted a mag, chambered a round, dropped the mag, and topped it off for a total of 8 rounds to start, then re-seated the mag in the weapon. He double-checked that the thumb safety was engaged and holstered the sidearm.

While briefing, Major Hearn exhibited his professionalism to the degree that one might think there was actually a standard procedure for the situation. There was not. He was thinking and improvising moment by moment. "We brought flak jackets, but I don't think we should use them. It is safe to assume the terrorists are using rifle-caliber weapons, so flak jackets won't help, anyway. They will slow down your reaction time, and in close quarters, might prevent you from getting your target. Maybe next time, fellas. We'll put body armor on our wish list to Colonel Strong. Next—forget caution. Once you get into the aircraft, we'll fail in our mission if you are cautious in the attack. Speed and quick reactions are the keys to success. You have to move quickly and accurately to throw the enemy off balance."

J.M. PATTON

0300 Hours
Heathrow Airport
London

"Heathrow is shrouded in darkness now. The rain commenced an hour ago. We've not been given access to the runway, so we are reporting to you live from the terminal area. In the distance behind me, you can just barely see the image of Pan Am Flight 630, where one hundred forty-three passengers are held hostage by three hijackers that have identified themselves as members of Komando Jihad. We interviewed a high-ranking British official less than an hour ago who is involved in negotiations with the hijackers. He refused to comment on this incident or what plans have been made to attempt a rescue, except to say that the hijackers have demanded six PLO members' release. This is Ann Borden, BBC, bringing you this update live from Heathrow Airport, London. We'll bring you additional coverage as events develop."

The red light on the camera, signifying it was recording every movement and sound, went blank, and Ann Borden changed her facial expression and slumped her shoulders. She was exhausted. She had been on the scene with the camera crew for nearly twenty-four hours, trying to get information on the hijacking and closer to the hijacked planes. Both efforts had been relatively futile. The officials on the scene were keeping security extremely tight. However, one official politely took the time to explain that any information given to the media would likely be heard by the hijackers, thereby thwarting any attempts to help the passengers on the plane. Ann understood their reasons well enough, but it still frustrated her that she could not get closer to the action.

The advent of satellite communications had been good for

both her and the British Broadcasting Company. Her section had become BBC's specialists on crisis events, and she literally thrived on the excitement of traveling all over the world without notice to report on bombings, hijackings, or political demonstrations. Ann Borden had a personal life once, but at the age of thirty-six, her career consumed every aspect of normalcy, leaving nothing but the rush of adrenaline experienced through crisis situations and exhaustion.

Walter Trent, a junior member of the crew, came rushing down the corridor and pulled Ann to the side. "Something is about to happen!"

"Calm down, Walter. Catch your breath and tell me quietly."

Trent took two deep breaths, then spoke almost in a whisper. "I was waiting outside that room, just like you said to do, and these two Naval officers came out. One of them said that the hijackers were starting to make the same speech they gave before. You know—about Komando Jihad—and American imperialism? You know?"

Ann's eyes grew wide. "So, you think that the hijackers are about to blow the other plane?"

"Yes! I don't know how long that last speech was, but I thought maybe you would want the cameras rolling when the plane explodes."

―――

THE A-TEAM HAD FINISHED ALL the preparatory activity twenty minutes earlier. Charges were set on a cargo dolly one hundred meters from the aircraft's starboard side. If the diversionary explosion caught the hijacker's attention for merely a few seconds, the team could enter the aircraft.

The team huddled directly under the fuselage next to the ladders that would be maneuvered into place seconds after detonation, shaking from both the cold rain and fear. Major Hearn maintained radio contact with the negotiators, trying to find the best possible set of circumstances to initiate the attack. He was beginning to favor sooner more than later. The cold rain and the waiting were doing nothing for the morale of his A-Team. They were ready, mentally on edge, to do the job, but he could not expect them to maintain that psychological pitch for long. It would be better for them to attack at their best than to wait and hope for the hijackers to be out of position.

The radio hissed. Major Hearn placed the receiver tight against his ear to shield it from the increasing wind, listened for a full minute, then said something into the handset before handing it to the communications NCO and turning to his huddled shivering men. "This is it," he said in a low voice. "Sergeant Gutierrez, blow the charges in two minutes. I say again, two minutes. The negotiating team thinks the hijackers are getting ready to blow the plane. We have to go now!" Gutierrez turned immediately to his equipment, checked the connections, and set the timer. Two minutes.

"All right, Captain Rigdon, the show is on. It's your baby now."

Rigdon stood and faced the eleven men. They were all ready—more than ready. "You all know what your positions are —you all know your assignment. Jacobs, you're first in on the starboard side, followed by Crocker. Yelton, port side with Bramlett behind you. Nelson and Fontenot set up housekeeping at the entry points." Captain Rigdon glanced another time into the faces of his men, then at his watch. "One minute and counting. Move out to your positions."

Jake and the others took their places, ready to swing the

ladders into place at the sound of the linear cutting tape charges. Poised, waiting for the seconds to roll by, the thought flashed through his mind how precious these sixty seconds might be. If the hijackers blew the plane, they, the A-Team, were already in harm's way. It did not make much difference if they were in the plane or under it if it exploded. They would all be dead, along with one hundred forty-three innocent passengers. The cold rain spattered against his face. In the distance, he could see the lights of the main terminal building.

WHAM! The blasts rang in the team's ears, and their bodies swung into motion. In the distance, Jake could see through his peripheral vision the fiery diversionary explosion and hoped that the hijackers were now rushing to the front of the aircraft, peering out the cockpit and starboard windows, wondering what had happened.

The two escape hatches under the aircraft's fuselage, and both emergency doors over the wing were blown simultaneously by their respective teams. The aircraft was breached. Jake's right leg, head, and weapon entered together, with eyes immediately focusing on the aisle leading to the plane's cockpit. He was inside. A woman screamed as he stepped in her lap. Then another screamed—and another. The exhausted, frightened passengers had no idea what was happening.

The diversionary explosion had worked. The terrorists inside had rushed forward to investigate the chaos on the tarmac and were busy peering out the windows and chatting nervously with one another. The scream of a woman back down the aisle alerted them that something was happening.

Jake riveted his eyes on the forward aisle as he scrambled. Out of the corner of his eye, he could see Yelton just entering the port side. He suddenly had a driving desire to turn his head to check the aisle behind him. The temptation was almost unbearable. With Yelton not yet in place, what if a terrorist were moving toward him from the rear of the plane? With his eyes focused on the cockpit, he would be shot in the back before Yelton was ready to react. *Forget it! Concentrate on my sector.*

The very moment Jake conquered that apprehension and stepped clearly into the aisle, the curtains separating the first-class section from coach, ten meters forward, opened violently, and a man with a full beard and an AK-47 sprang forward with a confused expression on his face. Jake's legs propelled him forward as he slightly adjusted the .45 automatic toward the terrorist, instinctively flicking the thumb safety off. BLAM!-BLAM!-BLAM! Jake's three rapid presses of the single-action trigger delivered three rounds to its mark before the soldier from Komando Jihad could raise his rifle, two rounds to the chest and one to the head, striking the bad guy in the center of the face. All of his involuntary functions ceased instantly, and he went down in a heap.

"Three rounds," Jake subconsciously counted to himself.

As his legs propelled him forward and his mind concentrated on the appearance of another target, Jake could hear Crocker a dozen steps behind him yelling, "U.S. Army—get down! U.S. Army—get down!" Without moving the focal point of his gaze, he leaped over the fallen terrorist and pressed on.

The cockpit cabin door flew open, and a terrorist in a sweat-stained white T-shirt came through with his automatic rifle blazing. His rounds were wild and high, firing without first finding his target. Jake immediately went to one knee and fired three more times. BLAM!-BLAM!-BLAM! The terrorist was first struck by a frangible round in his right cheek, which disintegrated what had been a face a moment before. The round severed the terrorist's medulla oblongata, instantly incapacitating him. He never felt the other two rounds decimate his upper chest before he fell to the floor.

"Three more rounds, two rounds left," Jake recorded instinctively and knew it was time for a reload. Without hesitation, Jake ejected the nearly spent magazine and seated a full 7-round mag before the first one hit the ground, all the while maintaining his focus on the front of the aircraft.

Simultaneously, Jake rose and continued his race to the cockpit. When he arrived, he kicked the door out of his way and entered, pistol still searching for another target. The airline captain, his co-pilot, and the navigation officer sat wide-eyed and speechless. Jake felt a sense of relief rush through his body as he realized that this was the end of the line. The bad guys on this end of the aircraft were dead. All Jake could say before he turned to make his way hurriedly back down the aisle was, "U.S. Army."

Less than a minute had elapsed. Jake and Sergeant Crocker walked quickly past the passengers, who were still stunned and frightened. Jake glanced over Crocker's shoulder and could see Yelton in the distance. He had not heard any of Yelton's shots but knew there had been a terrorist killed near the back of the plane. Jake stepped over the first target he had killed and stared at the massive pool of blood and the blank stare on what remained of the dead man's face.

It was time to get the passengers off the aircraft. One of the flight attendants deployed the emergency escape chutes, and the crew assisted with the order to evacuate the aircraft immediately.

It was over. The cold rain and wind hit Jake's face as he climbed through the hole to the outside and descended the steps. It almost seemed as though it had not really happened. The attack had been so fast that the event seemed like a hazy dream. Jake took a deep breath through his nose, exhaled slowly, then smiled affectionately at Major Hearn, who gave him an approving look as his foot touched the tarmac.

Several ambulances, fire trucks, buses, and cars raced toward the aircraft. A small bus, used to transport passengers to the outlying parking areas, came to a stop thirty yards from the aircraft. The passengers were whisked away to safety while another bus returned the team to the waiting C-130, which took off 5 minutes later

―――――

"Just moments ago, we briefly interviewed one passenger that has been debriefed and released by the authorities. Although the details are sketchy, a small detachment of soldiers of the United States Army entered the passenger compartment of Pan Am Flight 630, killing all three terrorists before they could detonate their bomb. Officials on the scene offered no comment on the specifics of this raid, nor would they identify the military unit involved. As details do evolve, BBC will be on the scene to bring you live coverage. Meanwhile, the sun is rising over London, and we are all grateful that the lives of those on Pan Am Flight 630 have been saved. We pray for the one hundred fifty that did lose their lives in this tragic and senseless event. May God be with them. This is Ann Borden, BBC World News."

―――――

0800 Hours
16 April 1974
The White House

Admiral Hollifield, General Jack T. Cushman, and Colonel Strong entered the Oval Office after a short wait. The President rose from his desk and briskly crossed the room to greet his visitors.

"Good morning, gentlemen. Have a seat."

"Good morning, Mr. President." General Cushman, the Chairman of the Joint Chiefs of Staff, was a frequent visitor to the office and had received his call shortly after midnight to let him know that this meeting was first on the President's agenda for the day. Hollifield and Strong had spent the night at the Pentagon and freshened themselves as best they could before the meeting. It had been a long twenty-four-hour period.

"That was a hell of a mess at Heathrow, wouldn't you say?" The President seldom wasted time with idle conversation, and this meeting was no exception. He sat and poured each officer coffee.

General Cushman spooned sugar into his cup as he spoke. "Yes, sir. The admiral and Colonel Strong did a fine job on this one, sir. It's a shame we lost that other plane and its passengers."

The president reflected on the general's statement as he sipped his coffee. "Tell me, John, just how lucky were we on this one? I mean, you came barging in here yesterday morning to get permission for that mission, and in hindsight, it's obvious that all of you were flying by the seat of your pants. Don't get me wrong. I'm damned happy about the results. Your men performed well, and many Americans are alive today because of your actions, but we weren't prepared for that sort of thing, were we?"

Hollifield set his cup on the table as he scooted to the last few inches of the sofa and cleared his throat. "No, sir. We weren't prepared. And, we were luckier than a teenager getting laid on his first date."

The President chuckled, and General Cushman grinned, shaking his head at John Hollifield's down-home manner with the president of the United States.

"Mr. President, the world is changing very quickly with respect to warfare and this nation's security. The Soviets have been very successful at getting us into limited engagements, like Vietnam, and they are sponsoring worldwide a new concept in warfare. Terrorism. They are supplying them with weapons and training in exchange for favors. They love seeing us off balance with events like Heathrow. We've all but eliminated our capability to defend ourselves against terrorism by pulling Special Forces out of the Order of Battle."

"The brass tells me we don't need Special Forces anymore. Isn't that right, General Cushman?"

"That's my opinion, Mr. President. Vietnam is over. They did a fine job, but we don't need an elitist unit anymore. We have no missions for covert operations or the training of foreign armies. Special Forces is an outdated concept, Mr. President."

Colonel Strong rattled his cup as anger gripped his neck. "Elitists! What you mean, General is exceptionally well-trained. Trained to handle situations just like Heathrow Airport. I dare you, sir, to attend all of those funerals and then report to the president that there is not a need for Special Forces."

The room fell quiet. Colonel Strong eased back in his

chair, fully aware that he had lost his temper when he should not have.

Hollifield cleared his throat again. "Well, sir, I'm sure that what Colonel Strong means is that perhaps the situation at Heathrow indicates that we should take a closer look at Special Forces and potential problems the unit might address in the future."

Cushman laughed loudly, which spread to the others once they recognized his sincerity. "Hell, that isn't what the good colonel meant at all. What he meant was that I'm full of crap." Again, everyone laughed, and the tension evaporated. "Perhaps Colonel Strong has a point, Mr. President. I'm an old tank soldier. I suppose it's hard for me to believe that a battalion of armor can't solve every problem."

The president liked Cushman. He was honest to a fault with himself and everyone else. "So, what do you recommend, Jack? Do you think we should give Colonel Strong a little more room to maneuver and see what he comes up with?"

General Cushman grinned as he looked at each anticipating face. What choice did he have? It was clear the president would order it even if he did not agree. "One condition I'd like to see in place, Mr. President. I'd like the lid on all this for now. The conventional troops don't like these guys, and we have morale problems everywhere."

"How about it, Colonel Strong? Can you live with that?"

Strong's excitement was almost as visible as his anger had been a few moments earlier. "Yes, sir. I can live with it. All I need is our facility at Bragg, a right to recruit quietly, and some time. We are developing doctrine and tactics to meet the need, and with your permission, sir, I'd like to report directly to Admiral Hollifield. He already has a feel for the direction we're going, and our plans call for coordination with the Navy SEAL teams."

General Cushman grinned and shook his head. "Ho-ly cow. What have I gotten myself into? Ok, Colonel. You've got your chance, but don't expect miracles."

The president rose, indicating to the others that the meeting was over. "Good. I feel like we are all in agreement here. Colonel Strong, I wish you well with your efforts. I happen to agree with your assessment that we are facing a new enemy. I'd like to see to it that each of your men is properly decorated for their heroism at Heathrow. See to it."

CHAPTER 13

1000 Hours
23 April 1974
Fort Bragg, North Carolina

IT WAS a Sunday morning and only the third such day that Jake had time to himself in seven weeks. He had a nice room in the BOQ, but he had not spent much time in it with the training schedule. It felt good to sleep late and have no plans for the day.

The action at Heathrow had not changed much for him. The moment they landed at Bragg, he climbed into the back of a deuce-and-a-half and was back in the field thirty minutes later with the training schedule as usual. If they knew about the mission at all, and he was sure they did, his instructors said nothing about it. After thinking about it, their reaction, or lack of it, was appropriate. He had simply done his job at Heathrow. Any one of the Special Forces men could have and would have done it if it had been their call for the mission.

For several days, Jake kept expecting to feel some remorse

or guilt about killing two human beings. It did not come. All he could feel was that he had done his duty, and in doing so, had helped save innocent lives. He had always placed a high value on human life. Still, there was a difference between volitional responsibility and murder. The terrorists had committed murder. Killing an enemy of the divine institutions of law and order, or even in defense of nationalism, balanced with his set of values and frame of reference. The terrorists had made a decision to hijack those planes and to kill one hundred fifty people. They were responsible for their actions, and the consequence, which was death, had been appropriately delivered. Though satisfied internally that his actions had matched his values, Jake sensed a warning from deep within himself to be watchful of how his choice of profession might someday challenge those values more directly. Perhaps someday, he might face a critical decision between expediency and his moral standard. Would he have the courage to choose correctly? Would he lay down his life to guard his values, or would he take the life of another to save his own? As Jake considered the potential of these things, which only Providence would provide, he recalled a part of the Cadet Prayer from West Point that clearly stated a guidepost. *Make us to choose the harder right instead of the easier wrong, and never to be content with a half-truth when the whole can be won.*

The phone rang as he stepped from the shower. Jake left a trail of water behind as he walked to the phone on his desk. "Lieutenant Jacobs speaking, sir."

"Where have you been? I've been trying to get your scrawny butt on the phone for a week. I'm gonna have to get you one of them aggravating beepers or something."

Jake laughed and sat, water pooling at his feet. "Hi, Patrick. Where are you?"

"Still at Rucker. Will be, I reckon, for another six months. But the great news is that you're gonna have the pleasure of my company in a couple of weeks. We're flyin' a squadron to Bragg for maneuvers with you snake-eaters. You guys will get to see how real soldiers get the job done."

"Get the job done? Oh, you're talking about after the fighting is done, and we're at the Officer's Club, right?"

Patrick laughed. "Right. What'd you think I was talkin' about?"

"That's great. If you're here long enough, maybe we can go up to D.C. for a weekend. I could use a weekend in civilian clothes."

"You're on. We'll be there for a month. Surely, we can get away. You guys aren't doing anything all that important at Bragg. Or maybe you are. What's the scoop on that hostage rescue at Heathrow Airport in London last week? They said it was a U.S. Army unit that saved the day. Had to be Special Forces."

Jake paused. It was the first time he had faced the conflict of classified information, and his best friend asking him for it.

"That was a long pause, ole buddy," Patrick finally said. "My fault. I shouldn't have asked. I reckon it's going to take a little gettin' used to for you and me not to be able to talk to each other about every little detail in our lives anymore. Anyway, that was one impressive raid. Whoever did it sure knew what they were doing. Took moxie, I know that. Who knows, maybe someday you'll be doing that sort of thing. You have my permission, but if there is going to be any shootin', you'll just have to tell your boss that Uncle Patrick said you couldn't go. I can't have you going and getting hurt on me."

Jake chuckled. "I'll let them know. If it's dangerous, Uncle

Patrick says I can't play. Hurry and get here. I'm ready to hear some of your bad jokes."

"I have some new ones. Oh, by the way. I ran into Wally Bidet. He said to tell you hello and that he was being assigned to the Pentagon in August. You guys will be next-door neighbors."

"Great. Never a dull moment with that crazy Cajun around."

"I have to go. Just wanted to let you know I'll be there in a couple of weeks. I'm looking forward to it."

"Me, too. Take care of yourself." Jake hung up the phone and noticed that he had drip-dried, leaving water pooled on the floor. After mopping the water all the way back to the bathroom, he stood facing his uniform shirt hanging on the back of the door. The sight of the little red, white, and blue ribbon above the pocket, the Bronze Star, still seemed strange on his uniform. Heathrow was not exactly a designated combat zone by Vietnam standards, but it had seemed close enough in the heat of the moment.

1500 Hours
29 May 1974
The Pentagon
Washington, D.C.

ADMIRAL HOLLIFIELD THUMBED through Colonel Strong's detailed report again while Colonel Carpenter and John Hanraty sat silent. The meeting time had been set a day earlier when Hanraty indicated to the colonel that he had sufficient information gathered for a report to the admiral. Hollifield had been offered a written report from Hanraty, but he declined. He wanted to hear it direct.

Hollifield drummed his fingers on the desk as he browsed through the report and thought. Strong's report held several surprises. The first being that young Lieutenant John Paul Jacobs had been a key member of the team and had killed two of the three terrorists. Had he known that beforehand, he would have been even more nervous about the deployment. He already knew that personal involvement affected his judgment. If Strong had asked him, Hollifield would have probably been tempted to put the nix on Jake's participation. He was proud of Jake for how he had performed, but he did not know if he could stand losing another one of his "boys." It had only been a few months since he had lost Steve. To lose another so soon would be unbearable for him and Suzanne.

Beyond the shock of finding Jake a central character in the report, Hollifield was fascinated with how effective the tactics had been against the terrorists. Strong emphasized the speed required and how critical the team's finely-honed skills were to the mission's success. It was clear from the description given that conventional training was simply not adequate for such an attack. To meet these types of situations effectively would require skill and practice. A team member had to be able to react by instinct, not reason. Reason was too slow. Hollifield drew his conclusion. *Perhaps that is exactly the edge we need. We need teams that attack by second nature against an enemy whom we force to stop and think. A mere second can make all the difference in the world.*

"What did you think of Colonel Strong's report?" Hollifield closed the cover and looked at Carpenter.

"Well, sir, it was enough to convince me to give him all the support he asks for. He seems to have proven his point. That is that the tactics his people are developing for counterterrorism activities are effective. It's a subtle twist on the doctrines and tactics of the Green Berets and the SEALs used in Vietnam, but when you think about it, sir, the basic team and individual skills developed within those units are the same needed for raids like Heathrow. There is definitely a common thread between the old and the new. It would be insane not to develop the capability to handle terrorist activity and even more insane not to utilize the assets we already have. My vote is to turn Colonel Strong loose on this idea."

Hollifield's expression did not change. "What would you have done differently? I mean, how would you have handled that attack?"

Carpenter grinned at Hollifield. "You mean as a career infantry soldier, Ranger, Pathfinder, and conventional warfare type, is there, in my opinion, a way to have rescued those passengers any other way?"

Hollifield leaned back in his chair and laughed. "You've been hanging around me too long, Colonel. I don't know if I like it when colonels and Navy captains start knowing what I'm thinking. It makes me think it's time for the rocking chair. Dang it, I guess I'm going to have to see to it you get a star when you leave this assignment."

Carpenter turned red. Becoming a general officer was a serious subject. Only those who had already made it could joke about it without feeling the butterflies churn in their stomach.

"Well?"

"No, sir. It couldn't be done. There are plenty of guys around to try, but that wouldn't be enough. Our soldiers are good, Admiral, but this type of combat is different. I hope you understand, sir. I'm not suggesting that Special Forces troops are better than conventional infantry or Rangers. On the contrary. Those troops are the best at what they train to do. They are the best combat infantry in the world. But you can't take men trained for basic infantry tactics and expect them to know exactly how to rescue hostages. Colonel Strong is absolutely correct. It's a special situation requiring special skills. It's just that simple."

"Then you're committed to this concept? Is that right?"

"Yessir."

Hollifield sat forward and stared sternly at Carpenter. "Are you really? Would you bet your career on it? Would you sacrifice your chance for two or three stars to see this mission successfully completed?"

Carpenter stared back firmly. He had been around the admiral long enough to recognize a challenge from him. The admiral did not waste words or disinherit his integrity for the satisfaction of watching a subordinate squirm. If the "Old Man" asked those questions, they were real questions deserving a direct and honest answer. "Yes, sir. I'm committed. I'd pass on getting a star altogether to see Strong give this country the capability it needs."

John Hanraty squirmed in his chair. He felt like he was in the middle of a conversation he was not supposed to hear.

Hollifield paused, then rose from his desk and walked to the window. He admired the beauty of the Washington Monument in the distance before he spoke. "We'll see. You're going to get an opportunity to choke on those words and that commitment." He turned to face Carpenter with Hanraty sitting next to him wide-eyed.

"I don't understand what you mean, Admiral."

"I'm creating a new operational area in the Department of Defense. It's not activated officially yet and probably won't be for several years. It will take years of hard work to make it happen. The Department of Defense tentatively likes the idea and is willing to support it on a prove-it basis. Over the next six months, we are to form the U.S. Army John F. Kennedy Center for Military Assistance and the U.S. Army Institute for Military Assistance. Both will be at Fort Bragg. The mission is to develop doctrine to train, deploy, and employ hostage rescue and other counterterrorism elements. Ultimately, this effort's primary long-term goal is to activate, within five years, the Joint Special Operations Command. As envisioned, this command is to be a joint service operation. Colonel Strong is now forming what he calls the 1st Special Forces Operational Detachment toward accomplishing this mission. In conjunction with Strong's Detachment, the 160th Aviation Group out of Fort Campbell, Kentucky, a new SEAL Team Six out of Dam Neck, Virginia, and the 23rd Air Force will be coordinated into this effort."

Colonel Carpenter could not believe his ears. Admiral Hollifield had taken this concept beyond idle discussion. He had bulldozed Washington into submission to develop a full-fledged Special Forces operation.

Hollifield moved back to his desk and sat. "As you know, Colonel Strong is the one who has rattled everyone's cage to get this thing rolling. The problem is, he's a junior colonel, and he is not the most diplomatic officer I've ever met. Besides, we need him in the field, hands-on with the men. I've discussed it with him, and he is in one hundred percent agreement with me that you are the man to take command of this god-awful mission. We need someone with your skills, experience, and diplomacy. You have the background for it. You're Infantry, a Ranger, Airborne, Pathfinder, and you spent two tours pounding the hills of Vietnam. Do you want the job?"

Colonel Richard Carpenter was stunned. "Yes, sir. This all comes as a total surprise, but yes, I'd be very pleased with the job."

"Good. I'm glad you said that because your orders have already been cut for Bragg. I want you out of my office at the end of the week and at Bragg on Monday. Oh, and by the way, stop by the PX on your way home this evening and get yourself a few sets of these." Admiral Hollifield extended his arm across the desk and opened his fist to reveal two silver stars. "These were my first stars. Unless you have some objection to wearing an old sailor's rank, I'd be proud if you'd wear them."

Colonel Carpenter, now Brigadier General Carpenter, was speechless. The promotion itself was unexpected, and the Admiral's desire for him to wear his stars left him without words.

"Come on, Hanraty. Help me pin these little suckers on the general."

General Carpenter could not believe what was happening to him. He knew he probably would be on the next promotion list for brigadier but never dreamed it could happen for another two or three years. Of course, with the early promotion, he was also accepting an enormous responsibility and challenge. The plans the admiral had laid out for a Joint Special Operations Command were on paper only. He and Strong, and all the others involved in the program, would have to move mountains to make the command a reality. Essentially, he was a brigadier general in command of an idea and little else.

"'That looks fine, son," Hollifield said as he shook Carpenter's hand and admired the stars. "You'll make a fine general officer, Richard. I'm proud of you. Congratulations."

Hanraty was all smiles. "I can't think of anyone who

deserves it more, Colonel, I mean, General. Who knows, Admiral, maybe you'll get another star out of all this."

Hollifield chuckled. "Don't you think four is enough, John? It's more than enough for me. Well, let's do a little business before I turn General Carpenter loose to call the wife and strut his stuff up and down the halls of the Pentagon. John, let's hear about Komando Jihad."

All three found a chair, and Hanraty immediately shuffled through the stack of notes he had carried from his office. In the excitement, he had almost forgotten the primary purpose of the meeting. "Admiral, we have made several assumptions throughout our investigation, but we have very little in the way of cold, hard facts. First, we think we know who is behind Komando Jihad and why they are suddenly so aggressive, and second if our assumptions are correct, we have a pretty good idea of what we can expect from Komando Jihad in the future. There's a pretty strong link between the bombing in Heidelberg and Komando Jihad. That ammonium nitrate keeps showing up. Heidelberg, though it actually wasn't ammonium nitrate, traces of it in the barrel Siegel was stuffed into, and again at Heathrow. It's been confirmed that the primary explosive used at Heathrow was ammonium nitrate saturated in fuel oil, with a plastique detonator. One of our early assumptions was that Komando Jihad initially thought they had ammonium nitrate. It wasn't, and ergo, Siegel ends up regretting his double-cross. Still, Komando Jihad made good use of the ammonium nitrate once they got their hands on the real stuff. Admiral, the first point is that there is still good reason to believe that Komando Jihad started to obtain bomb-making material and probably chemical agents. It appears to remain a part of their strategy. If they can find someone to sell them the goods, then we must assume they are prepared to use them again."

Hollifield frowned and cleared his throat. "What kind of fool would do that? The Soviets wouldn't get involved in this sort of thing."

"Well, sir, the Soviets might. They have a strong interest in developing revolutionary hot spots that potentially absorb our resources. It's certainly to their advantage to support third-party terrorist actions to divert our attention."

Hollifield frowned.

"Soviets or not, we think Komando Jihad has the financial means to buy whatever they need. If they want chemical weapons, biological or otherwise, then it's just a matter of time."

"Why's that?" The admiral was almost afraid to ask. John Hanraty's report was beginning to have all the components required to produce one of his massive migraines.

"Bangjar. Sukarno Bangjar. His father, Kuwat Bangjar, was in control of Indonesia's oil production a while back and absconded with some obscene amount of money. We're told that Kuwat Bangjar was found massacred along with his family, except his son, Sukarno, in Sao Paulo about a year and a half ago. Shortly after that, most of the money was returned to the Indonesian government, but not all. The word we have is that it's a gut cinch that Sukarno murdered his family, saved his neck by giving back most of the money, and pocketed millions of dollars."

"Seems like everyone has a beef with America these days. What's his?"

"Nothing we can figure, sir, unless it's simply lusting for power. He's in his early twenties, educated at the best

European schools, and a graduate of Princeton. And, apparently now extremely wealthy."

General Carpenter interrupted. "What makes you so sure he's our man, John?"

"Well, sir, you remember when I went to London when Siegel turned up dead? British MI-6 routinely tries to monitor those entering the country. They photographed a man traveling on the passport of one Sukarno Bangjar who came through customs two days before Siegel was killed and left a day later. That's no big deal, but he flew in again two days before the Heathrow hijackings, then out again the same day as the rescue. Another man, who has been identified as Rokus Sogiarto, entered the country the same day. He is probably our man with Komando Jihad. At this point, we have nothing but coincidence and speculation.

"Go figure," the admiral said. "Rich kid with the world by the tail goes and kills his family, then joins a fanatical bunch running around blowing up planes and schools. Princeton, huh? He's probably as socially American as you and I."

John Hanraty caught his breath, then continued. "Exactly, sir. He majored in American history and finance. If he's our man, and if he is on this terrorist track, then we can again make an assumption that he thinks he knows exactly what we will do in any given situation, at least politically, and he may be right. What we haven't figured is why this Bangjar fellow has an issue with the United States. Indirectly, through our economic and political involvement with Indonesia since World War II, Sukarno Bangjar owes everything he is and has to America. His father would not have had a job with the government had it not been for U.S. oil interests."

Hollifield laughed. "Welcome to reality, John. Don't waste

your time looking for a reason. There isn't one. Our history is full of this sort of thing. So, where are they going from here?"

John Hanraty lowered his head, almost ashamed that he did not have a better answer for the admiral. "We don't know for sure, sir. All we know right now is that Komando Jihad has money and that possibly a man ruthless enough to murder his family is building a power base. I'm sorry I can't give you a better answer, Admiral, but until we see more events, we are stuck."

CHAPTER 14

2000 Hours
18 June 1974
Durango, Colorado

STEPHEN PATRICK BREATHED DEEPLY. Sara tiptoed softly out of the room and closed the door to block the hallway light into the room. Bedtime for him was alone time for her. Although she only worked at the dentist's office half-days, she was usually exhausted by early evening after having done the day's routine chores and kept up with Stephen Patrick. He was at the age where if something was within his short reach, he was into it.

Sara descended the stairs to the kitchen, fixed a cup of hot tea, then strolled in her bare feet toward the porch. The sun was setting, and the view down the valley with its long shadows was peaceful and comforting. As she opened the screen door, the stack of morning mail caught her eye. Sorting the mail mentally into categories of importance as she sat in the old rocker and propped her feet on the peeled log rail, Sara pulled her mother's letter from the stack and set the other pieces on the porch floor.

The envelope opened easily with her long fingernail cutting the top edge like a knife, and when she opened the pages, a newspaper clipping fell to the porch. Sara was not surprised to find a clipping. There was always a clipping enclosed in her mother's letters. She had almost come to ignore them and their predictable advice on divorce or single parenthood or child-raising in the 1970s. Valerie Lowell could fret and nag in the most subtle ways.

Sara began the letter, and sure enough, the one-page letter covered the predictable. There was a short paragraph to let Sara know that she and her father were fine. Then, a long paragraph to render her opinion about Sara and Stephen Patrick living alone in the mountains of Colorado, notwithstanding advice on giving the boy a garlic capsule daily to ward off colds. Sara reached for the clipping on the floor as she read "Love, Mom" and a postscript about the clipping from the Comanche Herald.

Sara unfolded the clipping, and her heart started pounding. She saw Jake staring back at her. Though the photograph was in black and white, she knew that his uniform tunic and beret were green. She stared at the picture a full minute before reading the caption underneath. "2nd Lieutenant John Paul Jacobs, a 1969 graduate of Comanche High School and a 1973 graduate of the United States Military Academy at West Point, was awarded the Bronze Star on 21 April 1974. Second Lieutenant Jacobs is assigned to the 5th Special Forces Group, Fort Bragg, North Carolina."

The shadows were deepening as the sun fell to the west. Sara hardly noticed the light fade as she concentrated on every aspect of the photograph. She whispered aloud, "My Jake is a

Green Beret." Then suddenly, she re-read the caption and felt her pulse quicken as she realized that having received the Bronze Star meant that he had been in combat somewhere. Somehow, over the past five years, it had not occurred to her that Jake might actually get hurt or killed in action. At West Point, he was in the Army, but he was safe. And after West Point? Vietnam was all but over. Everyone said so. The troops were coming home every day.

Physically shivering prior to conscious thought, Sara could feel Jake's brother Charlie's death and the funeral as though she were standing graveside, experiencing it all again. No one ever really thought Charlie would die. Like others, he was the type of young man nobody expected to be lost. He was kind and talented and loved. Visions of the immaculately uniformed soldiers firing their salute, the folding of the flag, and its solemn presentation to his wife, Margie, sent waves of panic through Sara as she unconsciously squeezed the arm of the chair.

Sara had never before felt the horror that now ran through her veins. Without her knowing about it, the thought of Jake dying challenged the little hope she held but did not allow herself to think about. It terrified her. If Jake were to die, she might not know about it for days or weeks. If Jake were to die, would she know of it only from a folded newspaper clipping in the mail or from a much too late phone call like she had received when Steve was killed? If Jake were to die, being denied grief and mourning at the proper time would be unbearable.

Darkness came, and Sara sat alone with her sorrow. If life were to end for Jake, she would have to accept that she would be the last to know. Sara closed her eyes and whispered a prayer that it would not be so.

1500 Hours
20 June 1974
Mayflower Hotel
Washington, D.C.

JULIA PASSED HALFWAY through the Mayflower Hotel's block-long lobby, found a house phone, and asked the operator for Lieutenants Jacobs and McSwain's rooms. Jake had called her parent's residence at Annapolis to get her number in Baltimore. She had been reluctant to accept Jake's invitation for dinner, but he had her laughing so hard within five minutes, she could not refuse. Since Steve's death, she had hardly gone out at all and certainly not on a date. It had been over a year, and it seemed like yesterday. The hurt was still just as bad. "A date?" Jake had said. "This ain't a date. It's three old friends getting together just for fun. Besides, you have to come to rescue me. Patrick has gone and fallen head-over-heels in love. I mean, this is serious. She's flying into D.C. Saturday morning, and you and I have to be the old folks, so to speak, and scrutinize this situation. If we don't approve, that's it. Out she goes. We have outdone ourselves on this trip. First-class all the way. We reserved a suite at the Mayflower, and there's plenty of room and privacy." Julia was glad she had come. She was excited about the reunion, and after having thought about it, she realized that Steve would be happy to know she had done her part to keep the family together.

Jake and Patrick had arrived the night before, exhausted from a week of field exercises, and declined to do anything but try to catch up on the loss of sleep. The three weeks that Patrick had been at Fort Bragg had passed quickly. Patrick and

Jake had seen little of each other, but when they met in the field or back at the BOQ, it was as though they had never been separated. Patrick had declined a room of his own in the BOQ in favor of camping-in with Jake.

Patrick's eyes bulged when he noticed the Bronze Star on Jake's chest the second night on post at the Officer's Club. "What in the world is that?"

"What?" Jake asked as though he did not know.

"That's a gen-u-wine Bronze Star!" Patrick pointed at the ribbons, eyes wide in surprise. "Right there, son, on your scrawny chest. Wake up, boy. Right there!"

Jake turned red and chuckled. As usual, Patrick could not be casual or subtle about anything. "So what?" he said.

"So what?" Patrick asked. "Are you out of your mind? Unless you stole that little strip of heroism, which is certainly possible, since you're a Tex-i-kin, but if you didn't steal it, that means you're an ass-kickin' hero."

Jake simply smiled and lifted his glass for a drink.

"Ah-ha! No comment, huh? You sneaky little turd." Patrick leaned closer to Jake from across the table and spoke in a soft voice." It's not nice not to tell Uncle Patrick that you went to London and kicked some butt. When you got so quiet on the phone, I knew there was more to that deal than you were letting on." Patrick gave Jake a smile and a wink.

Jake paused. "Well, assuming you are right, which isn't likely, since you're one of those Tennessee hillbillies, I still couldn't tell you about it. Besides, didn't you know that they pass these Bronze Stars out to all Texans as standard issue just because they're the boys from the Lone Star State?"

"Sure, Jake. Well, I wish I knew all the grimy details so I could be even more proud of you than I already am. Congratulations." Patrick looked at Jake sternly and shook his finger at him. "But let me tell you this. You better play safe. If you don't, you'll really hack me off. You got that?"

Patrick said nothing more about the Bronze Star. Patrick understood that Special Forces work was highly classified, and he knew Jake preferred not to draw attention to his decoration. His fieldwork with Special Forces had been an eye-opening experience, and he was fascinated by the counterterrorist tactics under development. Rotary wing aircraft had a place in the doctrine. The tactics were different from those deployed with large infantry or armor units, but much of how helicopters would support counterterrorism activities was undecided. Patrick liked the idea of being on the ground floor to help determine how Special Forces would use the AH-1 Cobra. As a terrifyingly effective weapon in Vietnam, the Cobra could put air-to-ground firepower in support of Special Forces where field artillery would be unavailable.

Jake crossed the room quickly to answer the ringing phone. "Julia. Great. What took you so long?"

Julia giggled. "You know us women. It took me most of the morning to decide what to wear and what to bring."

"Good grief," Jake said, faking irritation at a woman's prerogative to use excuses like that. "You're only going to be here one night. Come on up. Room fourteen twenty-nine."

Jake met her at the door a few minutes later with a broad smile on his face and gave her a hug. He was elated to see her, and he could tell that she was glad she had come.

"Where's Patrick?"

"Oh, he and Rebecca took off a couple of hours ago to go sightseeing. They'll be back in a little while, famished, no doubt. I made reservations for us at F. Scott's. Dinner and jazz. What more could you ask for?"

"Well, tell me," Julia probed.

"Tell you what?" Jake asked, knowing full well what she meant.

"About Rebecca. I can't believe our Patrick has fallen in love. It's pretty scary, you know. I've never seen him serious about anything or anybody. I may not recognize him."

"Oh, he is serious, all right. I've never seen such a bad case of puppy love. The boy is sick, and he's almost sickening to be around."

Julia laughed. For the first time in a year, she felt relaxed and distracted from the heartache she had continuously felt. She had expected it to be otherwise. She initially dreaded seeing Jake and Patrick in some ways, anticipating that they would make the hurt of losing Steve even more acute than it already was.

"She's a beautiful girl." Jake walked to the small refrigerator, retrieved two colas, then removed the caps with an opener. "Not as pretty as you, of course, but I can see why ole Patrick is falling all over himself. And, as you might expect, she's quite enamored with him, too. She can't keep her hands off him, just like he was always saying about his female companions."

Julia smirked. "That's all Patrick needs is for someone to confirm how great he thinks he is with women. He'll be absolutely impossible now. Of course, he's right. He is a pretty terrific guy. I can see why she is attracted to him. He's a good-looking guy. She must like laughing a lot." She smiled and returned Jake's earlier compliment, "But he's not as good-looking as you."

Jake flopped his leg over the arm of the chair and laughed. "Well, now that we have swapped lies, don't be surprised if they announce wedding plans. Patrick hasn't said so, but I think they've been talking about it. She has dropped a dozen little hints about it since she hit D.C., and Patrick didn't flinch even once. They're talking about little Patrick's running around—God forbid—post housing and a station wagon swap for the Corvette, which would be the biggest tragedy of all. It's coming, Julia, I swear it."

"Sounds like they might be very happy together, and he is obviously in love, or he wouldn't be talking about trading in the Corvette. I hope so. One of us ought to get all those nice things, don't you think?"

Jake smiled back at Julia. "You'll have those things, too, someday. You just wait and see."

2000 Hours
F. Scott's
Washington, D.C.

"I LOVE these dress blue uniforms. You and Patrick are both so handsome. I wish I had met Patrick back when you two were at West Point. It would have been so much fun going to all the formal dances and all." Rebecca put her hand on Patrick's arm and gently rubbed the sleeve with her thumb.

Jake had difficulty withholding his grin through dinner because of Patrick's obvious feelings for Rebecca. Who could blame him? She was both charming and beautiful. Her long, raven hair and black dress contrasted perfectly with her skin tone and crimson lips. Her laugh was infectious, and her personality matched Patrick's. They had captured each other's hearts.

"And then, this guy refuses to tell me anything about why he was awarded the Bronze Star." Patrick animated his story by waving his arms in the air for emphasis and then raising his glass to indicate he was about to make a toast. "To 1st Lieutenant John Paul Jacobs. My best friend. A hero to his country. And the first in the Class of 1973 to be decorated for valor. May his career be brilliant, as we all know it will be, and safe. Jake, here's to you. We love you."

The glasses clinked as Jake sat red-faced. Julia was all smiles. She was delighted that Patrick had told what little he knew about Jake's decoration because she knew that Jake would never have said a word about it. And, like others not directly involved in the military, she would not readily know the significance of the tiny ribbon he wore.

Though Jake was embarrassed, he was thoroughly enjoying himself. Most of the past year had been hard work. Tonight he was relaxed, happy, and in the company of those for whom he really cared. Julia was laughing and enjoying the time with friends as well, and that alone made Jake pleased that he had made the trip to D.C.

Awkwardly, Patrick changed the ongoing conversation. "Rebecca's father was a young officer in World War II and remained in the National Guard. He was the commander of the Guard in Augusta for several years before retiring." Patrick lifted his glass again, indicating that he was about to make another toast. "Which brings me to the most important matter of the evening." He cleared his throat. "I spoke to Colonel Coulter last week, and I asked for his daughter's hand in marriage."

"Surely he said no," Jake said with a grin on his face.

"Funny you say that, Jake," Patrick said. "I haven't been that frightened since our first day of Beast Barracks. When he asked me why I wanted to marry his daughter, all I could think of was two of our standard answers. 'Sir, no excuse, sir,' and

'Sir, I do not know.' With a pause, I figured out that neither was appropriate."

Jake leaned closer to Julia and said, "That's my roommate. Smarter'n a whip."

"I'm engaged to Rebecca," Patrick said. "That makes me not only smart but brilliant. I know that Rebecca and I have only known each other for less than a year—and for a month of that, I was sleeping in the mud at Fort Bragg—but we knew from the moment we met that we were meant for each other. We love each other deeply and plan to be married in Augusta as soon as I return to Ft. Rucker."

Jake and Julia pretended surprise.

"Therefore, I propose a toast to my beautiful future bride."

The glasses clinked all around. Rebecca was all smiles and blew Patrick a kiss.

Jake rose from his chair and raised his glass. "Ah, Patrick, you are my best friend. In fact, I love you like we were flesh and blood brothers. I'm sure Julia joins me in wanting all the happiness in the world for both of you. We wish you and Rebecca a long and happy life together, but Rebecca, you'll have your hands full. This guy is one of a kind. So, here's to the future 1st Lieutenant and Mrs. Patrick McSwain. Congratulations."

Rebecca paused. "I know how dedicated you and Patrick are to the army life. It is a noble and honorable path you have chosen. And I know from my father that it takes the same dedication to be an army wife. There is much to consider when thinking about marrying a soldier. There are many unseen sacrifices to be made, even the possibility of the ultimate sacrifice. I have thought long and hard about a commitment to marry Patrick and the soldier's life. I'm committed with all my being."

Julia smiled, though saddened that she had made the same commitment with Steve and had not been allowed to live it. "Thank you for saying that, Rebecca. I am pleased that Patrick has chosen you to be his wife. You are both patriots. The only thing harder than being a soldier is being a soldier's wife. God bless you both."

'GET YOUR MOTOR RUNNIN'. *Head out on the hi-ghway. Whatev-er comes our way,*' Jake and Patrick sang, not well, but loud, along with the radio as the Corvette sped down Interstate 95 at eighty miles per hour toward Fayetteville, North Carolina. They had kissed the girls goodbye at the Mayflower in mid-afternoon and began their three hundred-mile road trip. Jake was at the wheel, and with luck, they would be at the BOQ in less than five hours. He downshifted to third, which caused the powerful engine to roar, jammed his foot to the floor, and accelerated the Corvette like a rocket to pass a semi-truck.

CHAPTER 15

1300 Hours
11 October 1974
10 Miles outside Bogota, Columbia

AS THE WHEELS of his Learjet 35 touched ground at the private airfield outside Bogota, Columbia, Sukarno focused on the vehicles gathered to meet him. After three months of meetings with Enrique Villalobos, he still expected him to arrive in a limousine, probably black, with an entourage of like-colored vehicles, all announcing his importance. But what he saw was the same half-dozen pick-up trucks, all a different color, and an Oldsmobile Delta 88, four-door sedan. His expectation of pretension was met with a degree of modesty.

Following a short ride in a Ford pick-up to the Oldsmobile, Sukarno was face-to-face with Villalobos in the back seat. In his late thirties, Villalobos was handsome. With intermittent strands of gray in his otherwise youthful dark hair, he wore a royal blue tailored suit, a crisply pressed white shirt, and a blue-on-crimson foulard tie. He carried the presence of a Wall

Street banker, not the stereotypical image of a leader of a Columbian cartel.

"Welcome to Columbia," Villalobos said as he shook hands with Sukarno. "I trust your trip was pleasant. Beautiful aircraft. I will have to look into the Learjet. I have an older model Gulfstream. I don't look as good in it as Mick Jagger or J. Willard Marriott do in theirs, but it will do.

Sukarno laughed. "Everyone looks good in a Gulfstream."

"Down to business," Villalobos said. "Where are we in terms of the agreement?"

Sukarno smiled. "I think we have a deal, so long as you recognize that it may take some time to set up the corporate conduits to launder the amount of cash you plan to have. I may not be able to meet all of your needs as your business expands in the United States. I need your assurance that there will be no demands beyond what I can do. Sixty to one hundred million now is acceptable. But I can't imagine having the capability to launder sixty million per week as you project in ten years."

"We will just have to learn as we go," Villalobos said. "The drug trade is not an exact science. I will follow your instructions to deliver the cash to the banks in the Caymans under several shell corporations. You take your percentage, and I will be out of the transaction. So long as I don't get pulled into your other activities, everything should make for a profitable relationship. I expect some losses in getting the money to the Caymans from law enforcement, but that is not your problem."

"That is acceptable," Sukarno said.

"You come highly recommended by our mutual friends from the Soviet Union," Villalobos said, "but to be clear—I'm not political. I'm not involved in their business, other than selling a product they think is useful, and they do me a favor from time to time. One such favor is our coming to this agreement. I am simply looking for a viable system to clean some of my dollars from the United States as my business expands there."

"And there is no heroin involved?" Sukarno asked.

"No. It is all cocaine." Villalobos slightly turned toward Sukarno to emphasize the details. "As we have already discussed, cocaine is more recreational, and the United States' potential market is much greater than heroin. And there is, at least for now, less law enforcement risk. I'll leave the heroin trade to the Asians. Heroin is a dirty game and has a limited market. Cocaine, on the other hand, is a social, recreational narcotic, and its market ranges from the elite to the soccer mom. The Soviets are smart. They know that a recreational narcotic will impact how future generations will think."

Sukarno paused. "Very well. My primary office is in New York, but I have an office now in Hong Kong to facilitate securities transactions between exchanges. I have established an investment fund with my own money, so the structure is legitimate. There isn't much regulation, so buying securities on one exchange and selling on another is not all that complicated. On the surface, I control investment and hedge funds—very little regulation. Clients, which is only me, funnel funds through several corporations. When the transactions are complete, the money goes back through the corporations and is clean."

Villalobos closed his day planner and pointed his fountain pen at Sukarno. "And you are certain of your expertise to make these transactions successfully?"

"I do have the expertise," Sukarno said. "And indirectly, the Soviets have provided me with experienced personnel. I pay their salaries, but they really work for the USSR. They have been trained well."

Villalobos handed Sukarno a file containing the names of corporations and account numbers. "Twenty million to start," he said. "If there are any problems, we can address them and triple the amount."

2100 Hours
1 November 1974
Jask, Iran

JASK WAS a small coastal city on the Gulf of Oman and the Strait of Hormuz's eastern side. The Bay of Jask was lively, with ships carrying all matter of cargo and brought seafarers from all over the world. Rokus Sogiarto had selected Jask as the ideal location to launch a long-term political attack against the West. The Soviet's advice to center operations outside Indonesia made sense. Giving the Indonesian government justification to attack and destroy them would be a grave error. By operating out of Jask, Indonesia remained home and a safe harbor.

The native people of Jask were ripe for revolution because their entire culture had been abused first by the British and now by other foreigners bringing heavy commercial traffic, which the Shah had encouraged. Sogiarto knew that the people would ultimately support any movement that preached a return to their cultural values and the riddance of foreigners. The West's presence was responsible for destroying their lives in terms of Muslim fundamentalism, and the Shah had brought that pestilence to them. The United States was deeply involved with Iran for oil exploration and development, and the Shah found the cultural changes a small price to pay for the wealth gained.

Sukarno both despised and admired the people he sought to influence. He despised their ignorance and disregard for a changing world around them, but he admired their simplicity and capacity for life. To him, they were all like children that were easily manipulated and ruled. Rokus Sogiarto was one of them. He was ignorant in some ways and misguided, but at the same time well-intentioned to serve the common person's historical culture. His goals were simple. All he wanted was to overthrow what he considered to be corrupt governments and replace them with governments that were honorable so that people could live in peace and prosperity under the laws established by Mohammed. As far as Sukarno was concerned, it was a fantasy he had heard all his life. His father had seen the world through the same eyes as Rokus, and both were wrong. Restoring nations to their original glory was not a viable goal, but unifying Muslims into one militarily powerful alliance was attainable. The divided Muslim world had to cease.

Sogiarto entered the room as Sukarno snapped the latches on his briefcase. "Are you leaving for New York?"

"Yes," Sukarno said without looking up. "I think we have covered everything. We have the local Mullah supporting our stay in Jask, and that will keep the shah at a distance. I will arrange a meeting with the exiled Ayatollah Khomeini in Paris as soon as possible. Just remember that we don't want to disturb the shah to the point that would cause the shah and his military, the SAVAK, to be threatened by our presence."

"Agreed," Sogiarto said. "It's too bad our Soviet friends are not willing to provide us with the Sarin gas we need."

"That would be best for us, but I understand their position. Any backlash on the USSR from an attack would be very bad for them. We will work it out. The Soviets will verify the gas when we have it," Sukarno said as he moved around the desk toward the door. "Just get it done with the American chemist, and after you do, bury him so deep no one will ever find him."

0930 Hours
11 December 1974
The Pentagon
Washington, D.C.

"What is it, John? You only have a few minutes to brief me on this."

"Sorry, admiral. I know you have an appointment at the White House this morning. I'll keep it short." Hanraty sat in front of Admiral Hollifield's desk and quickly found the notes he had made in red ink along his typed report's margins.

Admiral Hollifield straightened his dress coat as he sat and flicked a piece of lint from his right sleeve. "Go ahead. What's Komando Jihad done now to put me in a lousy mood?"

"Well, sir, apparently Komando Jihad has found themselves a home in Iran. As you know, they have been primarily gathering and training in Libya up until now, apparently with Colonel Muammar Gaddafi's blessing. He hasn't materially supported them, but he did give them a spot to organize. He may give them more support now."

"Gaddafi?" The admiral frowned at the mere mention of the man's name. Muammar Gaddafi had taken control of Libya in a bloodless coup in 1969, and he had been a growing concern ever since. He was a sponsor of terrorist activity, and the Pentagon analysts strongly suggested that he would instigate a great deal of the political problems, and perhaps military problems as well, for the United States for the next twenty years. "What does that maniac have to do with Komando Jihad?"

John Hanraty knew the admiral was intrigued and that his briefing would receive full attention. "Komando Jihad has settled in Jask, Iran, sir." Hanraty rose from his chair, walked quickly to the world map covering one entire wall, and pointed to the area. The admiral could see Hanraty's pencil point at the mouth of the Strait of Hormuz and recognized the strategic importance of Jask though he had never heard of it. "Sir, Komando Jihad apparently has the support of the local religious order in Jask and has been allowed to more or less set up a headquarters in the center of the city."

"Why doesn't the shah just kick them out of there?" Hollifield asked.

"Too risky, Admiral. He has enough problems with the mullahs throughout the country. If he removed them by force, he would likely have every region in Iran pitching a fit about his economic and social reforms. It looks like he's going to leave Komando Jihad alone for a while and hope they fizzle out, assuming they don't make the mistake of attacking the shah's government outright. But we don't think they will fizzle. We believe they have a pretty firm hold on the shah and that they have a good chance of causing our friend, the shah, a lot of grief. "

Hollifield leaned forward with his elbows on the desk. "Those two Indonesians are there, I suppose."

"We have no confirmation of that, sir, but Rokus Sogiarto, the leader of Komando Jihad, is probably there. We don't know about Sukarno Bangjar, and we haven't confirmed that he is even associated with this group yet."

"Is that it?" the admiral asked, ready to get on his way to the White House. He glanced at his watch and quickly calculated the amount of time he had to get there.

"No, sir," Hanraty said, unmoved by the admiral's impatience.

The admiral frowned.

"There's more and worse, Admiral. Our theory that Komando Jihad is trying to develop a chemical or biological weapon is confirmed. Intelligence reports that unusual amounts of sulfur trioxide and carbon tetrachloride have been purchased and were delivered to Jask by a freighter two days ago. That by itself does not produce chemical capability, but our Chemical Corps indicates that it's a suspicious start. A few shipments of the right chemical, a fairly sophisticated lab, and a couple of well-educated chemists would complete the list of components required to develop an effective chemical weapon. Last night, sir, Professor Harold Clinton Reiner at the University of Chicago was reported missing. Reiner is probably this country's foremost expert on chemical agents, specifically nerve gases."

"Kidnapped?" Admiral Hollifield's face slowly turned red as the anger rose upward from his neck. "You mean to tell me that one of the few men this country has that's been instrumental in the development of our chemical capability didn't have enough security on him to prevent some maniac, who shouldn't have been in the United States in the first place, from grabbing him off the street? I can't believe this. Who was in charge of Reiner's security anyhow?"

"Department of Defense. FBI. Kind of a conglomerate of responsibility, sir."

"Conglomerate my foot. Lack of responsibility is more like

it. What do we really know? I mean, has Reiner really been nabbed by someone, or did he just sneak off somewhere to cozy up with some gal half his age?" the admiral asked as he began to bounce the eraser end of a pencil on his desk.

John Hanraty sighed and shrugged his shoulders. "Doesn't look good, Admiral. Professor Reiner is in his mid-fifties, has a wife of thirty years, and four children. He's the ideal citizen. Church, fraternal clubs, and everything else you might think of as wholesome and American. He has a top-secret security clearance, sir, and is continuously monitored by the intelligence agencies. There is nothing to indicate that he would simply disappear by choice. He's clean as a whistle, sir. The clincher is that he's an assistant coach of his son's hockey team, and he did not show for the game last night. He would have been there, Admiral, if he could. We're almost certain he has been kidnapped.

Hollifield stood behind his desk and removed his coat. The White House meeting would have to wait on him or proceed without him. Duty first, reporting later. "Ok. Who? Komando Jihad is one. Who's next? The Soviets?"

"Not the Soviets, admiral. They already have their chemist and chemical weapons. A fact of life, sir, but they probably already know what we know, or more. They wouldn't have any reason to do something like this. If Reiner has been kidnapped for his knowledge of chemical weapons, it must be by someone who needs to develop chemical capability from the ground up. Potentially, there are several candidates, including our friend Gaddafi, but Komando Jihad is certainly a reasonable choice. Everything up to this point indicates that they are on the offensive, and those shipments to Jask fit the scenario.

Admiral Hollifield shook his head in resignation. "Delivery systems?"

Hanraty cleared his throat and leaned forward in his chair. "Not very complicated, sir. If we were talking about a government-sponsored army, then yes. They would need some relatively sophisticated delivery system in quantity, like artillery or missiles or even armor. However, if we think in terms of terrorism, then a delivery system can be painfully simple. Depending on what kind of agent they develop, a homemade bomb might be very effective for its purpose. A well-placed bomb of nerve gas and using weather as a facilitator would be comparable to the death rate of a small-sized nuke."

Hollifield's eyes widened as he more fully realized the potential danger. "What was Reiner working on, John?"

"Well, sir, as you know, nerve gas has been used militarily going back to the first world war, but the chemical agents used then were relatively mild compared to the killing power available today. In theory, our military interest is in protecting the flanks of an advancing unit, but it doesn't take a lot of imagination to think of offensive uses. Typically, sir, we tend to worry about some groups like Komando Jihad finding a way to obtain a nuclear device because of the fear it produces in our consciousness. It's loud and physically destructive. We overlook the threat of a nerve gas attack because it is silent. It doesn't destroy buildings and leave the landscape barren. It simply kills every living being that comes into contact with it. Unlike nukes, one doesn't have to steal nerve gas capability from an army stockpile. They can manufacture it with ease. After all, it is just a chemical."

"Get to the point, John. What kind of work was Reiner doing?" Hollifield asked again.

"Primarily phosphorous base agents, Admiral. Tabun, Sarin, and Soman nerve gases, sir. All three are bug spray for people. They are deadly beyond comprehension. Sarin is about ten times more potent than Tabun, and Soman is about three times more potent than Sarin. An interesting feature of these nerve gases is that they are not really in gaseous form. They are liquid. They are dispersed into the air as an aerosol, like out of a spray can, or by exploding a bomb under the liquid. These gases do not have to be inhaled to be deadly. The tiniest drop on the skin will cause death in minutes. The way these nerve gases kill is by causing the muscles in the body to contract. Excruciatingly painful."

Hanraty paused and quickly referred to his notes. The admiral loosened his tie, visibly agitated by the content of the briefing.

Clearing his throat, Hanraty continued. "Our chemical boys explain it this way. When a brain signal comes down a nerve telling a muscle to contract, the end of that nerve releases acetylcholine, which signals the muscle to contract. As soon as the muscle obeys the command, which is chemically induced, an enzyme called cholinesterase is released, which destroys the acetylcholine. This causes the muscle to relax again. If the acetylcholine is not destroyed, then soon every muscle in the body would be stuck in a contraction mode. As you can imagine, sir, this would result in a struggle of muscle against muscle and agonizing death. One molecule of nerve gas goes on a search and destroy mission for cholinesterase."

"Is there an antidote?" Hollifield asked without any tone of hope.

"Not in a practical sense, sir. In a laboratory setting, light exposures may be successfully treated with the immediate use of atropine. However, there is no countermeasure to save lives in an attack against an area of population."

Hollifield closed his eyes and shook his head. "My God. Who came up with this stuff?"

"Hitler. Who else?" Hanraty said. "Nazi Germany had factories manufacturing Tabun for most of the duration of the war. A fellow named Gerhard Schrader invented both Tabun and Sarin. The Nazis liked Tabun best because it is cyanide-based. You know how they liked their cyanide."

Hollifield glanced at his watch again. "Wrap it up, John. I've got to get down the street. What do you recommend?"

"Well, sir, first, I think we need to wait a few days to see if Professor Reiner shows up before we all panic. Meanwhile, I'd suggest that this potential problem be discussed up the chain of command and that we assemble staff immediately to gather more intelligence. All the effort could be a waste of time, but then again, we may have a real crisis forming."

"Very well," Hollifield said. Brief Admiral Limmerick and get the ball rolling. Tell him I would like to meet with him at 1500 hours today." Admiral Hollifield clenched his teeth. "I'll mention it to the Joint Chiefs and the president. They're going to be mad at somebody."

CHAPTER 16

1600 Hours
10 January 1975
Augusta, Georgia

"HOLD STILL. You've been dressing yourself for over twenty years. How come I have to start tying your bow tie now?"

Wayne rolled a cigar between his fingers while leaning casually against the wall, watching Jake struggle with Patrick's tie. "'Cause he's scared to death. That's how come."

"I ain't scared," Patrick said with little conviction in his voice.

"Yep," Wayne said. "He's shaking like a leaf."

Patrick smirked and rolled his eyes. "Shouldn't have invited him. Giving some guys a stethoscope is worse than giving them a loaded gun."

"There. Patrick is all dressed now." Jake stood back to admire his work and was satisfied that 1st Lieutenant Patrick McSwain was perfectly uniformed in his dress blues. All three of them were, but no one would have guessed the transformation possible a half-hour earlier. The guests had already started arriving at the church when Jake, Patrick, and Wayne had decided to shave the stubble off their faces and change out of their jeans and t-shirts.

"Where's the ring, Jake?" Patrick glanced at his watch, then at Jake.

Jake looked puzzled. "The ring. Well, let's see. I know I put it somewhere," as he methodically searched each pocket and consciously fought off the urge to laugh.

"Don't tell me you lost the ring."

Jake continued his search. "Well, I know I've got it. Nope. It's not in any of these pockets."

Wayne stuck the cigar in his mouth and walked slowly toward Jake with deep concern on his face. "Last I saw it; you laid it on the top of your car when you were trying to get your uniform bag in the passenger seat. Right before we drove over here. You reckon it's still there?"

"Maybe. Guess we better go check," Jake said, appearing at a loss as to where the ring might be.

"Jake, if you've lost that ring, I'll ...."

Jake turned his head and smiled at Wayne. "Touchy. Ain't he?"

"Settle down, Patrick. I'm sure Jake will either find the ring by the time you say your 'I do's', or he'll find a suitable substitute. Isn't that right, Jake?"

"Of course. I'm the best man, aren't I?" It was impossible for Jake not to smile at his suffering friend.

The door opened, and Reverend Joe Bradley's head appeared. He smiled and announced that it was time. Jake grabbed one of Patrick's arms and Wayne the other.

"Patrick, it's time for you to go marry your right woman,"

Jake said. "You are blessed, and I'm blessed to be a part of your wedding."

Patrick swallowed hard. "Thanks, Jake. Wayne, I'm glad you guys are here. It's like old times."

Wayne chuckled. "Kinda reminds me of when you and I use to navigate Jake into the boxing ring. Of course, boxing wasn't nearly as adventurous as matrimony. All Jake ever got was a broken nose, and his face beat black and blue."

Jake made the first step toward the door, pulling lightly on Patrick's arm. "He's joking. This is the best thing you will ever do."

Jake glanced around the sanctuary and was amused by the disproportionate seating of the guests. Many citizens of Augusta sat on the bride's side and less than fifty on the groom's. Patrick's parents were seated on the second row with Julia directly behind. The other guests there for Patrick were officers and two enlisted men from Fort Rucker, not including the six officers in dress blues with sabers that had ushered the crowd to their seats. Standing in place waiting for the groom was Captain Cantrell and 1st Lieutenant Wally Bidet. Cantrell traveled from Fort Benning, delighted to have been asked to be part of the wedding party. The plebes of the 4th squad, 7th New Cadet Company for the Class of 1973, were special to him, and he was a charter member in Admiral Hollifield's adopted family of cadets and midshipmen. Admiral and Mrs. H were certainly invited, but pressing matters in Washington prevented them from coming. The admiral made his contribution to the event by making his wishes known that Lieutenant Bidet be granted a few days off from the Pentagon. As usual, four-star admirals have a way of getting things done quickly. Wally was surprised when his commanding officer excitedly ordered him to take leave and return to work when convenient.

Patrick marched slowly to his position. Jake and Wayne followed while the folks of Augusta murmured how dashing the young officers looked in their impressive blue uniforms with bright yellow stripes down the side of each trouser leg and gold brass on their tunics. Rebecca had wanted the formality of a full military wedding, partially to signify her commitment as an Army wife and as an acknowledgment that the men who stood with him were as much a part of his family as his mother and father.

The groom and the groomsmen were in place, awaiting the beginning of the wedding march and Rebecca's entry with her father at her side. Jake took one step forward and whispered in Patrick's ear. "We've been buddies a long time, you and me. I just want you to know that I wish you all the happiness in the world. You deserve it."

Patrick turned his head and smiled as the wedding march began.

Rebecca and her father came through the doors at the back of the sanctuary. All eyes were on her. She was beautiful in her white dress and train that followed. Her father, Colonel Coulter, Georgia National Guard (Retired), wore a proud smile and a perfectly fitting dress blue uniform.

The wedding ceremony was perfect. Every detail capitalized on the moment's pageantry and emphasized the romanticism that one of Georgia's prettiest ladies was marrying a dashing young officer of the United States Army. It was a special moment— a moment where Rebecca and Patrick seemed the luckiest two people on earth.

Following the ceremony, the bride and groom passed under the traditional steeple of sabers to enter the black limousine for the short drive to the Augusta Country Club for the reception. It, too, was extravagant. A ten-piece band played a mixture of music. The towering cake was cut according to protocol, the bride was kissed on the cheek by most, and Patrick's hand was pumped by a couple of hundred people he did not know.

"Lieutenant McSwain," Jake said as the band returned to a genre more entertaining than elevator music. "May I have the honor of having this dance with your beautiful bride?" He bowed slightly at the waist toward Rebecca, and she, giggling, returned the formality with an equally out-of-fashion curtsy.

"Of course, Jake. Where's Cantrell? I haven't seen that slug since the reception line."

As a waltz began, Rebecca slid her arm through Jake's and smiled up at him as Patrick stretched to see over the heads of people in search of Cantrell. Jake led Rebecca to the dance floor.

"Congratulations, Rebecca," Jake said. "It was a beautiful wedding, and you just married the finest man I know."

Rebecca nodded in agreement. "We are going to be very happy. Years of happiness. When are you going to get married, Jake?"

Jake laughed. "Never. Didn't Patrick tell you? I'm a hopeless bachelor."

"Patrick told me about Sara. I'm sorry. You must have really loved her," Rebecca said in a tone of genuine sincerity.

The conversation made Jake more than a little uncomfortable. Throughout the ceremony, he had thought of Sara and imagined how he would have felt kneeling beside her as they exchanged their vows. "Well, that was a long time ago. I hardly think of her anymore," he lied. "There's not much time for family life in the Green Berets. Who knows, maybe someday when I'm a retired old goat, no offense to your father, I'll have time for that sort of thing."

Rebecca laughed. "Jake, you're lying through your teeth. You'll get over her. You just haven't had the right woman get hold of you to take your mind off her."

Patrick walked up and announced that it was time to start the honeymoon. "Let's change and get on our way to Cancun."

"Great," Jake said. "Wayne and I booked an adjoining room right next to yours. We are looking forward to the four of us playing in the sun for a week."

1400 Hours
12 January 1975
The Pentagon
Washington, D. C.

ADMIRAL HOLLIFIELD PUSHED the door to his outer office open and motioned for his secretary, Louise Brandt, to follow. "Call General Carpenter and ask if he would join me in an hour. He's wrapping up a briefing down in Lieutenant General Addison's office. Tell him it is important." Hollifield hung his gold-braided white hat on the rack and moved mindlessly to the window. The view of the Washington Monument in the distance had never before made him feel so low. "Ask Hanraty to come in as soon as possible. Admiral Limmerick, too."

Louise Brandt retreated from the room tense, sensing that Admiral Hollifield was in one of his rare moods of depression or overwhelming frustration. The mood was rare because Admiral Hollifield typically maintained his sense of humor and an optimistic viewpoint no matter what the crisis or circumstances. His facial expression was strained, and his voice barely audible.

Hollifield continued to stare out the window for several minutes, no longer consciously seeing the monument. The thoughts that raced through his mind overpowered his visual perception.

"Admiral? Mrs. Brandt said you wanted to see us." Admiral Kirk Limmerick had replaced General Carpenter as Hollifield's aide and had immediately become a welcome addition to the staff. A graduate of Yale, Limmerick had attended law school, then at the last moment, decided to join the Navy rather than his uncle's law firm in Boston. Hollifield's first impression had not been good. Limmerick bordered on slovenly. He was overweight by thirty pounds, balding rapidly at the age of forty-six, and had yet been heard to laugh. However, it did not take a week for Admiral Hollifield to cast away his first impression and gain a deep respect for one of the best military intuitions he had ever seen. Limmerick may not have looked like the naval officers in a recruiter's poster, but he was brighter than most. Others had worked with him over his twenty-year career and had unanimously recommended him for his stars though he had never set foot on a ship.

Concentration broken, Admiral Hollifield turned from the window with a faint smile. "Kirk, have a seat."

John Hanraty rushed through the door, trying to untangle his left arm from his blue blazer's sleeve. "Sorry, Admiral. I hope you weren't waiting for me."

Hollifield laughed. "Take that thing off, John. You're going to waste all your energy trying to look presentable when you and I both know that will never happen. I swear, between you and Admiral Limmerick, everyone in the Pentagon is scared to death to work for me because they think I never let either of you go home to take a shower or change clothes. Both of you look like you slept in those clothes."

Kirk Limmerick favored the admiral with one of his rare smiles. "In fact, Admiral, we did sleep, what little there was, in these clothes. We worked all night."

Hollifield did not know that. He had gone directly to the White House from Langley, Virginia, at sunrise. He laughed again. "Sorry, Kirk, how was I to know? You two dress this way every day."

Again, Limmerick smiled, then laughed aloud, both startling and pleasing Hollifield and Hanraty.

"These are pretty tough days, gentlemen. We knew it was coming, but it was still a shock. It is still hard to believe that the president of the United States resigned five months ago. History was made on August 9th, that's for sure. It's made our job much harder. History, I tell you. It has made me look forward to the rocking chair." Hollifield frowned and lit a cigar.

Brigadier General Richard (Dick) Carpenter tapped lightly on the door, then entered. "You wanted to see me, Admiral?"

"Dick. Come in and pull up a chair. We were just talking about the President's resignation in August."

Carpenter pulled a chair close to the desk, nodded at Hanraty and Limmerick, then sat without a word."

Hollifield drew deeply on his cigar and exhaled slowly before speaking. "Personal views aside regarding the resignation, the event in American history represents problems for us. The change of Commander in Chief is delaying everything we've been working toward. We are pretty much back to square one. All the initial briefings and approvals will have to start again from the beginning. That said, we can cut the president some slack because he had a lot dropped in his lap. Dick, what does this do to your program?"

"Not much, sir. We are still in the planning stages for the Joint Special Forces Command, and I don't see that our timetable will be significantly changed. I hadn't planned on briefings to the president for another twelve months."

"John, where are you on this Reiner situation?"

Hanraty frowned. "The president resigning is probably a major setback, sir. As you know, the president, I mean the ex-president, had taken a personal interest in our investigation into Dr. Reiner's disappearance and our theories on where he might be. You may disagree, sir, but I think it will be difficult to get the same audience on this matter again."

Hollifield blew smoke into the air. "I agree. The new president will be trying to find his fanny with both hands for the next several months. He's not going to be concerned about missing person theories and mysteries."

"What's the status of our intelligence-gathering operation, Admiral? Are we still active?" Limmerick already knew the answer. Admiral Hollifield would not be in the mood he was in otherwise.

Admiral Hollifield leaned back in his chair. "I've been ordered to stand down on all intelligence operations until the president has had the opportunity to be briefed."

General Carpenter leaned forward in his chair. "I must be missing something, Admiral. Obviously, you have been working on a mission that has to do with Dr. Reiner's disappearance, and it's just as obvious that you want me briefed, but so far, I don't know what we are talking about here."

"Sorry, Dick," Pointing the butt end of his cigar at Hanraty and Limmerick, Hollifield said, "Give him the quick and dirty."

Hanraty and Limmerick took turns over the next half-hour, providing General Carpenter with facts, theories, assumptions, and potential consequences. It was not a pretty picture. There were no hard facts concerning Reiner's kidnapping. Still, some investigative work provided by the FBI had uncovered the confirmed flight plan of a Beechcraft King Air, registered to a Delaware Corporation by the name of New World Farms, for a flight from Chicago to Mexico City on the night of Reiner's disappearance. New World Farms is owned by an ex-banker residing in North Carolina by the name of Stavanos. This is not unusual nor necessarily pertinent, but when the paper trail led to contacting Mr. Stavanos, he was dead. He was murdered, along with his wife, in his home in North Carolina the night of Reiner's disappearance. This coincidence threw a red flag in the air, and the FBI spread their investigation into the details concerning Stavanos. A week later, Admiral Limmerick met with the FBI and discovered that there is another coincidence. Stavanos had been an executive vice president at Chase Manhattan Bank and handled the accounts of Kuwat Bangjar, a high-level Indonesian government official who was murdered in Sao Paulo, Brazil. Also, on those accounts was Bangjar's son, Sukarno Bangjar. And Sukarno Bangjar is suspected of being a member and financier of Komando Jihad."

Hollifield interrupted. "That rat deserved what he got. He was a low six-figure earner and managed to retire in North Carolina with assets over ten million. We know Bangjar gave back a large portion of the money his father embezzled from the Indonesian government. Stavanos obviously helped Sukarno Bangjar keep a part of the money, and he paid off

Stavanos with several million dollars. Sukarno Bangjar's stolen money, proof or not, is financing all this activity with Komando Jihad. We don't know how much he has available, but if he paid Stavanos ten million, you can bet it's a bundle."

Admiral Limmerick continued when Hollifield paused and inhaled smoke from his cigar. "Bangjar probably used Stavanos' plane to snatch Reiner and killed Stavanos, thinking he was covering his tracks. Who knows? It may be that Bangjar just didn't like him. Trying to think like a terrorist is not easy."

General Carpenter leaned forward and lit a cigarette. "What about Mexico?"

"Nothing concrete, General," Hanraty said. "The Beechcraft pulled into a hangar, and it is still there. Abandoned, maybe. If they are holding Reiner in Mexico, finding him in a city of eleven million people will be difficult. But it doesn't make sense they would keep him there. The chemicals needed to construct nerve gas are in Jask, Iran. Reiner and the chemicals need to be in the same location. So, I think they changed to another aircraft and made their way to Jask."

"I agree,' Hollifield said. "We just can't prove it yet. Even if we could prove it, this bureaucratic circus called Washington is so screwed up Reiner is likely to sit there for years as a prisoner and give those rats all they need to develop chemical agents. That, gentlemen, puts thousands of innocent people at risk."

"Sounds like you need a reconnaissance mission, Admiral. Maybe a hostage rescue." Carpenter inhaled deeply, then smiled broadly. "Admiral, I worked for you a long time. I know how you operate. You called this little meeting because you wanted that kind of mission to be my idea."

Everyone in the room laughed. It was true. If there were to be such a mission, the admiral could not order it. He could not so much as order a plan and training for it. With an executive order some months away from possibility, if a mission were to be initiated, it would have to be done as a training exercise ordered by Brigadier General Richard Carpenter. He was the only one that could operationally start preparing for Reiner's rescue.

Limmerick was blunt. "So, when will your men be ready?"

"Whoa. Wait a minute," Carpenter immediately responded. "I've got a list, you know—a list of things that have to be in place before I send men into Iran with blazing rifles and hand grenades. First, I need a Presidential Executive Order to send U.S. troops into a hostile situation on foreign ground. Second, how about some intelligence? I can't put a team on the ground in Iran and have them stop people on the street asking for directions to the nearest terrorist's hide-out. We need to know that Reiner is there for sure, that he's alive, where he is specifically at different times of the day, and an analysis of the situation regarding guards, weapons, and a dozen other details. And third, I need time to put a plan together and train men on simulations."

Admiral Hollifield leaned back in his chair. "If you had all that, Dick, do you think you could do it?"

"You know the answer to that, Admiral. A few months ago, you told me I had five to seven years to develop the kind of capability you're asking me to deliver. If you're asking me to give it a solid effort, then the answer is yes. We can put together an operation with the capability we have, but don't expect miracles."

"That's a direct answer, and it's the one I expected from you." Hollifield snuffed his cigar in the ashtray, and the door opened. Louise Brandt set the coffee on the table in the corner of the room, and the officers rose to serve themselves.

"Louise, why don't you come to Bragg and work for me?" General Carpenter said. "I'll get you out of this nuthouse."

She smiled back. "It's not so bad, General. I notice you keep coming back." Mrs. Brandt did not wait for a response before she closed the door behind her. The general's smirk said it all.

Hollifield sat on the sofa and held his cup in both hands. "Dick, I understand all that you've asked for as a prerequisite, and we will try to give you everything you need. And I understand where you are with the capability for such a mission. It would be ideal if all the procedures and protocols for Special Forces handling this new war against terrorism were flawlessly in place. But you and your personnel will have to develop that capability over time and with creative training. If Reiner were out in the desert somewhere, this mission would be a cakewalk. But if he's in the center of Jask like we think he is, then I think you are looking at a percentage of success much less. Maybe fifty-fifty and with high casualties. This has to be a volunteer mission no matter how you plan it." He sipped his coffee and peered over the top of his cup, watching Carpenter's expression.

"Volunteers are no problem, admiral. This is what those soldiers signed on to do. They know the risks. How much time do I have to prepare?"

"A least a couple of months," Hollifield said. Admiral Limmerick handed Carpenter a manila folder with photographs and a sketchy intelligence report on the buildings held by Komando Jihad in Jask. "This is all we have right now. We won't get approval for the mission until the president gets his feet firmly on the ground. Meanwhile, we'll provide you with everything we can get."

Hollifield set his cup on the table and leaned forward. "Who will you send on this mission, General?"

The room fell silent, and the tension was palpable. The admiral had asked a question outside decisional authority, and everyone knew why he was worried and why he had asked it.

Likewise, General Carpenter set his cup of coffee on the table and leaned forward. "If you're asking me how 1st Lieutenant John Paul Jacobs is doing in the Green Berets, sir, I'm told by Colonel Strong that Jacobs is one of the best he has seen. He's a natural. I don't know whether he'll be selected for this mission. But that's Colonel Strong's decision. Isn't it, Admiral?"

CHAPTER 17

0730 Hours
15 January 1975
Fort Bragg, North Carolina

THE TWELVE MEN ran single file down the narrow path through a heavily wooded area characterized by sharp turns, steep slopes, and holes covered with dead foliage. The trail was treacherous. It was a sprained ankle lying in wait, but there was no cause to complain because complaints do not make a path less hazardous in live combat. Each man carried the load of his specific specialty, which made the daily run more or less difficult depending on one's job on the team. Master Sergeant Sam Carrigan had the heaviest load with an M-60 machine gun at twenty-three pounds plus ammunition, while Jake, the A-Team leader, had the lightest.

Depending on the training scenario, Jake had two long guns in his tool kit. If the mission was to clear buildings or attack physical structures, he carried a Winchester M97, the military version of the Model 1897 used in World War I. It was called a trench gun. The weapon was a twenty-inch barreled, pump-action, 12-gauge shotgun with a perforated steel heat shield over the barrel and an adapter for affixing a bayonet. It had an effective range of fifty meters, but it was an asset to the team should it be necessary to blow the hinges off a door. Jake's other long gun was the standard Colt M-16 rifle that fired 5.56 mm rounds, either in semi-automatic mode or full-automatic. In addition to the long guns, Jake had been selected to field test the German-made 9mm Volkspistole. It was manufactured by Heckler & Koch and called the VP70. Jake liked it. It held eighteen rounds and was the first polymer-framed handgun. It was a double-action semi-automatic. When it was attached to the H&K custom stock (which cleverly was also the holster), Jake could select it to fire three-round automatic bursts. The VP70 was being considered to replace the long-serving M1911A1 .45 ACP. The team had started teasing Jake in the field, saying that the tight-fitting, crossed bandoliers full of shotgun rounds across his chest and his custom of standing with the shotgun pointing downward and balanced in the crook of his arm gave the appearance of Pancho Villa on a duck hunt.

Jake was not in a relaxed stance at the moment. His team had run four miles of the hill trail with a grueling uphill mile remaining. Jake never turned to see how the men behind him were doing. He knew they were there, though he could hear nothing but his heavy breathing. This was a daily run. It was a warmup for a day of training about to begin or as the final effort at the end of a night of maneuvers in the dark. Usually, the team conducted techniques and methods in the daylight hours until they coordinated their movements, then the training continued through most of the night. It was the nature of the work. The darkness was an ally to Green Beret teams. They learned to love it.

Jake struggled over the crest of the hill, gasping for breath in the early morning humidity, and immediately noticed the jeep at the end of the trail some two hundred meters through the open meadow. As he drew nearer, the bright red plate on the front fender told him that a flag officer was present.

Brigadier General Carpenter and Colonel Strong cut their conversation short and walked toward the incoming A-Team as Jake raised his right hand high in the air to signal the men to a walk.

Colonel Strong lit the cold stub of his cigar. "That's your team, General. Jacobs has done a fine job, and the NCOs on the team are seasoned Berets. Ordinarily, a bunch like that would resent a young lieutenant, but Jacobs has earned their respect. They have confidence in him. He's demanding of the team. Since they've been training together, I've never seen an instance where age or rank was an issue. They work together to accomplish a task as well as any team I have seen, and I've seen a lot of teams."

Jake was about to regain normal breathing when the senior officers motioned to him. "Lieutenant Jacobs. Join us for a few minutes."

Jake saluted and dismissed his team for a rest before turning again toward Carpenter and Strong. It was not often he saw Colonel Strong, and he had only seen General Carpenter twice. On both occasions, it had been on parachute jumps over Fort Bragg, and he had been pleased to see the general doing what he had ordered others to do.

"Yes, sir," Jake said. "You wanted to see me?"

Carpenter spoke first. "Admiral Hollifield sends his regards. He regretted not attending the wedding ceremony down in Georgia, but I'm sure you can appreciate how little of his time is discretionary these days."

"Of course, General. We missed him and Mrs. Hollifield, but Lieutenant McSwain understood completely."

Colonel Strong pulled the cigar stub from his mouth and ended the informalities. "Jacobs, how would you feel about taking your team on a high-risk mission?"

Without hesitation, Jake said, "That's what this A-Team is here for, Colonel."

General Carpenter smiled at Jake's eagerness. "Well, it's a little more complex than you might assume, and the mission, if it actually comes together, is very high risk. It's an important mission, and it's likely to have significant costs associated with it."

Strong noisily cleared his throat and lightly kicked a rock with the toe of his boot. "I'll not candy-coat it, Jacobs. We need a volunteer team to go into an extremely tight situation, with little intel, and with a difficult extraction. Timing is not known, but probably in the next five months. If you want it, we think your A-Team is the best for the job. If not, we'll put together a volunteer team from around the command. If you and your men accept, then we'll start specific training immediately.

Jake thought for a moment about his answer and his men. "Colonel, I personally volunteer for the mission, and I think the rest of the team will, also. However, I feel that since you have emphasized that it is a volunteer mission, I should let each of my team members make that decision individually. With your permission, sir, I'll go present it to them right now so I can give you a clear answer."

"We'll wait at the Jeep." General Carpenter watched Jake walk the fifty yards to the grove of trees where the other eleven men of the team were lounging in the shade and approvingly nodded his head.

Colonel Strong stuck his cigar back in his mouth and leaned against the hood of the vehicle. "General. I can tell you already what those men will say. They didn't join this outfit just to look spiffy around town in their green berets. They are warriors."

Carpenter didn't reply. He leaned against the fender and watched Jake in the distance present the request. Only a few minutes passed when he saw Jake turn and deliberately walk toward them. He noticed that Jake's conversation had not caused much of a stir with the men in the grove of trees. They were again relaxing in the shade as though Jake had told them nothing significant.

"What are our orders, sir?" Jake said. "You've got yourself an all-volunteer A-Team." Jake's expression indicated only the expectation of instructions to proceed.

0800 Hours
15 January 1975
Jask, Iran

DR. HAROLD CLINTON REINER was fifty-six years of age and in excellent health. He was thankful for all the efforts he had made to stay in good physical condition over the years. The late afternoons jogging on the University of Chicago campus had paid off. Otherwise, he might be dead. It had been thirty-seven days since he had been pushed off the jogging trail by two men into a ravine with thick foliage on the backside of the campus, drugged, and carried away from his family and his life. After tumbling down the ravine, the last thing he remembered was being held by one man while the other punctured his arm with a syringe. He had awakened in the Beechcraft flying south to Mexico. Since that night and his arrival in Jask, he had been occasionally beaten, poorly fed, and often denied sleep. Another man his age, in marginal physical condition, might not have survived.

He had now accepted his circumstances and simply concentrated on survival, hoping that somehow someone would rescue him. His hope was thin. He had thought about it until his head ached. There was not much chance anyone knew what had happened to him, let alone his whereabouts. His most pressing worry was his family. Being a captive would be tolerable if he could let his wife and sons know that he was alive. Mary had always been much more concerned than he was about the nature of his work. Over the years, she had complained that he was a target, a valuable target, in the Cold War. She would know since she, too, held a doctorate and was employed by an international relations think tank. But, regardless of her admonitions, he played down the danger and tried to pacify her concerns with his humility. He had graduated from MIT, then had taken his masters and doctorate at Georgia Tech. Early in his graduate work, he was recommended to the government as a brilliant young chemist. Working for the military had been personally rewarding in that he felt he was making a significant contribution to his country. But, never had he realized that a foreign power, or in this case, terrorists, would single him out of hundreds of chemists and threaten him and his family.

The bruises were starting to heal. He had not seen his face in a mirror, but he did not need to. Scabs had formed where fists met his face. At one point, both his eyes had swollen shut.

Resistance to their demands had been his mindset for nearly thirty days. After all, he was a patriot, and even if he were not, he could not help the likes of his captors develop weapons of mass destruction. There was no doubt in his mind that they would use such weapons in irresponsible and evil ways. He would rather be dead than have the weight of such deaths on his soul.

The beatings had stopped one day. His captors gave him a hot meal, a full night's sleep, a shower, and fresh clothes before a well-mannered man entered the room. He spoke perfect English and introduced himself as Sukarno Bangjar. Reiner found him pleasant, but behind the pleasantness, he saw a coldness and an arrogance capable of much more brutality than the simple-minded guards who had beaten him. Sukarno told him that he had lived in the United States for many years and had graduated from Princeton University. Reiner deduced that his captor was only trying to have him mentally and emotionally associate with him and his political cause.

Through the conversation with Sukarno, Reiner made a decision. If he were to survive, he would have to provide Komando Jihad some level of cooperation. Perhaps he could buy time by delivering work that would appease his captors but not give them entirely what they wanted. Those thoughts evaporated when Sukarno plainly stated that they would verify his work. If he failed to produce a usable Sarin nerve gas in quantity and the means to reproduce it, they would execute him and his family.

Dr. Reiner tried to bargain for notification to his family that he was alive and well, but Sukarno refused. It was non-negotiable. Reiner could accept the loss of his freedom and his life, but not the murder of his family.

Since that day, he had been treated well. He ate well. He

was allowed to sleep. It was especially important to him that he was given an hour each day on the building's flat-top roof for fresh air and exercise. Under the circumstances, Reiner treasured this time.

After exercising a half-hour by stationary running and a few basic calisthenics, Reiner found that standing at the wall around the perimeter of the roof was a relaxing distraction from what had become his routine. He gazed down into the square at the crowds that had been forming in ever-increasing numbers daily. They were demonstrating. Chanting. He did not understand all that it meant, but one thing was clear. They were demonstrating against America and the Shah of Iran. Each day someone made a speech. The speaker would stand on the building's parapet across the square and, in a short time, have the crowd worked into a frenzy. Most days, the speaker was the local religious leader, the mullah, but other times it was a member of Komando Jihad.

0930 Hours
13 February 1975
Fort Bragg, North Carolina

WARRANT OFFICER-4 BRAD WASHBURN, the XO, the team's executive officer, was the first one out of the unmarked white van's door as it came to a stop in front of the simulated two-story building. Sergeant First Class Albert Vincento, the communications NCO, was directly behind him. Two silenced shots were fired simultaneously at lifelike silhouettes on each side of the doorway. Both silhouettes were fragmented in the chest area before Washburn's foot touched the ground. They ran up the three steps and entered the door with Jake, the team leader, while Sergeant First Class Miguel Gutierrez, medical NCO, and Sergeant Leonard Frasier, weapons NCO, followed close behind. Five seconds had elapsed, and five team members were inside the building.

Jake and Washburn moved to the first room on the right as Gutierrez fired a three-round burst into a silhouette at the top of the stairs. Jake kicked the door open, and Washburn slid past him, with his M16 in the firing position, searching for targets. Jake followed, scanning the left side with his Heckler & Koch VP70 at the ready. The room was empty. Washburn released the latch on the window, pulled it open, and then turned back toward the hallway with Jake.

Through the open window, Sergeant Larry Kim, a communications NCO, and Sergeant Benny Jaramillo, an engineer, came diving in, one behind the other, and quickly came to their feet, weapons up and scanning for a target. For the entry through the window, the second van had pulled to the side of the building, cleared it of anyone that might get in their way, and parked close enough to the window to enter it from the sliding door of the van.

The engineers had hurriedly constructed the simulated building at Bragg to resemble the outside of the building in Jask, but the interior was a guess. The building was a rough construction with no finishing touches. The layout was critical, not the cosmetics. The simulation exercise was designed to clear the lower level as quickly as possible while moving operators up the stairs where Reiner was likely to be, assuming he was there at all. Seven members of the team were in the building within thirty seconds.

The general plan was to use three nondescript vans for the assault and rescue. The first was to be driven by Sergeant First

Class Terry O'Banion, who would deposit the three members at the front door. He was to wait at the door for their return with Reiner, then drive out of the square, hopefully not under fire. The second van was to deposit Kim and Jaramillo at the window, then drive to the front of the building to provide covering fire, if necessary. First Sergeant Leroy Coats was the driver, and Master Sergeant Sam Carrigan manned an M-60 machine gun installed inside the van so the sliding door could bring the weapon to action quickly. The third van was to park on the right side of the square, its sliding door facing the center. Sergeant Mark Parrish drove while Sergeant Lucian Forest manned another M-60 for additional covering fire. If all went well, the team would be in and out of the building in less than three minutes with Reiner. O'Banion's van could drive away before other elements of Komando Jihad could react. If it went badly, the other two vans could apply enough firepower to support evacuation from the square.

Getting out of the town square was the second element of the plan, while the third was extraction. The vans had to drive out of the town as quickly as possible and rendezvous with a Navy CH-46 Sea Knight at the designated area two miles south of Jask on the coastline. To support the extraction from Jask and protect the SeaKnight, two Army AH-1 Cobras would provide covering fire on any Komando Jihad elements pursuing the vans. Once the Sea Knight was loaded with the A-Team and Reiner, all would return to the aircraft carrier orbiting in the Gulf of Oman.

Jake unslung his Winchester M97 from his right shoulder and holstered the Heckler & Koch VP70 while moving rapidly toward the staircase. Washburn and Gutierrez met him at the base. The remaining four operators immediately searched the first floor in pairs, with Frasier and Vincento to the left and

Kim and Jaramillo to the right. The stairs were ascended quickly, with Jake and Washburn concentrating on the landing. They moved together as one while Gutierrez provided rear-guard cover, ascending the stairs backward. Another fifteen seconds elapsed before Jake swung to the right on the second floor, with Washburn making an identical move on the left. Blam! Jake's 12-gauge slug splintered a silhouette at the far end of the hall, and the top half of the target toppled to the floor. The team could hear the men below yelling, "First floor clear. First floor clear."

Another full minute passed, and the second-floor team started the descent down the stairs with a large duffle bag, currently identified as the hostage. "Second floor clear. Second floor clear. Standby. Standby." The first-floor team understood that the team leader was coming down the stairs with the hostage and that it was time for them to leave the building for the van.

Kim and Jaramillo threw open the front door, then swung into a kneeling position, aiming left and right of the van, which was to their immediate front. "Clear. Clear."

Gutierrez and Frasier rushed through the door shoulder-to-shoulder, M16s at the ready, with Jake and the hostage pressing against their backs. Time elapsed from the door into the van was mere seconds, and Gutierrez and Frasier were right behind them. They were inside the van. The door closed, and Sergeant First Class Terry O'Banion accelerated away from the simulation in a route identical to the one in Jask.

O'Banion pulled the van to a stand of trees, and the team crawled out slowly. Colonel Strong sat on a rough tabletop with his feet on the bench, smoking a cigar. By his expression, Jake could not tell whether he was pleased or displeased with the exercise.

Captain March sat on a stool with his clipboard in hand as the men sat on the grass for the debriefing. "Not bad. Not bad at all. You broke the three-minute mark this time."

The A-Team members smiled and poked each other as if to say to the guy next to him, "Did you hear that? We did it."

March gave them a minute of self-congratulation, then continued. "The first phase entry was excellent. Twenty-five seconds. Eighteen seconds to the top of the stairs. One minute-ten to clear the second floor. Plus, there was one minute and some change to exit and drive away. Those are excellent times."

The A-Team sat silent. This was too good to be true. There had to be a "but" in this debriefing somewhere.

"There were eight bad guys terminated effectively on the first floor and five on the second floor. All shots were considered effective. Colonel, do you have any comments to make to the team?"

The team's eyes focused on Colonel Strong as he exhaled slowly without changing expression. "Yes. Well, gentlemen. You've come a long way in three weeks. That really was a remarkable job. That little demonstration would scare any bad guy."

The men chuckled.

"I think what we'll do now is change things up a bit for you. I'll have the engineers out here every afternoon to change the interior of that building. Remember, we don't have the slightest idea what the real thing looks like inside. It'd be embarrassing if you guys got in there and got lost. Captain March, put the other two vans into the exercise and design a course for the entire extraction. Let's practice all of it. The Navy is flying over a Sea Knight with crew tomorrow, and the day after tomorrow, we will have our two Cobras. They are yours for the duration. These are the crews that will be going on the mission, so I want all of you to get to know these men well. I want this entire mission team to be close. Every man in this team should know the other men well enough to know exactly what they will instinctively do under all circumstances. Success, if we go, demands that you think and act as one. Any questions?"

Jake stood. "Yes, sir. Can you give us an idea when we will execute the mission?"

Strong bit down on his cigar and spoke through clenched teeth. "Higher-higher, that is the slick-sleeves in Washington, still can't find their butt with both hands. That's not to say they aren't trying. They've finally got the president to okay delivery of the Cobras to the carrier in the Gulf and provide an increased intelligence effort. However, as you know, we can't go charging into a foreign country without being invited. The last word I have is no sooner than ninety days."

The men moaned. It was well known that once an effort is optimized, both mentally and physically, action should be taken immediately. There exists a point of diminishing returns where practiced skills become less effective, and the men become less precise in their execution.

Strong removed the cigar and smiled. "I know what you're thinking. I kid you not, boys. I wrote the course on "get ready then kick ass." I'll think of something. Don't you worry. I'll have you at your peak when the time comes."

The A-Team's disappointment vanished as quickly as it had come. They had confidence in Colonel Strong. He had literally written the book on Special Forces activity, and they knew he would not let them down. Each man's life was important to him.

CHAPTER 18

2000 Hours
14 February 1975
Fort Bragg, North Carolina

CAPTAIN TIMOTHY O'DONNEL, the aide to Lieutenant General Elvin P. Mitchell, stood next to Jake at the punch bowl and grinned when he saw Emily Parks wave and move across the crowded dance floor toward them. The general had left O'Donnel with Jake a few minutes earlier to continue the argument that airborne infantry was the path to a fruitful career while Special Forces was the road to ruin. "What on earth could you and your Colonel Strong be doing out there that's useful, Jacobs?" the general had asked. "Wake up and smell the coffee, Lieutenant. Special Forces died in Vietnam, and you're wasting your career. Come over to the 82nd, son, where you can be a real soldier."

"Who's the girl, Captain? Looks like she is zeroing in on you," Jake said as he watched the young lady maneuver her way through the crowded dance floor.

O'Donnel almost spilled his punch when he laughed. "Me? It's you she's after, Lieutenant. She nearly pulled my arm off in the reception line wanting an introduction. You lucky stiff. Half the men on this post would give a month's pay to take her out."

"Pretty. So, who is she?" Jake was skeptical. He didn't know O'Donnel well, and it would not be the first time a young lieutenant was sandbagged with the post weirdo.

"Major General Maurice Park's daughter. He's Bragg's chief surgeon at the medical facility, but he spends most of his time up at Walter Reed operating on big wigs."

Emily Parks finally cut her way through the crowd and approached Jake and O'Donnel. Jake met her smile with one of his own. She reminded him of Julia in that she had dark emerald green eyes, but her hair was much darker and longer. Her hair fell gently on the shoulders of her silver dress, and she moved her sensual figure with poise and grace. Though she was extremely pretty, Jake's attention was focused on her smile. It was confident and genuinely friendly. He immediately concluded that even if she was the post weirdo, he was going to like her.

She walked right up to Jake and extended her hand. "Lieutenant Jacobs, I'm Emily Parks. I asked this horrible captain to introduce me to you, but he completely ignored my wishes."

"Now, Emily, I was going to get around to it. General Mitchell put me up to trying to recruit the lieutenant into the 82nd Airborne Division. Duty first, you know."

"Bull," Emily said while maintaining eye contact with Jake.

Jake blushed. "It's nice to meet you, Miss Parks."

Emily grinned. "Miss Parks? If you and I are going to be

friends, you have to call me Emily. Sometimes I can't stand all this military formality. And you're Jake, right?"

Without realizing it, Jake took Emily's hand. "Would you like to dance, Emily?"

"Of course." She threw Captain O'Donnel a smug smile over her shoulder as Jake led her to the dance floor.

"You saved me," Jake said. "Captain O'Donnel and General Mitchell have been double-teaming me all evening."

Emily laughed while pulling herself a little closer to Jake as they danced. "From what I hear, they don't have much of a chance getting you out of the Green Berets. Oh, don't look so surprised that I know stuff about you. It's the seventies. I've seen you around the post, and I've asked just about everyone about you. I guess you can tell that I think you're cute. Well, so what? I do. So there."

Jake blushed but tried to act nonchalant. "And what did you find out about me?"

"Well, I found out that you are a bachelor. You're a West Pointer. You're in the Special Forces Group, where you are considered one of their real hotshots. You're from Texas. I already knew how good-looking you are, and everyone says you're a nice guy. They say you're a man with no enemies." Emily gave Jake a puzzled look. "That makes you pretty unique, considering the line of work you're in, don't you think?"

"Never thought about it," Jake said.

"Hmmm," Emily said as she pulled herself even closer to Jake. "I think I like the idea of a nice guy who doesn't have to think about it."

Jake laughed and admired Emily's honest interaction with people. She said what she thought. "What about you? Who are you, Emily?"

Without hesitation, Emily said, "I'm in medical school at Duke. I want to be a pediatrician. I'm pretty, or at least I hope you think so. I'm not shy, which I'm sure you already know, and I like people."

Jake grinned at Emily's description of herself. His first impression had been right. He liked her. "So, where's the guy? I mean, you're evidently smart and beautiful, so why are you alone at this dance twisting O'Donnel's arm for an introduction to the likes of me? I'd think you'd be beating men away with a stick."

"That's blunt," Emily said. "I like that, too. I hate beating around the bush. Fact is, I'm asked out plenty. I was asked several times for this Valentine dance, but I wanted to come alone. I'm like you, Jake Jacobs. I'm busy. Work, work, work. I don't have time for a normal relationship, just like you don't. Medical school takes all my time, just like Special Forces takes yours."

"Suits me. I'm not looking for a normal relationship." Jake did not know where this conversation was going, but he figured being honest about not wanting to get involved emotionally was a good place to start.

"Me either. What kind of relationship do you want?" Emily asked.

Jake was surprised by the question. "Well, since I haven't been looking for a relationship at all, I guess I can't give you an answer. That is unless good friends will do."

"I knew I was going to like you," Emily said. "So, who was she?"

"Who was who?" Jake asked, more than a little confused by her question.

Without any hesitation, Emily said, "The girl that broke your heart."

Jake was stunned. Sara was the last person he wanted to talk about with Emily or anyone else for that matter.

Emily could see how uncomfortable Jake was with the question. "Sorry. I didn't mean to strike a nerve. You'll have to tell me all about it someday. I have a feeling we will be friends for a very long time. I can wait."

Jake smiled. "How did you get so perceptive? You're right. There was a girl. A long time ago. While I was at the academy, she married another guy, has at least one child, and lives happily ever after. End of story."

Jake felt a tap on his shoulder and turned his head in annoyance. He was enjoying Emily's company and was not ready for some officer to cut in.

"Say, punk. Mind if I dance with the beautiful lady?"

Before Jake could process the familiarity of the voice or see the face, he felt shock and anger at his fellow officer's rudeness. When he saw the rude perpetrator, the anger vanished, but the shock doubled. "Patrick? What in the world are you doing here?"

Emily's eyes widened in puzzlement as the two officers excitedly shook each other's hands. Obviously, this tall, blonde 1st lieutenant was not the jerk she first thought him to be. Emily pushed Jake out of the way with a smile and extended her hand to Patrick. "Don't mind me. I'm just the girl who was having a marvelous time dancing with Lieutenant Jacobs before you barged in. I'm Emily Parks. Who are you?"

Patrick laughed loudly. "Howdy, Miss Emily Parks. I'm the West Point roommate that keeps this youngster out of trouble with beautiful women like yourself. Although, if he were to get in trouble, I think I would have to approve of him doing so with you. I'm Patrick McSwain, Cobra pilot extraordinaire."

"Charming and humble," Emily said with a broad smile on her face.

Jake handed Emily and Patrick a glass of punch. "So, are you up here on business, or did you just fly over to North Carolina to cut in on the first dance I've had with a beautiful woman in months?"

Patrick drank half of his glass, then looked at Emily. "Ain't my timin' absolutely perfect? You see, Emily, this boy can't get away with anything. Uncle Patrick is always watchin'."

Emily could tell that Jake and Patrick were extremely close, almost brotherly. She saw a side of Jake that was even more pleasing than what she had already seen. He was happy. Being around Patrick brought out a glow in him, and because of it, she had to like Patrick herself. What she saw between these two friends was rare. She saw total confidence and trust in each other.

"I just got in a couple of hours ago," Patrick said. "I drove from Rucker and broke into your BOQ. I hope you don't mind. I'll be getting my quarters tomorrow."

Jake had a confused expression on his face. "What do you mean you'll be getting quarters? If you're on temporary duty at Bragg, you can bunk with me."

Patrick grinned. "I've been assigned to Fort Bragg indefinitely, or at least for the next few months. Rebecca and I will have temporary quarters until that gets decided."

"Great, Emily said. "Sounds like we need to have a party. I'd like to meet Rebecca."

Jake heard what Emily said, but only part of it registered. "What kind of assignment do you have here?" Something in the back of his mind was starting to send out warning signals.

Patrick grinned again and filled his glass at the punch bowl. "Assignment? Oh, I heard this crazy 1st Lieutenant over at Special Forces needed a remarkable Cobra pilot sometime in the near future. You know me. Once a Tennessee Volunteer, always a volunteer."

Jake could not believe what he had heard, and of course, Emily did not have the slightest idea what he had said. She stood staring at Jake's expression of shock, then at Patrick's grin. For a large part of a minute, neither said a word.

"But ...," Jake tried to say.

"Thought you could do this without me being around to look after you, didn't you? Well, you've got another thing coming, Jacobs. As of 2000 hours this evening, I am officially a support member of your team."

2330 Hours
14 February 1975
Durango, Colorado

SARA STOOD on the cabin's front porch with a blanket covering her head and wrapped around her shoulders. The moon was full, piercing the cloud cover and making the large snowflakes falling a spectacular sight across the meadow. It was Valentine's Day again, and thoughts of celebrations with Jake in the past haunted her. Speculation on where he was and who he was with this night quickened her heart rate.

The thought of simply calling him had crossed her mind many times, but action to do so faltered when it came to picking up the phone to get a number from the Fort Bragg operator. Tonight was different. She felt discouraged to the bone that she had lacked the courage to talk to him but discouraged enough to pick up the phone and make the call.

Sara went back into the cabin, sat in her recliner, carefully covered her legs with the blanket, and set the phone in her lap. And then the fears and self-defeating thoughts crushed her resolve. With trembling hands, she set the phone back on the end table, covered her face with both hands, and cried.

1030 Hours
18 February 1975
Jask, Iran

Dr. Harold Clinton Reiner peered over the top of his glasses at the interruption. He had been constructing a series of chemical formulas, none of which would produce the results his captors wanted, and pretended to be nonplussed nonetheless from having his concentration disrupted from important work. Reiner had filled the past weeks with a series of mental games. For the most part, he had won. He spent hours each day working on formulas that bordered on producing Sarin nerve gas but always lacked a critical element. Sporadically, Rokus Sogiarto would come into the small room and question him about his progress. Luckily, Sogiarto lacked any substantial knowledge of the chemical sciences. As a result, the meetings were usually harmless. Although the makeshift lab was one of guaranteed contamination, that was the only limitation Reiner really had for the production of Sarin. He could give them what they wanted very quickly, but he played the game of delay.

Only once had Reiner regretted his game. Sogiarto had gathered several pages of his notes, only to return a few days later with two guards. They viciously slapped him around the room and kicked him repeatedly in the ribs when he fell to the floor. Sogiarto had said that he knew Reiner was stalling because he had the notes reviewed.

"Good morning, Dr. Reiner," Rokus Sogiarto said as he sat at Reiner's desk. Two guards rolled in carts and began to unload four tanks and stand them in the corner. "Do you know what those are, Dr. Reiner?"

A dreaded moment had arrived for Reiner. "Well, the tall ones, I guess to be about five feet tall, are probably liquid oxygen tanks. The small ones look like scuba tanks."

Without pause, Sogiarto said, "You are almost correct. The tall ones are propane tanks. New. They have never been filled. And you are correct about the scuba tanks." Sogiarto rose from the chair and walked the half dozen steps to stand directly in front of Dr. Reiner. "We have treated you well. Wouldn't you agree, Dr. Reiner?"

Reiner held his ground, though the inclination was to maintain a generous distance from Sogiarto and the guards. "Well, I don't mean to complain about the food, but I have a craving for a cheeseburger. Do you ever get a craving for a big, juicy cheeseburger? With French fries and a chocolate milkshake? I bet you do. So, there is that. And, I don't ever recall having people throw me down on the floor and break my ribs. Except here, of course."

Sogiarto laughed. "I do appreciate your sense of humor, Dr. Reiner. I think I can come up with that cheeseburger for you. I don't generally like American food, but I might join you."

"No offense," Reiner said. "But I don't mind eating alone."

"Me either," Sogiarto said, making the point that he, too, would not like the company. "On to business, Dr. Reiner."

Unconsciously, Reiner crossed his arms over his chest. It

was a subtle act of defensiveness. An act of defiance against whatever it was that Sogiarto had to say.

"Here are three photos you need to consider," Sogiarto said as he handed Reiner three 8x10 black and white photographs.

Reiner was shocked and emotional to the point of tears. They were photos of his family. His son was playing in one of his hockey games. His daughter was in a restaurant with friends, and his wife had been photographed shopping for groceries. Reiner was speechless.

"Dr. Reiner, we have lost patience with you. Those tanks will be full of effective Sarin nerve gas in thirty days, and you will have a written procedure for the reproduction of the gas that is easy to follow. If you do not meet that deadline, one of your family members will be executed. A month following that, those tanks will have a regulator that will atomize the liquid."

Reiner was horrified. His posture of stalling was over. His family's lives were now at stake, and he did not doubt that Sogiarto would order their execution.

Sogiarto turned toward the door without further conversation concerning the nerve agent. "You may keep the photographs."

1500 Hours
19 February 1975
Army Navy Country Club
Arlington, Virginia

General Jack T. Cushman drove the electric golf cart down the asphalt path with Admiral John Hollifield next to him. Neither played much golf, but they looked like they did. They were colorful, which was a discomfort for both, and they wore winter-weight windbreakers to help make the crisp winter air more tolerable.

"I feel ridiculous," Hollifield stated with his arms crossed. "Downright disgusting. All the trouble this country has, and we have to chase the Commander in Chief across half the country's golf courses. I wish he would get his priorities straight."

"Bitch-bitch-bitch," Cushman replied. "It's not so bad—fresh air and sunshine. This beats sitting in the White House waiting to get into the Oval Office. Actually, I think having a president make decisions from a golf course probably speeds things up a bit. After all, he has to make a decision before he tees off for the next hole. Eighteen decisions in one day? That's pretty good for a politician." Cushman chuckled at his assessment, but Hollifield did not find it humorous.

"Yeah. Don't let anything as unimportant as running the country get in the way of eighteen holes of golf. This is ridiculous."

Cushman laughed again. "You said that already. Besides, the president didn't exactly ask for the job. I'm sure he would rather still be in Congress so he could play golf every day."

The golf cart rolled over the crest of a small hill, and in the distance, a foursome could be seen on the fourteenth green. It looked like any other foursome but for the dozen Secret Service agents milling around the edges of the fairway. They were stopped twice and made to identify themselves properly before pulling alongside the president's cart.

"Afternoon, gentlemen," the president said as he slipped his putter into his bag. What brings half the Joint Chiefs to the links today? Would you like to play a few holes?"

Cushman smiled as he got out of the cart and met the president's extended hand. "Afternoon, Mr. President. Sorry to bother you out on the golf course, sir."

"That's all right. Let's take a walk. What's on your mind?" The president pulled a number one wood from his bag and began walking up the slope to the fifteenth hole tee box. Cushman and Hollifield fell in stride with him, one on each side.

"Well, sir. John has convinced me that we have a real problem brewing in Iran. I mentioned this situation to you three months ago, but I think it's time we seriously take a little closer look."

The president continued his stride toward the tee box while surveying the green in the distance. "Iran? What about Iran? I don't' remember anything about any problems over there."

Hollifield rolled his eyes and kept walking.

After clearing his throat, Cushman said, "Yes, sir. It's about that chemist, Dr. Harold Reiner. The chemist who was kidnapped from the University of Chicago campus. Admiral Hollifield has gathered intelligence reports that strongly indicate he is being held hostage by a group called Komando Jihad in Jask, Iran."

The president stopped short of the tee box and placed the club behind his neck and across his shoulders to stretch. "Go ahead. I'm listening."

The admiral continued the briefing. "Yes, sir. Reiner is one of our leading chemists with research in the area of chemical weapons. We have reason to believe that Komando Jihad is trying to use Reiner to develop weapons for their own use. If they get it, we know they will use it."

"So, what do you want to do about it?" The president

rolled from side to side, bending at the waist, to complete his stretching exercises.

Admiral Hollifield continued. "We have to move, Mr. President. The longer we leave Reiner in their hands, the bigger the gamble we take that Komando Jihad will get their weapon. Reiner is a patriot, but he can't hold out forever if they torture him. They could significantly influence the balance of power in Iran and the entire Middle East if we don't get him out of there. What we want, Mr. President, is a directive from you to send in a Special Forces team to get him out."

The president frowned. "Wouldn't we need cooperation with the Iranian government on something like that?"

Hollifield tried to keep a straight face. The anger rising in him was difficult to conceal. New or not, the president had already been briefed on all of this three months earlier and apparently remembered none of what he had heard. During the initial briefing, the president assured them he would immediately initiate a dialogue with the Iranian government. Now it appeared that all efforts to rescue Reiner were still at square-one at the political level.

Cushman sensed Hollifield's mounting frustration and quickly decided not to let his fellow officer answer what he, too, felt to be an incompetent question. "Well, Mr. President, we understood from our last meeting on this that your office had already initiated such cooperation from the Iranian government. If that isn't so, sir, then I'm afraid that a rescue mission, which is very much in the interest of national defense and foreign policy, has been dangerously delayed. Therefore, I believe Admiral Hollifield should have a clear directive to proceed with this operation immediately."

The president coldly stared at General Cushman. "I'll check on it. There won't be a directive to Admiral Hollifield or anyone else until I've had time to study it and all my advisors are brought up to date on the intelligence. Is that clear, General?"

"Yes, Mr. President," Cushman responded, personally feeling the sting of the president's reprimand.

"Damn. You people think I'm supposed to walk into the presidency and know everything that was going on immediately. It takes time, gentlemen. Be a little patient."

John Hollifield's first thoughts in reply to the president's last statement had to do with him wasting time and risking national security on the golf course, but he quickly searched his mind for a more productive approach. "Mr. President. Would you consider giving us a directive to increase our intelligence activity on the matter and officially place the operation in movement with men and logistics? Then, after you've had time to get permission from the Iranian government and made a decision, we'll be ready to get the job done. More delay than necessary could be disastrous."

The president glanced at the tee box and then his watch. "Okay. You boys get the ball rolling, and I'll chip it to the green."

General Cushman grimaced behind the president's back. "Fine, sir. We'll do our part. We'll set a meeting with your staff secretary to discuss the situation in two weeks. Is that fair enough, Mr. President?"

The president leaned on his driver with his other hand on his hip. "You really are pushing me on this, aren't you, Jack?"

Cushman motioned with his head, indicating that he and the president take a short walk in private. The president followed and listened intently as General Jack T. Cushman spoke in a low, deliberate tone. "We've known each other for many years, Mr. President. And you are my boss."

The president sensed a change in the conversation and who was in control of it. "That's right. You and I go back to when I was just a junior congressman."

"Since we've known each other for so long, you know that when I get angry, I can be about the meanest bull on the ranch. Ain't that right?"

The president's eyes grew wide. Jack Cushman did not get tough often with politicians, but when he did, it was because he was right. The president knew that, and like most men on Capitol Hill, he knew it was not wise to cross Jack Cushman. He could hurt you. Even with the tragedies of Vietnam, the American people knew him and trusted him.

Cushman took one step closer to the president and looked him in the eyes. "I briefed you on this situation three months ago. That's right. I said you. This isn't some Mickey Mouse political game we're dealing with here. We're talking about a lot of people getting killed and the balance of power in the Middle East. Now Admiral Hollifield over there has been busting his hump for months trying to solve this problem, and he, and this country, deserve a better shake than you sitting on your backside not doing your homework. You can fire me any time you want, Mr. President, but I'm putting you on notice that if you don't get off your ass on this, I'll go to the American people and do everything I can to sink your political ship come election time. And yes, Mr. President, you can consider that a threat. I'll back you all the way, Mr. President, but if you get sloppy like you have with this situation, I'll do all I can to break you."

The president held both hands up, palms forward, as a sign of surrender and a chance to reclaim Cushman's good graces. "Okay, Jack. I hear you. I admit it. I haven't done my homework on the situation, and it did fall through the cracks, as far as I know. But dang it, Jack, you of all people should know the pressure I'm under."

Cushman did not let up. He snarled at the president. "That's why we gave you three months to work on it. We don't expect miracles, but we do expect the kidnapping of this country's leading brain on chemical weapons by maniac terrorists to take precedence over eighteen holes of golf."

"Okay. I said, okay. I'll get my people right on it."

Cushman's tone softened. "Two weeks. We'll set a meeting with you on this in two weeks. Let's work on this together, Mr. President. It's important, and it's high risk."

Without another word, Jack T. Cushman walked briskly away from the president toward the white golf cart.

Admiral Hollifield followed.

CHAPTER 19

1015 Hours
20 February 1975
Fort Bragg, North Carolina

PATRICK'S BELL AH-1 Cobra responded immediately with a steep climb. He banked left hard, then dove toward the second target, a burned-out deuce and a half truck. Five hundred meters from the target, he leveled the gunship, flipped the safety cover off the firing button, and pressed it. The aircraft's frame hardly felt the vibration of the burst from the M134, 7.62x51mm, minigun. At a fire rate of up to six thousand rounds per minute, destruction on the ground was imminent. Rounds splattered the ground fifty meters from the front of the target, then sprayed chunks of metal from the truck before the impact of the gunner-fired 2.75-inch rockets. Patrick pulled out of the dive and banked right as the truck momentarily leaped off the ground in a ball of flames. "That's a hit, FAG," said Chief Warrant Officer 4 Doug Bright, call-sign NOTSO.

Patrick smiled at the callsign given to him, which stood for 'Funny Accent Guy' because of his Tennessee, Southern drawl. He was pleased with the armament on the Cobra and thought it appropriate to provide covering fire for the escaping vans down a relatively unobstructed stretch of road to the point of extraction from Jask. In addition to the minigun and 2.75-inch rockets, the Cobra had an M129 40mm grenade launcher fed by a three hundred round magazine. It was plenty of firepower to discourage pursuit.

Patrick's weapons officer was Chief Warrant Officer 5 Simon Keeler, better known as FISH. No one really knew why FISH had that callsign, but since he had been in the Army for twenty-four years and had seen rotary-wing aviation grow from the ground up, everyone assumed that there was an interesting and derogatory story behind the name. When asked about it, he would grumble something undefinable under his breath, stuff a large cigar butt in his mouth, and give the inquisitive a look that could kill. Patrick liked him and was glad FISH was in the rear seat. There had been many times the old man had coached him out of a tight spot or talked him through a difficult maneuver. Though FISH was not a pilot, he knew more about helicopters and how to fly them than any aviator alive.

NOTSO, CW4 Doug Bright, was forty-two years of age, a nineteen-year veteran with two tours in Vietnam, a recipient of the Silver Star, and had a chest full of other medals for valor, including the Purple Heart with three clusters. He was in command of the two-gunship support group to Special Forces. Everyone knew it, and everyone was glad. His reasons for volunteering for the mission were private, but Patrick was convinced that he knew why. It was Bright's last chance to fly a combat mission before retirement. To do so was just the kind of soldier he was. He and his wife would be leaving the Army in a year to retire in the woods along the shores of Lake Michigan, and the old pro wanted to go out of the Army doing something significant. Bright had already told Patrick that he thought him to be one of the best young Cobra pilots he had seen come through the program, but he also told him he figured him too green and dumb yet to survive without having some crusty old warrant officer around to keep him out of trouble. Patrick was honored by the old man's desire to teach him all he knew before retiring. He agreed with NOTSO—he needed the time and instruction that only the old-timers could give him before becoming the best.

"Roger." Patrick eased back on the throttle, fell in on NOTSO Bright's port side, and cruised at eighty miles per hour back to base.

0830 Hours
3 March 1975
The Pentagon
Washington, D.C.

THE LARGE CONFERENCE room in a sub-level of the Pentagon was elegantly furnished for comfort. In the center of the room was a cherry conference table for twenty and high-backed leather chairs. The room was equipped with a small stage to provide better visibility for those around the table, and equipment of every type was available for those giving a briefing with overhead projection and maps. It was a theatre for some of the most important briefings in the Western world, and the audience was composed of those in a tight circle of power that guided, rightly or wrongly, the actions of the United States. The president, or often Congress, would make the final decision and give the orders, but it was in this room that such decisions were already set in motion.

The meeting was scheduled for precisely 0830 hours. However, that time had come and gone while the invited participants casually strolled into the room and sought either their favorite seat or the place at the table that was understood by all to belong to them. There were power seats in this theatre, and then there were the other seats. The Joint Chiefs of Staff were present, as was the president's National Security Adviser, the Secretary of State, a senior agent of the FBI, the Secretary of the Army, and the Director of the CIA. In all, eleven powerful men were gathered in the room, not counting those from Admiral Hollifield's staff and General Carpenter. These eleven men represented separate and fiercely independent agencies or interests of the government. Each had his ax to grind or territory to protect. Concrete decisions from such a group were usually hard to achieve. But the president had ordered the meeting.

The president had kept his promise, but General Jack T. Cushman was not pleased to have the issue safely delegated to a committee where it would be almost impossible to generate its members into cohesive action. The meeting time had been set a week earlier, and he had anxious days and restless nights trying to imagine how he might obtain a committee recommendation to the president. Finally, he decided that there was only one chance.

Cushman stepped to the stage and flipped on the reading light attached to the podium. The other members of the committee quickly finished their social or political niceties and found their chairs. "Gentlemen. As you have been informed,

I've been appointed to chair this temporary committee." The room was silent as the general paused, then chuckled. "When the president told me who would be on the committee, I almost had a heart attack."

"You may yet," Drew Calvert, the Secretary of the Army, said, drawing nods of agreement and chuckles from the others.

"I might as well start this first meeting off right by pointing out what we all know already so we can bypass the minutia and get down to work. The fact is, the president could not have picked a more politically diverse group of senior officials to get together to agree on something. It's the American way, and I think we all fully accept that our system of government runs on checks and balances. Unfortunately, this system often works through territorial protectionism, but it works nonetheless in the long run. Every man here has been around the block. And some of you, several times."

Again, the members laughed.

"We are here today because the country has a serious threat developing, both in terms of national security and with respect to present and future foreign policy in the Middle East. I'm going to ask each of you to do something that I have never seen happen in my thirty-three years of service. I want each of you, for the good of the country, to set aside all departmental interests and simply bring your skills, knowledge, and best decision-making capability together on this matter. If you do that for this committee, then I will accept your judgment on the matter as honorable and valid. However, if that is not so, and I find that we are playing the usual political games, you can count on me to respond accordingly. This is not just another inconsequential committee. This is not an insignificant matter."

The room was silent. Each member considered mentally

what Jack Cushman had said. Over the years, they had each had plenty of contact with him, be it in committees, socially, or in the halls of the White House. His seriousness was noted and believed. Like the president, they knew that Cushman was a man that did not push his weight around without a cause. They respected him. If he was pushing now, it was because Jack T. Cushman felt he had to.

"We'll start with a briefing from Admiral Hollifield's aide, Vice Admiral Limmerick," Cushman said. Limmerick walked briskly to the podium and immediately jumped into an hour-long briefing on the details known about Komando Jihad, the Heidelberg incident, Heathrow Airport, Dr. Harold Reiner and his working knowledge of chemical weapons, the known leadership and military capability of Komando Jihad, and verified intelligence concerning the town of Jask. Following the first hour, Limmerick left the factual and entered the arena of the theoretical. All possible scenarios were laid before the committee, including the repercussions of an attack on civilians with nerve gas. Limmerick used photographs of the airliner wreckage with dead bodies dramatically strewn on the runway at Heathrow to convince the committee that Komando Jihad, though small in number, could murder thousands of people to reach its objectives and effectively wage war against the United States. Limmerick concluded his part of the briefing by emphasizing that Komando Jihad had the financing, the will, and potentially the capability of creating an international disaster.

After a thirty-minute break, General Carpenter stood at the podium, ready to continue the briefing and explain the preliminary plans implemented to attempt a rescue of Dr. Reiner.

"Before you start, General, I have a question." The

Assistant Attorney General stood and gripped the top of his chair while the others sat. "Why don't we simply ask the Shah to send in his troops, eliminate Komando Jihad, and rescue Dr. Reiner themselves? We've had good relations with the Shah since the end of World War II. I can't imagine him not cooperating on this matter. You haven't said as much, but I think you are about to tell us we need to recommend some military action."

Admiral Hollifield spoke for Carpenter. "That's true, Robert. We do have adequate relations with the Iranian government to solicit their assistance, and we agree that your suggestion should be our first attempt at solving this problem. However, as General Carpenter is about to go over, we have some concern that the Iranian government will only give us limited assistance."

Robert Walls nodded his acceptance that his initial thoughts had been considered and sat for the briefing to continue. Meanwhile, Leonard Jarvis, the Director of the CIA, silently considered why his agency had not already covertly been given the green light to eliminate Komando Jihad. At the same time, Ted Burch of the FBI reluctantly held his resentment in check over the Secretary of State's comment during the break about how it was the FBI's fault that Reiner had been kidnapped in the first place.

Due to the question from the Attorney General's office, General Carpenter began his briefing with the political environment existing between the Shah of Iran and Komando Jihad. Within twenty minutes, Carpenter had convinced the committee that the Shah could not militarily perform the rescue with Iranian troops because of the already existing unrest between his government and the Muslim fundamentalists. At this point, Komando Jihad had religion on their side.

Any show of force on the Shah's part would only further alienate the people against him and his government. Carpenter presented to the committee that if asked, the Shah probably would allow, or invite, a U.S. military operation so long as he could publicly avoid direct blame himself.

"Ok, General. Your point is well-taken. Of course, we won't know that to be a fact until we talk to the Shah, will we?" George Shire was Secretary of State, and his comment was intended to remind everyone at the table of that fact that though the general might be correct, any dealing with the Shah of Iran on the matter was his turf. Without actually saying so, he resented the conclusion that he could not resolve the entire matter diplomatically.

Carpenter did not respond to the Secretary of State but continued his briefing, which further infuriated the statesman. Without further interruption, he concluded his presentation by noon. He had explained in detail the who, what, and where of the special Forces operation awaiting their decision and subsequent recommendation to the president. He then closed with a realistic evaluation of the risks and chances of success. "Our men are prepared for this operation, and the plan will not get any better. Gentlemen, there is only a fifty percent chance of success, and the losses, on the high side, could be seventy percent. That's twelve men in the team on the ground and four air support personnel. No losses are a realistic possibility assuming the tactical plan does not encounter unforeseen circumstances. Komando Jihad is heavily fortified in Jask, well-armed, and our intelligence only takes the team to the outside of the building. Still, it is our assessment that this committee recommends the operation to the president."

The Secretary of the Army sat forward in his chair. "What's the name of this operation, General?"

"Heartbeat, sir. Operation Heartbeat. One of the enlisted men on the A-Team came up with the name during training. He kept reminding everyone that the team could be in and out of the building with Reiner in a heartbeat. The name stuck. So, that's what we've called it for the past three months."

Leonard Jarvis lit a cigarette and blew smoke at the ceiling. "Ah. This is a CIA kind of reasoning, gentlemen, but why don't we just eliminate Reiner? Intelligence puts him on that rooftop frequently. I hate to say it, but that might make more sense than sending several young soldiers to their death with only a fifty percent chance of success."

The room was silent for a full minute. The director's question had crossed the mind of every man in the room, and they were glad that Jarvis had asked the question instead of themselves.

General Cushman slowly rose from the table and stood behind his chair. "Leonard, thank you for bringing that alternative to the table. The assassination of Dr. Reiner is a rational possibility. It may not be moral, but it is rational. It's the most expedient solution to eliminating the threat that Reiner will ultimately create a weapon for Komando Jihad. However, there are several reasons why I will not ratify such a recommendation. First, I will not have any part in the assassination of this man. He has faithfully served his country, and I'll not be a party to his murder, no matter what the circumstances. Second, this country has just suffered the President of the United States' resignation because of a cover-up. Watergate was nothing compared to the cover-up that would have to follow an assassination of Dr. Reiner. It would inevitably catch up with the president and every man on this committee. Third, we, meaning this country, must have the courage to deal with the growing menace of terrorism. Assassinating our own citizens every time we get in a jam is not a solution. We simply cannot set that kind of precedent. It's open for discussion.

Again, Leonard Jarvis was the only one at the table who could talk about the option. "Point taken. And, I agree in principle. But how do the men who'll be risking their lives feel about our decision to send them into harm's way when one bullet would solve the problem? Everyone on this committee is in denial if they think they will escape having someone's death on their conscience. Face it, gentlemen. Some good guys are going to get killed."

Admiral Hollifield nodded to General Cushman, indicating that he would like to answer the director's question. "Mr. Jarvis, I understand your concern. We all, I think, have some of the same thoughts and concerns. It would be best if you remembered that the men who volunteered for the mission are professional soldiers. Believe me. This question has crossed their minds. They know that they can opt-out with no repercussion. You see, Mr. Jarvis, we all agree that Dr. Reiner has to be taken out of the hands of Komando Jihad. That is the right decision. But executing the right decision has to be done in the right way."

Jack Cushman smiled at Hollifield. "We've had a long meeting this morning. The bottom line is that we recommend two courses of action. The first being that we approach the Iranian government to send their troops to rescue Dr. Reiner. The second recommendation is that we seek an invitation to implement Operation Heartbeat with our personnel as soon as possible."

The committee members glanced around the table at each other to see if there was to be more discussion, then Leonard Jarvis made a motion in favor of General Cushman's recommendation. A vote was taken, and the motion passed unanimously.

George Shire was the first to speak following the vote. "I'll brief the president, and with his permission, I'll arrange to discuss the matter with the Shah. Let's cut through channels and go directly to him. It should take a couple of weeks, more or less, to get his answer."

Cushman smiled. "Thank you, gentlemen. Maybe I was wrong about having a heart attack trying to get you all to agree on something."

CHAPTER 20

1830 Hours
10 March 1975
Fort Bragg, North Carolina

THE WORKDAY in winter months brought darkness early. It was cold in the mornings and late afternoons. The A-team had more free time than they had ever had, but it was not because of the weather. It was because the training phases for the A-Team for Operation Heartbeat had become too routine, too practiced. The team worked hard during the daylight hours, both on simulated assaults and in the classroom, but near dark, the workday was completed, and the members of the team returned home. Colonel Strong was well aware that the delays meted out by Washington were causing an ever-increasing danger to the delicate balance between mentally peaked and physically worn. They were ready. The politicians were not. Strong was not happy that his A-Team for Operation Heartbeat could not execute the mission at its optimum.

Jake pushed the door to his BOQ open with his knee and

dumped his equipment on the single bed. He was exhausted. They had run five miles on the hill trail at sunrise under a full combat load, made three complete assaults on the buildings, including escape and extraction, two hours on the firing range, and another two hours of briefings and critiques. It had been a long week. In fact, the weeks were getting longer as they awaited orders to do what they could already do in their sleep. There were factors beyond their control that could quickly turn the mission into a disaster, but of the factors they could control, every man on the team was at the point of reacting automatically. They read each other's minds, anticipated a team member's next movement or action, and allowed the hours of training to control every move.

Jake stepped into the shower fully clothed. His mud-soaked fatigues sent rivers of mud to the shower floor to swirl around the drain. As the mud washed away, he stripped off the shirt, then the boots and pants, throwing them out of the shower onto the bathroom floor. The hot spray massaged his back as he rested his head against the wall and closed his eyes.

Through the soothing rush of water, Jake heard the phone ring. He did not move. "They'll call back," Jake mumbled to himself. The phone rang again. And again. Jake reluctantly stepped from the shower and paddled across the floor, leaving puddles of water as he went to his desk and the phone.

1830 Hours
10 March 1975
Durango, Colorado

SARA RETURNED to the living room with a glass of ice water from the kitchen, set it on the table next to the phone, and dialed with slow deliberation the numbers she had obtained for the post operator at Fort Bragg. The panic and self-imposed disappointment in herself were gone, replaced by a determination to place the call to Jake. No matter his opinion of her, or his feelings, it was time for her to face the truth. If he laughed at her and told her he hated her, then at least she would know that her dreams were nothing but an illusion. As hard as that would be to hear from him, and to accept, perhaps the knowing would free her somehow to live again.

When connected to Jake's room, the annoying sound of a busy signal was the response to her moment of courage. Sara held the phone and allowed the signal to continue for a full ten seconds, knowing full well that there would not be an answer. Finally, she hung up with the emotional conflict of relief that Jake did not answer and the sadness that to call again, she would have to overcome the anxiety to do so.

1830 Hours
10 March 1975
Fort Bragg, North Caroina

OUT OF THE SHOWER, naked and puddling water on the floor, Jake answered the phone. "Lieutenant Jacobs speaking, sir."

"Lieutenant, this is Sergeant O'Banion. Something

concerning Operation Heartbeat is happening. The colonel is calling in the team for alert status. We have orders to go to the training barracks by 0600 hours tomorrow. Looks like we may be there until this thing is over."

Jake was not surprised. He knew the order to sequester away from the main post would precede actual departure by days for security reasons. It was now formal doctrine to do so if a mission graciously allowed time. One of the gravest dangers to the success of a mission was a breach of security. Jake was glad for the call. "Have you called the rest of the team?"

"You're the first, sir."

"I'm having dinner with Lieutenant McSwain and his wife this evening. I'll let him know. Finish your calls, and I'll see you at the barracks at 0600." Jake hung up the phone and hurried through his shower.

2100 Hours
10 March 1975
Fort Bragg, North Carolina

RETURNING to the BOQ after dinner, Jake heard the phone ring its last ring as he rushed through the door to answer it. He knew it would not ring again, but he picked it up regardless, only to hear a dial tone. He wondered who had called, but it never crossed his mind that it was Sara.

0630 Hours
11 March 1975
Briefing Room
Fort Bragg, North Carolina

MAJOR NICHOLAS JANSEN stepped to the small stage and flipped the switch of the overhead projector. Jake's A-Team and several officers seated at the rear of the briefing, including Colonel Strong, set their eyes on the projected map of North and South Vietnam. Jake leaned forward, surprised that he was not looking at the town of Jask, Iran, on the coast of the Persian Gulf. The war in Vietnam was over, as far as the United States was concerned. His curiosity was piqued.

"Gentlemen," Major Jansen said. "In forty-eight hours, you will be on the deck of the USS Hancock in the South China Sea, twenty miles off the coast of South Vietnam, and another one hundred and thirty-five miles to your physical objective near Gia Nghia. Your mission is to extract The Army of the Republic of Vietnam, or ARVN, Major General Tran Van Nguyen to the Hancock. The team will be inserted by the Navy's CH-46 Sea Knight, which is similar to our CH-47 Chinook, and have air support of two AH-1 Sea Cobras adequately armed for close air-ground support. The team will disembark, establish a perimeter, load the VIP, and immediately return to the USS Hancock."

Most of the members of the team had had combat tours in Vietnam. They had no expectation they would return, based on the fact that there were no troops to speak of in-country. A remnant of military personnel in Saigon and the consulate was all that remained in South Vietnam. Jake was somewhat stunned that he was going to the battleground that had cost his family the loss of his brother.

Major Jansen changed the mylar sheet to present a detailed map of the insertion point and two designated alternative extraction points should the need arise. "Weather," the major continued. "Sixty to sixty-eight degrees Fahrenheit is expected, and the mission is about a month ahead of the monsoon season. Terrain. It is mountainous with dense foliage. Weapons? Standard A-Team issue. I am the B-Team commander, and the outpost will be on the Hancock. Specific Operation Orders will be developed in route. Are there any questions?"

Jake shifted in his chair and asked, "Just what is the military environment there now? And I won't ask, but I am curious about the extraction of an ARVN general officer when the Army of the Republic of Vietnam is under the pressure of a major PAVN (People's Army of Vietnam) offensive."

Colonel Strong stood and made his way toward the briefing platform. "I'll answer that," he said. "You men deserve a clear picture of what is going on over there." When he reached the platform, he leaned against the podium and paused, quickly formulating how to present a complex situation as a simple answer. "You, gentlemen, are about to be the participants of perhaps the last combat action of the Vietnam War by a United States unit. Theoretically, this mission is a cakewalk. You put boots on the ground, set up a defensive perimeter, load the VIP, and come home."

Jake and the team were silent. They sensed the significance of moving into combat when everyone else was moving out. It was not lost on them that they would be alone, though that did not particularly impact the mission.

It has been a long war," Colonel Strong said. "Fourteen years long, and fifty-eight thousand American soldiers, sailors, Marines, and airmen made the ultimate sacrifice. It will be formally over at the end of April, and make no mistake about it; there is no victory. Some of you may wonder how we got to this point of defeat. There are a lot of answers and plenty of blame. This current offensive started in March of last year. Much of the blame goes to the Paris Peace Accords ending early in 1973. The North didn't wait long to launch their offensive, and at that time, they were strengthened in every way, thanks to the Soviet Union and China. President Nixon promised the South more air power if the North violated the Peace Accord, and the South was assured continued financial and military support. The first blow to the South was when Congress passed the Church Amendment in 1973, which prohibited direct or indirect combat activities by air or land in Cambodia and both Vietnams. There have been many a soldier killed since our Congress told them they could no longer fight back."

Colonel Strong paused to let the men grasp the significance of Congress legislating our military's inability to fight in a war zone.

"Later in 1973," the colonel continued, "Congress overrode President Nixon's veto, which slashed the budget that upheld the ARVN troops by over fifty percent. In August 1974, Nixon resigned as president, and massive reductions in U.S. military aid to South Vietnam destroyed the ARVN's ability to continue fighting against the North. Gentlemen, it is not an exaggeration to say that when Congress finished gutting military aid, any PAVN offensive was going to be successful, and it has been. Communist Vietnam is now in the process of overrunning the country."

Jake took advantage of the colonel's pause and a drink of water to ask a question. "Sir, I didn't realize that the Paris Peace Accord allowed the North to maintain units in the

South while we essentially disarm and withdraw. That's a pretty sloppy negotiation. How did that happen?"

"Good question, Lieutenant," Strong said. "It certainly eliminated the possibility of a permanent ceasefire. The Accord was terribly flawed. Civilian governments make peace treaties, not the military. I know that those at the negotiating table were well-advised by the military, but the government people did it their way. That is one of the reasons this war is lost. But there are other contributing reasons. One is that the United States government outright broke its promise to take military action should the North violate the Peace Accord. Another is that the U.S. Congress simply abandoned South Vietnam in terms of military aid. We destroyed their ability to fight the war without our presence. And there are other reasons, too. People will be analyzing this defeat and pointing fingers for decades.

Jake could see the disappointment on Colonel Strong's face. A good part of his military career was directly connected to the Vietnam War. A defeat in Vietnam felt like a personal defeat, a feeling that all that he had done was meaningless.

Strong took a folded piece of paper from his pocket. "One final thing. I was at a meeting last week, and we were given a list of captured U.S. assets with a value of more than five billion dollars." He slowly unfolded the paper. "Communist North Vietnam has now captured five hundred tanks, thirteen hundred artillery pieces, forty-two trucks, twelve thousand mortars, a couple of million infantry weapons, which includes nearly eight hundred thousand M16 rifles, sixty-three thousand M72 LAWs, forty-seven thousand M79 grenade launchers, forty-eight thousand radios, one hundred and thirty thousand tons of ammunition, nine hundred ships, and eight hundred and seventy-seven aircraft and helicopters. So, I suggest that you never let anyone tell you that we didn't suffer a defeat."

Strong took another drink of water and a long pause. "Ok. The mission. I don't know why this Major General you are picking up is so important, but it's the job we've been ordered to do. He must be important enough for him to be saved while his troops are crushed in military defeat. Get this mission accomplished. Be safe. And God bless. Upon your return, we will continue preparation for that business in Iran. It looks like we are in a political spiral that will postpone any action for a least a couple of months." Colonel Strong stepped down from the platform, and the room was called to attention as he walked to the back of the room and exited the building.

———

1700 Hours
20 March 1975
New York, New York

AFTER SUCCESSFULLY LAUNDERING twenty million dollars for the Villalobos Cartel, another forty million in cash was now available to do the same. Sukarno was pleased with the ease of completing the securities transactions and earning three million dollars for making it happen. It would only take a couple of months to process the forty million and collect another six million in fees. The financing of Komando Jihad and the possibility of doing the same for others fighting the war against America was at hand.

The funds' placement had come from the cash being run through a number of shell corporations that had a mailing address and an offshore banking relationship. Actual ownership of those corporations belonged to Enrique Villalobos. However, each ownership was obscured by one appearing to own another, along with management companies all in the process of getting the funds through layers of corporations to Sukarno's hedge funds. Once the funds had been invested (appearing to be several hedge fund clients) and then sold, the reverse process began by delivering laundered money back to Enrique Villalobos through those shell corporations. The layering and integration processes made it appear that profits and return of capital had occurred. A thorough audit could cut through the fraud, but there was little risk of that. Sukarno had offices in New York and Hong Kong to utilize multiple securities exchanges. By buying equities long on one exchange and almost simultaneously selling on another exchange, the proceeds flowed back to Villalobos clean, making the huge sums of money available to invest in legitimate enterprises. Stock options worked equally as well, especially if the hedge fund held the underlying security. Sukarno was pleased. Villalobos was pleased.

CHAPTER 21

1600 Hours
15 March 1975
Coast of South Vietnam, NE of Phan Thiet

THE CH-46 SEA Knight and its two AH-1 Sea Cobra escorts cruised over the coast of South Vietnam from the North China Sea, ten miles northeast of Phan Thiet. Round trip to Gia Nghia and back to the USS Hancock was close to three hundred miles, giving all three aircraft adequate fuel margin.

Jake and his team leaned back for the ride, and from all appearances, relaxed. Relaxed perhaps, but Jake knew that each man felt electrified to some degree. It was the NAM. It was In Country. He was the only one on the team that had not had at least one tour. Their memories were not necessarily all bad, but they were life-long memories they might wish could be purged. Nonetheless, they were soldiers, fighting men, and their return to Vietnam was as natural as their call to serve.

When the team landed on the USS Hancock, they were briefed that the ground situation was not quite what it was when they left Fort Bragg. The North Vietnamese offensive was more effective against ARVN troops and moving faster than anyone had expected. In the Central Highlands on 10 March, General Dung had moved against Buon Ma Thuot, fifty miles north of the A-Team's objective at Gia Nghia, with an estimated eighty thousand PAVN troops. The four thousand ARVN troops at Buon Ma Thuot had been easily overrun. The North Vietnamese plan, called Blossoming Lotus, sent troops out like a flower bud, slowly opening its petals to engage South Vietnamese units and prevent them from reinforcing the city. At the same time, the vanguard prepared to drive southeast toward the coast and Saigon.

"Well, there's the pucker factor," Master Sergeant O'Banion had said. "Eighty thousand of them in the neighborhood, and twelve of us."

The Sea Knight Combat Search and Rescue (CSAR) was noisy. Too noisy to carry on a conversation without yelling in the recipient's ear. For the most part, the one hundred fifty-mile ride was in silence, each man to his thoughts or self-distraction from what might lie ahead. Cruising at one hundred miles per hour, well below its top speed of one hundred and sixty miles per hour, the time from the USS Hancock to the Landing Zone (LZ) was ninety minutes at an altitude of twenty-five-hundred feet.

As the Sea Knight approached the LZ, the pilot decided into a wide circling visual approach, looking for any sign of PAVN troops that could indicate a hot LZ. Except for the LZ, the foliage was too dense to tell one way or the other. The only activity spotted was Major General Tran Van Nguyen, his wife, and an ARVN Ranger officer making their way quickly from the wooded area to the LZ. The pilot executed a textbook CSAR low-level approach, a quick stop-flare maneuver to a no-hover landing to expedite the SAR mission.

As the Sea Knight settled into the LZ, the team egressed via two-man combat pairings. Within seconds, the team deployed into their predesignated positions, with weapons ready and each covering a one hundred eighty-degree field of fire. Jake oversaw the mission tactically from within the circle, commanding the perimeter. General Nguyen, his wife, and the general's aide came through the perimeter and hurriedly boarded the Sea Knight.

As Jake was about to give the team the extraction signal, small arms fire erupted from the tree line fifty meters to the Sea Knight's rear. Jake gave a hurry-up arm signal, a pump, and the team exfiltrated toward the helicopter via their combat pairings. One group laid down covering fire as their teammates retreated. Then the retreating group turned and provided covering fire for the first group to retreat, resulting in continual fire on the enemy. Jake continued to return fire as the last of the team boarded. Then, the circumstances took a turn for the worse.

The two Cobra gunships engaged the enemy with their 7.62mm miniguns in short strafing runs, but Jake realized that the attacking unit before them was at least company size of one hundred fifty men. Just as the Cobras completed strafing the NAVN infantry, killing a dozen, twice as many emerged from the tree line.

VAROOMPH! A mortar shell hit the ground twenty-five meters in front of the Sea Knight. Jake was now the only one on the ground as he continued to fire his M16 with deliberate aim. In a flash of thought, he became aware that most of the small arms fire was directed at the Sea Knight and that the mortars were in the process of adjusting their rounds to take out the helicopter and everyone in it. It was a matter of seconds before the pilot would have to take off and reluctantly leave him on the ground. Jake took a deep breath, exhaled, then waved the SAR helo airborne. As the Sea Knight lifted off and rotated to forward flight, a mortar round exploded in the now-empty LZ. Mere seconds earlier, that mortar round would have burst the Sea Knight into flames, killing all, and still left Jake on the ground alone.

The two Cobras continued their fire missions with minigun-deadly results as Jake scrambled across the open ground to the tree line. There were two viable extraction points. The first was a thousand meters to the southeast, a small clearing, and the second extraction point was a thousand meters south of the first to an abandoned Christian church. Jake knew that the second extraction point held a slight advantage because it was a structure identifiable from the air. With darkness approaching, a CSAR effort was not possible until sunup the next day. Jake squatted under the dense cover of trees and brush to get his bearings with a compass and map for a direct route to the second extraction point. He figured his decision would save about five hundred meters distance, making the journey to the church a little less than a mile. The objective now was to hustle through tough terrain before dark and gain his lead on the NAVN troops in pursuit.

While fifteen hundred meters is only nine-tenths of a mile, Jake found it difficult to move as fast as he would like. The brush tore his fatigues and cut deep scratches on his face down to the top of his boots, yet he felt sure that the pace would gain steps on the NAVN, perhaps enough for him to find a place not to be captured while he waited for dawn, and hopefully, a CSAR helicopter.

Finally, after an hour and several stops to maintain his

bearing, Jake came to a sizeable opening in the canopy of trees and the abandoned church. The sun was setting. Squatting well within the tree line, he surveyed the environment to surmise his options to make it through the night without capture. The church was not a viable option because the NAVN would surely search it on arrival. Climb one of the trees, perhaps? Or would hiding in the underbrush provide enough cover? "What if they have dogs?" Jake mumbled to himself. "If dogs, they will find me for sure if I'm on the ground. Okay. It's a tree."

Jake moved to his left, looking for a tree that he could climb, had dense foliage to provide him cover, and had a line of sight to the church. The NAVN troops following him were seasoned soldiers. He knew it was going to take more than an ounce of blessing not to be detected. Jake loosened the sling on his M16 and slung it across his chest, then shinnied up a tamarind tree with branches as low as ten feet and an abundance of leaves above. He moved around until he could not see the ground but had eyes on the church. While not a laughing matter, Jake grinned at the realization that he was thinking like an ostrich with his head in the sand.

No sooner had he settled into the branches that would conceal him than he heard voices in the distance. Jake whispered to himself, "They're here. The Lord is my shepherd; I shall not want."

First were slight noises of the soldiers moving slowly through the jungle. The snap of a dead branch, here and there, under the weight of men cautiously moving forward as though they were on the hunt for a dangerous animal. Then there were muffled voices, likely in a discussion about approaching the church. Jake instinctively held his breath when two NAVN soldiers stopped at the base of his tree and went to a knee. Their talk was barely audible. Jake could not see them through the foliage, but he could smell their cigarettes within a minute. Of all places in the vast jungle for these two to take a cigarette break, they had managed to pick Jake's tree.

It wasn't long before the two tree-squatters moved on toward the church, leaving Jake relieved. An hour passed, hearing faint conversations, then there was silence but for the night noises of the jungle, critters for the most part unfamiliar to Jake. He was convinced that the unit had given up on finding him. Recalling the briefing, Jake thought this company-sized unit was primarily running reconnaissance on the army's right flank marching toward Saigon. Still, the smart thing to do was to squelch all desire to do so much as twitch. Remaining motionless for hours was difficult, but it became impossible when a snake, four inches in diameter, crawled over his boot.

A dim light hinted at a new day. Jake slowly left the tree and cautiously watched the church for movement. There was none. In a crouched position, he slowly made his way to the stone-walled church. Nothing. The NAVN troops were gone. A stairway to the belfry and roof was still intact, and Jake took them, testing each step for integrity. As he reached the top of the stairs, dawn was displaying the beauty of the Central Highlands of Vietnam, and Jake thought it a perfect place to vacation, but for the eighty-thousand soldiers wanting to kill him.

As Jake stepped out to the low-pitched roof, he could hear the distinctive sounds of a helicopter in the distance. He waited until he had a visual, then set off an M18 yellow smoke grenade. The two Cobra gunships escorted a UH-1 Huey. A few minutes passed while the CSAR crew authenticated the smoke color with the USS Hancock, then it turned toward the church. The Sea Cobras covered ground quickly and set up a fire support mission on the church to ensure no surprises for the extraction.

As the Huey hovered out of ground effect above the church, the crew chief lowered the rescue cable with the SAR horse collar. Jake stood when the collar was within reaching distance, slid his arms through the middle, and signaled "thumbs up" to the crew chief for pickup.

Master Sergeant O'Banion was allowed to accompany the crew and was grinning as they hauled Jake into the Huey. "You look like hell, sir," O'Banion said, referring to Jake's torn fatigues and bloody scratches. "Are you wounded?"

Jake smiled. "No. But playing tag in the jungle beat me up pretty good."

O'Banion smiled back. "Well, welcome to the Green Berets, sir."

———

1400 Hours
15 March 1975
The Pentagon
Washington, D.C.

Admiral Hollifield walked ahead of General Carpenter into the conference room adjacent to his office with a full cup of black coffee. Admiral Limmerick and John Hanraty were already seated at the table. He could tell by their expressions that some sort of news had broken. But, whether it was good news or bad, he could not tell.

"Good morning, gentlemen. I understand we have some furtherance of business on Operation Heartbeat." The admiral sat at the long oval table's head and sipped the steaming coffee before setting it gently on a coaster. "Let's have it."

Limmerick cleared his throat. "Admiral, we received a message from the Secretary of State a few minutes ago. He's back in the air, headed home from Tehran. He's requested another committee meeting for 0800 hours, the day after tomorrow."

Hollifield thought audibly. "If George Shire is calling a meeting with such little notice given, he must have stumbled into a rat's nest in Iran. Not like him to rush anything."

"The only other part of the message was to stand down for Heartbeat."

Hollifield took another sip of coffee. "The Shah must have told him what we thought he would. He's not going to do it with his people, but he'll give us the unofficial blessing to go in and do it ourselves."

Carpenter rubbed his chin roughly. "Too easy. Shire wouldn't want a quick meeting if that's all there is to the Shah's approval. There's a catch somewhere, Admiral. I can smell it."

"John, what do you have?" the admiral asked.

"Admiral, about the only thing that has happened in Jask is an intensification of demonstrations against the Shah. The local mullah has the population all fired up. They have rallies daily. A lot of chanting, carrying signs demanding the removal of the Shah, and anti-American stuff. No violence yet, but who knows? Perhaps more important is a confirmation that Sukarno Bangjar is the money behind Komando Jihad, and the Drug Enforcement Agency (DEA) suspects his connection with a Columbian drug cartel. Without digging into his finances in detail, we don't exactly have solid proof, but he has been in and out of Jask in the past two weeks. So, circumstantially, we know he is our man."

Limmerick leaned back in his chair and unbuttoned the tailored blue jacket that had become snug over the past few months. He could care less, but if there was ever a senior officer in the U.S Navy who needed to take the time to exercise, it was Rear Admiral Kirk Limmerick. "Sir, this mullah, Du'ad, and his connection with Komando Jihad, has created more of an event over there than any of us initially imagined. Those people are ripe for rebellion. No one would've predicted that the synergy for the overthrow of the government would emanate from a place as obscure as Jask. But if left unchecked, that's what may happen. Could be that what Shire is going to tell us is that the Shah wants us to do more than just rescue Reiner."

"You mean the Shah wants us to somehow put this rebellion out of his misery without him being directly involved?" the admiral asked.

"Just speculation, sir," Limmerick replied. "That's interesting news about the source of financing. I wish we had reliable forensic information. It might not bode well to take action and then find out Bangjar showing up in Jask was only a coincidence."

Hollifield again sipped his coffee then pulled a fresh cigar from his breast pock. Limmerick's speculation was unsettling. "Nothing is simple anymore. If you're right, the Shah is holding a gun to our head and demanding that we be his mercenaries. It means he wants us to go in there and clean up his mess so we'll look like international aggressors, as if they don't already, while he sits back looking surprised and offended."

General Carpenter leaned forward. "To complicate that

scenario even further, Admiral, if Kirk is right, we have a significant delay on our hands. Operation Heartbeat is ready to go. Now. If this thing turns into a major political debate, we're going to lose precious time. Not only is Dr. Reiner a concern, but we'd have to make serious modifications to the plan. We can't leave the A-Team on hold indefinitely."

Hollifield felt discouraged. The situation had made a complicated and complex mission more so. "Well, we'll see what George Shire says. Then we will know the facts. Regarding Sukarno Bangjar, Kirk, contact the DEA and the Securities and Exchange Commission (SEC) to see what they come up with."

0830 Hours
17 March 1975
Pentagon Briefing Room
Washington, D. C.

SECRETARY OF STATE George Shire entered the room, visibly rushed, and hurried to his customary seat of power at the table. "Sorry I'm late, gentlemen. Thought I never would get off the phone this morning."

"No problem, George. It's your meeting. We couldn't very well proceed without you." Leonard Jarvis chuckled at his attempt at humor while the others merely reacted with a polite smile.

Jack Cushman tapped his first cigar of the day in the marble ashtray and cleared his throat. "Let's get right to it. George, we anxiously await the news of your visit to Iran."

"Well, I visited briefly with the president this morning on

the matter, and finally, Jack, he sees the urgency in the matter. He, in his special way, of course, sends his apology for not reacting sooner."

General Cushman nodded his acceptance of the apology.

"Gentlemen, the long and short of it is that the Shah of Iran won't lift a finger to free Dr. Reiner other than to turn his back while we slip a military unit into the country to do it ourselves. Yes, we have his permission, but he made it perfectly clear that publicly he'll deny it."

Robert Walls, the Assistant Attorney General, turned red. "What? George, that borders on not having governmental sanction at all, at least where international law is concerned. What good is his permission if he turns around and tells the world that we went in illegally?"

"I agree," Leonard Jarvis said without expression. "Perhaps we are back to the alternative solution that no one wants to face. If so, the Company can do it. We already have operatives on the ground there. It would be easy to send in a marksman."

Shire leaned forward in his chair. "Forget it, Leonard. The president and I discussed it this morning. It's not an alternative. Not under this administration."

The Secretary of the Army bumped the eraser of a pencil against his glass of water, making an audible clinking sound. "So, what do you recommend? Do we initiate Operation Heartbeat?"

Shire glanced at Jack Cushman with reservation, then to Drew Calvert. "Yes. But this committee and the president have to be aware that this incident could get very nasty. I did not get a clear answer from the Shah on what he intends to do about the political unrest in Jask. He has a major problem there. If that situation is allowed to continue, Komando Jihad might very well succeed in spreading a full-scale revolution.

The Shah said that once we rescue Reiner and remove Komando Jihad's hope for a chemical weapon, the secret police, the SAVAK, could quietly handle the political situation. But you know, the thought occurred to me on the flight home that we might be getting set up by the Shah."

"What do you mean?" Jack Cushman pressed.

"Well, Jack, suppose we send a team to get Reiner, and the SAVAK coordinates an attack against Komando Jihad at the same time or shortly thereafter. The Shah could send in his troops and kill everyone in Jask if he wanted to, and guess who would be the primary candidate to take the blame."

"My God," Cushman said as he bolted upright in his chair.

"I'm not saying that's what the Shah is planning, but that's precisely the point. He didn't, or wouldn't, give me a clear indication of how he intended to handle Komando Jihad and this Muslim leader, Du'ad. What he did do was remain closed-lipped about it. If that scenario is correct, our mission to rescue Reiner, even if successful, would be an outright disaster. Iran. The United Nations. The Soviets. All would have a field day. Not to mention that every Arab nation in the Middle East would violently protest. We not only have political and strategic interests at stake but major financial considerations as well. We have major investments there, both for petroleum import and the sale of military hardware. At least two major industries could be severely damaged."

Leonard Jarvis's interest was piqued. As far as he was concerned, the scenario smacked of truth. It was the sort of thing his agency would devise if they were working for the Iranian government. Make America the scapegoat. Let them have their little military operation, slide behind them with troops to completely obliterate the political opposition, then rush to the people's side with self-righteous indignation at

America's audacity and international misuse of military power. If he were the Shah, that's how he would handle the problem. It would be a safe bet that America would eventually forgive him. They would have to because of the region's financial interests, and he would be in the catbird's seat to graciously calm the other Muslim countries. He would have what he wanted. He would have the annihilation of his internal enemies with someone else paying the image cost.

The room was silent as each committee member reflected on the multitude of repercussions that could befall the United States if the Shah betrayed it for his gain.

"I know the president has already eliminated the alternative, but I see no other way," Jarvis said. Moral or immoral. Legal or not, the risks and potential consequences to the nation far outweigh one man's life. So, unless you gentlemen can dish up a way to guarantee that George's scenario isn't possible, I'm afraid I'll have to go on record as recommending that we send in a sniper to eliminate the national threat.

Again, the room was silent. Most had adamantly voiced opinions against such action, but a better or safer plan escaped them. The Shah blaming the United States for his dirty work seemed far less acceptable than Jarvis's suggestion. Each man felt heavily burdened with responsibility. They were where they were to serve the best interest and well-being of the United States. That was undeniable. But, none of them had anticipated that their careers would lead them personally to a decision to commit murder. Or was it murder? Maybe it was just duty. Duty to protect the country, its people, and in light of the destructiveness of chemical weapons, perhaps thousands of people in Iran or other parts of the world. Was the life of one man at the cost of moral standards a fair exchange for the well-being of countless others?

CHAPTER 22

1700 Hours
29 March 1975
North Point Mall
Dallas, Texas

NORTH POINT MALL was built in 1965 and was one of the world's largest indoor, climate-controlled retail malls. It regularly served as many as ten thousand customers a day. Texans and tourists came to shop, socialize, or to relax in a busy, festive atmosphere. It was a Saturday when the mall was most active.

Eight Komando Jihad volunteers entered the mall through different entrances, each carrying a large duffel bag with a large-hole mesh top containing two two-gallon canisters of Sarin nerve gas with aerosol release valves on a timer. The sixteen canisters were set to release lethal aerosol simultaneously at 1730 hours. Shoppers thought nothing of a duffel bag set in a rest area or storefront, with no apparent owner nearby because someone wishing them harm was the farthest thing from their minds. The terrorists set the bags as instructed, paused for two minutes, then walked away to exit the mall.

Sarin nerve gas dispersed by aerosol has an instant effect, and the ventilation system would carry the agent throughout the mall in a matter of minutes. A human's nervous system is generally in chemical balance, and the body functions normally. However, nerve agents disrupt the body's normal electrochemical processes. A build-up of the neurotransmitter acetylcholine causes an over-stimulation of the nervous system, making muscles and glands work overtime. Depending on the degree of exposure, an individual would experience blurred vision, difficulty in breathing, gastrointestinal distress, paralysis of the skeletal muscles, seizures, loss of consciousness, and finally, death. While those exposed to a light dose of Sarin can be treated with antidotes like atropine, an attack such as this allows no preparation. There are not any first responders standing by to save lives. Knowing what has happened comes much later when the aerosol droplets have prescribed death and panic.

William Teasdale, his wife Marianne, and their two children, Bradley, age six, and Mamie, age four, were a typical family enjoying the mall's busy activity before attending the movie theater to watch "Escape to Witch Mountain." The family was peering into KB Toys' storefront when the aerosol released from one of the duffel bags a dozen yards from where they stood. In seconds, all four were acutely aware that they were having difficulty breathing, and less than half-minute later, they were on the floor suffering violent involuntary contractions of their muscles, producing contortions of their bodies. Helplessly, William and Marianne watched in horror as their two beloved children suffered then died before they, too, passed into unconsciousness and death.

While the Sarin degraded as the droplets passed through cleaner air, the number of deaths and permanently disabled were significant. Worse, the attack was magnified by chaos and panic. Within minutes, everyone in the mall knew that something was terribly wrong as people fell to the floor, convulsing. People suddenly jammed the exits by simultaneously trying to get out of the mall. Those who were sick and worsening fell, blocking the exits until hardly any movement was possible through the doors. People were sick. People were trampled to death. Panic had made the attack a victory for Komando Jihad.

First responders were at a loss, fighting against an unknown enemy and ill-prepared with knowledge and equipment. Several managed to enter the mall only to find themselves overcome by the Sarin and join the ranks of the dead. Five hours elapsed before the gas had degraded, first responders had been appropriately equipped, triage had been established in the parking lots, and the carnage could be approached in an organized manner. Beyond the mall was a city, a nation, fearful of another attack.

0830 Hours
30 March 1975
The Oval Office
Washington, D.C.

THE PRESIDENT LISTENED ATTENTIVELY as General Cushman and Secretary of State George Shire outlined the situation in Dallas and how they thought it related to Dr. Harold Reiner in Jask, Iran, with the Komando Jihad. He winced almost imperceptibly when the CIA's preferred action was given its fair presentation of pros and cons but said nothing. Jack Cushman appreciated the president's total concentration on the options and his willingness to withhold his questions until each had been presented. George Shire appreciated the president's complete attention as well. However, he also knew that his brief meeting with him two days earlier had frightened him. Shire was an old friend, and formalities were never on the agenda. Within minutes, the president's ulcer was burning. He was a career politician. Congress and all its ambiguities were familiar ground, whereas being the president was an accident, a stroke of fate, or bad luck for his predecessor.

The image of hundreds of people dying horrible deaths at the North Point Mall in Dallas from nerve gas created by Harold Reiner got the reaction George Shire expected from the president. He sat wide-eyed, gripping the arms of his chair as he mourned the deaths and the political impact. Shire did not stop with the single, simple image of the terrorist attack in Dallas. He created another with the image of the Shah of Iran marching into Jask with the SAVAK behind our military rescue mission, murdering everyone in the town, then blaming it on the United States. The president felt trapped and doomed to political ruination.

"Sir," Cushman said. "Seven hundred four Americans died in Dallas. And that many more are permanently injured. Three things are clear, sir. The first is that Komando Jihad essentially declared war on the United States. It was a terrorist act against the American people on American soil. This act cannot go unanswered. The public is outraged, as they should be. The American people will demand action. Secondly, let's not kid ourselves. We knew months before this attack in Dallas that Komando Jihad wanted Reiner for his nerve gas expertise. It was obvious what they wanted from him. We, and I mean our slow, awkward way of dealing with his kidnapping, created the situation and the attack. We can't blame Reiner. Anyone can be broken, and he was. The blame is on us."

"And the third thing?" the president asked.

"Sterling and Brookshire Holdings Company," Cushman said. "We asked the Securities and Exchange Commission (SEC) and the Drug Enforcement Agency (DEA) to look into its dealings. When the surface layers of shell corporations are peeled back, an Indonesian named Sukarno Bangjar is the real owner. Bangjar is laundering large sums of money through securities trades between the New York Stock Exchange and the HKEX, the Hong Kong securities exchange. We know a couple of things. The DEA has seen this before. They are confident that the funds laundered are from one of the South American drug cartels, and we know that Sukarno Bangjar is financing Komando Jihad operations. At a minimum, sir, we need the SEC to freeze Sterling and Brookshire's assets and have the authorities in Hong Kong do the same."

George Shire leaned forward, took his cup from the coffee table, and took a sip. The pause gave time for Cushman's assessment of blame to resonate with the president. "Sir, the suggestion made by the CIA is no longer a consideration. Komando Jihad has the nerve agent. It is too late for the CIA option, even though it never was seriously considered."

"That's true," the president said. "Inconceivable."

"The circumstances now dictate that we immediately execute Operation Heartbeat to rescue Reiner and that we modify the mission as a response to the attack in Dallas. It is better to have an immediate military response than to let it fester with the public. The American people will have an overwhelmingly positive reaction to a quick military reply to Komando Jihad."

"Just as important, sir, is the absolute necessity to keep them from attacking again. We must put them out of business. Now." Cushman said.

"That's it, Mr. President," Shire said. "The committee agrees unanimously. We recommend Operation Heartbeat's implementation immediately to rescue Dr. Reiner and sanction any key leaders of Komando Jihad found in the raid. That also includes cutting off their financing. If we later identify leaders not present, additional operations may be advisable. If approved today, sir, we anticipate the raid to take place at 0300 hours, Greenwich Mean Time, on 5 April. That will be 2200 hours here on 4 April and 0700 hours on 5 April in Jask."

"So, it's a daylight raid?" the president asked.

"Yes, sir. Based on our intelligence reports, activity, and traffic around the building, that time of the morning would not be unusual. It's a slight advantage, but seconds count when you consider that the team will only be in the building for less than three minutes. Surprise and speed are critical to success. If we can get Reiner out and moved toward the point of extraction in under three minutes, then we aren't giving Komando Jihad much time to react."

The president looked at both Cushman and Shire with trusting eyes. "And you're sure this is our best option?"

Shire leaned forward and lowered his voice to emphasize his sincerity. "Yes, sir. It's not perfect, and there are risks. But Mr. President, we feel that this is our best chance to rescue Reiner, respond to the attack in Dallas, and eliminate the threat of more attacks with Sarin gas. Also, it's the option that offers the most flexibility should everything not go according to plan. Whether the rescue mission succeeds or fails, you will be in a position to react to the political aspects honorably."

A full minute passed in silence as the president thought.

He slowly drummed his index finger on his thigh. "Bad timing. The situation in Vietnam is deteriorating rapidly with this North Vietnamese offensive toward Saigon. We will be lucky to get everyone out of our embassy. I can hardly sleep at night, knowing that there are thousands of loyal South Vietnamese and ARVN troops that have no way to escape their doom. I'm afraid it will be a blood bath. It truly is a disgrace how we fought a war for fourteen years and leave with our tail between our legs in defeat. But this situation in Jask is what it is. Very well. Let's do it."

1600 Hours
2 April 1975
Bogota, Columbia

Enrique Villalobos threw the crystal water decanter as hard as he could, shattering it against the stone fireplace mantel. The three subordinates of the Villalobos Cartel stood without word or movement, knowing from experience that the boss's rage was likely to cause the death of several, whether they had any responsibility for the object of Enrique's wrath or not. People were going to pay, and those closest to him prayed that the payment did not include them.

"Forty million dollars of my money. Gone," Villalobos screamed. "I want Sukarno Bangjar standing right there," he said, pointing to the front of his desk. "He is a dead man. But first, I want him to wish he had never been born."

Enrique's most trusted advisor, Luis Munoz, quickly decided that it was better to say something than to remain silent. "He has left New York, Enrique. We know that he flew out yesterday, but we don't know where he is yet. We will find him."

"You better find him," Enrique yelled. "Don't you dare fail me on this, Luis."

1800 Hours
4 April 1975
USS Independence
The Arabian Sea

THE AIRCRAFT CARRIER USS Independence cruised the waters to which it and its contingent fleet support had been assigned for the past sixty days. Only twice had they passed through the Strait of Hormuz into the Persian Gulf, and only then for a slow cruise toward the northernmost tip of Qatar, approximately the midpoint of the Gulf waters. It was a typical cruise, the intent of which was merely to show the presence of the American Navy in the region. All governments concerned, including the Soviet Union, who monitored the American presence with their like-sized navy, were accustomed to the visible show of force. Scrambled fighter aircraft from the Independence deck, evasive maneuvers, and submarine hunting were common, everyday events. So accustomed were the Arabian Sea and the Persian Gulf to maneuvers, the presence was almost contradictory regarding its purpose. Their presence was commonplace. It was normal.

The Special Forces team, with its supporting Huey Cobra crews, had been flown courtesy of the U.S. Navy to the deck of the USS Independence as it pushed northward in the Arabian Sea. Security, even among the Independence's crew, was tight.

There was much scuttlebutt as to why they had taken on a load of Army Green Beret pukes. However, for the most part, they were glad that something was happening to break the monotony of only driving up and down the coastline of Arab nations they would never set foot on and playing footsie with the Soviet navy. Maybe, just maybe, they were going to get to kick some butt like they had trained to do, or at least get to watch some good guys, even if they were the Army, kick butt. The scuttlebutt's intensity increased on the second day, much to the delight of Admiral Davies' —the fleet's commanding officer—as it visibly had a positive impact on morale when an A-6 Intruder squadron was officially attached to the mission. The aviators were briefed for hours, and aircraft crews were given specific orders on ordnance to load. Rumors spread geometrically through the decks that the A-6 squadron would kill some bad guys in support of the Army pukes with the goofy green hats. Morale on board was the highest in two months as the Independence continued its course northward.

Jake and the team were comfortably quartered and had been provided a small briefing room twice daily to rehearse the operation via a tabletop model of Jask. The men knew every inch of the area, or at least what the intelligence branches had known to tell them. Each knew their assignments like the back of their hand. A Navy Seal team participated in the briefings and provided operational expertise on executing an over-the-horizon amphibious raid from the sea. From the Pentagon to the USS Independence, everyone was aware that Brigadier General Carpenter's work on developing doctrine and operational techniques for a joint-service Special Forces Group was critical for dealing with future situations like kidnappings and responses to terrorism. The timing for the raid to rescue Dr. Reiner was horrible. The time it had taken to make a decision in Washington was wildly unreasonable. Training for this type of operation should have been commonplace rather than unique, and once the orders were given for the execution of the mission, it should have taken place within hours, not days.

In the coming early morning hours, they would depart the USS Independence in two Combat Rubber Raiding Crafts, the Zodiac F470, with a single fifty-five horsepower outboard motor, each carrying six members of the team and a coxswain.

0900 Hours (1800 Hours)
4 April 1975
The Pentagon
Washington, D.C.

Vice Admiral Limmerick and John Hanraty entered Admiral Hollifield's office with tension visible on their faces. "Sir, we have disturbing intelligence from Jask."

Hollifield leaned back in his chair, picked up a pencil, and immediately started thumping the eraser on his desk. "I'm afraid to ask," he said.

"We are no longer confident about Dr. Reiner's status in Jask. His routine of showing up on the rooftop for an hour every day is no longer the case. He hasn't been on the roof for several days." Limmerick paused, waiting for Admiral Hollifield's response.

"Could be several things," Hollifield said, more as a thought than a statement. "Most of them not good. Well, we could speculate all day. Contact the team through Colonel Strong. The lack of intel on Reiner's status does not alter the mission from my desk."

"Yes, sir," Hanraty said. "One other thing, sir. The count was eighteen in and twenty-two out yesterday."

Hollifield frowned and shook his head. Their eyes on the ground in Jask had noticed that the count of Komando Jihad soldiers entering and leaving the building did not match on a day-to-day basis. Once they noticed, the count became a factor that could mean the difference between success or failure of the mission—and casualties. The training for Operation Heartbeat was based on six to ten soldiers inside, but now, there was no way to gauge opposition inside the building. Operation Heartbeat was now a blind mission in terms of combatants.

"The front door is all we can monitor, sir," Limmerick said. Traffic in and out of the adjacent building tells us nothing other than it is an operations area and barracks. It makes a difference if the buildings are connected."

Admiral Hollifield crushed his already cold cigar butt in the ashtray. "Contact Colonel Strong. I don't suppose there has been any communication from the team commander on these changes, has there?" It was impossible for Admiral Hollifield no to think of Jake under these circumstances.

"Yes, sir," Limmerick said. "I talked to Colonel Strong early this morning. He said that he asked Lieutenant Jacobs if he needed to modify the mission. Jacob's only response was that they might need a little more ammo.

2200 Hours
4 April 1975
USS Independence
Gulf of Oman

Patrick climbed the steel ladder to the upper deck railing, hoping to find Jake. He had checked his quarters to see an empty room and immediately knew that Jake had taken a walk to an inactive platform overlooking the long deck of the carrier. The breeze forced by the Independence's determined push northward and a black sky dotted with brilliant stars was a calming peace against foreboding danger. Jake stood against the railing, Patrick knew, with thoughts so private that even he, his best friend, refused to tread there.

As Patrick's head appeared above the platform's level, Jake's silhouette against the night sky was visible. Though it was impossible to ascend the steel stairs noiselessly, Jake had not turned to see who was disturbing his peace. Patrick joined him at the rail in silence.

"Glad you tracked me down," Jake said after a minute had passed.

"I've never been one for quiet time. You know that," Patrick replied. "But it is nice out here."

Jake shifted his weight from his left foot to his right. "Well, it won't be quiet in another five hours."

"No. Suppose not."

Without changing his gaze to the black horizon, Jake said, "If you hear me call to abort the mission on the radio, you do it. No heroics. I don't want you doing something dumb. Just do your job, then get back to this boat."

"It ain't a boat. It's an aircraft carrier. A ship. Everything is going to work out fine, Jake."

"Sure, I know, Jake said. "I was just thinking about my brother, Charlie, and Steve, too. One minute they're by your side, best of the best, and the next minute they're gone. Nothing left but old photographs and memories."

Patrick said nothing.

Jake turned toward Patrick. "By the way, do you remember Emily Parks? She went back to Duke medical school, looked up our old roommate, Wayne Barnes, and now they are getting married."

Patrick laughed. "Wayne Barnes. Smartest guy I know. And he is going to marry a wild mustang like Emily. Good for him."

CHAPTER 23

1800 Hours
4 April 1975
Bashagird Range, Iran

IMPERIAL GUARD COLONEL Hasan Khatami brought the armored column to a halt in a narrow valley in the Bashagird Range, thirty miles due north of Jask. His battalion-sized unit, supported by infantry transported on trucks, was relatively concealed. The movement had not gone unnoticed, but that was not critical to his mission. The local population had seen the Shah's army maneuver throughout Iran's desert and mountain regions many times.

Colonel Khatami gave orders to have the men bivouac for the night and post sentries. His battalion would roll through the pass at 0500 hours toward Jask. He was not to enter the city earlier than 0730. His mission order was to execute all Komando Jihad personnel, the Mullah Du'ad, and as many adult civilians as was practical within one hour, then withdraw quickly to concealment in the Bashagird

Range. Khatami had no reservations concerning his orders. Destroying one of their cities with a population of a few thousand was not a pleasant task but a necessary one. The mullahs wanted to return the country to strict Muslim rule, an absurd concept of turning the clock back on progress a thousand years. Allowing Komando Jihad to organize in Jask was a mistake. Though they had an agenda outside Iran, they were a bad influence on the people's revolutionary mindset. The Shah had to destroy the growing political movement in Jask. Otherwise, chaos and murder would destroy the country. The Americans? They would eventually see the wisdom of blaming this operation on them to sustain the Shah and his government. It was in everyone's best interest.

0100 Hours
5 April 1975
USS Independence

The USS Independence slowed as it approached the line of departure, and Jake stood by the other team members that would load into the two Zodiacs. Conditions for the twenty-mile, over-the-horizon transport to shore were near perfect. The sea state and Beaufort Force, or condition of the free surface with respect to wind waves and swell, was at level one. The wind was one to three knots, scaly ripples with swells less than a half meter. The team loaded water-tight equipment bags, and weapons were clean and ready for action.

"Well, Patrick," Jake said. "This is it. Shoot straight and hit 'em hard when you see our vans come hauling out of Jask. I suspect those guys will be pretty mad when they find out we robbed the candy store."

"You bet. We'll nail them if they come chasing after you. You take care of yourself, Jake."

Jake smiled. "Providence, buddy. We do our jobs, and Providence takes over."

"Humph. You sound like Stonewall Jackson."

A chief petty officer motioned to Jake that he was ready to load the Zodiacs. Jake tightened his beret on his head, smiled again at Patrick as he slapped him on the back, then moved quickly toward the Zodiacs without another word. Patrick gritted his teeth as he watched Jake walk away and climb into his ride to the shore of Iran. As the ship's crew lowered the Zodiacs to the dark water below, Patrick muttered the last line of the Alma Mater. "Live, serve, and die, we pray. West Point, for thee."

1600 Hours (0100 Hours Jask, Iran)
Durango, Colorado

SARA WET the tip of her finger with her tongue and quickly touched the hot iron to hear the expected hiss before pulling a wrinkled blouse off the back of a chair and spreading it on the ironing board. Steven Patrick was in his room playing while she did her chores to get ready for tomorrow's work at the dentist's office and his morning at the daycare center. Across the room, the noise of the television kept her company as she ironed.

The afternoon was as routine as the afternoon before and the afternoon before that. Sara had told Sam Gale that she did not want to go out with him anymore. Though he had persisted in convincing her otherwise for a week, he was now dating a cocktail waitress at the Diamond Belle Saloon and was quite happy drinking beer until two in the morning while he waited for his new girl to get off work. Sara was happy about his new distraction, too. The only anxiety she felt about Sam was the awkwardness of occasionally seeing him in town.

True to her commitment, Sara dialed Jake's number at the BOQ at Fort Bragg every night before she went to sleep. Some nights the try was easy. Other nights, dialing those numbers was as frightening to her as any risk she might ever take. And, nightly, as the phone rang with no answer, she felt both disappointment and relief.

Sara pressed the iron along the back of the blouse while, from the television, a CBS anchorman discussed the latest news from the terrorist attack at North Point Mall in Dallas. The anchorman switched to a clip of a United States senator calling for the president to take military action against those terrorists involved in the murder of hundreds of American citizens.

"Stephen Patrick? Do you have your toys picked up yet?" Sara said, loud enough for him to hear her in his bedroom.

Sara set the iron upright and shifted the blouse, exposing another wrinkled surface as the senator continued to make his argument that an attack on American soil demanded immediate military action. "Did you hear me, young man? Do you have those toys picked up?"

No sound from Stephen Patrick was audible. Sara pressed the iron back and forth on the sleeve of the blouse a half-dozen strokes, then set the iron upright again, slightly irritated. As she did, the CBS anchorman said, "There you have it. A military response seems to be what is expected from the president."

Sara looked up from the ironing board toward Stephen Patrick's room as though she might see through the wall. "For Pete's sake. What is that boy into now?"

0657 Hours
5 April 1975
Jask, Iran

THE NARROW WINDING streets of Jask were quiet. Only a few civilians had begun their daily chores as the three vans placed by the CIA approached the square in the heart of the small town. The A-Team was on target to converge into position exactly as planned.

"Two minutes," Sergeant First Class Terry O'Banion said calmly.

The four men in the back of the van hardly flinched at O'Banion's announcement as they sat firmly planted on the floorboard, weapons at the ready, rounds chambered in silenced pistols. The two minutes slowly ticked by, and the van droned onward at a casual pace. Miguel Gutierrez sat relaxed, unwrapped a stick of gum and savored the first few chews, then silently offered the others a stick.

Sergeant First Class Albert Vincento was the only one to accept. "This have chile powder on it, Miguel?"

"Naw. But when this is over, you come home with me to Santa Fe. My mama, she'll fix you some enchiladas that'll make your eyes water."

The vans slowed as they entered the square and started a

slow counterclockwise drive to the target building at a north, twelve o'clock position. Jake slid closer to the door and placed his right hand on the handle, ready to slide the door open.

"Parrish and Forest have stopped on schedule," O'Banion stated of van number two when it came to a halt at the ten o'clock position, prepared to provide supporting fire. "Coats is here as well. Right on schedule." First Sergeant Leroy Coats, the driver of the third van, had arrived thirty seconds earlier and had parked according to plan next to the window on the right side of the building. O'Banion continued his approach. "Two guards at the door. Otherwise, the area is clear. I see no other resistance."

The van came to a smooth halt at the front door, and Jake tightened his grip on the door handle. The guards were still unaware of the situation. A lack of recognition of the driver had not disturbed their complacency. That complacency was to be their death sentence.

Jake pulled the handle hard to slide the door open as quickly as possible. Brad Washburn's hand bucked, and a silenced round caught the guard on the right in the forehead. Again it recoiled to deliver a hollow-point to the terrorist's chest, and Albert Vincento fired simultaneously over Washburn's shoulder with the same effect to the guard on the left. Washburn and Vincento reached their victims with three long steps while Jake, Gutierrez, and Frasier brushed past them and crashed through the door. As Frasier entered, Vincento and Washburn followed, pulling the dead guards inside and dropping them on alternate sides of the doorway.

Jake's mind did not mentally process what his eyes told him. He reacted from his training. Two Komando Jihad soldiers stood within three feet of him as he came through the door, their eyes wide with surprise. Their slow recognition of the situation gave Jake all the time he needed. Two rounds to the chest of each dropped them. On the stairway in front of him, another terrorist reached to unsling his weapon, screaming that the building was under attack. Frasier unleashed his Winchester M97, twelve-gauge Trench Gun. Jake heard the report of the shotgun, turned toward the room on his right to let Kim and Jaramillo in the window, holstered his Heckler and Koch, and unslung his M97 Trench Gun. Without waiting to watch the outcome, he knew that the terrorist on the stairs was now only recognizable by his Allah.

Jake pressed his back to the wall, and Washburn simultaneously kicked the door with the heel of his boot. The door swung open as Jake entered, stooped low, focusing on the left, and fired at a hostile. Washburn followed. His M16 joined the chorus in quick three-round bursts. Targets seemed to be everywhere. The small room was crowded. Jake stood up and continued to pump and fire the shotgun. Two terrorists down, three, then five. The engagement lasted mere seconds, and the room was cleared. The room had not been occupied by just one or two terrorists as planned. It was a convention of hostiles. Jake could hear the battle behind him and knew that they were fighting combatants coming into the building from the adjacent building. Jake glanced toward the door and felt his heartbeat accelerate at the sight of Washburn lying face down on the floor, a huge bloody exit wound spanning the center of his back. The still-in-trials Kevlar vest he was wearing was only protective from small-caliber handguns and shotgun projectiles, not a 7.62x39mm AK-47 Kalashnikov.

Gutierrez entered the door, low and ready to fire. "Lieutenant?"

"Get the window. We've got to get Kim and Jaramillo in the building," Jake said over the roar of gunfire.

Gutierrez rushed to his side. "No can do, sir. All hell has broken loose. They caught fire from the rear and had to pull out. They're in the square with Parrish and Forest, trying to keep the front clear with supporting fire."

"Ok," Jake said, fully aware that there was no way they would be out of the building in three to five minutes, if at all. "We have to get to the second floor. We are clear here." Jake shoved shells into the trench gun and moved out of the room, through the foyer to the staircase. Frasier and Vincento had stopped the infusion of Komando Jihad soldiers, but a glance told Jake that Frasier, who was still a shooter, was shot up pretty bad. Jake moved up the stairs, focused on the landing above, while Gutierrez backed up the steps to cover their rear and flank.

At the top of the stairway, Jake positioned himself to cover the doorways to two rooms as Gutierrez passed him and cautiously entered the first. "Clear." Then Jake moved forward to the second room as Gutierrez covered the other. The third room was the last down the hall, and they knew it was the only room remaining for Reiner to be held.

Before they reached the door, Rokus Sogiarto threw the door open and opened fire with an AK-47 on full automatic. A dozen spent casings spewed from the rifle's ejection port, and two rounds ripped through Miguel Gutierrez's chest. He was dead before he hit the floor and before Jake pumped two twelve-gauge shells through the trench gun. Sogiarto was launched three feet backward, slamming his lifeless body against the wall. His knees buckled, and his torso slid down the wall to a sitting position.

Jake paused a moment as he unholstered his Heckler & Koch 9mm and simultaneously passed the sling of the trench gun over his head to secure it across his back. He focused on the room in front of him, resisting the urge to look at Guitierrez

Jake entered the room cautiously, immediately seeing a man facing the back wall, hands held high and legs spread apart. Jake was hypervigilant for any movement the man at the wall might make as he probed every detail of the room through the sights of his pistol. It was clear.

"Turn around. Keep your hands up," Jake said in a commanding voice.

The man turned slowly. Jake recognized him immediately from the photos he had seen in the briefings. It was Sukarno Bangjar—his face pained from the shock of the raid.

"What is your name?" Jake aggressively interrogated.

Sukarno's respiration was high, near gasping for air. "Sukarno Bangjar."

"Where is Dr. Reiner?" Jake asked.

Gripped with fear, Sukarno didn't answer.

Jake took an intimidating step forward. "Where is Dr. Reiner? Tell me now."

"He is dead," Sukarno said timidly. Rokus Sogiarto had him executed and buried in the mountains. "I had nothing to do with that."

"You had plenty to do with it, Mr. Bangjar. And over seven hundred Americans died because of you."

"Arrest me," Sukarno said. "I'll go with you and take my chances in the courts."

Jake shook his head as he studied Sukarno's arrogant, expectant expression of a trial and a good lawyer. "I'm not the sheriff, Mr. Bangjar. I'm the United States Army, and I am here to put you out of the Sarin gas business." Jake raised his pistol to Sukarno's face and pulled the trigger. Sukarno sank to the floor, and Jake fired two more 9mm rounds into his chest.

J.M. PATTON

0720 Hours
5 April 1975
Bashagird Range

Colonel Hasan Khatami glanced over his shoulder and was satisfied that his armored column was intact. Now that they were on a hard-surfaced dirt road, they could sprint into Jask. It was twelve miles yet to the city, but it was already too late for any Komando Jihad units to react. They could not stop him now.

Satisfied, Khatami turned around with a smile. He lit a cigarette and was about to tell his aide to pass his command to increase speed when the first U.S. A-6 Intruder, flying at treetop level, became frighteningly visible through the windshield of the staff car. The Intruder did not pull up, and Khatami's driver turned hard to the left, fearing that the huge aircraft screaming above the road toward them would crash into the front of the car. The staff car skidded on the dirt road, slid through the bar ditch, crashed through a stone fence, and came to an abrupt stop. Disheveled and shaken, Colonel Khatami staggered from the car and looked skyward. Another Intruder followed the first and fired an AGM-65 Maverick missile, exploding two hundred yards in front of the column. The colonel threw himself to the ground as the Maverick destroyed the road. Seconds later, two more Intruders, approaching from the rear, roared down both sides of the column. There were no casualties.

The U.S. Navy had accomplished its mission without a single inflicted dent on Iranian military hardware or personnel. Panic struck the Iranian armored column as tanks and trucks attempted to get off the road, and in doing so, scrambled right and left, running into each other. Colonel Khatomi stood, dusted off his crisply pressed uniform, and watched his column in a rout. He was angry. He was embarrassed. The Americans had made their point. There would be no attack on Jask by Iranian forces. Not today.

0722 Hours
5 April 1975
Jask, Iran

JAKE EXITED THE ROOM, squatted down next to Gutierrez, and pulled his lifeless body over his shoulders in a fireman's carry before moving down the stairs. Vincento and Frasier were managing the threat from the adjacent building.

Jake thought quickly, then pulled the handset from the small radio on his back. "Heartbeat-2. This Heartbeat-1. Do you read?" He released the button and waited for a response.

Warrant Officer-4 Doug Snow responded from his Cobra. "Heartbeat-1. This is Heartbeat-2. Go ahead."

"We are exiting the building to the van," Jake said. "Two casualties. I say again. We are exiting the building."

"Roger, Heartbeat-1. Standing by to cover your extraction."

Vincento pulled Washburn's body up for a fireman's carry as Jake threw open the front door. Jake took a deep breath. Then, with Vincento leading, they rushed to the van's side door. Vincento turned around to drop Washburn on the floor, then helped Frasier through the door before taking Gutierrez off Jake's back. As Jake turned to climb into the van, he felt a hard slap on his right leg above the knee. He knew that he had been hit.

O'Banion pushed the accelerator to the floor as Jake slammed the sliding door. Jake peered out the windshield and saw the two cobras using their miniguns to blanket both buildings with a wall of 7.62mm rounds an inch apart.

The van lurched forward but gained yards slowly with both rear tires and the right front shot flat. "We're in deep kimchi, Lieutenant," O'Banion yelled over the pandemonium.

"Try to make it over to Parrish's van," Jake said. "We'll transfer to it."

"Roger, Lieutenant," O'Banion replied. "I'll ..."

Terry O'Banion's sentence abruptly ended as the windshield shattered from the impact of a well-placed round before it struck his lower right cheek, taking his two molars and bone fragments through the exit wound in his lower jaw. A moment passed before he was again working the accelerator and turning the steering wheel from side to side to get the van moving again.

Parrish and Forest moved toward O'Banion's van as Patrick maneuvered his Cobra to hover between the building and the two vans. When positioned, he immediately engaged the M134 7.62x51mm minigun set at four thousand rounds per minute. The hostile fire ceased, and the transfer to Parrish's van took less than a minute.

The moment the van was out of the square, Patrick fired a hundred grenades at the building with the M129 Grenade Launcher, then lifted off and rotated to forward flight to join Doug Snow's Cobra. As the vans exited the city, the Cobras hovered out of ground effect to cover them should any vehicles attempt to follow.

The short two-mile drive to the extraction point gave only

minutes to tend to Frasier's wound, and Jake slapped a bandage on his leg to stop the bleeding. It was a through-and-through wound, and he was thankful the bullet did not break a bone. The initial sensation of no pain had left him, and he was now aware that he had a hole in his leg.

Upon arrival at the point of extraction, Vincente pitched an M18 green smoke grenade out the window. The CH-46 Sea Knight immediately radioed the USS Independence to authenticate the smoke color, and the two Cobras remained prepared to engage any pursuit of the vans. Within two minutes, the Sea Knight was on the ground, and the Combat Search and Rescue crew loaded the A-Team.

Jake noticed that he was trembling as he watched the Sea Knight's crew tend to Frasier's wound. He glanced at his watch. The three-to-five minute, easy raid had turned into a forty-minute nightmare. "I failed miserably," Jake mumbled to himself. "Two of my men are dead, three wounded, and we didn't save Dr. Reiner."

1000 Hours
5 July 1975
USS Independence
Gulf of Oman

"LIEUTENANT JACOBS. I am Commander Ned Parsons, Naval Intelligence. I understand from the doctor that your leg will require some surgery when you get back home, but I hope you've been made comfortable."

"I don't know what they gave me, but I'm pretty relaxed," Jake said.

"You and your team had one heck of a morning, Lieutenant. You will have a more detailed debriefing later, but I need to ask a few questions to satisfy the higher-highers in Washington. They all get their feelings hurt if they don't know what is going on."

Jake sat up and put another pillow behind his back. "I don't mind, sir. Ask away."

"Sukarno Bangjar told you that Dr. Reiner had been executed. Do you have any reservations about that being the truth?"

"No, sir. Mr. Bangjar was very frightened. I was convinced that he was telling the truth. He said that Dr. Reiner was executed and buried somewhere in the mountains. But he didn't know where."

"Ok. Your mission orders were to sanction, or terminate, any Komando Jihad leaders, which would have been Rokus Sogiarto and Sukarno Bangjar. Do you know that those orders were successfully carried out?"

"Yes, sir. The mission in that regard was successful," Jake said in a business-like manner. "Sogiarto came out of the room, firing an AK. He killed Master Sergeant Miguel Gutierrez. I put two 12 gauge triple-ought loads into his center mass. Sogiarto is dead. Sukarno Bangjar was in the room, willing to surrender and be taken back to the United States for due process under the law. I shot him in the head with my 9mm, then two more rounds in the chest. Sukarno Bangjar is dead."

Commander Parsons paused and looked Jake in the eyes. What he saw was a slight hint of tears. "Well, Lieutenant, that couldn't have been easy. But those were your orders, and you did your duty. You probably saved hundreds of American lives by stopping their use of Sarin nerve gas in the future. Bravo Zulu, Lieutenant."

CHAPTER 24

1000 Hours
20 April 1975
Walter Reed Army Medical Center
Washington, D.C.

WITH SURGERY on his leg nearly two weeks behind him, Jake sat in the chair next to the bed, his right leg stiff from the bandages and metal brace. He was tired. Though he was walking respectably well with a cane, he moved at a snail's pace. Every step was painful. The doctors had told him that the difference between a disabling stiff leg for life or a functionally stiff leg would be up to him. The sooner he used it, and the more he used it, would be the determining factors of the end result. A disability for life was not something Jake wanted to accept. The thought worried him. Special Forces and a full career in the Army was his choice, and the idea of having it taken away from him was frightening. No one had said so yet, but Colonel Strong would eventually talk to him about his ability to remain combat-qualified in the Green

Berets. He had a significant investment at stake. He had invested years and sweat and blood to be what he was. And now? He could lose it all or have to prove himself all over again. But until that time came, he was determined to walk, to fight the pain. He would do whatever was necessary to prove that he could recover and be as good as new.

"How about some visitors?" Suzanne Hollifield said, peeking her head through the open door with a smile.

Jake smiled when she, the admiral, and Julia entered with a bouquet of flowers and magazines. He clumsily tried to rise, but the admiral gently pushed him back into the chair, voiding the protocol that an officer and a gentleman rise in the presence of senior officers and women.

"The brass, his beautiful bride, and my best girl. You sure know how to brighten up a guy's day," Jake said.

Mrs. H. and Julia leaned over to kiss him on the cheek, and the admiral shook his hand. "Brass?" the admiral said. "If you're shy around brass, you better stay in the room. Walter Reed has more military heavyweights running around than in the Pentagon. This place gives me the willies. Suzanne, if I get sick, just lay me down in the garage. I'd rather smell motor oil than all this medicine and antiseptic."

"Me, too," Jake agreed. "I'm ready to get out of here. The doctor said I could leave in about two weeks. Physical therapy twice a day. Patrick and Rebecca have been up a couple of times from Fort Bragg. He has a way of motivating me to get back to work."

Suzanne squeezed his hand. "That's wonderful, Jake. Then your leg must be feeling much better. I'm so glad. We've been worried about you.

"It's coming along fine. It'll take me a few months to get it in top shape, but I'll be running and jumping out of airplanes again pretty soon."

Admiral Hollifield frowned, disbelieving Jake's optimism. He had heard otherwise. An hour's visit passed quickly. The admiral sat quietly, enjoying the conversation, while Suzanne and Julia made Jake feel like he was truly back home. Finally, the admiral cleared his throat and asked the ladies if he could have a few minutes alone with Jake. Reluctantly, they said their goodbyes, but not before dragging their exit out for another five minutes.

"Running the women off is pretty serious, sir," Jake said jokingly.

"They do brighten up a room."

Jake laughed. "No doubt about it, sir."

Hollifield walked to Jake's chair and sat on the bed next to it. "Well, our visit today is mostly pleasure, but you know admirals. We seldom get a whole day off."

"Guess you could have been a screw-up, sir, and stayed an ensign."

"Sometimes I wish I had," the admiral said. "General Jack Cushman retired. I guess you knew that already."

"Yes, sir. I heard that. I was surprised. I thought he had a few more years."

Hollifield pulled one of his cigars from his breast pocket, lit it, and found an empty glass to use as an ashtray. "Oh, Jack could have stayed. Damn fine military man. The best, actually. You know, most men returning from Vietnam got to put it behind them, in one way or another, maybe with a different assignment or getting out of the military altogether. But not Jack. He did three tours over there, and when he wasn't in-country, he was here in the states fighting the war with

Congress. The man fought the Vietnam War for fourteen years. Did you know he was against the war?"

"No, sir," Jack replied, somewhat surprised.

"Yes. Jack did everything possible to get Congress to act responsibly. He wanted them to either let the military fight it to a swift conclusion or pull out. Well, we are out now, and North Vietnam will overrun South Vietnam in the next few days. It is a total defeat for the United States."

"Yes, sir. Looks like Korea, only worse."

"Well, anyhow. Jack sure took a stand for you on Operation Heartbeat. It was his last fight with the politicians, and he did a fine job of it. You can thank him someday if you get a chance. He would appreciate that."

Admiral Hollifield thumbed his cigar on the rim of the glass to remove a lengthening ash. "Well, the real reason I needed to have a little chat with you is that in the president's excitement over scoring political points for taking action in response to the Dallas attack, he wanted to award you the Distinguished Service Cross and the Purple Heart, of course."

Jake's eyes could not open any wider, and his jaw dropped. "But. But. I."

Hollifield laughed with the cigar clenched between his teeth. "Close your mouth, Lieutenant. You might catch a fly or something."

"But, sir, I didn't do anything to be awarded the DSC."

"The president thought so. Or, more likely, he thought it would get him more political points," Admiral Hollifield said. "I told him that was a bad idea."

The admiral continued, "Oh, I think you should be awarded a medal, and I'm sure you will be. Maybe another Bronze Star, but the Distinguished Service Cross is not a good thing for you. It's not in your best interest. It would be an albatross around your neck. Senior officers would go through the roof. Other units are already suspicious and resentful of Special Forces. The DSC would make that situation worse, and you would be the one to pay for it."

Jake shook his head in agreement.

"The military is a peculiar community, Jake. Little petty jealousies can be the death of a young officer's career. When one gets a little further along and has some rank, that kind of thing can be handled easier. People don't criticize officers of high rank, but everyone is willing to step on you if you are a junior officer. It makes them mistakenly think more of themselves at your expense."

Jake smiled. "That's true, sir. I was an athlete in high school, and friends criticized me for being good at it. I received an appointment to West Point, and many of my friends simply couldn't be happy for me, so they ran me down. After some confusion about it, I figured out that they were not friends after all."

Hollifield tapped the ash from his cigar into the glass. "Well, Jake. If one is an achiever, he will run into that kind of pettiness their entire life." He looked down for a moment and cleared his throat. "One other thing, Jake. You will have to make some hard decisions about your career at this point. You will make first lieutenant with your class in another month. Your doctor tells me that your leg is a game-changer. I respect you for your attitude. You are an overcomer, but you will not likely see combat again as a Green Beret. Your leg is not going to be one hundred percent, and that would put your combat team in jeopardy."

Jake was suddenly uncomfortable with the conversation. "I am an overcomer, sir. I can get back to one hundred percent."

"Maybe," Admiral Hollifield said. "An outstanding officer,

which you are, always knows his limitations and makes decisions accordingly. My advice is to take this time to get your master's degree and then take a three-year assignment back to West Point as an instructor. That will give you time to make your leg as good as it is ever going to be, and a teaching assignment and masters would be good for your career."

"I'll give it serious consideration, sir," Jake said, appreciative of the logical proposal.

Admiral Hollifield smiled, knowing that his proposal was not what Jake desired but that it would receive a productive examination. "Lieutenant General Parker has invited me to visit West Point for a tour of the post and to say a few words to the Corps of Cadets in the mess hall. I thought you might like to join me."

"I would love to go, sir. I know it sounds crazy, but West Point is home."

1130 Hours
2 May 1975
West Point, New York

Springtime at West Point is beautiful. The mountains are teeming again with multi-colored trees in contrast to winter's stark lack of foliage, and the Hudson River flows unhindered by ice. Jake walked beside Lieutenant General Lloyd S. Parker, still superintendent of the academy, and Admiral Hollifield as they entered the front doors of Washington Hall, the cadet mess hall. A yearling, a second-year cadet, stood his guard duty post at the front door. His gray uniform, white three-inch wide belt with a large brass buckle, and white gloves were all immaculate. Jake smiled, remembering the days he stood guard in the mess hall and unconsciously tugged on the bottom of his dress blue coat to match the cadet's wrinkle-free appearance. Jake walked up to the cadet while General Parker and Admiral Hollifield stood aside, discussing the grandeur of the mess hall. "Where are you from, mister?"

The cadet's expression told Jake that the cadet was pleased that he had the courtesy to speak to him. "Sir, I am from Upper Saddle River, New Jersey." Jake saw the cadet's eyes fall to the few campaign ribbons and Combat Infantry Badge above his left breast pocket. "Welcome back to West Point, sir."

"Thank you," Jake replied. "What is your name?"

"Cadet Marino, sir."

"Have a nice day, Mr. Marino." Jake gave the cadet a friendly smile and turned to the senior officers for the fifty-yard walk through one wing of the mess hall to the poop deck. Jake leaned heavily on his cane, each step painful, and observed many of the sensations he had felt that first day as a new cadet entering the massive building. The battle flags hanging from the wall, the overpowering stained-glass windows, and the all-too-familiar sounds of the cadets standing at their tables ready to eat flooded Jake with memories of a time when life inside these walls had set in motion all that he was and forever would be. He was home. West Point embraced him like a mother would a returning child.

The brigade commander, Cadet Captain Michael Graves, was a gracious host and formally introduced his staff to Admiral Hollifield and Jake. It was not often that a Navy admiral walked the post or dined with the Corps of Cadets. Aware that the admiral was present, the Corps yelled Army cheers in unison and chants of "Beat Navy" for his benefit.

"Perhaps an apology is due, Admiral, for the Corps enthusiasm," Graves said jokingly, albeit a respectful expression on his face.

"I understand completely, Mr. Graves. I certainly feel outnumbered here today," the admiral said.

"You're safe up here in the poop deck," General Parker said. "Here, sit in the traditional chair for our honored guests."

"Battalions. Atten---shun." The mess hall fell silent as each of the four thousand cadets came to attention behind his chair. The brigade adjutant made two short announcements, followed by a mealtime prayer. Graves returned to the microphone.

"We, the Corps of Cadets, have visitors in the mess hall today. At the command of take seats, standby. Admiral John Hollifield, Chief of Naval Operations (CNO), will address the Corps." Immediately, the sound of applause rose from the five wings toward the poop deck, expressing their approval. "Also, we are honored to have with us today our superintendent, Lieutenant General Lloyd S. Parker, and First Lieutenant John P. Jacobs, Class of 1973." Again, applause rose from the floor.

The Corps fell silent. Not a sound was heard as Admiral Hollifield approached the microphone. He cleared his throat, now tight from the emotions that consumed him. "Lieutenant General Parker, distinguished guests, and gentlemen of the Corps." He paused, surveying the sea of cadets he saw before him.

"Unhappily, I possess neither that eloquence of diction, that poetry of imagination, nor that brilliance of metaphor to tell you..." The laughter and applause from the cadets were spontaneous. Each recognized the admiral's opening line as General Douglas MacArthur's speech to West Point upon accepting the Thayer Award in 1962. The Corps again silenced, pleased with the admiral's sense of humor. "Actually, gentlemen, I was hoping to deliver General MacArthur's entire speech without getting caught, but since you are not going to allow me to do that, I hope my brief words to you today, my alternate speech, will be of value."

"Two days ago, 30 April 1975, is a day that should be remembered for generations to come. The thirtieth of April was the final day of the Vietnam War for the United States of America. It was a day of chaos and panic as military helicopters attempted to rescue as many people as possible from our consulate. The enemy successfully moved their army into Saigon to claim victory. It was the day that the United States Congress could see the reality of their abandonment of the commitment to South Vietnam, both militarily and financially, and the degree of success of their armchair, micro-management of war strategy and tactics. It was the day that those of us in the military profession mourned for the fifty-eight thousand servicemen and women that died for their country."

"Some contend the United States should not have been involved in the affairs of Vietnam at all, and there is arguably some validity to that position. Whether true or not, our military went honorably to Vietnam on orders from the collective will of the people, through those that govern. Others contend that this war was lost from the beginning because of a faulty military strategy based on a fear of escalating the war with the Communist Chinese or the Soviet Union. And, arguably, there is some validity to that position as well. Regardless of position, our military was sent into combat without a declaration of war, nor was our military allowed to fight the war to victory. The aftermath is that our military organization and morale are in disrepair."

"As objectionable as this may appear, you, cadets at West Point and future officers in the United States Army, along with those cadets and midshipmen at the other service academies, are tasked to rebuild our military. It is you who must set the standards of character that define the essence of military excellence. It is you who must remain focused on the mission, your only mission, to win our wars. General MacArthur stated it accurately, 'There is no substitute for victory.'"

"West Point's traditions and methods of preparing officers to serve our country have proven successful from its founding in 1802 to the present. While it is true that the service academies are institutions of higher learning, the result of that learning is like no other institution. You are the guardians of the Constitution and freedom. Upon entering the academy, your sworn oath was to support and defend the Constitution of the United States against all enemies, foreign and domestic. There is no expiration to your oath. Let this oath be your guidepost for all your God-given days."

"The Vietnam War is an American tragedy, yet it is for others to debate the intricacies of governance. Your calling, your beacon of light, resides in these words you know so well: Duty. Honor. Country."

"Gentlemen. Thank you for allowing me a moment of your attention. Let's eat."

2330 Hours
4 May 1975
Fort Bragg, North Carolina

THE STAFF CAR pulled to the front of the BOQ and stopped. A few lights could be seen in the three-story building, but the building showed little activity. It was late, and tomorrow was another workday. Most of the officers were asleep, resting for the 0500 rise for physical training or other duties.

"You need help with that bag, sir?" the sergeant driver asked.

"No thank you, Sergeant. I'll manage." Jake began the slow walk up the building's steps and struggled with the door. He was already exhausted from the trip to West Point, and the hassle of trying to do something as simple as open a door with a cane and bag was frustrating. "I'll get up for PT with the others," Jake mumbled, then laughed at the fact that he was talking to himself. "I've got to get rid of this cane. It's more a nuisance than a help."

The BOQ orderly saw him struggling and came from behind his counter to help. "Lieutenant Jacobs. Welcome home. Let me give you a hand with that bag."

"That's all right, Sergeant Bridegan. I can manage."

The sergeant reached for the bag. "Now, you may be an officer and me only a sergeant, but I'm gonna carry the bag, Lieutenant. Might as well not argue with me."

Jake laughed and let the sergeant take the bag from him. "So, what's been happening that's exciting in the BOQ, Sergeant? You still screening calls for Lieutenant Morrow?"

"Yes, sir. Lieutenant Morrow has too many girlfriends. He's gonna get shot one of these days. He'd be dead already if it weren't for me juggling his calls. As they slowly walked toward the elevator, the sergeant said, "I figure he will be a general someday if he will divert all that tactical planning into his official duties instead of his love life."

On the third floor, Sergeant Bridegan took the key from Jake, opened the door, and turned on the light. Jake walked in and slowly looked around the small room. It seemed strange to him. It seemed like he had been gone longer than he actually was. The sergeant set the bag at the foot of the bed then wished Jake a good night before leaving.

Jake limped around the room, looking and touching all his things, perhaps recognizing for the first time how lucky he was to be alive to see his meager material possessions again. The thought of losing Gutierrez and Washburn on the mission caused him to wonder why them and not himself. He took off his uniform and turned on the shower.

As the hot steaming water sprayed onto the top of his head, he became more relaxed as the minutes passed. He would report to Colonel Strong tomorrow, and thoughts of Admiral Hollifield's skepticism about his leg and duty status caused him to dread the meeting. "Providence," he mumbled. "It comes in the most unexpected ways."

Jake toweled himself dry, put on a pair of athletic shorts, and opened a soft drink from his small refrigerator. He pulled the blanket and bedsheet back with one arm and then slowly eased himself onto the bed. The phone rang. Jake was startled by the noise and unconsciously tried to jump off of the bed to answer it. The sharp pain in his right leg canceled the sudden move. The phone rang again. Slowly swinging his legs over the side of the bed, Jake pushed himself up with the help of the cane then took slow steps toward his desk while the phone rang twice more. "Lieutenant Jacobs speaking, sir," he said as he sat in the desk chair.

"Lieutenant, this is Sergeant Bridegan. You have a long-distance call being transferred from the post operator. I didn't know if you wanted to be bothered with the call or not."

"Long-distance?" Jake asked. "Who is it?"

"Don't know, sir. A call from Colorado."

"Colorado?" Jake said as he wondered who he knew in Colorado. "That's all right, sergeant. I'll take the call."

The line clicked twice while the operator made the connection through the post's main switchboard. "Your call is connected, sir," Bridegan said.

"Lieutenant Jacobs speaking, sir."

"Jake?" the soft feminine voice asked. "Jake, is that you?"

Jake couldn't answer. His heart was pounding from the sound of the voice on the other end of the line.

"Jake. This is Sara."

Jake's eyes gravitated to the small picture frame on his desk, the picture of a fifteen-year-old girl he had set on his desk that first night at West Point, and every desk he had since. "Sara. I still love you. I've never stopped loving you."

EPILOGUE

DRUMS OF WAR ends with 1ˢᵗ Lieutenant Jake Jacobs having a permanent injury to his leg from combat in Jask, Iran. Though he clung to the hope that he could overcome his limitations with determination to do so, moments of pure objective thinking brought him closer to realizing that his days as an effective Green Beret officer were over. The leg wound would endanger him on demanding missions, but worse still, his limitations could endanger his team members and the mission itself. The thought of such possibilities was devastating to him. It was a personal loss, and to accept it, he sought to find a meaningful career alternative as an Army officer. As good as that alternative might be, it would be second-best to his days as a Green Beret. With Admiral Hollifield's guidance, Jake requested a transfer to Military Intelligence and applied to enter a Master's program at the Walsh School of Foreign Service, Georgetown University, for Russian and East European Studies.

Sara's persistence at contacting Jake opened the door to revive what had been lost between them. The starting point is the recognition that their idyllic teenage perception of love and marriage was flawed and that a mended relationship had to be built, not assumed. Both had matured, partially through suffering, which granted the prospect for a capacity to build a relationship stronger than they had before. Jake and Sara and Stephen Patrick savored the moments together, overcoming the disadvantages of distance. Two years quickly passed. Jake was promoted to Captain and was one of a few under the rank of Major to be assigned as an instructor in the Political Science Department at West Point. A three-year assignment at West Point is as good as it gets for an Army officer.

There are plans – both foreign and domestic – to weaken America's military capability to defend herself. And the way her enemies intend to initiate that plan is to change the character of the U.S. Army's highest pinnacle of education for its leaders – the United States Military Academy, known as West Point.

Thundering White Crosses, book #3 in the *A Full Measure* trilogy, concludes the series in a full-out assault, culminating in a rich, exciting, and rewarding climax.

ACKNOWLEDGMENTS

I would like to sincerely thank those who helped in the narrative of this second volume of the trilogy, *A Full Measure*, especially my wife, Debbie, for her support of this project through many hours of writing. Thank you, James Roth, for your hours of dedication and hard work to ensure the completion of the work. I want to thank my West Point roommate, Col. Scott Cottrell (U.S. Army, Ret) for graciously writing the forward for this novel, and I am grateful for the professionalism and integrity of Frank Eastland, Raeghan Rebstock, and Nancy Laning at Publish Authority.

There were many who helped make this novel a reality. Of great importance were my first readers who provided valuable feedback and insight: My NMMI roommate, Captain Mike Herbert (U.S. Navy, Ret.), my lifelong friend and NMMI classmate Greg Graves, MSgt Steve Foust (U.S. Air Force, Ret.), my NMMI faculty colleague Dr. L.D. Swift, PhD and wife Dana, and my NMMI classmates Tom Berry and Stephen Romberger. Their willingness to participate in this project is greatly appreciated.

ABOUT THE AUTHOR

J.M. Patton is a retired Assistant Professor of Mathematics at New Mexico Military Institute (NMMI). His academic major was mathematics: NMMI '69JC, USMA x1973, Baylor University, M Ed Wayland Baptist University. He has a love for Christ and a passion for strict construction of the Constitution. He and his wife Debbie live in rural New Mexico. They are the parents of five sons and have sixteen grandchildren.

Mr. Patton's website > https://jmpattonauthor.com

facebook.com/J.M.Patton.Author

THANK YOU FOR READING

Publish Authority

If you enjoyed *Drums of War*, book #2 in the trilogy *A Full Measure*, we invite you to share your thoughts and reactions online and with friends and family.

Made in the USA
Monee, IL
06 August 2023